Losing Faith

A Rutherford Novel

By Robbie Cox

Losing Faith
By Robbie Cox

Second Edition
Copyright © 2016 by Robbie Cox
All rights reserved
Cover art by SelfPubBookCovers.com/Shardel
Cover graphics by Teri Edney
Editing by CTS Editing & Weis Editing/Proofreading Services
Formatting by Brenda Wright, Formatting Done Wright
& Sarah Mick

ISBN: 9780990522003
Library of Congress Control Number: 2014914834

www.robbiecox.net

This book is a work of fiction. All names, characters, locations, and incidents are strictly products of the author's imagination. Any resemblance to actual persons, living or dead, is entirely coincidental.

Other Books by Robbie Cox

Warrior of the Way

Reaping the Harvest

The Rutherford Series

Losing Faith
Roll the Dice

Fangirls
Nikki
Lily
Cassie
Olivia

The Harper Twins
Sibling Rivalry

Come Halloween
Ribbons & Bows
A Confused Life

Short Stories

Circle of Justice

Dedication

To Charleen, Teresa, and Sarah,
three ladies who keep me grounded
in the real world while my mind
drifts in fantasy.

Author's Note

The one thing about writing fiction is that writers can create the perfect environment for our stories. Sometimes that means we don't have to necessarily worry about the possible consequences that those of us in the real world have to consider, such as unexpected pregnancies and sexually transmitted diseases, unless it fits into the story we are telling. In *Losing Faith*, I assume that everyone is drug and disease free and taking fantastic birth control. Or just very lucky not to get pregnant. However, please don't confuse fiction with reality. If you are sexually active, please be aware of the dangers that are lurking out there with very serious and life changing consequences and practice safe sex. After all, we only want surprises in our novels and around our birthdays.

Acknowledgments

Losing Faith is a tale five years in the making and there are several people that deserve my gratitude. First and above all, my girls, Charleen, Teresa, and Sarah, who deserve a standing ovation for all they constantly do to help me see my dream come to fruition. They are the biggest Candle Lighters of anyone I know and I shudder to think where I would be without them. They are my encouragers, supporters and idea givers. They edit, promote, and tolerate all of my craziness. I love them dearly and beyond words.

Next, I have to thank Katie Weisenberger and Stephanie Neighbour for reading the final draft and catching all of those things we missed. Their critiques and encouragement is a benefit every writer needs.

Furthermore, I want to thank all of the friends I have made through social media who have not only encouraged me, but continuously share my work on their newsfeeds and streams. A debt of gratitude goes to Margie Miklas, James Jackson, Taylor Fulks, David Brown, Sherry Rentschler, Lydia AsWolf, Gary Alan Henson, Jeanette Bolt Smith and Roberta Goodman for helping me with shout outs and promos. I greatly appreciate all they have done for me.

And last but not least, to my parents who have always supported me in my crazy ventures and our children who have put up with their father's silly space-outs when a thought entered my head or for putting up with me when I ramble on and on about a story line or character. To Nathan, Christopher, Zachariah, Heather, Chad, Christina, Dylan, and Amanda Lowery, our daughter in heart, thanks for your tolerance when I stop mid-step to write an idea down. I'm proud of each of you and hope you are of me, as well.

One

I hate Mondays. Why can't we just go straight from Sunday to Tuesday and forget this whole Monday concept? The alarm screamed at Faith Greer as she yanked the covers up over her head and attempted to stuff the excess into her ears. It didn't help.

"Rise and shine, gorgeous." Selby sat on the edge of the bed and strove to pull the covers from his wife's head. "It's a beautiful day and you're wasting the best part."

"I thought being in bed was the best part." She sighed as the covers disappeared. She hated morning people.

Selby only laughed as he set a hot cup of coffee on her nightstand. "Only if we're having sex and since we're not, it's time to get up."

"I'll let you fuck me if I can sleep through it." She spread her legs and laid her arms out flat.

"You could sleep through me fucking you? I'm wounded." Selby left the side of the bed and grabbed his shoes.

"I'm tired. Get over it. Pretend my snores are moans." She kicked the covers back within arms' reach and snuggled down. "I'll even snore loudly."

"Oh, no, no, no. Upsie daisy." Selby walked back over and ripped the pillow from under her head. As she reached for it, she felt the covers being yanked away as well.

1

She opened her eyes only enough to glare at him. "You, Selby Greer, are an evil man."

His smile was better than morning coffee. "So I've been told." He patted her tummy and then walked out of their bedroom, his shoes dangling from his fingers.

Faith couldn't help but watch him leave, her eyes mesmerized by his faded Levi's snug against his ass. His blond hair, even washed and combed, was a shaggy mess. He needed a haircut and she knew he'd get one soon because he hated the way it hung around his ears. Still, she loved that brief period where he let it go. It gave him a rugged, unkempt, beachy look, which she adored. It was during this period that the thin strands swished across the top of his shoulders, drawing her eyes to his casual but confidant stride. He was fit, with an athletic build, not that of a body builder, which suited Faith just fine. She liked to lay her head on a firm chest, not a rock.

Selby turned the corner and was out of sight before Faith turned her gaze to the ceiling. Why couldn't she be born rich so she could pay someone else to deal with Mondays? Oh well, she thought, nothing for it but to get this day started.

Faith forced herself out of the warm spot that had cradled her throughout the night. She turned the shower on to allow the water to heat up and then stared at herself with blurry vision in the mirror over their dual sinks. It was definitely a Monday. Her wheaten hair was all knotted and resembled the aftermath of a cat toy rather than her hair. She pulled down on her cheeks examining her forest green eyes, for what she didn't know. With a groan, she pulled her burgundy nightie over her head and tossed it onto the counter. Freckles dusted her slim body, her torso an hour glass shape that she was proud of and her breasts, while not huge by any means, still were pert and perky. She hadn't always been so fit. When she had met Selby she was a pencil stick with hips. It didn't help that at a quarter inch shy of five-ten she was only two inches shorter than he was. Heels were not her friends.

Steam billowed over the shower door, drawing her into the small stall where she allowed the scalding water to beat her pale skin. She hung her head under the pulsing jet and allowed it to massage her brain into wakefulness. She hated Mondays. The weekend was free and unstructured and the two of them made the most of each moment.

Mondays always seemed to give her separation anxiety and she struggled those first few hours against feeling lost.

By the time Faith had finished getting ready for work and downed that first cup of coffee, she had come to life. Selby had packed her lunch and fixed her a cinnamon and raisin bagel with blueberry cream cheese, which was waiting for her as she emerged from the master bedroom into the kitchen. He took her Winnie the Pooh mug and refilled her coffee, adding two sugars and just a splash of cream. She might actually make it through the day.

Selby stood by the kitchen counter sipping coffee out of a mug with a giant picture of Grumpy on it. Besides his jeans and deck shoes, he wore a blue and yellow Hawaiian shirt. Casual. He owned his own used bookstore, so every day was casual Friday for him. She envied him. She worked in a construction office and had to have some sort of business casual attire, which to her point of view was the same as business dress up. There was nothing casual about it. Edwin Coldwell, her boss, wanted the girls at the office ready to meet a client at all times. While Faith didn't really mind dressing up, she would have preferred jeans and a tee-shirt.

"Want to trade places with me today," Faith said as she held her mug with both hands in front of her. "I'll run the bookstore and you can sit in an office with Cherish all day." Spending the day with her younger sister had lost its appeal after the first week of working together, even if there were muscle-bound men to distract her at times.

He just smiled at her. "I really don't think the guys would appreciate my ass as much as they do yours. Besides, I prefer the solitude of my shop. Work place politics don't get along with me too well. And it's Monday, isn't it?"

She gave him a quizzical look. "Meaning?"

"Cherish always calls out on Mondays, according to you."

Faith nodded as a slight laugh escaped her. "Very true, which means it'll be quiet today. I can handle that."

Selby placed his mug in the sink before leaning over and giving Faith a kiss on the forehead. "That's my girl. And speaking of handling it, I need to get going. Have a great day, love."

"Oh joy," Faith said as she watched him scoop up his briefcase and the latest Terry Brooks novel. As the door to the garage shut, Faith took a deep breath. She might as well get the day underway.

As she crossed the Melbourne Causeway her phone dinged. Glancing at the text she read, *Tracey wants to have dinner Wednesday night. She says she misses you. You up for it?* Faith couldn't help but smile knowing what Selby's meaning behind "up for it" meant. Tracey owned Joe's Bakery & Cafe across from his bookstore and ever since he had introduced the two women he had been hoping for some girl-on-girl action between them. Tracey was a hot little redhead, but Faith had never crossed the girl-on-girl line and wasn't sure she wanted to start. There were still so many other lines Selby and her were crossing.

Dinner, yes, she texted back and could picture his mischievous grin as he read it. Well, at least the dinner date would give her something to look forward to as she struggled through another Monday.

Before she knew it, Faith was driving her Toyota pickup onto the grounds of the new Rutherford Construction, Inc. offices. They had recently relocated the business from within the city to four acres west of I-95 on Eau Gallie Boulevard, one of the more isolated areas in Melbourne.

One of the major construction conglomerates in East and Central Florida, Rutherford Construction handled office buildings, hospitals, and million dollar homes and even did some work for the major amusement parks that filled Orlando. The founder, Neal Rutherford, was a self-made man who started flipping houses in the '90s and then just kept stretching his reach until he was one of the most sought after contractors in Florida. Rumor had it he was even putting his fingers into projects in Georgia, Alabama and Mississippi.

Faith had only met Neal once at a Christmas party three months back. He was a powerful looking man, still in perfect shape at fifty-two with short salt and pepper hair and a trimmed mustache to match. He caught the eye of every girl in the office, all four of them.

She parked her small pickup on the side of the building, snatched up her purse and headed for the front door. The morning sun brought a smile to her face as it warmed her hair contrasting the breeze that cooled her face. Neal had wanted the Brevard offices close to the interstate since their jobs were located in so many different locations. Of course, some of the bigger locations had a trailer on site for immediate needs, but the bulk of the operation was housed on this small four acres of land practically in the middle of nowhere. It housed two buildings, the offices and a warehouse, and had plenty of room for trucks and materials. Eau Gallie Boulevard dead ended into Lake Washington and was always crowded with air boats and lovers in parked cars, but was otherwise pretty quiet. There was an animal shelter, a giant flea market, a Park & Ride parking lot that always seemed to be empty and the new Fire and Rescue Training School. Otherwise, it was a gravel road surrounded by palm fronds and alligators. It was peaceful, even if a little scary at night.

Most of the men were getting the materials they needed for that particular day's assignment loaded into their trucks and ready to go. Some were still arriving, however, and honked at Faith as she walked to the main doors. She turned, waved, and then sashayed her ass into the office. Forget sexual harassment. She wanted to be flirted with and whistled at and working with construction workers definitely boosted a girl's self-esteem. It turned her on for them to want what they couldn't have.

With a smile at the wetness between her legs from the attention, Faith pulled open the door to Rutherford Construction and entered her day.

~ ~ ~ ~ ~

Selby finished adding several Sue Grafton novels that someone had traded in the previous week to the mystery section when he heard the cowbell over his front door jingle. "Lunch time," he heard the soprano voice call out. He glanced at his watch, surprised it was already quarter past noon. This Monday was flying by.

He slid *T is for Trespassing* onto the shelf and then left the rest of the books in the box in favor of food. He hadn't realized he was hungry until the call for lunch rang out. "Be right there." He slid to the back room, snagged a Coke and a Dr. Pepper from the ancient fridge he kept in the back, and then made his way to the front counter where Tracey was opening a Styrofoam container and already sitting on a stool that was kept there for her visits. He could smell the sauerkraut and knew the selection of the day was Reuben sandwiches. "Smells delicious."

"Well, you know it is. I made it." She nibbled on a corn chip as Selby handed her the Dr. Pepper. Tracey's vibrant red hair kept falling into her face, forcing her to keep tucking it behind her ear. Even sitting on the stool she couldn't look Selby eye to eye. Standing, she was only five-five and every inch was a treat for the eyes. Her hair fell just below her shoulders, pointing to a firm heart-shaped ass that Selby just loved to watch walk back to the bakery. Her breasts were firm handfuls that always seemed to have hard nipples pointing out of her blouses. She was petite, but strong. Tracey Williams was not a lady to be taken advantage of and she ran her business with a firm hand and a gentle smile.

Selby sat in his big black leather office chair, twirling it so that he was facing the tender frame of his lunch companion. "How's your day going?"

She merely shrugged. "It's Monday. Joe's there, grumbling about the way I'm running his bakery as if he forgets he sold it to me. Joanie screwed up two cakes and a strudel and Darrell was late with my food delivery this morning. I'm ready for a drink." She gave him her fake grin with her lips pressed into a thin line.

Selby finished chewing a bite of sandwich before answering. He nodded as he said, "Yeah, that sounds like a Monday. Why don't you just tell Joe to stop coming in?"

She slipped a slice of corned beef into her mouth, sucking the juice from her finger as she withdrew it. Selby had to shake the erotic thoughts out of his head. "I feel sorry for him," Tracey said. "His kids moved away right after he sold me the place, so he doesn't have anyone here. Besides, he's not really that bad. He's like my father, if my father still talked to me."

Selby nodded his head. "I just can't understand a father turning his back on his daughter, for any reason."

Tracey shrugged. "It is what it is. My choices in life didn't get his stamp of approval. Of course, when dear ol' Dad is against you, Mom has to follow suit, so she ignores one of the children that shot out from between her legs."

He almost choked on his lunch at her brutal description. "You've never told me what decision you made that caused them to exile you." He doubted she would now, but it didn't stop him from being curious. As far as Selby knew, only her brother kept in touch with her.

"What does it matter? No one bullies me into their way of thinking. My life is mine to live as I see fit and I won't be controlled or manipulated." She dropped her sandwich back into its container. "People have to accept me for me, even my parents."

Selby took another bite of his sandwich. He agreed with Tracey, up to a point. Some choices, he knew, were just too much for traditional people to handle. Most would not be able to accept the decisions Faith and he had made, but then, not everything is meant to be shouted from the rooftops. Selby was a firm believer in living your life and only answering questions when asked. There was no need to volunteer things for the shock value.

The rest of their lunch was just idle chit chat about other shop owners Downtown. The man who ran the British store was secretly seeing the lady behind the counter at the candle shop and it was all hush hush which meant everyone was talking about it. Another street party was being planned to try and attract business. Selby never worked one and Tracey thought the only thing they attracted were drunks. Still, since it was the bars organizing it, they were reaching the crowd they wanted.

"Oh, Faith said yes to Wednesday night. Where do you want to go? Our place?" Selby tried to look innocent, but Tracey's laugh told him it wasn't working.

"I know Faith is becoming adventurous, but I doubt she's become that open. Yet." Her smile told him, however, that she would be willing, if it were ever to happen. He was halfway there. "How about that small Italian place by the interstate?"

Italian sounded good to him, so they set a dinner date for seven and then lunch was over; all too quick for his taste. Selby watched her perfect ass sway back across the street to her bakery to finish her day. He smiled the entire time wondering if he was ever going to see her without those white shorts covering that ass.

The bell over his door rang as an elderly couple entered, said good afternoon and started browsing. Selby went back to organizing the new additions to his mystery section with images of Faith and Tracey spread upon his bed making him wish he was either alone or at home.

~ ~ ~ ~ ~

Faith had been right. Not that there had been any doubt in her mind that she wouldn't be, of course. Cherish had called out for the day claiming she had hurt her back over the weekend moving furniture. Faith knew it was a lie, or at least a cover up. Knowing Cherish, she wore herself out over the weekend or merely hated Mondays. It had become a pretty common occurrence. Her sister may not call off every Monday, but it was frequent enough to be noticeable; at least to Faith it was. Edwin either didn't notice it or didn't care. To be honest, Faith didn't care either. Cherish was moody, her emotions sometimes coming out like a roller coaster ride that's gone out of control. The office was a much more pleasant environment to work in when she was gone.

The day had seemed set on fast forward, which was great for a Monday, and Faith was pleased there were only two hours left to her daily prison sentence. She glanced at her list of To Dos and gave herself a satisfied pat on the back when she saw all but two things checked off. Four girls worked at the Brevard office of Rutherford Construction. Ashlynn Leighton was the receptionist and worked out in the front lobby. She was a sweet girl, but not the brightest. Her sole purpose seemed to be eye-candy for the male clients who could stare at her store-bought tits and not care if they were kept waiting.

The other three worked in what the men affectionately called the Girls' Den, a small office with three desks and several file cabinets. Cherish was human resources, in charge of all employees, the hiring, firing and keeping track of vacation days and sick days, which was ironic considering how often she called out. Nessa Sanchez was a part time employee who was there to tend to the overflow of assignments the other girls couldn't do, which quite often relegated her to answering phones when she was there and filing.

Faith kept track of everything else, job assignments, trucks and equipment inspections, and customer complaints. She had started out as Nessa, part time and doing the filing, but Edwin Coldwell had been impressed enough with her work ethic to make her full time and dump a heavy load of responsibility on her. She had loved it, but her sister hadn't been the same toward her since. Of course, they had never really been close, but her promotion had made it worse.

"How's it going in here?" Edwin stood in the doorway. Faith saw him glance at Cherish's desk and then turn to Nessa and her.

"Almost quitting time, so I'd say pretty well," Faith said as she paused from going over a contract and turned to face her boss. He was a powerful man, standing three inches over six feet with broad shoulders and thick arms. His stomach was just beginning to gain that middle age paunch, but he still looked solid with strong arms and legs that could pin a girl to the bed as he drove into her. A Salem cigarette perched behind his right ear almost hidden by his raven black hair. So far the color gray had left him alone.

Nessa glanced up at him, a smirk giving her a mischievous look. "Forgot Cherish wasn't here?"

Faith glanced at the dark haired girl, woman really, even if she was ten years younger than Faith, not understanding the question. Then she saw him take the cigarette from behind his ear. "Well, it is time for a smoke break." He put the cancer stick between his lips and left.

Nessa just chuckled and went back to her files. Faith stared at the empty doorway, at the spot where his ass had been just seconds ago, and could still see the way his tight jeans had highlighted its firmness. *Maybe I should take up smoking.*

The rest of the day went by just as fast and before Faith knew it, Nessa was packing up to go home. Faith looked up at the clock. 5:05. It was definitely Monday and Cherish wasn't there. If she had been there, then the office would have started closing thirty-five minutes ago. With a sense of pride, Faith checked the last thing off her list and began shutting her computer down. Nessa said goodbye and was gone before Faith could return the farewell.

She just chuckled to herself as she put pens and reading glasses into her purse. She couldn't blame the younger girl. She was ready to go as well. Work was great, but home was better.

"Heading out?" Faith turned and saw Edwin walking into the room.

She stood, slinging her purse over her shoulder, keys dangling from her fingers. "I was, unless you needed something else." She waggled her eyebrows at him as she pursed her lips into a smile.

Edwin laughed, the sound deep and inviting. "Too many people still here, otherwise…"

Faith walked by him and patted his ass on the way out. "You always tease me."

He turned and watched her walk down the hall. "As if you'd let me do anything else." His eyebrows lifted as he gave her a challenging smile.

Faith paused at the door that opened to the lobby and smiled back at him. "I'm not the one who keeps giving excuses." She blew him a kiss. "Goodnight, Edwin." And then she left.

On the drive home she wondered what she would do if Edwin ceased teasing and acted on his taunts. He flirted with all the girls, offering services outside of their job descriptions, but Faith had never known him to follow through on any of it. Of course, Nessa called him a dog and a player, insinuating that their boss did anything and everything in a skirt. Still, Faith had never seen or heard any evidence suggesting it was true.

Furthermore, even though Selby and she had opened up that part of their lives to new adventures, Faith wasn't sure she was ready to venture in that direction. She liked the security Selby provided, the strength to allow her inhibitions to fall away and explore that dark side she had always ignored. Up until a year ago, she denied those fantasies even existed. Yet, they were there and she was nervous about where it would take her.

By the time she arrived home, Selby's car was already in the garage. As she entered their quaint beachside haven, the sound of Journey telling her to *Don't Stop Believing* mingled with the aroma of stir-fry. Selby stood at the stove pushing food around in the wok, dressed in shorts and a blue Quicksilver T-shirt. As the scent of cooking vegetables and sizzling meat assailed her senses, she was glad that he had made it home before her. She loved when he cooked.

Dropping her purse on the white Formica counter, Faith snuggled in behind him and slid her hands around his waist and up his firm chest. She laid her cheek against his back as she squeezed, breathing in the scent of him. "I missed this." Her voice came out soft and content.

"What? My cooking?" She could hear the smile in his voice.

Faith squeezed again. "Nope. You. I missed you."

Selby set the wooden spoon on the stove and turned to face her. She never let go, allowing his body to turn in her arms. As she glanced up into his deep ocean blue eyes, he leaned in and kissed her nose. "You mean all those burly construction workers couldn't keep you from missing me?"

She gave an exaggerated sigh. "Well, they are nice to look at, but I fit so much nicer in your arms."

Selby licked her nose, laughing. "But in order for you to know that you would have had to try their arms around you."

She shrugged. "Perhaps." Her grin was mischievous and he just shook his head, laughing, before returning to the stir fry. Faith kissed the back of his neck. "I'm going to go get as comfortable as you. How long do I have?"

"Fifteen."

She kissed him again as she gave his ass a squeeze and then passed from the kitchen to the master bedroom. From the speaker system throughout the house, Journey had finished and Styx was urging her to *Come Sail Away*. She unzipped the side of her dress pants as she kicked her heels toward the closet and her breathing relaxed as the business attire slid down her thin legs. It was a different mindset being in work clothes and only now as she shed them like unwanted skin did she feel as if she could relax. The cream-colored blouse and bra were next, followed by her black thong. She was tempted just to stay nude, but then they would never eat. Instead she grabbed a lavender sundress and slipped it over her head.

"All comfy," she said as she spun in front of the mirror. "Selby Greer, you are one lucky bastard."

"Don't I know it." He leaned on the doorframe, watching her with insatiable eyes. "Now, let's eat."

Faith felt the blush warm her cheeks at being caught staring at herself. "You mean dinner, right?" She walked toward him and slid the sundress up, tantalizingly close to her pussy as she gave her husband a sultry come-hither glance.

Selby groaned and went back to the kitchen. "Grab the wine, vixen," he called as he picked up both plates and headed to the back deck.

Faith smiled and did as she was told.

Two

Faith sat at her desk spinning a pen in her fingers as Jed Jorrell went over the Polawski file with her. Rutherford was in charge of building a series of office buildings off Babcock Street for Mr. Vincent Polawski and while everything Jed was reciting was routine, not to mention boring, Faith enjoyed listening to him talk. His voice was deep and playful and you could always hear a smile in it, even when he was reading boring reports. She had never noticed before how intoxicating his voice was. Nor had she noticed his hands with their long thick fingers that she could imagine caressing her nipples into taut little pebbles aching to be pinched.

Faith gave her mind a mental shake, bringing it out of its bedroom thoughts, and sat up straighter in her desk chair as she focused on what Jed was saying. However, she found herself blushing at the moisture between her legs. She couldn't believe how easily her mind went to sex these days. She had worked with these people for four years and for the first part of that, the majority of her time at Rutherford really, she had only seen them as coworkers. Now, everyone had the potential of being a fuck buddy, at least in her fantasies.

She blamed Selby. Ever since he took her to that festival in Key West, sex seemed to be a permanent fix in her mind. The past few months had been a whirlwind of sensation she never thought possible

13

and which now battled inside her mind against what she had been told growing up was right and wrong. At times, it was all very confusing.

"Did you hear any of that?"

Faith glanced up and saw Jed handing her the manila folder, which held the report he had just finished reading, and which she had ignored. She felt her face flush as she took it. "Of course I did." Yet, she knew she had been caught daydreaming. It was a good thing he couldn't read her mind. Her pussy grew wetter at the embarrassment of being caught.

Jed just laughed. "Sure you did," he said as he stood. "Well, everything's in there if you need to look it up."

"Thanks," Faith said as she watched him leave her office, still chuckling.

When he was gone, she closed her eyes and took a deep breath. *My god, Faith. What has gotten into you?* But she knew. What she didn't know was why the embarrassment of being caught, lost in her private fantasies, had caused even more excitement between her legs.

As soon as Jed had cleared the doorway, Edwin walked in, his cigarette resting behind his ear. Faith glanced at the clock. 10:15. He was right on time. "How are you girls doing?"

"Doing well," Faith said as she watched Cherish stop what she was doing and grab a cigarette from her purse. "Break time, I see."

Edwin smiled at her. "Lung killing time. Be glad you don't smoke."

"But why? If I smoked, I'd get extra breaks." Faith smiled back. "Maybe I should just pretend, so I can stand outside for a while."

"Perhaps you should just work." Cherish walked over to where Edwin stood. "Shall we?"

Edwin glanced at her and then back at Faith. "Did you want to take a break and join us? It's a gorgeous day outside."

Cherish's mouth dropped open for just a moment before she caught herself and clamped it shut. Still, it was obvious to Faith that her sister did not care for the idea of Faith joining them. Of course, that alone made her want to join them. Instead, however, she said, "No, thanks. I was just giving you a hard time. Maybe next time, though." Faith didn't understand the relief on Cherish's face. Did her sister hate her that much?

Edwin didn't seem to notice Cherish's reaction. "You can give me a hard time anytime you want." He winked at her. "Feel free to step away from your desk anytime you need. Everyone needs a break. Just be glad you don't smoke." Smokers always tended to tell non-smokers that, but they never took their own advice.

Faith just nodded as she told them to have a good time. She spun around to her monitor and read back over the file that Jed had handed her. As she glanced over it she realized she had been daydreaming through most of what he had said. She found herself having to reread the entire file. *But man, it was worth it.*

"Hey, Faith, do you know where Cherish is?"

Faith was about to groan at not being able to get anything done because her office had a revolving door. However, when she noticed the lady standing behind Ashlynn, she was glad she had kept quiet. "Mom? Is something wrong?" She stood to her feet and took a couple of steps closer to the two women.

"Why on earth would anything be wrong? Does anything have to be wrong for me to visit my daughter?" Faith noticed the singular "daughter," but didn't comment.

"No. No, of course not." She glanced at the blonde receptionist and smiled. "I've got it, Ashlynn. Thank you." She didn't watch the girl leave. Instead, she turned Nessa's desk chair around for her mother and offered it to her with an open palm. "Cherish stepped out for a minute, but she'll be right back. What brings you by?"

Valerie Driscoll sat rigid in the desk chair, her legs pressed together and her back ramrod straight. Her hands rested on her thick black purse perched on her lap as if she needed the barrier between her and everyone else. Her short black hair stopped abruptly at the base of her scalp as if afraid to grow any longer. Faith had always thought her mother had a harsh look about her with thin lips that always seemed pressed into disapproval and a narrow nose between tiny brown eyes. She was thin, too thin for Faith's taste, and made to look even more so by her five foot ten body. She was a cold lady and Faith had always thought her born too late in history.

"I was going to let Cherish take me out to lunch. Do you know how much longer she'll be?"

"Lunch sounds fun. You should come up sometime and let me treat you one day." Faith forced her voice to sound pleasant. "There's a nice little café down on John Rhodes that has the best chicken salad."

Her mom's lips never moved into a smile. A smile would have been nice, at least a faint sign of promise that lunch could happen. "Oh, I thought you were too busy to have lunch away or that you would be having it with your husband or one of your many new friends."

"New friends? And my husband's name is Selby."

"I know."

"Mom? What are you doing here?" Cherish stood in the doorway, Edwin a step behind her.

Valerie Driscoll stood up, her purse strap still clutched in both hands. "Obviously being told I'm too stupid to know her husband's name."

Faith looked at her mother's back, which was all she saw of her now and just rolled her eyes. Edwin wasn't sure what to do as his eyes flicked back and forth between all the women in the small office. Faith wanted to tell him to run.

"Edwin, this is my mom, Valerie. Mother, this is Edwin, our boss." Cherish didn't move from the doorway. "Now, what are you here for, Mom?"

"Lunch. I thought you and I could grab some lunch and discuss Jordie's upcoming birthday. I have some great party ideas and I was nearby." Valerie ignored Edwin, as if the introduction hadn't happened.

Cherish just shook her head. "It's only ten-thirty, Mom. I can't take a lunch, yet."

"No, no. Why don't you go ahead and take it, Cherish," Edwin said as he pushed into the office. He glanced at Faith and concern filled his eyes. "After all, she did come up here to see you. Matter of fact, make it a family thing and all three of you go. Ashlynn can handle the phones for an hour."

Faith's eyes widened at the suggestion and she wanted to kick him. Cherish saw the expression and smiled, but Valerie's back stiffened. "No, I'm good," Faith blurted out. "I need to get this file that Jed gave me finished."

Valerie's back softened as she turned to face her middle child. "Are you sure? You did say you wanted to do lunch."

Faith smiled. If only her mother meant those words, but Faith knew the truth. It was only a show now for a man that Valerie had already dismissed as unimportant. "I'm good. You two go and enjoy."

With a nod, Cherish grabbed her purse and locked her desk. Mother and daughter walked out the door without so much as an "I'll bring you a doggie bag back." Faith watched them leave, both saying goodbye to Edwin on their way out as she sat there wondering what she ever did to her mother.

"I, um, screwed up?" Edwin sat on the corner of Nessa's desk. His hard body was soft with concern at having caused trouble or hurt feelings. His dark eyes were tender and Faith just wanted to crawl into them and hide.

She put on a strong smile as she leaned back in her chair. "No, it's all right. Mom and Cherish have always been close, which has never made sense to me. Then again, Cherish allows Mom to dictate some of her life and I don't. My mother has always been a control freak."

Edwin nodded. "Family politics are never fun, and from what you've shared before, your family has a lot of inner politics."

Faith turned and stared out the window. It had been the politics that had made her rush into Selby's arms. He had been her escape. He still was.

~ ~ ~ ~ ~

Selby entered the house through the garage and was assaulted by Disturbed blaring through the house speakers. *Well, something has set her off.* He weaved through the house to his office where the music originated and turned down the volume on electric guitars and drums. He inhaled the silence.

Dropping his briefcase by his desk, he went in search of Faith. It didn't take long. She was in the kitchen butchering carrots and hurling them into a pot of boiling water. "I want to hug you, but I think I want you to put the knife down first." He stopped at the edge of the counter and bent his head, attempting to peer into her eyes. "Bad day at work?"

Faith kept chopping at the carrots and Selby assumed he would need a new cutting board before long. "Work was fine. At least, it was until my mother showed up."

He should have known. No one could work Faith up more than Valerie Driscoll. Selby always believed that to be the older woman's super power. He chose not to say anything, though. Instead, he just walked around the counter, turned her to face him, and wrapped his arms around her, careful of the knife. He never knew what to do when Faith's mother decided to be a bitch, so most times he did the only thing he could and just held Faith, letting her know that he was there for her. The only other option was illegal; if they ever found the body, that is.

He felt her squeeze him tight before wiggling out of his arms. "I have to finish dinner," she said as she turned back around.

Selby kissed the back of her head. "I'm going to wash up." Faith just nodded as he gave her ass a pat and headed for the master bedroom. Once he was in their room he took a deep breath. He could kill Valerie Driscoll, at times. She was the only rough spot in their lives. The sad part was that he saw no reason for it. Faith had never done anything to antagonize her mother. Valerie was just a bitter old woman.

He ran cold water over his face, washing away the work day and the bile that erupted in him against his mother-in-law. No child should be treated that way by their mother. Of course, Cherish and Dennis, Faith's older brother, were never assaulted with their mother's vile disposition. For some reason, it was only Faith that bore the brunt of her hatred. Selby stared into the mirror as if it were a crystal ball. *I wonder why that is?*

Dinner was served on the back deck while the waves of the Atlantic beat a steady cadence in the background. Almost all of their meals were taken there because Selby enjoyed it. What was the point of living on the beach if you never took advantage of it?

Faith had everything set up and the Goo Goo Dolls now played through the speakers, a sign that she was calming down. She had even lit the tiki torches that edged their wooden paradise. The March breeze had a bit of a chill to it, but in Florida it was never truly cold, at least, not to Selby. While he loved traveling, nothing compared to Florida for tropical paradise.

"How about a walk after dinner?" He slid into his chair as he picked up his glass of merlot.

Faith had changed into a tan sundress, foregoing the bra and, with any luck, the panties, too. Her hair was pulled back into a ponytail revealing her small ears and slender neck. She must have laid out within the past few days because her dusting of freckles was more pronounced as it led down her shoulders and chest. Selby couldn't help but smile at how beautiful she was and he wanted—hungered— to lean over and kiss her small nose. "We can do that if you want," she said as she scooped cooked carrots onto her plate.

Throughout dinner Selby tried to engage Faith in conversation, but she wasn't having it. Her answers were clipped and simple. Perhaps she hadn't calmed down as much as he had thought. Her gaze was lost in her plate, even though she barely nibbled at its contents. It was pretty much just him and the Goo Goo Dolls.

After dinner, he helped clear the table and, even though she said she'd get the dishes, he stood there, dried them, and put them away. Faith would talk. She just needed time to get through the storm of emotions that churned inside of her. As much as Faith said she didn't care, Selby knew she did. Deeply. Yet, nothing they had ever done had changed her mother's bitchy behavior, and truly, there was no reason for it. Faith had always done everything her mother wanted. It wasn't until the past few months that Faith had decided to shed her conservative skin and explore her sexual side. Of course, her mom didn't know about their exploits. Still, her newfound lifestyle had altered the way Faith carried herself. Perhaps it was that change in confidence that Valerie Driscoll despised. Faith was no longer under her mother's thumb and the woman hated it. She would never be controlled by her mother again if he had anything to do with it.

And he had a lot to do with it.

"What are you thinking?" Faith held a plate out to him.

He smiled as he took it, running the rooster covered hand towel over it. "I was thinking of stripping you once we got on the beach and taking advantage of you."

19

"Were you now?" Faith leaned back against the counter, drying her hands, dishes done. "And what makes you think I'd let you?"

Selby put the plate in the cupboard as he dropped the towel on the counter. He slid in front of her, gripping the counter with a hand on each side of her, so she couldn't escape. "Because, Mrs. Greer," he leaned in and dusted her neck with kisses, "I know you," he kissed her throat feeling her lift her head giving him access, "for the little tramp you are." His tongue brushed her flesh like an artist painting as he licked down her throat to the top of her dress, kissing his way to her chest.

Her groan filled his ears as her hands draped over his. "Am I now? Is that what I am?"

Selby pulled his hand out from under hers and slid the strap of her sundress off her shoulder, following the string with soft kisses as he slid it down her arm. "Yes," he moved to the other side, "you are." He slid the thin strap off her other shoulder and down her arm. "And you love," he kissed her warm flesh, "every minute of it." He leaned back, grinning at her as he pulled the dress down over her chest, freeing her small globes to the cool air. "Don't you?" He lowered his head and ran his tongue over her hardening nipple, feeling the small pearl contract from his touch.

Faith's hands came up to his head, her fingers threading into his hair. He could feel the tightness of her body as passion replaced the cold emotions of the day. "I'm beginning to." Her voice was husky, filled with the lust she was feeling.

He slid his hand up her thigh, pulling the dress up with it. Her flesh was warm to the touch as he slid his hand between her legs. She eased them apart as his fingers grazed higher. Her pussy dripped with need as he plunged two fingers into her, making her gasp with pleasurable surprise. As his fingers strummed her sex, Selby used the other hand to free his swollen cock from the confines of his pants.

Faith never moved, her head tilted back, hair falling behind her. With his cock free, Selby slid his fingers from her wetness and lifted her into the air, his hands around her thighs. Faith braced herself with her hands on the counter, wrapping her legs around his waist as he eased his cock into her sweet cavern. He held her in place as he fucked her, his cock driving into her with a slow, steady rhythm, her whimpers feeding his hunger.

Selby leaned down and kissed her chest, her shoulders, as his hips pounded into her thighs. Faith was helpless to move, her hands on the counter and his under her thighs keeping her airborne. Her moans echoed off the kitchen cabinets as he felt her body tense and her legs begin to stiffen with the orgasm he knew was close to exploding. He gripped her thighs tighter, thrusting into her faster, spearing her with his hardness.

Her inner walls pulsed around his cock, sucking him as well as her mouth could. He could feel his balls tighten, ready to explode. Faith cried out as her body started to shake and buck against him. His own orgasm hit as he felt his cock erupt deep inside of her as her passion dripped between them. Her tits bounced and he wanted so bad to lean in and take her taut nipples in his mouth, but he was frozen in place, holding her up until her body relaxed.

The ripples of pleasure subsided as she lowered her head to gaze into his eyes, a smile widening her cheeks. "So much for the beach."

Selby lowered her feet to the floor as he felt their juices drip between them. He pressed up against her, kissing her neck. "I couldn't wait."

Faith wrapped her arms around him, hugging him tight. "I'm glad you didn't."

Three

So far the morning had been pretty smooth, so Faith knew something was about to blow up. Quietness at Rutherford Construction never lasted long. As she reached for another file from the stack of never-ending paperwork, she spotted Edwin as he poked his head through the doorway. A quick glance at her computer clock told her it was smoke break time. Cherish was already reaching into her purse for her own cancer stick. With a deep breath, Faith decided that today she wasn't going to say a thing.

As it turned out, she didn't have to mention it. Edwin did.

"Faith, care to join me for a cigarette break?" He leaned against the doorframe, his strong hand gripping the wood as he smiled at her. He didn't even glance at Cherish.

Confused, Faith glanced back and forth between Cherish and Edwin. "I don't smoke."

"So? Come breathe in my habit secondhand and keep me company." He patted the doorframe before disappearing back down the hall, already assuming she would follow.

She glanced over at her sister who was already throwing her cigarettes back into her purse. The look on her face showed that the day had definitely taken a turn for the worse. Oh well, might as well earn the bad mood she was going to have to tolerate for the rest of the day. Faith grabbed her bottled water and headed for the back door.

"Enjoy your private time with the boss," Nessa winked at Faith as she passed out of the Girls' Den.

The late morning sun blazed overhead as she stepped around to Edwin's Tundra. It was barely ten in the morning and already the Florida heat was causing the plants to droop. The chill that came with the morning hadn't lasted long. Edwin stood, his right foot on the rear bumper, hands resting on the tailgate while a Camel already sent a strand of smoke into the fresh air. He smiled at her as she exited the building and joined him at the rear of his truck. "Welcome to Smoker's Alley," he teased.

She smiled back, still not sure what was going on, but deciding to just go with it. "Thank you. Is there some sort of hazing that goes with inductees or is it open to anyone?"

"I'm sure I could come up with a private initiation for you." He wiggled his eyebrows at her as he took a pull from his cigarette. "Truck windows are tinted."

Faith laughed as she shook her head. "If this is what Cherish and you do on your little excursions, no wonder she's miffed. Who would want to miss an afternoon romp with Mr. Coldwell?"

Edwin glanced at the building a moment before shrugging his shoulders. "She'll get over it." He turned his dark, mischievous eyes back to Faith. "You, of course, seem to be the fun sister at the moment."

"Is that so?" Faith leaned back against the tailgate and stared out at the woods behind the property, the midmorning breeze tugging through the branches. A jet flew low, preparing to land at the nearby airport. "And why is that?"

"You're the one with stories of parties and dancing." Edwin flipped around and sat on the rear bumper, sliding a little closer as he did. Faith didn't scoot away. "No longer the wallflower, I hear."

Faith shrugged. "Life is too short not to have fun. Selby and I have decided we only get one shot at this life and we're going to live it to its fullest. There are plenty of adventures out there for someone with the guts to go for them. We just so happen to have the guts."

"Good way of looking at life. Is that the reason for the warm reception from your mom or why Cherish seems bitchy toward you?"

"Cherish hates that I'm happy. She doesn't approve that I can enjoy life."

"What is it she doesn't approve of?"

Faith gave a bitter laugh. "That's the funny part. She doesn't know. I don't talk to people about my life. All they know is that I'm out having a good time instead of kowtowing to their wishes for my life." She took a sip of her water before continuing. "Mom is Mom. She's been cold toward me since the day I said I was marrying Selby."

"She doesn't like your husband?"

"She doesn't like that she no longer has control of my actions. She blames Selby for me finally standing up for myself."

Edwin nodded as if he understood, but Faith knew he didn't. He couldn't. People who have a good relationship with their family can never really understand those that don't. It's a foreign concept to them. Parents—normal parents, that is—love their children no matter what they do. A parent's love is supposed to be unconditional. Faith only received that from her father. Her mother had nothing except conditions attached to her love.

"Well, I'm sorry for yesterday," Edwin said after a moment of silence. "It seemed to be my day for screw ups." He took another drag from his Camel and dropped it to the ground, grinding it under the toe of his work boot.

She gave him a reassuring smile. "How were you to know? Hell, I'm part of the family and half the time I don't even know what's going on."

"That has to suck."

"It is what it is." She glanced up at the climbing sun. "I better get back in before her highness takes her anger out on Nessa."

"Well, if you ever need to talk, I'm here." His face was sincere. Then in a blink it turned to playfulness. "Or if you want to take me up on that initiation, we can always pop into the cab of my truck."

Faith laughed as she pushed away from the truck. "You don't think they'd see it rocking?"

"I hope they do." He grinned at her and she felt the heat flush in her cheeks. "It would only boost my sagging reputation."

"I'm sure nothing sags on you."

"Not when you're around."

Faith glanced at his crotch and then caught herself. Jerking her eyes back to his, she knew she had been busted and the smirk on his face only made her pussy drip. He patted the truck and grinned at her. "Just food for thought."

"Edwin! I need your signature," Terry called from the warehouse, waving a clipboard.

Edwin gave her a suggestive wink as he walked over to his warehouse supervisor. Faith watched him walk away, his jeans outlining his firm ass and powerful legs. From sweet to sexy in one sentence, Edwin had managed to show concern *and* stir her passion at the same time. He made some wisecrack as he took the clipboard from Terry about the other's lousy timing and then gave Faith another playful smile before turning back to work.

She stared a moment longer before returning to the office. Her thoughts, however, weren't on work, but on the inside of Edwin's truck. What would it be like to be alone with him there? Was he as good in bed as he thought he was?

"I see all the buttons are in place," Nessa said with a shake of her head as Faith entered the Girls' Den. "Too bad."

Faith gave an overdramatic sigh. "I know, right? Rejected. My feelings are deeply hurt. I don't think I'll recover."

Nessa winked at Faith. "I can sooth those hurt feelings."

"I may just…"

"Can we just work around here?" Cherish slammed a manila folder down on her desk. "That type of conversation is not appropriate for the office."

Both Nessa and Faith just stared at Cherish. Her lips were pressed into a tight thin line and instead of her normal light tapping, she pounded the keys on her keyboard. Faith just gave Nessa a shrug as she swung back around to her own computer. She couldn't believe her sister had become so riled up over one cigarette break. Missing one fifteen minute break was not going to cause her to lose her queen bee status within the Rutherford walls. Faith had been right, however. Quietness at the construction company never lasted long.

~ ~ ~ ~ ~

"And she just snapped? Over a fifteen minute break?" Selby stood in front of their bathroom mirror, wearing just his jeans as he ran a brush through his hair. Just as he would get his hair the way he wanted, Faith would come up and tousle it, saying she preferred his blond locks with a rough look to them. He finally just surrendered.

"Isn't that the stupidest thing you ever heard?" Faith wore a purple thong with a matching push up bra as she stared into the walk-in closet for some outfit to volunteer itself to her for the evening. "It's like if she gets passed over for anything she has to throw a temper tantrum. I swear she never grew up."

"Well, don't let her ruin your night," Selby said as he walked up behind her and slid his arms around her bare belly. "I hear a glass of sangria calling your name."

Faith leaned her head back, resting it on his shoulder as she nuzzled into his neck. He could feel her take a deep breath. "This, right here, is better than any drink," she whispered.

He glided a hand up her smooth stomach to her bra and dipped his fingers inside, toying with a nipple that was hardening to life. Her moan filled his ears as she pushed her ass back into him, grinding it against his cock. She had no problem finding his manhood as it started stiffening inside his tight jeans. His lips discovered her neck, peppering the curve of her shoulder with kisses, knowing that he was sending shivers throughout her body. He felt one of her hands gripping his leg as the other held his forearm.

"You know, we could just call Tracey and cancel," he whispered in her ear. "This seems a much better meal than Italian." He slid his tongue over her bare flesh.

Her groan filled his ears, proving she was tempted. "Knowing our friend, she'd show up to join us."

"And that's bad how?" He kissed her ear as he rolled her swollen nipple between his fingers.

Faith gave his arm a squeeze as she turned in his embrace. "Get dressed. Knowing Tracey, she's early."

Selby kissed her forehead and gave her a disappointed frown. "No fun at all."

"I'll remind you of that later."

Another hour passed before they found themselves sitting around a small table with the short redhead who was already two glasses of pinot noir ahead of them. Her hair hung loose around her shoulders and seemed more an accessory to her peach dress than her actual hair. A silver charm bracelet dangled from her wrist, every once in a while clinking against her wine glass. Her makeup was light and Selby was quick to notice the transformation between work Tracey and off-duty Tracey. He much preferred the off-duty versions.

"I was about to give up on you two." She smiled at them as they slid into their seats. "You decide to have fun without me?"

Selby shrugged. "I tried, but Faith was insistent that we not leave you waiting and ordered me to get dressed. It hurt being rejected for a plate of wet noodles and a moist breadstick."

Faith rolled her eyes as she draped her cloth napkin over her lap. "I'm sure you'll survive. And if you don't stop pouting, *your* breadstick won't get moist later."

"Forceful. Nice." Tracey winked at Faith as she gave a tiny laugh.

The waiter appeared and drinks, as well as appetizers, were quickly ordered. The small place was alive with customers and busy serving staff. The air conditioning was in full force causing the flame in the fancy red glass candle to flicker with violent sparks. Soft music played in the background trying to offer a peaceful, perhaps romantic, atmosphere. To Selby, it beat all of those places that had a television on every wall.

"So, how was the day of my two favorite people?" Tracey sipped her wine as she held the glass with both hands.

Selby's day was boring. Stocking shelves. Cataloging books. Chitchatting with whoever wandered into his store. Quiet. Predictable. Just the way he liked work to be. His philosophy was to save the excitement for after work. That was when life was to be lived.

Faith, however, could talk about work forever, and Selby noticed one name kept popping up as she did. "So, I think Edwin really pissed Cherish off today by asking me to join him on his cigarette break and not her," his wife said.

"Is that a euphemism?" Tracey wiggled her eyebrows. "Is our Faith playing naughty secretary?"

Faith's cheeks turned red as she laughed off the notion. "No, I'm not. Although, we do flirt quite a bit and I'm sure he'd jump if I gave him the come hither." Faith shook her head a little after she took a sip of her wine. "No, he was feeling guilty about the other day and he thought he hurt my feelings and caused more family tension. As if my family needed help in that area."

"How did he hurt your feelings?" Tracey leaned forward as she pulled a breadstick apart to nibble on while they waited for their entrées. "Mine are better, by the way," she said, glancing at the garlic stick in her hand.

"No doubt. Anyway, my mother, bless her icicle heart, showed up at work yesterday." Faith related the whole story from the cigarette break to Edwin's giving them all permission to go out to lunch together. His intention for asking her out on a break was to apologize for putting her in an awkward place. Of course, there had been some playful flirting involved and by her second glass of wine and the first bite of her lasagna, Faith was sharing some of the teasing quips they had passed back and forth.

Tracey was good at getting Faith to talk and Selby just sat back, sipping his Maker's Mark, while the short redhead coaxed every dirty detail out of his wife. He wasn't worried about Faith keeping things secret from him. They had a great relationship and after making the decision to branch out sexually with other people, it was the stories and the flirtatious games that they enjoyed sharing the most. However, this was about someone at her work, her boss, and in Faith's eyes, he could see where she might see the flirting as something out of bounds. Personally, he loved seeing her all worked up. It made things quite a bit steamier when they were alone.

"So, are you going to pursue it?" Tracey asked, her eyebrows arched with eager anticipation. "Sounds like you want to."

"What? With Edwin?" Faith stared at the redhead, and then glanced at Selby who only smiled back. "I mean, he's hot and all, but he's my boss. Wouldn't that just be weird in so many ways?"

Tracey leaned back with a shrug. "People sleep with their bosses all the time. It's only weird if you make it weird. I know you two like playing with other couples, but have you ever thought about having adventures without the other one around?"

Selby had to admit he had never thought of it before and by the look on Faith's face, neither had she. Their rules so far had been easy. They were allowed to tease and flirt. They were even allowed to talk out a sex scene with someone they were interested in via text, sexting the young crowd called it, as long as each other knew about it. However, any physical contact required that they both be present. There was no solo dating with a sex interest. How would they handle opening up their game a little further? He smiled at Faith as he took her hand and kissed it, her skin warm against his lips. He wasn't sure how they would cope, but he could tell that Edwin made his wife's panties wet and that in turn made his cock twitch.

~ ~ ~ ~ ~

Faith stared at herself in the mirror as she finished washing the day's makeup away. The rest of the evening had been full of stories and flirtatious bantering back and forth. She knew that Selby would love to see Tracey and her together, but she wasn't sure she was there, yet. Besides, there wasn't much she knew about the fiery redhead, except she seemed to have an insatiable mischievousness about her. Tracey had befriended Selby because of how close they worked together, and from there she had insinuated herself into their lives. Not that Faith minded, of course. It was good to have a female to talk to about things, and Selby seemed to really care for her.

Still, even with how often they talked, Tracey never revealed much about her past. She seemed to be all about the "Now."

Of course, Tracey was quite the instigator and a tease on top of it. Yet, her suggestion of Selby and Faith playing without each other present had started Faith wondering if she wanted to go that route. So far, Selby and she had played with others while everyone was in the same room. But, what if Selby wasn't in the room? His presence made her feel safe and allowed her the freedom to give herself over to the experience. But, what if he wasn't there? Would she feel as if she had more freedom or be more afraid? Would she go deeper or hold back from whoever she was with?

And what if it were Edwin?

Faith slipped out of her clothes, tossing them into a laundry basket at the rear of the walk-in closet and then slipped an old Florida State T-shirt over her naked body. The room held a slight chill as she left the bathroom and crossed the master bedroom to join Selby who was already in bed, under the covers and enjoying a Mercedes Lackey novel. A cup of hot tea sat on the night stand beside him, probably turning cold as he became lost in whatever fantasy world he was reading about. She scooted in beside him and draped an arm across his waist while laying her head on his chest. He kept his eyes on his book, but wrapped an arm around her shoulders, squeezing her tighter to his body.

"You okay?" He caressed her arm with his fingertips as he spoke. His attention was still on his book, however.

"Just thinking." She ran her fingers over the small trail of hair that traveled from his belly button to his cock, gliding her finger back and forth.

"If your finger is any indication of what you're thinking, I'm game."

She couldn't help but smile as she gave his blond body hair a playful tug. "No. I was thinking about Tracey's questions, about us playing apart."

She felt him close his book before she saw him set it to the side. "And what thoughts have you had?"

"Not much, really. Just whether or not it would be fun or scary as hell. I'm used to you always being there. You're like my security blanket."

"All warm and cuddly?"

She lifted her head and looked into his eyes. "Tattered and frayed around the edges." She pulled his hair again. They both laughed as she laid her head back down. She stared at the picture of the two of them on her dresser. It was of the two of them sitting on the Mad Tea Cup ride at Disney, smiling as they waited for the ride to spin them out of control. "I was just wondering how different it would be."

His hand went from caressing her arm to teasing her hair. "Is it something you want to experiment with? I'm sure there are guys who would be more comfortable if I wasn't around."

"I don't know if I want to or not. It was just something to think about. What are your thoughts? Is it something you'd want to try?"

"I hadn't really thought about it before, to be honest. It would have to be someone we both trusted. I don't want you with anyone that I'm not sure you're safe with or who I don't know about." He was silent for a while, and she knew he was mulling it over. "I suppose we could give it a run through and see how it pans out with the agreement that if either of us becomes uncomfortable, we put an end to it, immediately."

She nodded her head, feeling his hard stomach against her cheek. She ran her fingers back down his abdomen, only this time she kept going until she felt the soft curls around his growing member. She wrapped her hand around his shaft and smiled as she heard him moan. Turning her head, she kissed his flesh, tasting its warmth. As she ran her tongue over his stomach, she glanced up into his eyes. She pumped his cock with a slow, teasing motion, feeling it come to life in her hand. She grinned up at him. "Well, well, Mr. Greer, I do believe the idea of another man ravaging your wife excites you."

He sucked in a deep breath, his eyes widening a little as she gave his cock a tender squeeze. "It does have an exciting air about it," he said, his voice full of the lust she was drawing out of him.

"Does it? Does the idea of you being home alone while another man uses me for his pleasure turn you on?" She lowered her head to his testicles and ran her tongue over the wrinkled skin, eliciting a moan from his lips. She nuzzled her face into his sac and breathed him in. She continued to pump his cock as she kissed around the base, teasing him. "Can you imagine me being taken, maybe in a car or cheap hotel, my legs spread, as another man's cock plunges into me? You won't hear my cries of pleasure, but you'll know I'll be making them, making a story to bring back to you."

Selby reached down and gripped her shoulders, flipping her hard onto her back. Before she could tell what was going on, he was on top of her, her hands pinned above her head. He kissed her ear as he drove his swollen rod deep into her pussy, making her cry out. "And you'll love every minute of it, playing the cheating wife." His voice was a growl in her ear. "But I'll take you the minute you walk in the door." His cock drove in and out of her as her honey dripped. "I'll make you relive every moment of every detail." His hips pounded hers while his balls slapped against her.

She wanted to grip him, claw at his back, but he had her hands clasped tight. Her moans echoed off the walls, her hips rising to meet his. She wanted him deeper, harder. He gave her what she needed, reading her body and her groans. Her body tensed. She cried out. Her orgasm hit like a current ripping through her, making her body jerk

31

and twist under him. As her body started to calm, she felt his cock twitch and his body tense as his lust erupted inside of her.

Faith wrapped her legs around him, holding him to her. He collapsed on top of her, his breathing heavy in her ears as he kissed her, his lips soft against her flesh. She returned the kiss, her body the glowing embers of their passion.

When he finally rolled to the side, arms at his side, his eyes staring at the ceiling without seeing it, she propped herself on her side and smiled at him. "Yeah," she said, her own breathing ragged with the exertion. "I'd say that idea excites you."

Four

Faith Greer hooked her pinkie into the bar handle of the sliding door pulling it open just enough to wedge a foot between frame and door to scoot it open the rest of the way. Her right hand held two glasses of cranberry juice with a carafe of coffee dangling from her index finger while the other balanced two plates of eggs, bacon, hash browns and blackberry jam on toast. She could have been a waitress with that balancing act. Selby finished setting the table on their wooden deck as Journey serenaded them from the speakers. The salt spray brushed against her face as the breeze pulled playfully at her wheaten hair, whipping it around her face and shoulders.

"Will you take these please," she laughed. "I can't see where I'm going."

Selby laughed with her, but instead of helping her, he pulled the strands of hair from her face and licked her nose. "But you look so cute helpless."

"You won't think it's cute when your breakfast hits the deck."

He continued to laugh but unwrapped the carafe and juice glasses from her hand. "I can think of something better for breakfast." He wiggled his eyebrows at her as he set the glasses upon the table.

Faith set the plates down and wrapped her arm around Selby's neck. "I thought men's sexual peak was in their twenties?" She kissed his ear softly, her moistened tongue licking his lobe as she pulled away.

He smiled at her and her breath caught at the sparkle in his eyes. "You, my sweet Faith, make me feel like a teenager."

"Oh, great! Now I'm a pedophile." Her laughter mixed with the crashing waves not far away.

His grin threatened to consume her. "Take me, Mrs. Greer. I've been a very naughty boy."

She laughed and her forest green eyes glinted with mischievous desires. "You *are* a naughty boy, wanting me to be late for work."

Selby laughed as he ushered her to the flower-patterned chair, holding it out for her to sit. "You're just eager to get to those construction hunks. You don't have me fooled one bit."

Faith tucked her hair behind her left ear as she sat. "What can I say? Every girl loves eye candy and most of those guys can give me a sugar high to last all day. Rippling muscles, six pack abs, strong powerful hands that can grip…"

"Okay, okay," Selby held his hands up in surrender, laughing even harder. "I get it. My scrawny frame doesn't compare to those well-toned hunks." Selby let out an overdramatic sigh. "Your puny husband doesn't measure up."

Faith picked up a crisp slice of bacon as she patted his cheek with her right hand. "It's okay, my stick man. You have other uses."

Selby arched his eyebrows and bit her bacon. Faith laughed and bit off a piece herself.

Within the next thirty minutes, Faith dressed for work—gray slacks, a black pull-over low-cut blouse that showed off her orange-sized breasts, and sandals. She was five minutes late, but it wasn't the end of the world. Edwin was pretty easy going. He had to be to put up with all of the nonsense Cherish kept putting him through. The office was casual as long as work got done. And there was plenty of work. Besides, it's hard getting construction workers to be businesslike. It just wasn't part of their job description.

"Morning, Ashley." Faith waved as she passed the young receptionist on her way through the front lobby.

"You're in a chipper mood this morning," the twenty-two-year-old said, her store-bought tits overflowing her blouse.

Faith paused at the door leading into the warren of offices that made up Rutherford Construction. With a playful grin pushing at her cheeks, she turned back to the young blonde. "It's Friday. Who can't be chipper on the last day of the week?" She pulled the door open and entered the inner world of Rutherford Construction and all of its trappings. She was in a great mood and she was determined to keep it that way.

~ ~ ~ ~ ~

Selby took the small, white bag from the short redhead behind the counter of Joe's bakery. "One Everything Bagel and the freshest black coffee in Melbourne."

"The only way to start the day," Selby said.

Tracey Williams just smirked. "Oh, there are other ways, but this is what I'm offering."

Selby Sighed. "All the women in my life insist on teasing me."

"Poor baby." She reached behind her to pour another cup of coffee for a customer. "Speaking of teasing, I won't make our lunch today. I have an appointment I can't miss."

"Anything fun?"

She shrugged. "No, but something I can't get out of. Life throws us crap sometimes and we just have to deal with it."

He gave her a quizzical look. "Everything okay?"

"Yes, I just have to take care of something. So you'll have to fix your own lunch today, you mooch."

"Now, I'm teased and abandoned."

"My heart is breaking for you." She took some money from a man in a suit and tie and wished him a good day. "I'll make it up to you. Now, don't you have a store to open?"

Selby smiled at the fiery woman as he waved two fingers at her from over the white bag. As he turned, he spotted the original Joe of Joe's Bakery engrossed in a game of checkers with another elderly man. Joe still wore his typical all-white clothing as if he still worked at the small bakery. Selby said hello, but didn't stop to chat.

After crossing New Haven, Selby unlocked the wood-framed glass door of his tiny bookstore in Downtown Melbourne. No matter how hard he tried, the place still held that antique store smell left over from the previous owner. The morning downtown traffic came awake as thrift stores, antique shops, bakeries, and small over-priced restaurants came alive. He loved this part of town. The older people walked the shops during the day and at night the young crowd wandered from one pub to another until they couldn't wander anymore.

Setting his briefcase on the counter, he flipped the three light switches bringing Selby's Downtown Books to life for another day. It was not a fancy place, but then again his was not a fancy life. That's the way he wanted it. He was happy and that's all that mattered. Well, Faith's happiness mattered, of course. He glanced at two pictures of Faith on the small desk he used behind the counter, the photos a total display of contrasts if ever there was one. The first was a snapshot of Faith wearing blue jeans and a baggy Florida State sweatshirt, her hair pulled back in a ponytail, sitting under a tree at a local park. The other was of both of them taken by a random passerby at a festival they attended down in Key West the previous October. In one you got the sense of how shy she was, how insecure. The other was a breaking out moment.

He picked up the photo from Key West as he smiled at the changes in his wife, or at least the transformation that she had undergone that week. It was a festival that happened every year down in the Keys that celebrated life with wild parties, parades and exotic costumes. Some people, however, didn't wear costumes at all, but rather had their bodies painted instead. Faith, with a lot of convincing had agreed to go see what it was about. They had been talking fantasies for a while and that trip was a way for her to safely open up a hidden side of her. He was afraid that it might ruin her in the beginning, make her fold in on herself. As soon as she had agreed, Selby called some old friends and booked a small condo. He wasn't giving her a chance to back out.

They left on a Friday night, taking their time and enjoying the road trip. He could tell she was nervous. Faith always fell asleep in the car if she had to be in it for more than thirty minutes and Key West was an eight hour drive. Yet, she was wide awake and as talkative as ever, even without the Mountain Dew intake that was standard fare.

"Nervous?" He had asked her.

She pressed her palms together and slid them between her thighs. "That obvious?"

He had laughed. "I've never heard you talk so much about palm trees before. You seem utterly fascinated with them."

She gave a sheepish smile and a shrug of her shoulders. "What if someone finds out we went?"

"Who could possibly find out?"

"What if we see someone we know?"

"Then they'll be doing the same thing we are with no room to judge." He reached over and squeezed her hand. "It's going to be fine, love. I promise."

She smiled, but he knew she wasn't convinced. Hell, it took him almost eight years to get her to share a fantasy with him. Faith never talked about sex. He knew that she had a boyfriend in high school, but he didn't know how far they had gone beyond kissing and when he would ask, she just changed the subject. After a while, he just quit asking.

Upon their arrival, Faith was still in her jeans and baggy shirt, hiding as much of herself as she could. Selby didn't push, just casually suggesting the sexier shirts and ass-hugging shorts. Everyone at the festival was in lingerie costumes or walking around with their breasts painted, acting out fantasies they had dreamed about the entire year. Anyone wanting to show off their exotic outfits to the cheering crowds was allowed to walk in the parades. By Wednesday, Faith was down to shorts and a bathing suit top that made her creamy globes cry for attention. She was laughing and openly ogling the other visitors and all they displayed. Friday, she wanted to have her breasts painted like so many others she had seen.

"They have them painted so that they can walk around like that. You know that, right?" Selby asked.

Faith blushed. "I know. I want to do it."

"I'm not paying to have it done so that you can hide it under your shirt. And it'll look ridiculous if you put your bathing suit back on."

"I won't. I promise. Please?"

Selby let her have a shot of tequila and led her to the air brush artist. She picked a scene with a white tiger in it and quickly sat in the chair, waiting.

"Honey, he can't do it through your shirt."

Faith blushed even more but pulled her shirt off and unhooked her bra. As far as he knew it was the first time another man had seen her tits. He smiled as he watched her sit there, eyes closed, as the man moved her breasts around preparing to paint. Selby could see her tense at the other man's touch, but she didn't back out, which made him proud of her.

The art work came out great and Selby carried her shirt and bra as Faith walked out on to the street, nipples harder than he had ever seen them. It brought his cock to life just watching her walk in public showing herself off.

The rest of the trip she remained that way and by Saturday night she was only wearing her bathing suit bottoms. People would brush up against her and she wouldn't flinch as she engaged each in conversation. They even met a man named Jake that they spent Saturday evening with helping Faith live out her fantasy.

The whole experience cracked open a door for Faith that she had kept bolted all her life. On the way home they kept reliving the weekend and she kept thanking him for taking her.

"You sure you're not mad at me?"

"Why would I be mad? I took you, remember?"

"Yes, but..."

"Faith, I promise. Nothing happened that I wasn't okay with."

When they got back to Melbourne, Faith wanted to go to the adult toy store. She heard other women talk about vibrators and dildos and wanted to try those next. That in itself was a switch for her. He had suggested buying her one early in their marriage and she had gotten angry at him.

"It would be like cheating on you," she said. "You satisfy me enough. I don't need battery powered toys."

Now, she wanted to try every toy they had. Of course, not everything changed and she was still very timid with sex, even with him. When they first played with them, it had to be under the covers where Selby couldn't see what was happening.

"This way I can pretend it's all you."

"Faith, I'm not an octopus with two dicks."

Of course, by December she was thoroughly enjoying the new sensations and even confessed to using them when Selby wasn't home. He didn't mind. He just wanted details.

One night, Selby came home to find Faith on their couch, naked with one leg draped over the back of the sofa. She had an eight inch dildo they had called Fred shoved between her legs as her vibrator rested on her clit. Selby stripped down and stood beside her, his hand gripping her lengthy hair, pulling her mouth to his sprouting erection. Faith didn't blink. She opened her mouth and he slipped his cock inside, her tongue swirling around his throbbing member as her head bobbed up and down on it. Her hands were shoving Fred in and out of her soaking pussy with abandon as she pressed the dolphin shaped vibrator harder onto her clit. It was amazing to watch and soon the scene before him made him pull his cock from her mouth and shoot his cum onto her darkened breasts. That was all Faith needed to reach her own release. Her back arched as her eyes rolled back into her head and her body rocked violently with her orgasm. Her cries of pleasure echoed off their living room walls as her head rolled side to side. Selby stood in silent awe at his wife who never before would have even touched herself, nevertheless brought herself to an orgasm.

The bell over the front door of the bookstore sounded and Selby snapped back to the mundane present.

"Morning, Selby," Mrs. Patterson, one of his Friday regulars, greeted as she made her way to the Civil War section.

Selby greeted her, but realized he would only embarrass himself if he stood right then. Instead, he recounted the day's starting cash.

~ ~ ~ ~ ~

Faith sat at her desk sorting yesterday's work orders. She never heard Edwin come in behind her and jumped as his hands gripped her shoulders and started massaging them.

"Oh, geez!" Faith yelled at him. "Bark or something, will ya?"

She couldn't see him, but knew he was smiling. "Should I stop?"

Faith lowered her head and relaxed, allowing herself to enjoy the shoulder massage. "Maybe in a year. For now, keep going. I like."

Edwin Coldwell just laughed. "If you turn around we can both enjoy it."

Faith spun her chair around without warning, her face stopping before his waist. With a mischievous grin, she said, "Sure. Let's see what you've got."

He tapped her nose with his finger, still chuckling as she wiggled her eyebrows at him. "I came to tell you that your sister is going to be late."

"And that's different how?"

"I know. I know." Edwin leaned back on Cherish's vacant desk. "Apparently little Jordie was sick this morning. She's taking him to the doctor and will be here at noon."

"I hope she brings lunch."

"If you need something to eat...." Edwin pointed to his crotch, grinning.

"I already said whip it out. You're the one that backed up." She held up her hands and spun back around to her desk. "Hurt a girl's feelings, why don't ya."

Edwin pushed himself off the desk, walked up behind her and kissed the top of her head. "One day, I'm going to surprise you and do it. Then what'll you do?"

"Surprise me and we'll find out."

She heard him chuckle as he kissed her head again and walked out.

Nine minutes after noon, Faith's sister walked in and dropped her purse on her desk. "I hate doctors." Faith swiveled her chair to face her sister who wore the look of aggravation on her pale face.

"What was wrong with Jordie?"

Cherish plopped into her chair, glanced at the list of to-do's on her desk, then quickly ignored them. "A cold. That's it, a cold. They gave me a fifty-six dollar prescription for medicine and a 'Have a nice day.'"

"Well, it is March. Cold weather and warm weather flipping back and forth every few minutes. Florida weather breeds colds throughout the year."

Cherish just shrugged. "So, what did I miss?"

Faith turned back around. "Not a thing. Morning paperwork is done. Everyone's at their jobs and the guys are at lunch. A typical day."

Cherish picked up the thick manila folder of applications that sat in the middle of her desk. "Yea, typical."

Faith just laughed as she returned to the task of answering emails. Cherish had worked for Rutherford Construction two years prior to Faith's getting hired on and was, in fact, the reason Faith got the job. Cherish was the human resources person for their office and three years ago when the previous secretary, Betsy Farmer, moved to one of the offices in West Palm Beach, Cherish got Faith hired on. Not wanting her younger sister to regret hiring her, Faith busted her ass at her job and soon became more valuable to the company than Cherish.

And Cherish knew it.

"Hey, Faith," a baritone voice interrupted her thoughts as she was entering the laborers' time sheets for the Nasa Medical Complex. Jed stood in the doorway. His smile was bright in the center of his dark beard and mustache and his chocolate eyes always matched his smile. "Edwin needs you to do a check on the spare trucks for the teams he has to send beachside for those new condo units."

"I'll get right on it." Faith couldn't help but smile back. She finished her email and then scooped up her clipboard. "I'll be out back," she told Cherish as she passed by her desk.

"Whatever," was all the response she received back.

Faith shook her head once as she passed through the door, but came up short as she was instantly tangled up in another set of arms.

"Where to, Gorgeous?" Deon wrapped his arms around her waist and held her tight.

"Oh, for....You scared the hell out of me, Deon." Faith didn't push away. Deon was half Mexican and half American and thought he was a god to the ladies. At twenty-two he was merely a player.

He squeezed Faith's ass before letting go. "You're all Heaven, Baby." He winked at her and then walked off.

Faith closed her eyes and took a deep breath. She could still feel the kid's hands on her ass cheeks and that brought a smile to her face. With another deep breath she continued down the hall to the office's back door. Deon was a player all right. He would nail any girl he could and brag on it to everyone who would listen. Still, it was fun to think about it. And Faith thought about it.

Faith, Faith, Faith. What on earth are you thinking? He's a kid. She turned and caught a glimpse of the young, muscular youth as he turned the corner, probably on his way to harass Ashlynn. He was definitely nice to look at. *Faith, stop that*, she scolded herself as she passed out the back door and into the afternoon sun. Her thought processes had changed so much since their time in the Keys last October. Sex had been a major no-no before that, at least enjoying it was. Not that she didn't enjoy sex. She did. Very much. It's just that she had to shut that away. She had discovered what she liked in high school, but it was wrong. All wrong. And it was contrary to what her parents had raised her to believe, at least her mother. Her father tended to shy away from any conversation dealing with sex of any kind. Faith's mother had raised her in a very strict legalistic Southern Baptist way and discussing sex was forbidden.

"Your husband will teach you on your wedding night how to please him. He's the one that will matter, so there's no sense discussing it until then." Her mom gave the same answer every time. Faith couldn't remember a time when her parents would have had sex. No child wants to know about their parents doing it, but there were usually signs that it was going on. Yet, there never were.

The Driscoll girls weren't even allowed to comment on whether a boy was cute or not.

That was purely "of the flesh and Satan." Faith didn't know much about it being from Satan but it was surely from the flesh as her panties were soaking wet quite often. It wasn't until she married Selby that she wore her first pair of thongs. He had bought them for her and it took her forever to try them on for him. Her entire ass was exposed, after all. Good girls didn't wear such dental floss, she had been raised to think.

Faith couldn't help but laugh as she remembered how her mom had found a pair when she had been helping Faith fold clothes one morning. It wasn't an approving reaction.

"What's so funny?" Edwin came out from between two of the trucks, the wind whipping his raven black hair, a Salem cigarette in his fingers.

Faith hugged the clipboard to her chest as she leaned back against one of the vehicles. "I was thinking of my mom. Remember Cherish and I telling you how strict our family was, well, my mom anyway?"

Propping a foot on the rear bumper of the red Ford F150, Edwin nodded, his hands resting on the closed tailgate. "Your dad was pretty easy going, but your mom was rigid. Then Cherish broke all the rules and got away with it."

"She was mother's baby and now she's momma's bitch." Edwin arched an eyebrow at that but Faith ignored it. "Anyway, Mom was visiting shortly after Selby and I were married and helping me fold some laundry. Selby had bought me some lacy thongs and Mom picked up a pair. Oh my god, you would have thought she had picked up a snake." Both started laughing as Faith told the story. "'What has that boy done to you?' my mom squealed, dropping the thong on the bed. She only believed in granny panties. I don't think she came back to our 'house of sin' for a couple of months."

"Now see, if I had your thongs in my hands, I'd be back daily." Edwin grinned at her.

Faith blushed as she tucked a stray strand of hair behind her ear. "Promises, promises."

"Oh, I promise."

"I can only imagine." Faith laughed as she pushed herself off the truck. "Now, let me get these inspections done. When do the new crews start?"

Edwin took a drag from his cigarette as he stared into her eyes. "I bet you went back to granny panties."

Faith laughed and reached a finger into her jeans waist and pulled out the string to her thong. "Nope."

Edwin tossed the stump of his cigarette into the yard as he laughed. "That's not what I was hoping for."

"I know." Faith grinned at him and walked away. "Maybe if you're a good boy."

"Edwin!" Jed called from the back door.

Edwin waved that he was coming. He turned back to Faith who was unlocking the first truck's passenger door. "Oh, and I can be very good. Very." He smiled at her and then walked away, hands tucked into his front pockets.

"Don't you have a new girlfriend?" She called out to him.

He spun, walking backwards now. "And you have a husband." He shrugged and spun back around.

Faith watched him walk away, wondering just how good Edwin Coldwell could be. And if his girlfriend knew how much of a flirt he was.

Five

Faith was putting the baked ziti on the table as Selby walked in and dropped his briefcase on the chair by the front door. "Something smells great," he said as he passed through the house on his way to the dining room. Their house was a single story structure over-looking the beach in Indialantic. The front door faced A1A with a garage on the north side. When you entered the front door, to your left was what they called the television room with two sofas and a massive entertainment center housing a 56-inch flat screen. To the right was the sitting room with a solid granite wall encircling a fireplace. Directly in front of the door was another doorway leading to the kitchen. As soon as you passed through that, to your right was the master bedroom. The kitchen was a large affair with a huge walk-in pantry and an island in the middle. The dining room was to the left of the island with a hall leading to a couple of small bedrooms, Selby's office, and the guest bathroom. Behind the kitchen were the Florida room and then the back deck with stairs leading to the ocean.

Faith handed Selby a glass of white Zinfandel as he wrapped an arm around her and brushed her neck with his warm lips. She tilted her head as her eyes closed. "I hope it tastes good."

He kept kissing her neck. "If it tastes half as good as this neck, then it's a gourmet delight."

Faith moaned with pleasure. "That's dessert."

Selby bit her neck playfully before pulling away and taking the glass of wine. "And how was your day, brat?"

Faith smiled at him as she grabbed the salad bowl from the counter and took her spot at the table. "I was surrounded by strong, tanned men. My day was awesome."

"My wife, the slut." Selby laughed before sipping his wine.

"I'm not a slut. I'm a tease. Big difference."

He nodded. "True. One engages men while the other enrages them."

Faith shrugged her shoulders as she scooped the ziti onto both of their plates. "They seem to enjoy it."

"And what guy wouldn't enjoy that body of yours?"

"So true, so true."

"So tell me how you flirted with them today." And she did without leaving anything out. It was their ritual. Faith could flirt and tease all she wanted as long as she recited everything to Selby that night. Sometimes, they even added it to their sexual play with her telling him how the guys fondled her ass and tried to sneak peeks down her low-cut blouses to catch as much of her breasts as they could with their eyes. It made her feel sexy as hell that those men wanted to touch her and grope her. For so long she had thought of herself as too fat or not pretty enough or some other flaw thanks to her mother. Selby had entered her life and changed all of that. He had made her feel beautiful and even more, he made her believe she was beautiful.

"I swear that sister of yours just needs a good fucking," Selby said around a mouthful of garlic bread.

Faith choked on her wine almost spewing it across the table. "Okay, I do not want to mix my sister and sex in the same conversation."

Selby shrugged, sitting back in his chair, wineglass in hand. "I'm just saying for the black sheep of the family, the wild child of the Driscolls, you would think she'd have more life in her."

It was Faith's turn to shrug. "She's more like Mom than my brother or me. I think she's trying to make up for her lousy behavior in her younger days or maybe family life has drastically changed her. Who knows?"

She could feel Selby staring at her, but she really had no answer for him. Her family was a bunch of self-righteous hypocrites who could do no wrong; at least, everyone but Faith. Everything she did *was* wrong in their eyes. Yet, she was the only one who had never gone down a dark street in her life. Cherish had started acting out in high school, dating the wrong kind of boys according to her parents. Then it was sex, drugs, and drinking and she never bothered to hide any of it. Still, she was the baby and that was the excuse.

Faith had given up trying to please her family. Selby was the one she focused on now. It was more than enough to keep her content.

"Let's change the subject. Cherish is a bitch. Case closed." Faith sipped her wine. "What are we going to do this weekend?"

Together, they scraped the dishes and cleaned up. Faith washed while Selby dried and put away. As they wiped the table and counters, they batted around ideas, not only for their weekend, but other adventures they wanted to take.

"Let's get out of town," Selby finally suggested.

"Now?"

"Tomorrow morning. We'll get up early, watch the sunrise, then head to Madeira Beach and watch it set. We'll get a room and come back on Sunday. It'll be fun. You can ride naked." He waggled his eyebrows up and down at her.

"I'm sure the truckers would love that." Faith laughed as she dried her hands.

"I know I would."

Of that, Faith had no doubt. She put the towel down and thought about it. Audrey watched the bookstore on the weekends for Selby, so there really wasn't a good reason not to do it. She left the towel on the counter and walked over to her husband, her hands sliding around his waist as she kissed his neck. "Why not? Romantic and spontaneous. I love it."

He kissed her softly on the forehead, his warm lips lingering. "Good. I'll get the car ready while you pack a bag. No nightie needed." He grinned again.

"That was already assumed, my love."

That night, after their small Accord was fueled and packed up, they curled up in front of the fire, wrapped in a thin blanket, each holding a glass of wine. The sap in the wood popped and sizzled, the dancing flames hypnotizing the two of them. Faith leaned back against Selby's chest, losing herself in the fire and the beating of his heart. She could easily drift off to sleep sitting in his arms. Peacefulness washed over her, taking her breath away even seven plus years later. He had been the one to anchor her heart, her soul.

She reached up, her hand sliding up his arm and over his neck, up into his blond hair. With a deep breath, she pulled him closer, needing that contact.

Selby wrapped himself around her, his arms snaking around her waist. He buried his face into her neck, breathing her in. "What are you thinking, love?"

She stayed quiet a moment, lost in the feel of him, his strength around her. She closed her eyes, wrapped in the heat of him behind her and the fire in front of her. The warmth filled her, surrounded her.

"I was thinking how growing up, people would tell me not to be afraid of who I am and then proceed to tell me who I was, or rather, who I was supposed to be." She held onto him as she spoke, her hand pulling him closer. "I was always afraid of disappointing people, my family, church members, even you for a while. For so long, I never knew who I was because I allowed others to dictate my actions. A good wife does so-and-so. Christian ladies behave this way. Don't like that, but do like this." She shrugged a little.

She felt him shift behind her, and then felt his lips on her neck. "I love who and how you are."

She laughed. "You like me naked and spread."

He moved a finger to her chin, turning her face, so he could look into her eyes. "I love you because you're you and I'd love you even in sackcloth and ashes. I don't want a robot or a doormat. I want you. You're not the same quiet girl I married seven years ago or the girl I dated the two years before that. We've both grown and changed, but together and, in my opinion, for the better."

She stared into his deep ocean blue eyes and leaned forward to kiss him, his lips warm and tasting like the wine they had finished off. She felt his hands squeezing her, pulling her into his embrace, into him. His warm breath brushed her cheek as they kissed, lost in each other. Backwards, she pushed him, the kiss never breaking, until he was flat on his back, her body bearing down on him. Harder, she pressed her lips into his, gliding her tongue over his teeth before fencing with his tongue as their mouths opened in passion. Selby's hands roamed up and down her back, hard, pressing her into him and she could feel his reaction pressing into her abdomen.

"This is what you like." Her voice was deep, sultry as she broke the kiss. The warmth of their bodies now moistened her special places. Her fingers raked down his bare chest until his hardness filled her fingers. She kissed her way down to his neck and around until she could suck his lobe into her hungry mouth. She bit his ear, feeling his body tense under her from the pleasure and pain mixed. "You love that your wife is no longer the timid church girl, don't you?" Her hand stroked up and down the stiffness filling his pants.

He whispered, "Yes." His breathing heavy from her hand's playing.

She sucked on his ear more. "You love that your wife's a horny little slut now, don't you?"

"Yes," he groaned.

She unbuttoned his jeans, and then eased the zipper down, teasing him with a fingernail down his shaft as she did. His hips moved upward, his body wanting more. With soft kisses, she followed a trail down his chest to his nipple, flicking it before sucking on it. Her hand slipped inside the opening of his boxers and took his hardness in her hand, caressing the sides, one finger rubbing the moisture that had leaked out of the tip. "You've made me hungry for more. This is the me I am now, Selby. Is this what you want?"

"Yes, Faith. Oh god, yes." One of his hands played with her hair, fondling her head. "I just want you. Anyway you are as long as you are mine."

She nipped at his nipple, looking up at him. Pulling away, she smiled at him, lifting the sundress she was wearing to her waist as she straddled him. "Oh, I believe you, love." She slid her thong to the side and placed the tip of his cock at her dripping opening. "But you love this me, don't you?" She lowered herself down onto him, taking his full length into her, her mouth opening just a little at the sensation. "Don't you, Selby?"

His hands pressed on the carpet, his eyes closed. "Yes!" She felt his body tense as she rocked back and forth on him in a slow rhythm, her clit rubbing against him. Her head bent, eyes closed, she allowed her hair to brush against his face as her hips rocked back and forth. She enjoyed the way he felt inside of her, pressing against the top wall of her pussy as she controlled the angle as well as the depth. She sped up her gyrations as she felt his hands slide up her dress to massage her breasts. God, it felt so good having his hands on her.

She heard him talking, but no longer could make out what he said. His fingers pinched her nipples, twisting them. Her mouth opened with the pleasure-pain and she felt her body shudder as her release finally spread over her.

"Oh, god," he grunted as she felt his cock throb inside of her before filling her with his seed. His fingers gripped her, holding her as his orgasm erupted through them both.

Still lost in the moment, she ground her hips back and forth on him until she felt him slip from her passage. Unable and unwilling to move, she laid her head on his chest as his arms enfolded her.

"That's what I am, my love. A woman so hungry for you she can't even wait to be naked." Her voice was soft, heady.

He kissed the top of her head as he squeezed her to him. Together, wrapped in their love and each other's arms, they drifted off to sleep.

~ ~ ~ ~ ~

Sometime in the night Faith woke and they stumbled to their bed, stripped down and slept again. At five thirty, the alarm went off and their weekend adventure began. It was in the beginning of their marriage that they began to take spontaneous trips, much to her parents'—more her mother's—grumbling. Weekend trips were fine as long as you were still in your pew come Sunday morning. The difference between going to Heaven or Hell was how many times you skipped church. Valerie Driscoll blamed Selby for Faith's downward spiral.

"Plenty of boys for you to marry here at the church and you go and find a dreamer that's never graced a church step in his life," her mother scolded when Faith brought Selby home.

"Selby has more personality than those sheep at church."

"We are called to be sheep. Those men are following the Lord's path for their lives."

"Sheep are brainless animals, Mother. They'll follow one another over the side of a cliff unless someone stops them. Do you ever wonder why you are called to be a brainless animal?"

"It is called faith, Faith. God directs our lives and we follow."

"Even if he leads you over a cliff?"

Selby was not a sheep. Faith's mother called him a wolf and Faith his meal. Faith preferred her husband's free thinking to the rote conversation of people who talked of doing good, but never actually did anything.

"The car is loaded, love," Selby said as he came in. He wore a Hawaiian shirt with khaki shorts and flip-flops. Dark narrow sun glasses rested on his head just waiting to be pushed down.

Faith handed him a mug of coffee and the thermos before picking up the blanket that rested on the barstool. "Something to cuddle in as we watch the sunrise."

The morning was damp with dew and salt spray as they made their way through the dark, across the patio and down the steps to the sand. The beach air was chill and Faith had already wrapped the blanket around her, trying to save as much warmth from her bed as possible. The darkness of night was being nudged away by the pink of dawn as the barely-seen waves crashed upon the shells, scattering and rearranging. She found a soft, clear spot and sat among the ocean's discards and left-over seaweed from the tide, offering Selby some of her blanket. He took it, wrapping his left arm around her waist and snuggling in close. He sipped his coffee as Faith leaned her head on his shoulder.

"It's so peaceful on the beach in the morning," she whispered, almost as if her words would ruin the serenity of the moment.

Further along the beach, another couple could be seen awaiting the dawn of a fresh day.

"That it is, love." Selby rested the mug on his knee as he caressed her side with his free hand.

The pale yellows and oranges mixed with light blues as the sun peeked over the horizon. Seagulls glided along the breaking waves, a new dawn starting a fresh day with new opportunities. She had seen each day like that for the past few months. No longer pleasing family, friend, or church, she was determined to live each day to its fullest for Selby and herself.

"You know what I love about the beach?" Selby asked.

Faith snuggled into him. "What's that?"

"While it's always the same, it's also always changing. The tide brings things in as well as steals things. Even the shape changes due to erosion. Coquina rock and shale are either covered or revealed. It's a changing constant."

She found herself smiling as she thought of his words. "Sounds like us this year." He kissed her forehead. "My private beach."

The sun climbed with greater speed, it seemed, after that first break of dawn, and the dark night was replaced with the pale rays of day. It always took Faith's breath away. This proved there was a God, even if not what typical man thought.

Soon they were in the Accord and driving west. It almost felt like they were in a race with the sun. Faith had worn a lavender sundress with a bra and a matching thong. Sandals set on the floorboard as her feet rested on the dash. She loved road trips and missed taking them. There were so many places she wanted to see and explore. Once past the toll booths on the Beeline, they'd hit I-4 to 275 and the Gulf Coast. They'd be in the car for almost three hours. She grinned with a wicked delight at all of the possibilities.

It didn't take Selby long with those thoughts, either. Once they were on I-4 he ran his hand up her calve, over her knee, and along her thigh. Faith's legs fell open, giving him better access to her pink slit. He slipped his hand under her dress, reaching his fingers closer to her passion. A moan escaped her as the fingers grazed along her moistening mound.

Selby said nothing, nor did he look at her. With his eyes on the road as he weaved among Saturday traveling traffic, he slipped one finger into her wetness, feeling her body surrender to the intrusion. She put a hand behind her, holding onto the headrest, her hips pushing downward to meet his fingers. "More please," she practically groaned.

"Lift your dress so that your ass is sitting on the seat." He didn't give her another finger. Waiting. She complied, sliding the dress up to her waist, her ass sitting back down on the cold seat. "Now, slide that pretty little thong off." Without hesitation, she hooked her thumbs into the sides of her panties and slid the thong down her thighs and off her legs. "Put it on the dash." She obeyed. She knew that only truckers would probably see her skimpy panties, but the fact that anyone could sent a humiliating, naughty thrill through her.

Selby's finger slid back inside of her sweet wetness, his thumb pressing against her swelling clit. Again, Faith pushed down and asked for more, her voice soft and raspy.

"Turn so that you face me."

Faith slid around, putting her back to the door and opening her legs wide, exposing her most private part to his pleasure. As soon as she was still, he shoved two fingers into her causing her mouth to drop open with a gasp as her back arched against the door. "Yes!"

He curved his fingers slightly so that they rubbed the underside of her pubic bone to get to that most sensitive of places. Her ass raised inches into the air as her head shook back and forth. Her wetness covered his fingers as his thumb continued to press against her clit, swirling it in small tight circles. When he slid his fingers out, he added a third and shoved them harder back inside of her.

A truck pulled up alongside them. The driver was a young kid with shaggy, walnut hair and two days growth on his face. He was passing by on the right side, apparently about to yell at Selby for being in the passing lane and not passing, when he glanced over and saw what was going on. He slowed down without yelling, matching Selby's pace.

Selby continued to fuck his fingers in and out of Faith's slick channel, pressing the inside of her. Her moans and whimpers bounced off the interior of the car as her hips thrust up to meet his hand.

"Oh god, Selby. Selby!" Her inner walls squeezed his fingers tight as her body shook with her climax. Her left hand beat the seat while her right gripped the dash with all of her strength. Her cries drowned out the Black Eyed Peas' "I Gotta Feeling" that had been coming out of the radio.

Selby continued to finger fuck her until her body relaxed, her breathing ragged, spent. After pulling his fingers out of her wetness, he held them up to her. "Clean them, please."

Faith sighed. She hated tasting herself, but she leaned forward taking all three fingers into her mouth, suckling them, her tongue sliding around and between each one until only her saliva was left.

As she slipped them out of her mouth, Selby smiled. "Very nice. Now, turn and wave at our new friend."

Faith looked confused, but turned as she was told. The young truck driver just waved, a satisfied grin on his face. Faith blushed, the heat rushing to her face. She waved back with an embarrassed smile as Selby pushed on the accelerator.

Six

Madeira Beach is a small community below the Clearwater area on the West Coast of Florida with a Key West feel to it. It was more of a beach community than a city. Bike paths out-numbered the streets and a canal ran alongside the road opposite the shoreline. Furthermore, most restaurants and businesses had a boat dock for customers to arrive by water. The beach back home was more laid back than the mainland, but you could still feel the city encroaching on your location. Madeira Beach was different. Faith had not realized how much she missed the place until they pulled up into their condo rental.

Selby always found a room directly on the beach close to a place called John's Pass, which was full of specialty shops and small cateries. Everything was low key, laid back. They checked in, put the bags in their room and locked the car knowing they wouldn't get into it again until they were ready to return home. Breathing in the calmness that filled the air, Faith doubted she'd ever be ready to return.

Together, hands clasped and swaying slightly, they walked down the sidewalk that ran parallel to the two-lane road. Even the cars driving by had a laid back speed to them. No one was in any hurry to get anywhere. The two-story buildings of John's Pass were what Faith thought of as beach colors, sandstone, light peaches and faded yellows with driftwood used as business signs. There were your normal shoe stores and tee-shirt huts, even a leather-works shop. However, there were also crystal shops, a nautical store, a winery and a cigar store specializing in hand-rolled cigars. It was one of her favorite places to visit.

"Shop first or lunch?"

"Food first," Faith answered. "Who can shop on an empty stomach?"

They climbed a flight of rickety stairs and found a sandwich shop toward the south end. With BLTs and Coronas ordered, they enjoyed the outside breeze on the deck as people buzzed around. Eating outdoors was one of the many pleasures they both enjoyed about living in Florida. Some, if not most, dreaded the sticky humidity that seemed too thick on an average day, but they loved the sun and freshness of its warmth.

"Did I tell you Tracey had some appointment yesterday she wouldn't tell me about?" Selby was watching people walk in and out of a shoe store across the street as he spoke. "It's not like her to be so close-lipped."

The waitress arrived and plopped down a couple of bottles with limes poking out of the opening. Faith shoved hers down into the Mexican beer with her thumb and gave it a slight shake. "It's probably nothing. We females do enjoy our secrets." She gave him a small smile before sipping the beer. She knew that her husband had grown fond of the fiery redhead and would worry no matter what she had said. As she set the tall bottle back on the table, she admitted to herself that she had grown pretty fond of the younger woman as well. "You know, it's funny that with all of our little adventures, none of them have included Tracey. I mean, it's obvious that you two are attracted to each other, and you have teased me quite a bit about playing with her."

Selby nodded. "True. Yet, most of our encounters have been out of town with strangers. We haven't exactly had this kind of fun close to home."

"Right, but if we're going to venture out solo as we talked about, we'll have to do it back home. No trips alone. Perhaps now is the time for you to test the waters with her, see if she really is interested."

Selby laughed as he stared into her eyes, his fingers toying with his bottle. "I love our conversations. They would freak the average person out."

"We are far from average and nowhere near normal. Besides, you have to admit, as soon as we talked about this your mind went straight to Tracey."

It was cute the way her husband blushed and Faith took pride in the fact that she could still make him do it. "It did. I won't deny it. I would just hate to ruin a friendship."

Faith reached over and patted his hand. "Babe, it's obvious how she feels toward you. It's not going to ruin anything. Besides, it would definitely liven up your lunch dates."

Selby nodded and refrained from saying anything else as the waitress arrived with their sandwiches. However, Faith knew her husband. His mind was reeling with ideas of how to have that conversation with Tracey Williams and follow where his cock was pointing.

The rest of the day was spent browsing the novelty shops and dreaming of redecorating their small house. Faith bought a butterfly wind chime and Selby picked up two of the hand-rolled cigars. When they weren't in the stores touching this and that, they were touching each other. Selby would run his fingers through her hair, letting the wheaten strands cascade off his hand like water over rocks. Faith would hold his hand and walk with her head on his shoulder as they whispered among themselves.

"You have an admirer it seems," Selby whispered to her as they entered the winery.

"Oh?" Faith tried to look without looking. She was surprised she hadn't noticed anyone watching her. Usually, she was more observant than that. She wasn't, however, surprised that Selby had. He noticed everything.

As Selby led them to the portion of the bar where the gentleman waited for people to sample his vintages, Faith saw him. A dark haired man, slightly tanned with a surfer's body, had followed them into the wine shop. She had seen him before, but had paid no attention to him. He had been at the leather shop when Selby and she had teased about the belts and the intense things they could use them for that didn't involve holding up a pair of pants. Pants weren't even to be worn while the belts were used.

He smiled at her when their eyes met. Faith felt her cheeks flush as a quick smile crossed her face before turning back to Selby and squeezing his hand. Selby chuckled at her and she dug her fingernails into his palm. He only laughed harder. "Perhaps today's fun has just arrived."

"What do you say, folks?" The silver-haired man behind the counter smiled at them. "Care to sample this year's delights?"

"A wonderful idea," Selby said as he ushered Faith to the wooden bar. She leaned on the polished wood and put one of the oyster crackers that sat in a bowl in her mouth to start with a fresh palate.

"Mind if I join you?"

Faith turned and saw the dark-haired man slide up beside her on the bar. He reached his arm across her to shake hands with Selby. "My name's Paul, Paul Butler."

"Selby Greer," Selby said, shaking the man's hand. "This is my lovely wife, Faith."

Paul took Faith's hand and kissed her knuckles. "Lovely is an understatement."

Blushing, Faith only whispered, "Please, join us." And in her mind, the phrase was colored with many shades of meaning.

Paul took one of the crackers and popped it into his mouth. Faith couldn't take her eyes off his long fingers as he placed the cracker in his mouth with a seductive push, allowing his finger to linger as his deep hazel eyes took her in. Her breath caught and she forced herself to focus on what the man behind the counter was saying. She felt her heart beat harder as the heat went from her cheeks to between her legs. Concentrating was going to be hard.

~ ~ ~ ~ ~

"This is something new we tried this year," the older man was saying as he poured two swallows into each of the clear wine glasses. "When tasting a wine for the first time, you should ignore the first sip as it's a shock to your senses. Always judge the wine by the second swallow as to whether you like it or not; never the first." He then proceeded to explain the mango and peach combination they were sampling.

Selby only half paid attention. His main focus was on the images in the mirror behind the bar, which gave him a perfect view of Paul and Faith. He thought it cute how flustered Faith became with Paul's arrival. He had watched her blossom into an adventurous woman over the past year, allowing herself to explore a side of her she had kept buried for so long. It was a side that had been embarrassed in high school and yet, while buried, it never completely disappeared.

Breathing in the fruity aroma of the chardonnay, Selby's mind drifted backwards to a day at the beach that had set their present course. The day for the most part was uneventful and typical. The cool ocean breeze slid around their barely clad bodies, contrasting the skin-burning heat from the sun overhead. Their house was in a less populated area so the beach was almost deserted. Faith had risked tanning topless a few times as few beachcombers walked that far down the dunes.

"Now, this is from watermelon and has a very sweet taste." Selby slipped a cracker into his mouth.

It was more the conversation that day on the beach as they lay upon their blanket that had opened them up to their present adventures. Selby had always tried to get Faith to share her sexual fantasies with him and she always balked at the thought of even possessing them. It embarrassed her every time the topic came up.

"I'm sorry, Selby. I'm not built to think that way. It's just not right."

He shook his head. "That's your mother talking," he said. "After all, aren't you the girl who picked the song we danced to at our wedding? You know, the one that sang about us making love."

"It was not! That was a beautiful song."

He nodded. "It was. But what do you think they were doing face to face, sweetheart?"

Her face flushed at the thought and he smiled as he ran a hand down her sunburned arm. "Faith, it's just us. It's okay to think outside the church box. I've seen the books you read and experienced your love after certain chapters. I know that some things excite you. I just want to know what those things are so we can have some fun."

She had squirmed as she sat there, delaying her answer by drinking from her water bottle. She almost drank it all.

"Selby, I just…"

"I won't be mad or jealous. Trust me."

She paused again, took a deep breath and then answered. "I've thought those scenes where two guys took the girl were pretty hot."

They spent the day talking about the novels she read and how certain things caused her sex to burn. He assured her that it was all okay and told her how he thought it was all pretty hot as well. He could tell that she was holding something back, but wasn't going to press. Her revelation was a beginning and the next day they made their plans to attend Fantasy Fest.

"Shall we try some reds now?" The man at the winery asked as he rinsed the three glasses used for the Zinfandel samples.

~ ~ ~ ~ ~

Faith wished that they had more crackers to eat as they were on their sixth wine sample and she was beginning to feel the effects. Paul had scooted closer to her and she felt his breath caress her arm. Selby was nuzzled in on the other side and would lean down occasionally and kiss her ear lobe every once in a while. Her body was reacting to more than the wine, and it seemed both men were encouraging it.

When the wine tasting was over, both men bought a bottle, one white and one red. They tipped the silver-haired man and walked back out into the pre-evening air. The conversation was casual as the three of them started off toward the rented condo. Faith knew why Paul was tagging along and knew Selby was giving it to her. The butterflies started as she worried about disappointing either of them. However, her body was burning from the excitement and need that was engulfing her. Her mind screamed that she shouldn't, but her body knew she would. This was the real reason they escaped on their occasional weekend getaways, for both of them to see what sexual encounter would present itself to them. Sometimes, it was a couple or a single guy. Other times, they made their own excitement. Either way, they always had fun and came back with stories to repeat to each other.

Unconsciously, she wiped her sweaty palms on her sundress. The battle warred within her to turn this man around and send him on his way. It was the same battle that always waged within her before one of their adventures. It was wrong! Yet, her body burned for it. Part of her felt like it was cheating on Selby while the hornier part, the part that her husband had pushed open, wanted this stranger, wanted his cock, wanted him to take her and ravage her. It was the same battle every time. As much as she wanted it, she fought her upbringing that was against it.

The walk was short and soon they were climbing the weather-worn steps that led to the front door on the second floor. She gripped the rail with shaking fingers as she ascended, the two men conversing as if nothing out of the ordinary was about to happen. Yet, she knew it was.

Once inside, Selby took Paul's bottle of wine, setting both of them on the table. Faith panicked, not knowing what to do, afraid of doing the wrong thing, afraid of doing anything. There was no protocol for "Hey, let's go to your place and fuck." It wasn't something that always happened to her.

But it was happening. Right then. Right there.

Paul was standing in front of her and she had to look up to see into his eyes. A hand slid around her neck and under her hair, the calluses from his palm rough on her flesh. Her eyes never left his lips until they were pressed to hers with warmth that went straight to her sweet passage. She didn't know where Selby was, but could feel his presence in the room. Paul's breath was still sweet with the merlot they last sampled, his lips soft and gentle. He sucked her lower lip into his mouth, licking it with his tongue.

Hands went around her waist and she felt her sundress sliding up her thighs. Selby. His lips moistened her bare shoulder as he slowly raised her dress enough that his hands could caress her naked ass. Her mind reeled with the passion that coursed through her body, the sensations of so many hands roaming her body. She surrendered to the two men, the battle decided, her frontier about to be conquered.

Paul trailed kisses down her chin and throat to her other shoulder as his strong hand slid the spaghetti strap down her arm. He continued a trail of gentle kisses down her chest to the slope of her breast as his other hand slid from her neck down her throat to her hardening nipple on her other soft globe. Both at once shriveled with desire and hardened as tongue and fingers flicked the swollen nubs back and forth.

61

She couldn't concentrate. Hands roamed all over her. So lost was she in the pleasure, she hadn't noticed when her sundress had been taken off or even who had done it. She stood in the middle of the living room completely nude, one hand inside Paul's shirt as the other wrapped inside Selby's hair. Her husband knelt behind her planting tender kisses on her ass. She felt his hands roaming up and down her thighs as Paul's stronger, rougher hand pinched her nipple, twisting it, bringing a yelp from her lips. She felt her wetness increase. Selby had pinched her before, but was always afraid to get too rough with her. Paul seemed not to have her husband's reluctance. It hurt, the pain coursing through her as he twisted her tiny nipple, pulling it downward to her stomach. She found herself yearning for more of his hands, his roughness.

Paul's lips were at her ear, his breathing heavy, his voice growling. "A little tart, aren't you? You like that pain, don't you, my toy?" His smile teased her, almost mocking her.

His words inflamed her passion, stoked the flames that burned between her legs. She should be insulted, but instead she only grew hotter. She should slap his face and order him out of their condo. Instead, she groaned, "Yes. Yes, I am."

The pain sharpened in her tit as he twisted even harder. "You didn't answer my other question, Tart. You like the pain, don't you? Or would you rather I stop and just take you?"

The pinching pain stole the breath from her voice as she felt herself ease up on her tip toes. Selby's lips slid across her ass as she was pulled away. "Yes!" She finally screamed. "Oh god, yes. I...I like the pain. I like it all."

Paul slid a finger down her slender stomach to her bare pussy. His finger grazed her pulsing clit, sending shivers through her before slipping between her velvet folds. Her body ached from his touch.

Again, that grin. "I heard that conversation in the leather shop, the control you like to feel. Your wetness reveals your body's desire." It was almost as if he laughed at her. "Kneel."

No! But her body ignored her mind's protest as she lowered to the floor to kneel before him, her face level with the bulge in his jeans. He was right. She craved it. Yet, Selby never took it. He was always the playful one. Her feet touched Selby behind her, but she could only think of the dark-haired stranger before her.

He reached down and grabbed her head, bringing her face to his crotch, pressing her into him. "Do you want it, my little tart?"

"Yes." The word fell from her lips before she could stop it. Oh god, she felt like such a slut, naked before this man, this stranger, her face pressed against his manhood. Yet, that feeling sent shivers through her and every time he called her his tart, she felt her pussy get wetter.

"Tell us what you want."

Her brain fought her. This was wrong. This slapped the face of what she was raised to believe was right. Yet, she couldn't help it. She surrendered to a desire that had always lay buried; she surrendered to whatever he wanted. "I want your cock. I want to feel it, taste it. I want you to take me, use me."

Now she heard his laughter, cruel, yet so passionate. There was power in his voice. "Your husband sits behind you. Don't you want his cock?"

"I want yours. His. Both. God, please, fuck me."

His hand tangled in her hair, holding her head still. "Unbutton my pants. Pull out what you want."

And she did, with a hunger that surprised and scared her. He kept his hand on her head as she unbuttoned, then unzipped his pants, pulling the flaps open as she did. She slid them down his sun-browned legs and his erect cock pointed straight at her. It was large, larger than Selby's, and thicker. She couldn't take her eyes off of it, the hood leaking a small drop of pre-cum that she longed to lick off. He stood there, allowing her to take in the fullness of him before pulling her mouth to the dark curls surrounding his balls.

Faith needed no instructions. Her mouth opened and she kissed each one, her tongue sliding over the dark skin, smelling the mustiness of him. She felt hands behind her and knew Selby was there as his hands slid up her thighs to her passion, his fingers probing her glistening folds. She spread her legs wider, giving him more access.

She ran her tongue up the shaft of Paul's cock to the head and back down again. Her hand cupped his balls, massaging them as she licked and kissed his hardness, while her free hand slid around his waist and over his ass, cupping a cheek in her hand, squeezing him to her. She ran her tongue back up to the tip of his cock and this time swallowed him, savoring the salty taste as she took half of his shaft into her mouth. It was all she could take. She gave herself over to his hardness, her head bobbing up and down on him, her tongue swirling around his thickness licking the head as her mouth slid to the tip and then back down. He filled her mouth with his cock; her ears with his groans.

Selby had slid two fingers into her, pumping in and out of her slick channel as he kissed her back. Her skin was on fire, her mind a dizzy mess.

"My little tart craves more, doesn't she?" Paul's voice, deep and husky, reached down to her.

She slid her mouth back to the hood of his cock. "Yes." Her voice was hoarse with lust.

He pulled her by her hair off his hardness and turned her so that she faced Selby. Her husband sat there, naked. She had never heard him strip down, but there he was, cock erect and fingers coated with her honey. Paul pushed her head forward until she rested on all fours.

"Spread your legs, Tart."

Eager for his manhood, she opened herself to him. She felt his hands on her ass as he positioned her face between Selby's legs. However, instead of his cock, she felt his hand smack her ass hard. She yelped and jumped closer to Selby. Another smack on her ass, harder. She felt the heat rising in her flesh. It hurt, but it made her cunt ache more. Again he spanked her, his hand resting where it reddened her flesh. And again.

"What do you want, Tart? Tell us."

Selby's cock brushed her nose. "Your cock! I want you to fuck me."

Again he spanked her and she fell forward into Selby's crotch, her face buried in his lap. She could feel tears in her eyes, but she wanted more. She couldn't believe what was happening. Another man was spanking her in front of her husband and she was begging for it. "Please, fuck me. Please! Fuck me!"

It was a sudden, hard thrust. No warning. He smacked her ass once and then his cock was buried in her until his balls slapped her clit. She cried out into Selby's balls, her husband's hand holding her head down.

Paul filled her slick heat, burying himself in her. His body rocked back and forth, fucking her. She felt his hands sliding up her back and into her hair, replacing Selby's. He pulled her head back and shoved her mouth down onto Selby's cock. As Paul worked his hardness in and out of her pussy, Faith sucked on Selby's cock, her mouth sliding up and down as he sat spread-eagled for her. She wanted to cry out, but could only moan around her husband's shaft. She ran her hand up and down Selby's manhood, masturbating him as she sucked on him. Paul's grunts filled her ears until she felt his cock throb and jerk inside of her as his hot liquid erupted into her. She pushed back on him, bouncing against him in time with her mouth on Selby's cock.

Paul fucked her for only a bit longer before he slid out of her. Faith almost groaned in protest. She wanted more!

Then she felt herself being pulled off Selby and her body spun. Paul was turning her as Selby closed his legs. Faith was then pushed down onto Selby's cock.

"I do believe it's his turn, Tart."

With her cunt full of Paul's seed, she lowered herself onto Selby's cock, fucking him, her body rocking back and forth. Her lust drove her as she thought of another man's come as her lube for her husband. Then she felt Selby's cock twitch as he exploded into her. As his warmth splashed against her cunt walls, Faith was pushed over the edge, her body shuddering with her orgasm. She settled down onto Selby's cock, her hands bracing her up on his legs as she savored every shiver, his hands gripping her waist.

When she opened her eyes, Paul was sitting in front of her, legs stretched toward her. His erection had shriveled by half but it was still impressive. He grinned at her with that seductive smile of his and suddenly Faith was very aware of being naked.

Seven

The sun was a bright pale yellow as it started it's descent into the west. The sand underneath them felt like sugar with its softness. It was nothing like the beach back home, where the sand had a rougher texture. People were scattered everywhere to watch the night spectacle. Of course, it was easier to be awake to watch the sun set than it was to see it rise, so it had a greater audience.

Selby's hand caressed her skin as his arm wrapped around her back. She felt the cool air caress her face as they nestled in the soft sand, watching the pale sun slowly sink into the horizon, changing from pale yellow to a vibrant orange.

Paul Butler had left their lives as easily as he had entered. After a glass of wine and some small talk about their trip so far and their plans for the rest of it, he made his departure by again kissing her knuckles. "Truly beyond lovely." His smile caught her breath again and she felt the heat rush through her. He only chuckled at her blush. Paul then shook hands with Selby. "Thank you, dear Sir, for sharing your afternoon with me."

"Was my pleasure, and obviously hers," Selby said.

Paul laughed and left. That was it. No numbers swapped or addresses exchanged. No "Next time you're in town promises" made. He had entered their day, fucked her and left.

She sat with her feet in the white sand now, her fingers wrapped around Selby's bicep as she rested her head on his shoulder. Instead of enjoying the sunset, her mind couldn't release the afternoon. She had just given herself to that stranger. To make matters worse, he had no doubt in his mind that she would. He followed them home and took her right in front of her husband. More than that, he made her fuck Selby while his own seed dripped from her. As much as her mind fought the idea, scolded her for her actions, she couldn't deny how excited the whole encounter made her. Even now, thinking about it caused her passion to drip.

But Faith, you're no longer in high school. You're married to a loving man. This will only lead to trouble. She squeezed Selby's arm tighter.

And what about how he had ordered her around, took her and called her names? Selby never did those things to her. Yet, it was those very things that drove her crazy, made her melt with sexual heat. It was those cravings that she had buried way back when.

The sun dipped under the horizon and faded from the day leaving the evening sky a faded blue as the darkness of night was close on its heels. Selby leaned over and kissed her head, pressing his lips softly on her wind-tousled hair. He had been quiet most of the night, allowing her time to sort through her thoughts and emotions. Faith took a deep breath, taking his strength into her. He always knew what she needed and when.

"I love you," he whispered into her hair.

She pressed into him. "I love you, too. So very much." Of that, there was no doubt. That was part of her confusion. How could she love the man beside her so much, more than life itself, and yet crave the Paul Butlers using her body as their playground? She had been taught all her life that even to look at another with sexual thoughts was evil and adulterous. She had crossed that line once in high school and it ended badly. Yet, over the past several months she couldn't stop. Her body was almost always on fire and Selby seemed to enjoy fanning those flames. If only he knew the fire he flamed within her.

They sat staring at the water, the waves mere ripples compared to those on the East Coast. This beach had a more serene feel to it where the Atlantic had a churning raw power that beat upon the shore. She smiled to herself at the analogy. That was her afternoon. Selby was the Gulf Coast, serene, peaceful, and constant. Paul had been the Atlantic with his raw passion, his power. Is that what she hungered for? Selby was her safety, her serenity. Yet, she also needed that wildness that threatened to drown her.

"Come. Let's find our way to some food, shall we?" Selby took his arm from around her waist and started to rise. Once on his feet, he reached for her, drawing her to him. He would always take care of her and be her arms of comfort.

"Good." She leaned up and kissed him softly. "This day has made me hungry."

He grinned and kissed her nose. "Me as well, love. Me as well."

After brushing themselves off they clasped hands and strolled toward the eateries along the beach.

"Beautiful sunset, wasn't it?" He asked, the sand sinking slightly beneath their feet as they walked.

"I love watching it. The colors are so vibrant. It always amazes me how light it still is after the sun disappears, though. I guess I always assumed that the darkness swallowed it up as soon as it was gone." She laughed at herself. "Silly, I know." It was that raw power that had excited her today, the unknown of what she would be made to do next and then doing it. The humiliation of it all was confusing her mind.

"Not silly at all, love. Until you see it, it's all hard to imagine," Selby said, his hand warm in hers. "I have to admit, the first time I saw it I was surprised, as well. Are you in the mood for anything in particular for dinner?"

She knew he meant food, but her mind was still filled with sex and power. "Anything is fine."

He smiled down at her, his eyes studying her. He squeezed her hand and led her to a small seafood restaurant on the boardwalk. "Your mind is busy."

Understatement. "Did you enjoy....you know...back at the condo...with Paul?" God, she felt stupid. Even with Selby she sometimes found herself embarrassed to talk about sex when others found it so natural. Flirting was one thing. Talking about how she actually enjoyed being fucked was quite another.

Selby didn't look at her, which would only have embarrassed her more. "I thought it was hot as hell. You were so turned on, it was unbelievable."

"But he just took me. That didn't bother you?"

Now, Selby paused and turned to face her, a look of concern pinching his face. "Did it bother you?"

"Why do you always answer my questions with a question? No, it didn't bother me and that's what's bothering me. I let him do whatever he wanted to me and got off on it. It didn't hit me that you were right there and I wasn't with you."

He placed a finger on her chin forcing her to look into his eyes. "But I was right there, watching, ready to step in the moment you showed any sign that anything was amiss. It was hot as hell watching you, even the part of him making you do what he wanted as his little tart."

Faith felt the blush in her cheeks as she closed her eyes. She tried to look away, but his one finger held her head firm. He was waiting, she knew. With an embarrassed reluctance, she opened her eyes again.

He slid his finger down her throat to the spot on her chest just over her heart. "This is mine, correct?"

"And only yours." Her voice was a hoarse whisper, catching in her throat.

He smiled. "Then as long as that always holds true, nothing else matters. It's all just a game you and I are playing."

She smiled up at him. "I do love you, Selby, so very much." And then she wiggled her eyebrows at him. "And it was hot as hell being his little tart."

They both laughed as she felt herself being pulled into his embrace. "Let's eat, Tart."

"Oral sex. I love it."

He took her hand and together they crossed the beach to Mr. Frog's Crab Shack. "Liar. You love receiving it, but hate giving."

She shrugged. "I just suck at it."

Selby laughed. "Nice play on words. Isn't sucking the point?"

"Brat."

"That's me, just a bratty boy."

"Maybe I'll give you the spanking this time."

"Promises, promises."

~ ~ ~ ~ ~

Selby held her hand with a firm grip as they crossed the beach to the Crab Shack. As it turned out, it was an actual shack. The rustic walls had the appearance of driftwood thrown together haphazardly. Crab traps, nets and boat paraphernalia decorated the inside and the tables were, for the most part, a collection of picnic tables with benches. The food, however, was well worth it.

He had ordered them wine and allowed Faith a couple of glasses to help her unwind. He knew her well and knew the battle that raged within her. What excited her and what she wanted fought against the way she was raised, the teachings that had been ingrained in her as to the difference between right and wrong. When Selby entered her life, he had shaken those viewpoints.

"You don't believe in morals?" She had asked him as he drank an Amber Bock while she sipped sweet tea. They were at a friend's party and she had made it clear that drinking was evil. He responded by opening a cold bottle.

"Sure I do. I just don't believe they're as detailed as you churchy people believe them to be. Who makes the decision between what's moral and not moral?"

"God."

He lifted his eyebrows at that. "God thinks it's evil for women to wear pants?"

"Now you're being ridiculous."

"Really? But don't some groups teach that?" He wasn't mocking her, only testing traditional thought.

"Well, yes, but they've taken something that someone said at one time and twisted it to their way of thinking?"

She grew quiet and he could see twenty years of teaching fighting for control. Faith was smart and he had not pegged her as a blind follower of the blind. She didn't disappoint him.

"We just take it on faith." By the look in her eyes, he could see she had trouble swallowing the cliché.

He sipped his beer again and then pointed at her with the tip of the bottle. "Nothing wrong with faith, but I prefer a less detailed version of morals." He settled the bottle between his legs, holding it with both hands. "Murder is not a very moral action except, say, in self-defense or to protect one's loved ones. Rape is immoral, but to me, sex isn't. It's the motive behind something that makes it right or wrong. Not necessarily the action. I don't like people trying to force me into their mold when what I'm doing isn't hurting them."

They had dated for two years before they were married and during those two years they had dozens of discussions on morality and the difference between right and wrong. He never pushed her or asked her to give up any of her beliefs. Likewise, Faith didn't try to convert him to her religion. Soon, they were engaged and then married and once she had escaped the thumb of her parents, Faith began to "rebel" in subtle ways. It began with her wearing lingerie for him, then thong underwear. She would sip wine and soon moved to cocktails. Sexually, she was pretty straight forward, missionary position and dressed again right afterward. Oral sex was a major taboo.

"You pee out of that!"

It took him forever just to get her to touch his cock and when he touched her between her legs she froze as if an animal trapped. Over time, he got her to relax and even admit it felt good. He had to get her drunk to go down on her, which was a challenge itself, but well worth it. Since then, Faith had grown and opened herself up in amazing ways, ways that always made his cock twitch.

Dinner was quickly ordered and soon they were chewing on hot rolls with honey butter while waiting for their meals to arrive. The restaurant was loud, but to Selby that only protected their conversation.

"How did it make you feel," Selby ventured as he set his glass on the table, "to be made to do what Paul wanted, even fucking me with your pussy still full of him?"

"Selby!" Her eyes widened and she jerked her head back and forth to see if anyone had overheard. He loved making her fidget like that. She took a deep breath and tried to hide behind her wineglass. "It drove me wild to be honest. That's what I was saying earlier." She paused, staring at the burgundy liquid in her glass.

He didn't rush her. He learned years ago that Faith would always explain herself if given the time and silence to do so. He sipped his wine while he waited.

"It was all bizarre in my head. It was humiliating, that control he had on me, the way he pulled me by my hair to do what he wanted, the way he called me tart in front of you, shaming me. Yet, that humiliation drove me wild inside. It was like being drunk. I honestly think I would have done whatever he told me to."

Selby smiled with playful mirth. "You did."

She didn't blush this time. "But I probably would have done more. And then he added to it by giving your used wife back to you. It was like he was doing it to both of us, making me humiliate you, which gave me power over you while he had power over me and..." She shook her head, her words trailing off. "The whole thing was intoxicating."

Their food arrived, grilled salmon and crab cakes, and they changed the topic. Still, Selby had to agree with Faith. The whole encounter had been heady with passion and emotions. They'd had threesomes before, but nothing like this afternoon. Then, it had been pure sex, a living out of Faith's fantasy. This afternoon with Paul was something beyond sex. It was powerful. It was almost like they had been willingly raped. Paul had used Faith, taken her and fucked her and then tossed Selby the cum-soaked scraps and Selby had been completely eager to have it happen. To be honest with himself, it was exactly that which had gotten him off that afternoon. Listening to Faith talk, it had gotten her off as well, and not just physically.

A door had been opened to their appetites they never knew existed. Selby could only fantasize what they would do with it.

~ ~ ~ ~ ~

After dinner they went for another stroll on the beach. The sun had been replaced by stars and daylight by darkness. The number of people had dwindled, leaving them almost alone. Most of the locals as well as visitors had gravitated to the two beach clubs that offered live music and dancing and two-for-one cocktails. Faith and Selby walked, fingers intertwined, while the Gulf of Mexico licked at the shore.

At one point, her mom called while they were walking. "Your dad wants to have a cookout with the family tomorrow, so I'm calling you to ask if you'd like to join us." Faith rolled her eyes, but accepted. As much as she disagreed with her mom, Faith loved visiting her dad, and would never refuse a chance to see him.

"We drove by your house to invite you in person, but you weren't home," her mother said. "Sounds like you're at the beach. Why would you go to another beach when you live on one?"

Faith took a deep breath. Here it goes. "Because you can't see the sunset on our beach."

"The sunset? Where can you see the sun set on our beaches?" Her mother's voice was gravelly, as if coming down with a cold.

"You can't. Selby and I drove to Madeira Beach to spend the weekend."

"You're on the West Coast? You didn't tell me you were leaving town."

Another deep breath. As if her mother cared about what she did. She suddenly regretted saying anything to her mother, but she knew that whatever answer she gave would be the wrong answer. "Selby surprised me with a trip at the last minute. I didn't even know we were going until we were in the car."

She looked at Selby with apologetic eyes as he mouthed the word "Liar" and did a tsk-tsk with his fingers.

"Well, isn't he Mr. Sweetie." Valerie's condescending tone told Faith her mother meant the opposite.

"What was....Mom...hear you....signal." And Faith closed her phone with a sigh.

Selby laughed. "You faked a lost call on your mom."

Faith stuck the phone in her shorts pocket, her head hung low. "I know. I know. It's just…"

"Hush, sweetheart." Selby pulled her to him and hugged her. "No need to apologize to me. I've met your mother, remember?"

Faith looked up into his eyes and then kissed him. "Let's go back to the condo so I can take advantage of you."

"Does that mean I have to fight you?" He snaked his arm around her waist and guided her back in the direction of their rental.

"Might be fun. I'm always up for something new."

Selby laughed and it made her heart glad. "Whatever you want, Tart."

What Faith wanted was more of what she had that afternoon, but she was afraid to tell him that. She feared how it might make him feel. Yet, it was so much on her mind as they walked back that by the time they reached the door, her panties were soaked and her pussy craved something hard pounding it.

Selby tossed the keys on the counter. When he turned to face her, she was already there, pulling up his shirt and yanking it over his head. She ran her hands over his chest and across his abdomen, her nails digging into him as she kissed his shoulders and neck. His skin was cool to her warm lips. She sucked on his flesh, running her tongue across his pale body. A groan escaped his lips.

He slid his hands underneath her blouse, over her back to her bra strap. Within seconds, her bra and shirt were on the floor and he was returning her kisses on her body. She slid her hand down his stomach, running a finger around his waist, teasing him before working his button open and sliding his zipper down. She wanted him, to feel him. Her body still ached from earlier and she hungered for more. She reached inside wrapping her hand around his hardening cock, moaning as she felt it grow in her hand. She wanted him. Correction. She needed him.

Kissing her way down Selby's chest, she slid his shorts down his legs until his hardened pride stuck out free and hungry. She knelt in front of him, one hand stroking him while the other gripped his firm ass. "Did you like watching me kneel like this in front of Paul, knowing your wife was going to take another man's cock into her mouth?"

She felt his hands on her head, stroking her hair. "Mhm, I did. You looked sexy as hell."

Faith leaned into his legs, nuzzled her face into his balls as she ran her tongue across the loose skin, tasting him. Her right hand stroked his shaft as she sucked each of his testicles into her mouth, rolling her tongue around them. His hands tightened on her head and she licked her way from his base to the hood of his cock and back down again. She remembered Paul's cock in her mouth and the salty taste, the power with which he had ordered it and she obeyed. Just thinking about it while Selby's cock filled her mouth made her passion rise. She couldn't believe she was thinking of another man while she was with her husband, but she couldn't stop. She took Selby's cock fully into her mouth, her head bobbing up and down. Ravenous. That was the only word for it.

She sucked on his manhood for only a moment until her pussy needed his cock more than her mouth wanted it. She jumped to her feet, sliding her shorts off as she stood. "Lay down," she ordered and couldn't believe that she had commanded it once it passed her lips. Yet, just saying it sent heat through her slick channel. Power. Was that it? Was that what was driving her crazy with lust now?

Selby did as she ordered without hesitating. He lay naked on the beige carpet, his hands at his sides, his cock sticking straight up like a stripper pole she was about to twist on. The look in his eyes was raw excitement. He was there for whatever she wanted and even that sent shivers through her body. The head rush was again intoxicating. She wanted more.

Faith stood straddling Selby's waist, her glistening lips directly above his erect manhood. "I liked it, too. Very much." She lowered herself, taking his cock in her hand and guiding him to her wetness. She kissed his chest, covering it with small spots of moisture. "I liked him taking me, Selby. He didn't ask you if he could. He just did it." She lowered herself down onto him, letting him open her wide, spreading her. "He stripped me, put me on my knees and drove his cock into my mouth." Her pussy swallowed Selby's cock, sucking on him as she replayed the afternoon in her mind's eye.

Selby's hands went to her waist as she rocked herself back and forth on his cock. She pushed down so that her clit rubbed against his pubic bone. Her body shuddered from the vibrations it sent through her. She had taken Paul's cock in her mouth not even caring that she was no good at oral sex. He had not given her a choice.

"He fucked my mouth. You watched as he held my head and made me take him. And I loved it, Selby. I loved being used in front of you. I loved when he dragged me by my hair, spinning me so he could fuck me." She rocked harder, driving Selby's thick cock into her burning passion. "And he did. He fucked your wife like a little bitch, filling me with his cum." Faster, she rocked, pounding harder as she talked. "He used me like the tart he kept calling me and then made me fuck you with his cum dripping from me."

She felt her body tense, felt her orgasm building inside of her as her vision blurred, lost in the lust that filled her. Selby grunted below her. His cock throbbed inside of her as she pounded on top of him, trying to drive him even deeper into her wanton sex.

"And, god help me, I loved it. I loved fucking you with my used little cunt, making you feel his cum inside of your wife. The humiliation of it all drove me...drove me..." She felt Selby's cock jerk, felt his hips push himself into her as he sprayed her hungry channel with his hot liquid, felt his body tense as he emptied himself inside of her. "Drove me..." And then her own orgasm flooded through her. She cried out as her body jerked and shuddered, tremors of pleasure coursing through every core of her being. She pressed down hard on his chest as the tremors of pleasure racked her body.

She wasn't sure how long it lasted. It seemed like hours. Selby held her until her orgasm subsided.

Faith took a deep breath as she laid her head on Selby's shoulder, eyes closed. "Drove me crazy." And then she was asleep.

Eight

"I don't want to do this," Faith said as Selby pulled into her parents' driveway.

"Then why did you say yes? I was quite happy with you naked in our room."

Sometime during the evening, Selby had carried her to bed and wrapped his arms around her as they drifted back off to sleep. She had woken up early and served him breakfast in bed, her mind in turmoil over her behavior during their lovemaking. She wanted to apologize, but was too embarrassed to even bring up the subject. Selby had been the gentleman and not commented on it. She knew he was waiting to talk about it. Nothing fazed him and he seemed to relish the verbal play of their sex. Yet, she knew he would wait to talk about it until she was ready. She wasn't. Nowhere near ready.

"Like saying 'No' is ever an option with my mother." She sighed as she released her seat belt. "Besides, I love my dad. It's my mom that's the bitch."

"Such strong language from such a little girl." Selby took her hand and kissed it. "Let's go see what's for dinner, shall we?"

"Probably poison."

Selby came around and opened her car door and together they walked up the drive. They timed their departure from Madeira Beach so that they could go straight to her parents' house in Melbourne. The ride over was spent talking about other trips they wanted to take and about work. Selby's bookstore was doing well and he was tossing around the idea of adding a magazine rack like the big chains to draw in more regulars. Faith's position was secure at Rutherford Construction and they teased about the different people there and who Faith thought was attractive and who the assholes were. At one point, Faith found herself talking quite a bit about Edwin and stopped herself. However, before long the conversation would come back around to her boss.

"I do believe someone is smitten," Selby teased.

Faith just blushed, but she couldn't deny it. Yet, what would happen if she did play with someone at work?

"Faith! Selby!" Turning, Faith saw her father leaning against the garage, a Don Nikki cigar in his hand. Arnold Driscoll was a tall, well-muscled man who preferred the outskirts of gatherings rather than the inner circle. At sixty-two, he still had black hair with just some salt at the temples.

"Daddy." Faith walked over and hugged her father, squeezing him as if she hadn't seen him in years as opposed to just last week. He was the only reason she kept coming around.

"Arni." Selby shook the older man's hand with a firm grip. Using his head to point to the house, Selby asked, "The topic made you escape already?"

Arni rolled his gray eyes. "You should go back to Madeira Beach, only this time take me with you."

Faith smiled at her father as Selby laughed. "I picked you up something while I was there." Selby reached into his shirt pocket and pulled out one of the two cigars he had tucked inside. "Honduras. Hand rolled."

Arnold Driscoll slid the cigar under his nose, breathing in the aroma. "Nice. I'll save this one for when I need to escape after dinner."

Selby laughed as he pulled the cigar that remained in his pocket into view. "I'll join you."

"Great. Leave me to the wolves," Faith said with a sigh.

"Actually, I was out here making notes for another article." Arni tapped at a notepad in his shirt pocket as he shrugged. "Have to get my thoughts down while I can before your mother screams them out of my mind."

Faith laughed as her father just smiled at her, giving her a wink as he did. She was very proud of her father. He taught high school history and in his spare time wrote articles for different magazines based on varying time periods that he found intriguing. She supposed it offered him some quiet time away from her mother, which she could understand completely.

"So tell me about your trip." Arni cut the burning end of his cigar, dumping it on the drive and snuffing it out with the toe of his shoe. After tucking the remaining portion back into his shirt pocket with the one Selby had just given him, he wrapped an arm around Faith and walked them inside.

Faith took her time and shared Selby's idea for the trip. She told her father of the shops and sunrise, of the condo and the sunset. She shared everything except the part Paul played. Her father listened and asked questions, smiling and nodding. He had thought it a most romantic idea and congratulated Selby on his spontaneity.

"You should make a weekend of it, Daddy," Faith said as they walked through the house and onto the back porch where the rest of the family sat while Faith's brother, Dennis, worked the grill.

"A weekend alone with your mother? You trying to kill me?"

"I heard that." Valerie Driscoll sat in a camp chair staring at her grandkids in the backyard. "And there's too much to do at the church to escape on weekends. Isn't that right, Dennis?"

Dennis was tall like his father, just breaking six feet. A thick-bodied man with a balding head peaking a ringlet of black hair, he served as youth minister at Trinity Baptist Church. Two of the three kids in the backyard were his, the third being Cherish's son, Jordie. "Well, there is a lot to be done for sure, but sometimes you just have to get away and rejuvenate for a while. Even our Lord pulled away from the crowd for periods of rest."

Faith could tell by the glare her mother gave Dennis that she didn't approve of his answer.

"Well then, Valerie, if you're too busy, I might be able to enjoy the trip after all." Arni winked at Faith when he said it. Faith hid a smile.

Cherish sat next to her mother as always, a lit Salem in her hand and a Budweiser beside her. How Cherish got away with it all without her mother lecturing her, Faith would never comprehend.

Dennis was the golden child, because he had entered the ministry, married a nice enough woman, even if she was one of the biggest Faith had seen, and given their parents the first two grandchildren, a boy and a girl. Cherish was the baby of the family. Still, she had more balls than most men Faith knew. Faith was just Faith.

"So, Mom says you took a mini-vacation this weekend," Cherish said, blowing smoke as she spoke. She looked like an amusement park dragon. "Must be nice to get away whenever you want."

"Quite nice, actually," Selby said. "How come you two don't try it?"

"Glen works weekends mostly and it's hard to travel with Jordie." Cherish took another drag from the cigarette. "I'll just live the high life through Faith here."

"Really, Cherish, it wasn't anything fancy." Faith's words came out in an apologetic ramble. "Drive over, see the sunset. That's it really. Just a quiet night for two."

"Those burgers ready, yet?" Arni broke in as he walked to where Dennis was flipping meat on the grill. "I'm about famished."

Soon, everyone was scattered around the back porch, paper plates propped in their laps, enjoying burgers, baked beans and Valerie Driscoll's famous potato salad. Faith and Selby described their impromptu trip again, ignoring Valerie's snide remarks. They talked of grandkids and Dennis described his youth's upcoming trip to Haiti to help build an addition onto a school.

"Now, that's a trip you should take," Valerie said to Selby.

As Selby opened his mouth, Faith stood. "Who's done? I'll gather the plates."

"I'll help." Cherish collected some of the plates and followed Faith into the kitchen to help clean up. Faith had never known her baby sister to volunteer for work of any kind before, always content to allow someone else to do it, but Faith didn't say anything. Once they

80

were alone in the kitchen, Cherish started in on work. "So, I hear my prudish sister has become quite the flirt at work."

So, that's why she followed me in. "I was a prude? And, I don't flirt. I merely joke around. What's wrong with that?"

Cherish brushed her bangs out of her eyes with her forearms before dumping paper plates with uneaten food into the trash can. "Yes, you were a prude. You were more holier-than-thou than mother dear out there."

Faith was used to Cherish's comments knocking their mother. "Really? Hmmmm. Well," she shrugged, "I'm enjoying my life and having fun."

"If your prince out there ever found out what a flirt you're becoming, he wouldn't be too happy."

Faith turned and leaned on the sink, drying her hands. "That prince is my savior and Selby knows everything. He trusts me and I trust him. You're not getting jealous are you?"

Cherish popped a lid on the potato salad and put it and the beans in the refrigerator. She was in her typical men's gym shorts and a worn-out over-sized tee-shirt, no makeup and barely brushed hair. She seemed more the boy of the family than Dennis. "Jealous? Of those men thinking you're a slut at work? Hardly."

"No one thinks I'm a slut, Cherish." But the words bothered her. *Did* they think of her that way?

Cherish laughed as she uttered, "If you say so. Hey, if it works for you, then go for it. The men get to feel your ass and you get whatever you want. Personally, I couldn't do it, let men grope me when they want, but hey, that's me. You're having fun."

Faith stared at her sister. She wanted to scream, but with family so close by, she only whispered, her voice strained. "I do not let the men grope me whenever they want."

Cherish smiled and her face seemed to twist into a sneer. "They swat your ass all the time, especially Edwin. Hell, the last time Morgan was in town inspecting our office he teased you about getting you a stripper pole and you swung on every word."

"Oh, for crying out loud, that was a joke. I think you're the one who's become the prude," Faith said.

~ ~ ~ ~ ~

Cherish dropped the subject as they went out on the porch with the others. Yet, as the conversation flowed around them, Faith's mind kept hearing Cherish's accusation in her head. She had become more brazen and playful at work, but other than Edwin massaging her shoulders, no one had laid a hand on her or her on them. Wasn't a slut someone who readily opened her legs for people? Then she thought of Paul. She had hungrily opened her legs and mouth for him. There hadn't even been a doubt or hesitation that she was going to fuck him. She had known it as they left the winery. She had known it and wanted it.

Selby reached over with his right hand and took hers in his, squeezing. Cigars were lit, their strong aroma taking over the back porch. His eyes asked her if she was all right. She smiled back at him. She *was* all right, just confused, but that had been a typical state for her since October.

How could she be a slut? She had had sex only once before meeting Selby and that had been in high school. She had been twenty-seven before having it again and until October, Selby had been her only sex partner. She never should have told Selby her fantasy. She should have stayed closed in on herself as she had always been.

"Mo-om!" Little five-year-old Denise stood in front of Debra, pulling her walnut hair out of her eyes. "Danny's picking on me. Make him stop."

Debra tucked her daughter's hair behind her ears. "I think someone's tired."

Dennis patted his knees and then stood with a groan. "She's not the only one. Sundays are long days."

"We should be going, as well," Selby said, squeezing Faith's hand.

"I would figure Sundays were restful for you," Valerie quipped.

"Ah, well, all this hedonistic living can take a toll on a person." Selby helped Faith to stand, ignoring her shocked expression.

Arnie laughed. "You really need to tell me more, one day."

Valerie just glared.

As they had been the last to arrive, they were the first to pull out of the driveway, for which Faith was extremely thankful. Selby held her hand as they drove over the bridge and back home, allowing Faith time to shake whatever funk had overtaken her at her parents'.

As they came down the east side of the Eau Gallie Causeway, Faith had to ask. "Am I a slut?"

"I wish."

She turned to look at him. "I'm serious. Have I become a slut?"

"No, but I'm working on it."

"Selby."

She kept staring at him. He pulled into the small boat ramp park on the south side and drove to the covered picnic table on the far east end. He pulled between the picnic table and bushes that lined that section of the Indian River. A couple of cars were parked on the west end, couples lying on top of their hoods staring up at the stars that dotted the night sky. He parked the car, turning off the engine before turning to face her.

"Faith, as of yesterday, you've only had sex with a few people. Most of those were one time adventures. The amount of sex you've had in thirty-five years hardly makes you a slut. What did Cherish say to you?"

Faith looked out at the river. The water was glassy and deserted. "What makes you think she said anything?"

He leaned his back against the door frame as he stared at her profile. "Because you were fine until you came out of the kitchen with her. After that you were pensive."

Faith didn't answer right away. Instead, she replayed the conversation with her sister over in her mind.

"Cherish is just a bitter woman angry at life in general," Selby said, his eyes never leaving her.

"She said the guys at work think I'm a slut."

"Are you fucking them and I don't know about it?"

Faith whipped her head to look at him, her eyes wide. "No! I would never."

"Then you're a prick tease at best and they wish you were a slut." Selby was smiling as he spoke. "You worry too much about what your sister thinks and says." He reached over and stroked her cheek, brushing her hair back. "And even if you were doing them all, what does it matter to her? It's not like your sister wants to protect me of all people."

"She thinks my prince would be devastated."

He waggled his eyebrows up and down. "On the contrary, your prince would be highly turned on."

Faith laughed, some of the tension leaving her shoulders. "That you would."

"Pull down your pants."

She turned, looking around to see who was nearby. "Selby, this is a public park."

"I know." He grinned at her. "It's also dark and we're in our car. Now, pull down your pants."

With a nervous tilt of her head, keeping an eye out for passersby, Faith unbuttoned her jeans and slid them down to her ankles.

"Panties, too."

"Selby," she whined, but her fingers went into her thong and slid it down to join her jeans. As she sat back in the seat, she opened her legs, exposing her pink slit to the air. "You're going to get us arrested."

"Might be fun. Then you could be Big Bertha's bitch in the slammer." Selby gripped her left leg, spinning her so that she faced him, pussy open. "Now, pull your shirt up. Bra, too. Show me how hard your nipples are by all of this."

His words were sending warm shivers throughout her body. She knew her nipples were going to be tiny pebbles even before she pulled her shirt and bra up to her neck, just as she knew that Selby could see the wetness between her legs. He was taking her. Right there in the car on the side of the road and she was going eagerly.

"Play with your titties. Show me how you like them touched."

Faith started at her navel, both hands palms flat, sliding up her torso until she could feel the small globes of her breasts. She closed her eyes, no longer caring if someone could see her. She slid her fingers over her breasts until each hand had a swollen nipple. She heard herself moan and felt the heat between her legs grow. With her thumb and index finger, she twirled her nipples, now shriveled into tight buds with her excitement, back and forth in small circles, pinching them as she did. Her hips lifted off the seat, her pussy wanting attention.

"Seems they like the notion of being someone's little bitch." She could hear the grin in his voice. "Of course, we found that out this weekend, didn't we?" She couldn't deny it. She answered by pulling her nipples out, stretching them the way Paul had. A whimper escaped her lips.

"Now, slide your right hand down to your sweet cunt and play with yourself until you come." As she started to slide her hand down as he had commanded, he stopped her. "But you must ask before coming."

Ask? *Oh my god.* She slid her hand against her skin, her nails scraping along her bare flesh sending tremors through her. Over her clit and between her velvet folds she slid her index and middle finger using her own nectar to moisten them before sliding them back up over her sensitive clit. With both fingers, she pushed against her swollen nub, swirling it in small, quick circles, and with her other hand, she kept pinching and pulling on her left nipple.

She groaned, her mouth open as her body tensed from the pleasure she was giving it. Faster, she fingered her clit, feeling her mounting passion take her. She couldn't believe she was doing this, playing with herself in front of him. Yet, she didn't care. Oh god, she didn't care. So good, this feeling.

"I think your sister's comments about you being a slut bothered you because you want it to be true," he taunted her. She could feel his hands on her calves, sliding up and down. The strength in his hands as he squeezed and caressed her added to her desire, her lust.

But his words were not true. "No. No. I don't want them to think of me that way. No." Did she? Oh god, she really didn't know. Her head leaned forward from the ecstasy pulling at her wet channel.

Selby laughed. "Liar. You love the attention. You love all of those men hot to get between your legs. You would love to know what their cocks felt like as they make you their bitch."

Faith shook her head. "No. It's not true." Her body began to shake.

"You love the attention. Don't you, Faith?"

"No." Her body betrayed her. "Yes. Oh god, yes! I love the attention." It was going to rip from her. "Please, Selby. I gotta come. Please!"

"You like the idea of playing the slut?"

"Yes. I'm sorry. Yes! Please."

"Now." One simple word, but with it the dam she was forcing into place broke. "Aaaiii..." Her ass lifted off the seat as waves of pleasure broke over her. Her back arched and her cries echoed off the car's interior. She opened her eyes wide and saw Selby grinning, watching her. She couldn't believe she had done what she just did.

Her chest rose and fell with her heavy breathing as her body dropped from its high. Selby started the car, still smiling. Faith rushed to reach for her pants.

"Leave them." She sat back, having no energy to protest. She laid her head back on the seat, praying they didn't get pulled over. She was past the point of caring if anyone could see in the car. Selby had at least allowed her to pull her shirt and bra back into place, so she was partially covered.

Their home was less than ten minutes from the causeway and soon Selby was pulling into the garage. Neither had spoken since he had started the car. She had to believe that he was furious at her. For crying out loud, she had just confessed that she liked the idea of being a slut. How could she be so stupid?

The car was off and the garage door finished closing. Selby left his side of the car and came around to hers, opening her door. She started to reach for her jeans, and then stopped. She was so confused. She wasn't sure what to do.

"Leave them." Selby's hand was out, waiting to assist her from the car.

Faith took his proffered hand and slid herself around to step out of the Accord. Selby didn't let go of her hand. She tried peering into his face, but there was nothing there. She had never seen it blank before. She took a deep breath. Oh, why had he asked her those questions?

He closed the door and she started toward the door to the house. Selby stopped her and spun her so that she faced the car and forcefully bent her over onto the car's hot hood. The warmth hit her stomach through her shirt.

"Now, now," Selby said. Was his voice playful? Angry? Oh god, she wished she could read him right now. "You were able to come. It's my turn now." She heard him opening his pants, could picture his erect manhood as he slapped her thighs. In her mind, she saw the bulbous head as he pierced her, shoving his cock deep into her with one thrust. His hands gripped her hips as he pounded with a ferociousness that was not to be denied. She laid her cheek on the car; the warmth against her cool skin had a calming effect. She was still wet from where he made her finger herself to an orgasm. He spread her slick channel without pause. Her hands pressed on the car near her face, bracing for the onslaught of his cock.

Within a few thrusts of his thick manhood, her body started reacting. She began pushing back on him, her ass meeting his hips.

"That's my girl," she heard him say. "C'mon, fuck me, slut. Feel that cock inside of you." His fingers dug into her ass and she wanted to yell from the pain. Instead, she pressed harder against his cock, banging back against him as he continued to thrust inside of her. She left herself. She wanted his cock, needed it now.

"Fuck me!" His voice boomed and she obeyed. Within a few more thrusts, she felt her climax hit her. She groaned loud against the hood, pressing her face into it as her orgasm took hold of her. Her pussy tightened around his cock and pumped and soon she felt his seed hit the inside of her, warming her even more. He grunted loud as he drove into her until his balls slapped against her clitoris and he emptied himself.

She was panting heavily, spent, when she felt his hands on her arm pulling her up. When he spun her so that she faced him, she could see the gleam in his eyes. He was smiling from ear to ear.

He took her into his arms and held her tight, kissing the side of her head. "You're so fucking hot." He kissed her some more.

"You're not mad at me?" She clung to him, afraid of letting go.

"Mad at you? Why on earth would I be mad at you?" He pulled back and looked into her eyes. "You were amazing."

"But, you know, the stuff I said, about being a slut. That didn't make you mad?"

He smiled at her. "You suffer from short term memory loss." She must have had a confused look on her face because he went on. "I know you love the attention, sweetheart. I also know that you're having fun exploring your sexual side. I'm fine with that. It's a game. As long as I don't share your heart, everything else is merely fun." He kissed her nose. "Besides, we both know how much you like being someone's bitch." He was smiling, but Faith knew he wasn't teasing. Her experience with Paul had opened her curiosity for a whole new set of adventures.

She leaned up and softly kissed his lips, warm against hers. "I love you, you know."

"And why wouldn't you? I'm adorable." He wiggled his eyebrows at her again.

She kissed him. "Yes, you are."

Selby opened the car and retrieved her clothing. Together, they went inside and jumped into a steaming hot shower. As they lathered each other, Faith wondered what it would be like to be someone's toy. Or, as Selby put it, someone's bitch.

Nine

Ashlynn sat behind the receptionist's desk, typing away when Faith walked through the front doors of Rutherford Construction. She looked tired from the weekend and Faith found herself wondering what the younger woman did for fun. Behind her stood Jed, sipping coffee from his University of Florida coffee mug. He seemed as perky as ever. He was one of those morning people. Morning people were weird. Yet, Faith felt like one today when usually Mondays were a dreaded disease.

"Good morning, folks." Faith bounced over to the counter and leaned forward. She wore a low-cut black sweater, which fell forward when she bent over, allowing people who dared to see the fleshy portion of her breasts before her black lace bra took over. While her tanned globes were only a third the size of Ashlynn's, she loved the attention they brought.

Ashlynn and Jed both tried to sneak peeks.

"You look even perkier today than you did Friday," Ashlynn said, pulling her eyes from Faith's cleavage. "Since it's not Friday and that was your reasoning then, what is it today?"

"An amazing weekend." Faith told them of her excursions west—minus their time with Paul— and how romantic her husband was. Jed was glad she had a great time and Ashlynn was envious. "I wish I could find a man like that."

89

"By the way, Cherish called in sick," Jed said with a smile on his face as he spoke.

Faith laughed. "Of course she did. It's Monday."

"And what does that mean?" Everyone turned as Grady Parrish entered the lobby from the hall. Faith's gut tightened. Grady was the only employee besides her own sister that Faith detested. He was scarecrow thin and just as drab as the stuffed figure that was left out in the rain for years. Black stringy hair fell to his shoulders and probably had never felt a comb as it perched on top of his long, thin face. His nose was narrow and long, reminding Faith of a bird's beak.

"It means that Cherish usually calls out on Mondays," Faith answered. She turned to Jed. "I'll be at my desk."

He nodded. "Okay. Those new crews will be coming by for their truck keys. Terry has them loaded up."

Faith nodded and left the front lobby as fast as she could. However, the door didn't close fast enough. She heard Grady call out, "You should lean over more often." His grin was more a leer. She shut the door, turned right, and found her sanctuary.

If anyone could ruin a good mood it was Grady Parrish. And she had been in a good mood. After Selby had taken her in the garage, they spent some more time talking. He wanted to make sure Faith was okay, that she knew they could quit at any time. If she wasn't happy with their game, they could go back to the way things were. She didn't want to stop, she told him. She just didn't want to betray his visions of her.

Yet, Grady knocked her mood out of whack. If his power trip wasn't bad enough, his laziness was worse. He was supposed to be in the field most days making sure crews were on the job. He usually wound up at a bar drinking his lunch or back at his apartment banging his girlfriend, Tiffany Collins. Last week was one of those times. He had been told to go to a doctor's office that they were refinishing the stucco work on and make sure that the crew working on it had gotten the right set of plans. He told Edwin that he had done it, but John Steinman, the stucco foreman, said otherwise. The stucco had to be redone and Grady made John look incompetent. Edwin had just shrugged it off, making excuses for Grady, something he always seemed to do.

Faith flipped on her computer, brought Pandora up on her web browser, typed in the band Disturbed and let the heavy chords beat out her frustration. With Cherish out for the day and Nessa not due in, no one would really complain.

"I see someone's already ruffled your feathers," Edwin's voice came from the doorway. He almost had to yell to be heard over the heavy guitar.

Faith turned the music down as she turned to face him. He leaned against the door frame, arms crossed over his broad chest. A cigarette tucked behind his right ear told her he was about to go out for his morning smoke. His raven black hair was perfect and his smile seductive. He was the same height as Selby, just over six feet, but broader in frame. Edwin looked like a construction worker. She felt her breath catch just looking at him and the heat between her legs grew.

"Grady is an ass," she said, and then jerked her eyes up to Edwin's face as she caught herself staring at his crotch. His jeans were tight and, even limp, his cock left an imprint to be seen. His hunter green pullover was tight over his biceps and Faith focused on his dark emerald eyes beneath his... She shook her head, spinning her chair around to her desk to get Edwin and his crotch out of her line of sight. "Why you keep him, I'll never understand." It had to be the weekend. She was still worked up from all that had happened.

She heard him crossing the floor, his steps heavy as he walked. His voice held a smile and Faith knew he had noticed her staring at his crotch. Her cheeks flushed. God, she was blushing a lot lately.

Edwin perched himself on the edge of her desk, his legs open and his cock aimed at her. He had definitely noticed, she thought, and was sitting that way on purpose. Faith straightened things on her desk, setting up for the day.

"Everyone has their purpose, Faith." He was smiling. She could hear it in his voice. "Even Grady. True, he's a fuck up, but he comes in handy for the shit jobs we need done that neither Jed nor I want to do." He paused and she was sure he was delaying on purpose. "I've got Nessa coming in at eleven to help in here since it's Monday and Cherish pulled her typical bailout."

"Thank you."

He laughed. "You're cute, you know that?"

She glanced at him. "How so?"

Edwin shrugged. "Friday you told me to whip it out and now you're blushing because you keep looking at it. Do you want to see my cock or not?" He was smiling, teasing but not teasing.

And he was right. She was acting like a blushing school girl. Where was the flirt she had been? "Sorry. It's been an interesting weekend." She turned and grinned. "Now, whip it out."

Edwin laughed, rubbing his legs as he did. "Too busy now. Maybe you should work late."

"Now that's an interesting proposition."

He reached out and placed his hand on her shoulder giving it a squeeze. "So, surprise me." Edwin pushed himself off the desk, squeezed her shoulder again, and left.

Faith picked up the manila folder on the truck assignments, but could not focus on what was inside. Surprise him. What would Edwin Coldwell do if she did just that? Would it be worth perhaps risking the end of his flirting fun by calling his bluff? Of course, there was the flip side to that coin. What if he wasn't bluffing? She felt the heat between her legs grow at the thought of Edwin before her, his manhood exposed for her pleasure.

She giggled. Oh god, she actually giggled. She would have to talk to Selby, but they had been talking about this since dinner with Tracey the other night and he had gotten off on it when she talked about it during sex.

"Surprise me," Edwin had said.

Maybe she would.

Her hands grew clammy, causing her to drop her pen. Butterflies fluttered in her stomach at the thought of what she was contemplating. Men in other cities were one thing. This was not only her hometown, but her work place.

Maybe she wouldn't.

It wasn't long before her office was busy with new crews and phones ringing. Nessa arrived at eleven as promised and immediately hopped on the phones. A small girl from Columbia whose family moved to the states when she was twelve, Nessa Sanchez had five older brothers and knew how to survive in the world of men.

Before Faith knew it, it was lunchtime and she ran as fast as she could from the mayhem. With a nervous knot in the pit of her stomach, she snatched her purse and lunch and slid out the back door to her car. Usually she ate in the break room with whoever else was there, but today she needed a private talk with her husband. She started her car and cranked the air, not even wanting to risk her words carrying to unwanted ears. She pressed two on her phone and Selby's began to ring.

"What's up, Baby Cakes?" Good. He was in a good mood. Now, would he stay that way? With a nervous lightness, she told him of her day up to that point and ended with Edwin's "Surprise me."

"Oh really?" She could hear her husband's grin. "He's been panting after you pretty heavily as of late. Do you think he means it?"

"I honestly don't know." She was almost sure he did, but Faith had never been good at reading people. "He could just be teasing and flirting and, if I actually showed up, it might scare the shit out of him. Then where would I be?"

Selby grew quiet on the other end of the phone. Faith heard the cowbell above the bookstore's front door clamor and knew he had a customer. Hopefully, that was the only reason he went quiet.

"You want to find out, don't you?" His tone was curious, not accusatory.

"I don't know." And she really didn't. "Part of me is scared to death and mad at myself for even thinking it. The other part is horny as hell and wants to see what he does."

Selby laughed. "That's my girl. Well, you know we've already talked about the what-ifs. If this is the adventure you want to try, I'll support you and whack off to your stories." She could picture the wiggle of his eyebrows.

"You wouldn't be mad or jealous?"

"Jealous? Perhaps a bit, but as I told you, your heart is mine and we're playing with our bodies. I saw how you were with Paul. I love seeing you that worked up. Mad? Why would I be? We've agreed to this and you aren't sneaking around behind my back." He started to whisper, which told her whoever had come in was close by. "Surprise him and see what happens. Sounds to me like you want to."

She did but she was scared as hell. Selby wouldn't be there. This was her game and if she did it, she'd be alone. It was high school all over again.

"I've got to get back. I love you."

She heard the playfulness in his voice. "I love you, too, Baby Cakes. Have fun this afternoon. Can't wait to hear all about it."

~ ~ ~ ~ ~

"What can't you wait to hear about?" Tracey Williams tucked a stray strand of her auburn hair behind her right ear as she was finally able to set down the hot coffee and Styrofoam containers she was holding on Selby's counter. Lunchtime.

Selby set his cell phone on the counter and took the steaming cup of coffee. "Faith may be on an adventure at work this afternoon and I'm eagerly awaiting the outcome."

Tracey raised her eyebrows. "Oh? So you two decided to explore without each other?"

"We did. And it seems Edwin's name keeps popping up." He watched as Tracey walked around the counter and straddled a bar stool he kept back there just for her, her forearms crossed and resting on the back. Her shorts opened slightly, giving Selby a small glimpse at her bare sex, which he kept staring at without embarrassment. "We talked about guidelines and promised each other if it became an issue, we'd stop."

Tracey reached over and grabbed her cup of coffee. "And what of you? Does this allow you to venture out on your own?"

Selby had shared quite a bit with Tracey over the past few months. She knew about all of their escapades as she liked to call them. The two of them had teased and flirted, but how did you come right out and say, "Hey, my wife says I can fuck you." He sipped his coffee and if Tracey knew he was stalling, she didn't let on. Finally, he just decided to say it. If Tracey was only flirting, then he would at least know. Hopefully, it wouldn't ruin a great friendship. Sex sometimes does.

"Me? Your wife thinks you and I should hop in bed?"

He nodded. "She said it might make our lunches more enjoyable. I can't say that I disagree." He watched her eyes for some sort of reaction, whether it be excitement or disgust.

94

Tracey stared at him, her eyes twinkling with a familiar mischief he had seen before plenty of times. "And what do you want? Do you want to have sex with me?" She spread her legs a little wider as she said it.

His eyes went to where he knew her pink lips to be as a smile, which was more of a grin, pulled his cheeks up. "Yes, actually, I would. However to be honest, I'd love to see the three of us in bed together."

She took another sip of her coffee, but he could see her smile behind the white cup. When she pulled it away, she was giggling as she shook her head. "I can't believe that was so hard for you to say. After all of the sex talk and teasing we've done."

"I don't want to ruin a friendship. Besides, teasing is one thing. Taking it serious is quite another."

"That it is." She smiled as she took another sip.

She still hadn't answered the question and Selby felt his gut tighten. He had made the wrong decision by telling her, he knew it. "Let's just forget the whole thing. You ready to eat?"

"What? You don't want to have sex with me now? Selby Greer, are you leading me on?"

"No!" He jerked up straighter in his chair, suddenly not knowing what to do or say or even think. "No, I wasn't leading you on. I just thought…"

"Well, don't. I've made it quite clear that I wanted to be with both of you and I meant it. If I can't have both, however, I'll be happy with just the one. Quite happy. So, relax and dish out the food, lover boy. And tell me about this weekend's getaway."

Selby sighed with relief as his cock twitched. He could feel his stomach stirring with excitement as he reached for the bag containing their sandwiches. It was out there. They both wanted each other. Now came the hard part. Sitting back and seeing if it actually happened.

In-between bites of pastrami on rye, Selby related the entire weekend to Tracey, leaving nothing out, including Paul Butler. Through the gap between her shorts and thigh, which she probably kept there to torment him, he could see her mound begin to glisten with the excitement of his stories. Or was it the previous conversation? She was really excited when he told her how Paul had taken control of Faith and used her as his fuck toy. Her nipples poked through the fabric of her blouse and Selby fought the urge to reach out and touch them.

He then related how he made Faith masturbate on the side of the road and then took her home and fucked her over the hood of the car. Tracey squirmed as she listened, almost forgetting to eat.

"How did you feel getting her used snatch?"

"Believe it or not, very hot," he admitted. "It's weird, but it was such a turn on to see her used and then given to me as scraps. What's more, it really got Faith going. I've never seen her so turned on. It was incredible."

Tracey spread her legs and ran a finger inside of her shorts between her pussy lips as she stared into his eyes, her mischievous grin back in place. She pulled the moistened finger out and slowly sucked on it. After sliding her fingers out of her lips, she said, "Yes, this is going to be a lot of fun."

Selby just stared at the wet fingers.

~ ~ ~ ~ ~

The latter part of the afternoon dragged by as Faith found it hard to focus. More contracts were thrown at her to type and organize and with Cherish out of the office, Faith was in charge of the human resource aspect of the company, as well. Nessa maintained the phones and Jed pitched in here and there, so it went pretty smooth, just busy. Her mind, however, was just not in it.

"Okay, Faith, I'm out of here." Nessa was shutting down her computer and packing up her purse. The clock read five. "You should go home, too."

Faith smiled. The day hadn't gone as slow as she thought. *Surprise me.* "I will. I just need to finish this one contract and then it's home to a glass of wine and crashing waves."

"Sounds good. I'm going home to a screaming kid and a bossy mother. Enjoy your night."

Faith watched her leave and wondered how many were still in the building. Deon was working at a new hotel in Cocoa and would go straight home since he lived in the same city. Grady was supposed to be checking on crews in Palm Bay and Faith knew he wouldn't come back to the office. He'd be afraid of being assigned more work. That left Terry in the warehouse, Ashlynn at the front desk, Jed somewhere and Edwin, if Edwin was still there, that is. Faith hadn't seen him since right after lunch and knew he had a meeting at town hall over some permits. Did he ever come back?

Suddenly, she felt very foolish. What if she had been nervous for nothing? What if it had all just been innocent flirting and she read more into it than was really there.

"Still working away?" Jed walked into her office carrying a couple of personnel files, which he plopped down on Cherish's desk.

"Yeah, I wanted to get this one contract finished. Everyone else gone?"

"Almost. I just locked the door behind Ashlynn and I saw Terry driving off. I think Edwin's in his office. He just got back from that permit meeting. And I'm outta here. Doors are locked. Just turn out the lights when you're done, please."

"Especially on Edwin?"

Jed laughed. "But of course."

He then said "Goodbye" and left. She was alone in the building with Edwin and his two words, "Surprise me."

Faith tried to focus on the contract on her computer screen, but she couldn't get rid of the fluttering feeling in her stomach. Her hands were sweaty and she suddenly felt like she couldn't breathe. She closed her eyes, placing her hands palms down on her desk. She forced herself to take deep, slow breaths trying to calm her nervousness. It suddenly felt as if she were back in high school.

Surprise me. Okay, Mr. Coldwell, let's see if you're all talk. With another deep breath, Faith pushed herself away from the desk and stood up. The building was quiet as she walked down the hallway outside of the Girls' Den to Edwin's office. His door was open as he sat behind his desk thumbing through some paperwork. She stood still for a moment, just taking him in, his bronze face crowned by the darkest hair she had seen. His shoulders were square with the chest and arms to carry it. He brushed the hair from his emerald eyes with long, strong fingers and Faith wondered what they would feel like pumping inside of her swollen slit.

"I see I'm not the only one working past closing time," Faith said as she leaned sideways against the door.

Edwin glanced up and a twinkle brightened his eyes, matching the smile that covered his face. He waved her inside. "Come in. I was just browsing through my notes from the zoning and permits meeting."

Faith walked into his office, ignoring the two chairs that sat empty in front of the mahogany desk and instead perched on the corner to face him. "How'd it go?" It could have waited until tomorrow, but she was nervous. How does she go about saying, "I'm here to see that dick that you wanted to show me?" Selby usually broke the ice when meeting new people and even then everyone knew why they were there, so it wasn't too awkward.

Edwin leaned back in his chair, his hands steepled in front of him as his elbows rested on the chair arms. His smile never vanished as he studied her while he related the boring business news of fighting to rezone for businesses in what used to be residential zones and the permit codes for the new medical high-rise they were to build on the river off Highway One. She listened with real interest as it would affect her job in some way, but the nervousness never left her stomach. Finally, he finished recounting the afternoon and just stared at her, smiling. Always smiling.

She took a deep breath. "Well, you said to surprise you. Surprise. I'm here to see what you keep bragging about." She wiggled her eyebrows at him as she leaned back on his desk, holding herself up by her hands.

Edwin's eyes sparkled; his grin grew as he nodded his head. He never took his eyes from hers as he stood to his feet, his hands unbuttoning his pants and sliding his zipper down. In a slow, teasing motion he hooked his thumbs into the waistband and slid pants and boxers to mid-thigh. He straightened, placing his hands on his hips and waited.

Faith's heart pounded. She couldn't believe what had just happened. Her boss stood in front of her with his cock hanging out. She raised her eyebrows in a pleased manner as she leaned forward and took his limp cock in her hands. His dark curls matched his hair and she felt her hunger rise as she stroked him gently before sliding her hand down to fondle his balls.

She heard him take a deep breath of surprise at her touch and looked up into his face. He watched her, still smiling. "Very nice," she said, her voice back to its playful tone.

"Why, thank you, Mrs. Greer." He pulled his pants up and sat back in his chair. "Not to sound like a school boy, but I've shown you mine, now show me yours."

Faith grinned as the moisture dripped from her heat. "Yes, Sir." She stood facing him, keeping her eyes focused on his. She slipped out of her sandals as she unbuttoned her jeans and slid them off her long legs, laying them on his desk. He wanted to see hers and she was going to let him see it all. Still watching him, she grabbed the bottom of her shirt and pulled it over her head and off her body, tossing it on top of her pants. With her fingers she hooked her lacy thong and slowly slid it down to her ankles, allowing her ass to stick up in the air as she stepped slowly out of them. They joined the growing pile. Standing back up, she reached behind her and unstrapped her bra. Staring into his dark green eyes, she slid each strap down her arm and then dropped the bra onto the pile of clothes.

His eyes soaked her in as she sashayed to sit in front of him on his desk. She placed a foot on each arm of his chair, revealing her glistening slit to his hungry eyes. "Your view, Sir."

His eyes swallowed her as his hands slid up her soft legs to the swollen pussy lips in front of him. He glanced up into her eyes and she merely raised her eyebrows at him. He slid his fingers to her slick folds, wetness making it easy for him as he slowly slid a finger into her slick channel.

Faith gasped, both from the pleasure and the shock that he had actually done it. Her mind reeled at what was happening even as her legs opened wider. He slid his one finger out, added another and shoved them both inside of her with more force. A moan slipped past her lips and she felt her eyes close partway. She was being fingered by her boss on his desk. It dawned on her that the door was still open. Anyone could come in and see her. She was completely nude, spread before Edwin for whatever he wanted. The fire of passion rushed through her. Oh god, this had gone far enough. She needed to stop it. She opened her eyes, opened her mouth to tell him, but...

Edwin's hand pumped faster, his fingers going in and out with harder force. She watched as he eased closer, lowering his head to her sensitive bud. She felt his hot breath brush against her inflamed heat just before his lips kissed her clitoris.

She forgot what she was going to say. She let her head fall back, her hair a waterfall behind her as Edwin's tongue flicked back and forth over her sensitive nub. He sucked it into his mouth while he fucked her with his fingers. She felt his knuckles slamming into her pussy lips as her inner walls sucked on his fingers, urging him deeper. Her moans filled the office. She was sure her cries echoed down the halls.

She didn't care. "Oh god, harder! Please harder."

Edwin fucked her with rapid jerks as his tongue licked her honey from his hand and her passion. She lifted her hips to meet his hand wanting—no needing—more of him. He sucked harder on her clit and she felt her body begin to shake.

She grunted loud as her orgasm ripped from her, shoving her pussy into his face. Her legs tightened on him and her mouth opened wide. "Yes!" Her breaths were heavy gasps as the intensity of her climax rolled through her until she was left panting and spent.

Edwin kissed her drenched pussy one more time as he slipped his cum-soaked fingers from her passion. He wiped them on a napkin under a cold coffee mug as he leaned back in his chair, watching her.

Faith's eyes were closed. She didn't move, needing a moment to catch her breath and her thoughts. Eventually, she lifted her head to look into his face, almost afraid of what she would see. Her fear was unfounded.

His face shone with her wetness and his smile was pleasing. "Wow. Now, that's a surprise."

Faith found herself giggling. "Um, yea. For both of us." She leaned forward, suddenly self-conscious about her nudity. She quickly began to reach for her clothes, pulling them on as fast as she could grab them.

"Are you okay?" Edwin reached out and touched her arm.

She kept dressing. "I'm fine. Really. It's just...well...wow." She shook her head. When she finished dressing, she sat back down on the desk, but not before noticing the wetness of where she had sat before.

"You should clean that. And wash your face and hands before you go home." She stopped, took a deep breath and turned to him. Placing her hand on his chest, she looked up into his deep green eyes unable to keep the satisfied smile from her face. "And I am truly fine, Edwin. I've never done anything like this before, at least, not without Selby."

His eyebrows rose at that and she felt her face flush. "Without Selby?"

"A story for another time."

He ran a hand down her hair, watching his own fingers as he traced the outline of her head. "Does that mean I get more surprises?"

"Why not? This one was kinda one-sided." She smiled as she patted his firm chest. "Turn off the lights when you leave." She winked and then turned to leave. "See you tomorrow, Mr. Coldwell."

Ten

She kept playing with the steering wheel as she drove home, twisting her hands back and forth over the gray ridges. The nervousness that had filled her stomach since lunch was now replaced with a giddiness that reminded her of her first days with Selby. He had invited her to go on a walk on the beach at night looking for sea turtles laying eggs. She remembered being so nervous the whole day that her father made her wash all three cars just to give her something to do.

Selby knocked on her door at seven fifty-five that night and insisted on meeting her father before they left for their date. He not only met her dad and shook his hand but sat down and carried on a twenty-five minute conversation. Faith wanted out of there and Selby showed no sign of being in a hurry to go.

When they finally did make it to the beach, she had forgotten her jacket, so he had given her his hoodie from the backseat. The wind off the Atlantic was strong carrying a salty chill with it. She had pulled the jacket tight around her, crossing her arms across her chest as they walked. It wasn't so much from the cold as to keep her from throwing up because of how nervous she had been. She hadn't been much on dating, avoiding it at all cost. Truth was Selby had been her first date in five years.

After strolling away from the rickety steps that led down to the sand, they finally came upon one of the giant turtles digging its nest.

Four men surrounded it with dim flashlights, watching. Without thought, Selby had slid his hand into hers and pulled her over protectively. They stood among the small group for a bit, amazed at the miracle of nature, before Selby nudged her and started walking her back the way they had come.

At the car, they knocked their shoes against the tires, freeing them of sand. She didn't know what to do. Her stomach had been in knots the whole time. He helped her onto the hood of his truck while he stood there and they talked. Just talked. When he finally returned her to her doorstep and walked her to her front door, he simply kissed her hand and said, "Good night." He had never even tried to kiss her on the lips. She thought she had done something wrong. It had been her experience, little that it was, that all men tried to get as far as they could with a girl the first time out.

Selby had her home by midnight, and yet, it was another three hours before she could fall asleep. She was so giddy. Nervous. Afraid. Cherish was also living at home and Faith had talked her ears off as she lay there staring at the ceiling. Faith had decided Selby had just played the role of gentleman, but Cherish just called him a wuss. Faith didn't care. Selby had captured her heart that very first night.

It was that feeling that coursed through her now, but for totally different reasons. She had stepped out of her box and grabbed the adventure. She had also grabbed Edwin's cock. She giggled again. Oh god, she couldn't believe the feelings coursing through her, the adrenaline. She had been naked in front of him, on her own. And he had gone down on her right there on his desk.

She closed her eyes at the memory and then opened them again, quickly, remembering she was driving. Faith guessed they could call her a slut now. Another giggle. She couldn't wait to get home and tell Selby. She needed him to fuck her, she was so horny. Edwin had definitely got her off, but just the fact of what she had done had caused her to heat up again and she could feel the wetness between her legs growing. Need was an understatement.

~ ~ ~ ~ ~

By five thirty, Selby knew that Faith had decided to give Edwin his surprise. He glanced down at his phone. Nothing. *Edwin must have liked his surprise.* Selby dropped his briefcase on the counter and grabbed a highball glass and the bottle of Jameson, carrying both to the back deck. Setting the glass on the wood rail, he poured two fingers and stared at the breaking waves. The game had begun. He wondered how she would handle it. It was a big step in their adventure and he still wasn't sure how he felt about it. Nervous. Aroused. Excited. Scared. Okay, he knew how he felt, but wasn't sure how they would handle it.

Their sexual adventures were just that—adventures. They had them together, shared them, and repeated them to each other during their own sexual play. She would tell him how hot she had felt, how much she loved being taken by another man, feeling his hands on her and his cock in her. She described, in detail, how she felt and as she would replay her orgasms, Selby would get off. Their lovemaking had always been hot, but their games made it even hotter. He could see what she was describing, because he had been there. Now, she was alone. The game had changed, but was it for the better or worse?

And what of Tracey? Faith had given him permission to have his own adventure with the fiery redhead, and Tracey had implied that she was more than willing. He had to admit he was, as well. Tracey intrigued him. She seemed so open about everything, and yet, so much of her was still a mystery. Was it that characteristic which pulled him in?

He glanced down at his phone, tempted to call her and just…chat? What would he say to her? He had been with Faith so long he wasn't sure how to begin another dating adventure. He laughed as he lifted his glass. Knowing Tracey, she would make all the moves and he would just be going along for the ride. He took a large swallow of his whisky and that first swig burned its way down his throat to start a fire in his belly. He couldn't deny that he wouldn't mind if she did take the reins. It would be a pleasant change to him always leading. He stared out at the crashing waves. It would definitely be a change.

Selby's phone beeped. He glanced down expecting a text from Faith letting him know she was heading home. Instead, it was Tracey. *I enjoyed our lunch today. I look forward to what's to come. How did our girl do?*

He smiled as he texted back. *I haven't heard from her, yet, so I assume she's having fun. And I'm looking forward to future days, as well.*

He drained his glass and poured another as an elderly couple walked hand-in-hand along the shore in front of him. Selby took a deep breath of the ocean air. Faith and he were going to be that couple one day, enjoying retirement and spending their days meandering through time, lost in each other. Of that, he had no doubt. However, now they were having fun exploring everything they could so they *would* have something to talk about when they were doing that meandering.

His phone beeped again. *So what are our ground rules? Do we have certain times or places or can we have whatever we want whenever I want it?*

He laughed even harder. She was already taking the lead. Yet, she had a valid question. What were their ground rules? Faith had asked to stay and surprise Edwin, but would she always? Was she expecting him to tell her everything about his play with Tracey? This was beginning to sound more like relationship issues than sexual boundaries. This was definitely more involved. *I'll find out. I haven't thought that far ahead. How was your appointment?* He had forgotten to ask her at lunch, so caught up in Faith's surprise.

"I should have known you'd be out here."

He turned just as Faith wrapped her arms around his neck. Before he could say anything, she pressed her lips to his and her passion ignited a flame within him. She pulled away and he couldn't help but smile at her school girl grin. "I take it that your surprise went well?"

She squeezed him hard and he could hear her giggle. A twinge of excitement mingled with jealousy knotted his gut. "I did it. I actually did it! And then, well, then he did it."

"He fucked you?" His eyebrow went up as did the tone of his voice.

However, Faith shook her head. "No. He did go down on me, though. Oh god, Selby. I was so nervous and so excited at the same time. C'mon, I need you. Come fuck me and I'll tell you all about it." She pulled him toward the sliding doors. "Please, Selby. I need you to fuck me."

"Okay, okay," Selby said as he set his glass on the table as he passed it as he was being hauled inside. He couldn't help but laugh at how eager Faith seemed. His phone beeped, but his attention was focused on his wife as she tugged him all the way into the master bedroom, stripping him as they went.

~ ~ ~ ~ ~

He couldn't sleep. It should have been no problem. After what Faith had put him through in the bedroom before they fell asleep, he should have been exhausted. Yet, his mind wouldn't shut off. There had been no denying that Faith's afternoon had turned her on. She couldn't stop talking about it; she was so excited that she carried out her surprise with Edwin.

Selby slid out of the bed, careful not to wake Faith up. In the kitchen, he poured himself some orange juice and stood over the sink as he drank it. He knew he shouldn't be feeling jealous over Faith's experience. After all, he had started this whole journey. He had even agreed to the solo adventures and was looking forward to exploring with Tracey. Yet, he was jealous. He hadn't been there to share the experience and it was driving him nuts. He'd get over it, he knew. In time.

"You okay?" Faith's voice came from behind him.

He forced a smile as he turned to face her. "Of course. Just thirsty. You can dehydrate a guy, you know that?"

Faith stepped up to him and put her hand on his chest as she leaned up and kissed his forehead. "And yet, I'm the one that gets all wet."

Selby set his glass on the counter and then wrapped his arms around her waist, pulling her tight against him. "That you were." He leaned down and kissed her, their lips warm against each other. He ran a hand up her back, caressing her.

When they pulled back from each other, he could see the concern in her eyes. "Are you really okay? If this afternoon bothered you, I can stop everything right now."

He smiled down at her. He wasn't about to make her stop her exploration simply because he had a twinge of jealousy. "No, sweetheart. I want you to have fun. It's just that first time gut feeling. It'll pass by morning. Promise."

"Selby, I don't want to do anything that's going to hurt us. If this isn't fun, then we need to call it quits. We made a promise to each other, remember?"

He gave her nose a quick kiss. "I remember. And I promise. I'm fine. Now, let's hit the sheets."

~ ~ ~ ~ ~

Faith could hear his breathing as he lay beside her, a steady rhythm of in and out. She could picture his chest rising and falling in the dark. He had wrapped his arm around her and then drifted off to sleep. There was just enough light in the bedroom that she could make out his profile. She stared at him as he lay sleeping, wondering if he was indeed okay with what happened between her and Edwin. She knew that the two of them entering the swinging lifestyle had been Selby's idea, but this latest step was hers. While he had eagerly agreed, she knew that sometimes fantasies didn't always transfer well to reality.

She also knew that he would hate himself if he didn't get to explore with Tracey. For that matter, Tracey would probably kill her if she changed her mind now. It was obvious that her husband and friend had a lust for each other. What's funny is that Selby was the one acting jealous and not Faith. Usually, she was the insecure one. She fell asleep wondering what that meant exactly.

Eleven

Selby parked in front of his bookstore, left his car, and clicked the automatic lock button. He turned and faced Joe's Bakery and decided against coffee and a bagel that morning. He still wasn't sure how to approach Tracey with the new direction their relationship seemed to be heading. To compound things, he wasn't sure how to handle his jealousy with Faith and Edwin. Everything about their sexual exploration thus far had excited him more than anything else he had experienced. Yet, he wasn't sure how to handle her being off on her own with these adventures.

Flipping on the lights, he dropped his copy of the latest Mercedes Lackey novel on the counter and kicked down the air conditioning. The March weather was already humid, getting ready for summer. He had dressed casual as always, blue jeans, button-down, short-sleeve shirt and Dockers, his normal business attire.

Faith, on the other hand, had dressed to entice. She had worn tight jeans that morning with a low-cut black sweater and sandals. She was ready to make a statement and see what Edwin would do. Selby watched her leave that morning, giddy and already moist between her legs. Jealousy of her behavior for another's attention yanked at his gut. However, he shook the feeling as fast as it came. Her heart was his. Everything else was a game. He had to keep reminding himself of that or he would go crazy.

He carried his stained coffee pot to the back to fill it with water as he wondered how much of the game Faith actually wanted.

Or if Edwin was even playing a game.

~ ~ ~ ~ ~

"You seem unusually happy this morning," Cherish noted as Faith seemed to bounce into the room, plopping her leather purse on her desk.

Faith turned to her sister and shrugged. "I am happy. It was a wonderful night." She thought for a moment about how happy she actually was. She should be nervous after her little tryst in the office, worried about how Edwin would act today. Yet, for some odd reason, she wasn't.

"Oh? And what did you do?"

Faith grinned. "Just hung out."

"And how are you ladies this morning?" Deon pranced into the room. "Deon here could make you feel all better."

"Do any of the girls buy your shit?" Cherish shook her head as she opened up some files on her desk.

"Mexicans know all about the art of love. Try me and find out the truth of that."

Faith sat in her chair and laughed at him. "Well, since you're only half Mexican, I think I'll wait for the full package before trying it out."

Cherish laughed even though it was obvious she didn't want to.

"Deon, don't you have jobs to get to?" Grady Parrish stood in the doorway, wearing the same dirty shirt he had on the day before.

Faith rolled her eyes as she spun around to her desk and flipped on the computer. She still had no idea what use Edwin had for Grady. Others would be more reliable.

"Just waiting on Terry to give me supplies." Deon wiggled his eyebrows at Faith. She rolled her eyes as she shook her head.

Grady crossed his arms. "Then I suggest you get to the warehouse."

Deon waved at Grady to say he was going. First, however, he leaned down and whispered into Faith's ear. "One day I'll show you how much Mexican I am."

"Promises, promises," she whispered back as she shook her head.

Deon laughed as he walked out of the Girls' Den, completely ignoring the glare on Grady's face.

Grady then turned to Faith. "Do I have a list of the crews I'm supposed to be checking on today?" His voice already held a pack of cigarettes.

"Probably, but seeing as how I just got here, I have"t had a chance to pull it up yet. Give me a sec and I'll get you out of here." She wanted nothing more than to get him out of there. Fast.

He ran a hand through his greasy hair as he crossed the room to Faith's desk and leaned his ass up against it. "Did the princess have a rough night last night?" Grady tried to grin, but it always came out more as a leer. "Is that why you're behind?"

"Who said I was behind? My work day doesn't start until eight and it's only 7:58 now." Faith sat back in her chair, hands in her lap. "Technically, I can sit here for another two minutes."

"I'm supposed to be in the field by seven." His dark eyes widened a little as his voice took on an edgy tone.

Faith shrugged. "I'm not in charge of scheduling. Cherish is." She hooked a thumb in her sister's direction.

"Are you giving my girl a hard time, Grady?" Edwin walked in and handed Cherish a stack of files before crossing to where Faith sat. He placed his hands on her shoulders, massaging them. "Since the job list is the same as yesterday, you already know where you're going. You just want an excuse to put off working." Edwin nodded his head toward the door. "Now, get going."

"And don't call me princess." Faith said.

Grady glared at her as he pushed himself off the desk, but didn't say a word. He stalked away, leaving behind the odor of stale smoke. Cherish pulled out a can of mountain-scented air freshener and showered the room. "I smoke and even I hate the reek he leaves behind," she said as she put the can back in her drawer.

Edwin gave a soft chuckle at Cherish's statement before turning back to Faith. He continued to massage her shoulders as he spoke. "How's your morning look?"

"Typical." She couldn't turn to look at him, so she dropped her head and allowed him to work his magic on her shoulders. "Typing, filing, more typing, teasing you men so you go home to your wives and they wonder what you've been up to all day."

Edwin laughed as he squeezed her shoulders harder. "For which their wives probably thank you." He slid around the side and sat on the edge of her desk so that he could see her face.

Faith turned and looked into his dark emerald eyes. "Did you need something?"

"Well, you're always complaining about the supplies I purchase and the quantities. So, I was thinking you should tag along and make sure I get it right."

"Road trip." Faith smiled and then waggled her eyebrows up and down. "I love road trips."

Edwin shook his head. "Just make a list and be ready to leave in an hour." He patted her shoulder as he walked past her and left the office.

Faith watched him leave, enjoying the shape of his ass in his tight jeans. Once he was out of the office, she glanced over at her sister and saw Cherish just staring at her. "What?"

"My girl? Road trip? What's going on with you two?" Cherish's tone was not only accusatory but also disgusted. "You trying to earn that slut title?"

Faith rolled her eyes as she spun back to her desk to make a shopping list. "Nothing is going on. I'm just having fun. You should try it sometime. It might make you smile." She then turned back to Cherish feeling mischievous. "Of course, the effort might cause you some discomfort so be careful. It might seem like work." Faith could feel her sister's dagger gaze. There was an empowering feeling to her new freedom. Life was to be enjoyed, not trudged through, and Faith had every intention of drawing every ounce of life out of it. She had held back way too long.

~ ~ ~ ~ ~

Selby heard the cowbell over his front door jingle while he was adding Sue Grafton novels to the mystery section in the back of the store. "I'll be right there! If you need help with anything just call out." His morning had been hectic. He had four boxes of books to sort, price and shelve along with an endless stream of ladies from the

Trinity Towers nursing home that had wheeled in for their weekly fix. He was ready for the day to be over.

"You really drink this shit and call it coffee?" Tracey's voice echoed from the front of the store.

Selby froze and glanced to where she would be, except several rows of shelves blocked his view. He should have known that she would have come to him if he didn't go to her. The day had just been so chaotic that he hadn't had time to think. Now, he was out of time. He placed the books casually on the shelf and made his way up front. "There is no such thing as bad coffee, only better."

"Spoken like a man who has burned his taste buds off." She stood by the counter, holding two Styrofoam cups with steam coming from them. A plate on one of them held a sesame bagel lathered with strawberry cream cheese.

He walked over to take one of the cups from her and she turned a cheek to him before she would release the coffee. Selby surrendered with a smile and gave her a peck on the cheek. Pulling away, he suddenly felt like an idiot. "Sorry about not making it over to you this morning. I was running real late and already behind."

"Liar." She was smiling as she took a sip from her coffee. "I know why you didn't come over this morning and I understand. There's no need for falsehood between us. Deal?" She perched herself on the stool behind the counter.

"I'm sorry. You're right, of course. Deal." He took a bite of the bagel as he sat in his chair by the register. "Thanks for this. Breakfast kind of got skipped this morning." He gave her a sheepish smile.

Tracey waved the appreciation off. "My pleasure. Now, tell me about our girl's adventure."

Selby laughed. "I think you love hearing these stories as much, if not more, than I do."

Tracey shrugged, her breasts rising and falling slightly with the motion. "Of course. It's been too long since I've had an adventure of my own. Can you blame me for living vicariously through yours?" She grinned down at him and gave a playful wink. "Hopefully, that dry spell ends soon, though."

Selby felt his face heat up as he gave a nervous chuckle. Before the conversation led them down a path he wasn't sure he was ready for, he repeated everything Faith told him the night before. He found himself staring at the picture of his wife he kept on the desk behind the counter as he continued the erotic tale and had to force his eyes away to avoid the jealous emotions sprouting up again. He did, however, tell Tracey about his inner struggle.

"I can understand that, the newness of the whole thing and the uncertainty of what is going on. It allows your imagination to wander too much and sometimes that's just dangerous." She stretched her foot out, slid it along his thighs and teased his hardening cock with her toes through his jeans. "However, it does seem that her little adventure still has you excited."

Embarrassed, Selby shifted on his chair trying to pull his erection from Tracey's probing toes. He couldn't deny how excited he was remembering the previous night's passion, and the thrill Faith had held in her voice as she shared how she sat on Edwin's desk, naked and open. She had relived every tongue lick and tremor, and the sexual intensity of what she had experienced had caught him by surprise.

"Now, now, dear Selby, are you suddenly bashful?" Tracey set her coffee on the counter as she slid off her stool. She approached him, mischief in her eyes.

He sat still, eyes glancing at the door, hoping someone would come in and rescue him. This woman was shorter than him by about a foot as well as eighty pounds lighter. Yet, he sat paralyzed as she approached. She reached her right hand down to his crotch and stroked his erect prick through his jeans, rubbing up and down, pressing on him.

"Your wife got to show off. I think it's your turn. What surprise do you have?" She stared into his eyes as she slid her hand up his pants and undid the button. Grinning, she gripped the zipper and slowly slid it down.

Selby sucked his waist in, allowing her more room. He couldn't believe she was doing this; couldn't believe he was allowing it. He glanced at the door again. Tracey didn't care. She reached into his jeans, slid her hand into his boxers and gripped his manhood, which was at full attention. "Feels like a nice surprise." She grinned at him as she stroked up and down his thick shaft. She pulled his cock out and for the first time took her eyes off his to glance at his hardness. "Oh, yes, very nice."

His breathing grew heavier, more rapid, as Tracey gripped his cock, pumping it. She returned her gaze to his as she masturbated him, her index finger gliding over the ridge of his cock's hood. Faster, she worked his shaft. His body tensed as he felt his hips lift from the chair with her hand.

"That's a good Selby. Just relax and enjoy my hand just like your wife enjoyed Edwin's mouth." She smiled at him. "You know he's going to fuck her, right? He's going to spread your wife's legs and cram that cock of his deep into her cunt and use her pussy for his own."

"Yes." Selby's eyes closed. He knew it was true, knew Faith wanted it, too. Hell, Selby wanted it.

"She's going to come home one night and her tight little twat is going to be dripping with his seed and you're going to fuck that used little wife of yours, getting off on what you're sinking this cock into. Aren't you, Selby?"

"Yes." He groaned. His cock throbbed and he felt his balls shrivel up to the base of his cock. "Yes."

"Interesting." Tracey chuckled.

Selby looked at her, his eyes wide. His cock twitched and he felt the riding of his orgasm deep in his balls. She pumped twice more, and then leaned her head over, taking his throbbing cock into her mouth as hot liquid erupted from the top. He held his body rigid, his mouth hung open as he stared at the cascading red hair filling his lap. She swallowed every drop of his salty seed and her mouth stayed in place until his cock ceased throbbing and his breathing slowed.

Licking her lips, she lifted her head. Selby was about to say something when the cowbells announced the opening of the door. He yanked his shirt over his exposed cock as two elderly ladies walked past his counter, smiling and waving.

"Good morning, Selby."

"Morning, Selby."

Selby waved. "Morning, ladies."

"Are you okay? You seem out of breath." One of the older ladies narrowed her eyes at him as if trying to diagnose some ailment by sight.

Selby glanced at Tracey who just leaned against the counter smiling. "I'm fine. Thanks. Just overdid it with the morning load."

"I'll say," Tracey quipped.

He glared at her as he waved at the other two ladies. "I added some more mysteries this morning. If you need help just let me know."

"We will, dear."

Selby watched as they turned the corner. When he couldn''t hear their footsteps any longer, he quickly stood to his feet and zipped his cock back into his pants. "That was close."

"And fun." Tracey moved back over to her stool. "I need to get back but we should really talk more. Very interesting."

He stared at her, not really sure what to say. She picked up her cup and left the bookstore as if nothing out of the ordinary had taken place. Selby watched her start across New Haven, her ass swaying back and forth. When she reached the middle of the street, she turned and blew him a kiss. Selby smiled, shaking his head. How had she known he was even going to be watching her walk away?

~ ~ ~ ~ ~

When the hour was up, Faith locked her desk, grabbed her list and went in search of Edwin.

"Enjoy your little road trip," Cherish said, each word dripping with bitterness.

"Of course." Faith waved her fingers at her sister as she passed her desk. "It gets me out of here for a while."

Edwin was standing in the hall outside his office, right hand on the doorframe holding him up. He was talking to Jed who was leaning against the bulletin boards that decorated the outside of Edwin's wall. As she neared the men, she could hear them talking about Morgan Brewer's upcoming visit, wondering why Edwin's boss was stopping in. When they spotted Faith, they both smiled at her.

"There's my girl. I thought I was going to have to come get you." Edwin raked her with his eyes.

"Oh, no. I'm eager for any excuse to get out of here for a while."

"I can create some excuses for you if it means getting you alone in my truck," Jed said, his lips turned upward in a mischievous grin.

Edwin took a step toward Faith and put his arm around her waist, pulling her close to his side. "This is my girl." He said it in playfulness, but Faith had the feeling she had just been claimed. She liked the feeling. "You're just going to have to find your own."

"Ah, the perks of being the boss." Jed walked over and pinched Faith's cheek. "One day..." His phone started ringing. "Ah, well, you two have fun and bring me back a burger." He turned and went into his office.

"Shall we?" Edwin offered her his arm.

She slid hers through his and nodded. "Lead on, Mr. Coldwell. I'm at your service."

"I was hoping you'd say that."

She walked with Edwin down the hall and through the back door where his red Ford F150 was parked. Faith loved their company trucks. They were massive in size and powerful in speed and visibility. Edwin had a camper top on his and Rutherford Construction's logo blazoned on both front doors. It was a man's truck and she wanted it.

Edwin opened her door and helped her inside by placing a hand on her rump and pushing up. She giggled as she slid into her seat. Soon, he was sitting behind the steering wheel and they were pulling out of the parking lot.

At first, it was normal, idle chit-chat. How was your day? Questions about different job sites. How's your husband? How's the new girlfriend? We broke up. Sorry to hear that. She could tell that he was a tad nervous, so she kept everything as easy going as possible. It was funny, in an odd sort of way, considering she had been the buffet spread out on his desk, yesterday.

"Are you okay about yesterday?" He finally drew up the courage to ask.

She made sure she had her most confident smile on as she turned to face him. "Very much so. Edwin, I went to you, remember?"

He nodded. It was quiet a moment and then he asked, "What was it you meant when you said that was your first time without Selby?"

116

Faith leaned back against the truck door so she could see her boss better and be comfortable at the same time. She debated for a second how much to tell him, but then decided it didn't really matter since he had already seen her fully exposed. "October was a…hmmmm…what would you call it?" She struggled trying to decide the best way to describe the changes in their lifestyle. Finally, she shrugged. "A new chapter? A course direction? I don't know. Selby has always tried to get me to open up and share some of my fantasies with him. Being raised a legalistic Southern Baptist, fantasies were greatly frowned upon, especially sexual fantasies. October, I finally shared some."

"And what was your fantasy?"

Faith blushed slightly but answered. "To have sex with two men at once. I wanted a cock in my mouth while another guy fucked me." She had never told anyone except Selby that before. Yet, she wanted honesty with Edwin. If this game she was on was going to work, he needed all the facts.

"I take it that's happened." He kept glancing over at her periodically as he weaved in and out of traffic.

She gave a slight chuckle. "That and more. The first was at Fantasy Fest last October. We went down to explore our wild side without risking running into people we knew. It was the first time I was semi-nude in public. By the end of the week, I had seen so many other women walking around with their breasts airbrushed with the most amazing art work that I was envious. So, our last Saturday there, I sat down in front of the guy, peeled my shirt off and said, 'Paint me.' At first he fondled my tits, pushing them this way and that. Up until then Selby had been the only one to see me naked nevertheless touch me there. Well, there was my boyfriend in high school, but that is a longer tale."

"Wow. You're not kidding about being conservative. You and your sister aren't anything alike are you?"

"Thanks. That's a compliment." She laughed. "Anyway, that night was to be our last night there, so we went into this quaint little bar that the locals seemed to enjoy. Some guy, I don't even remember his name, started talking us up and buying drinks for us. I danced with him and I remember his hands all over my back and ass. He was good looking, dark blond hair, deep bronze tan and strong, muscular arms.

As we danced, I ground my pussy into his crotch and I could feel the effect I was having on him.

"After the dance, Selby asked him to come back to the hotel with us and the guy was eager to tag along. When we shut the door, Selby made us all drinks and I sat on the edge of the bed with the guy. He put his hand around my waist and pulled me to him, his lips going for my neck. I was nervous and just sat there as his mouth and hands slid over my body. Selby joined us and started kissing on my ears. My timidity soon gave way to lust as four hands and two mouths ravished me.

"Selby was the one who started stripping me, not that there was much left to take off, pulling my bathing suit bottom off. I was already basically topless, with just the paint covering my tits. The guy had already slid his hand inside and was fingering my cunt. Both men started sucking on my nipples as I leaned back, giving them complete access to my body. The guy—Jake, maybe?—started kissing his way down my stomach. I remember going crazy as he spread my legs and licked between my pussy lips up to my clit, which he sucked into his mouth.

"I don't remember Selby stripping, but I felt his cock in my hand as he guided my head to his lap. It was my fantasy come to reality and I grabbed it. Or rather my mouth did. I took his cock into my mouth, sucking him as Jake started fingering my pussy. I was so wet and soon he had three fingers pumping in and out of me. My moans were bouncing off the walls as I worked Selby's cock with my mouth and Jake used my cunt.

"I felt Jake's fingers leave my pussy and was about to protest when suddenly I felt his cock slide into me. Selby says my back arched and he could feel my moans around his cock as the other guy fucked me. Within only a few moments of watching Jake pound into me, Selby pulled his cock out of my mouth and came all over my tits.

"Anyway, Jake bent my legs out and up, spreading me wide and just kept fucking me, his balls slapping against my ass. I remember crying out, begging for more until I climaxed with the loudest scream ever to come from my lips. As my pussy tightened around his cock, I heard Jake grunt as he finally came inside of me. It was the most intense sex I'd had up until then."

Faith glanced out the front windshield as they passed businesses and restaurants. "Jake hung out for an hour talking. When he left, Selby and I had sex again and then fell asleep. It was that weekend that opened us up to sex as an adventure. We've shared fantasies and talked about role-playing different scenarios. It's become a game to us. Sex, that is."

"Pretty intense." Edwin glanced over at her. "But you said 'and more.'"

"You just want all the fun facts, don't you?" Faith shifted in the seat to a more comfortable position. "We've met up with others. Single men. Couples. Never around here, of course. Our trip this weekend was the most recent and had an interesting twist." Faith told him about meeting Paul at the winery and how he had just followed them back to the condo. She told him everything, even how Paul had used her as a sex toy and then made her ride Selby while the man's sperm dripped from her.

"I'd never been used in such a fashion." She turned back around in her seat as they pulled into Offices Plus. "He got off on taunting me and ordering me around. It was like I couldn't not do what he said. I allowed him to pull me where he wanted and use me. It was pretty intense."

Edwin pulled into a parking spot and turned the truck off. "And how did Selby handle watching his wife be under the control of another man?" He turned and watched for her answer before opening his door.

"Honestly? It was the horniest I've ever seen him. After Paul left, we went at it again, both of us still so turned on. It was pretty awesome."

Edwin shook his head, laughing. "You've really opened up your legs, er, life."

Faith shrugged as she reached for the door handle. "I'm having fun and enjoying myself." She opened the truck's door and slid out. It was almost like falling out because the truck was so high.

"I envy you." Edwin stepped out of the truck and they walked toward the store entrance.

As they walked the aisles, Edwin pushed the cart while Faith dropped things into the basket; the conversation went back to work.

Faith had a fascination with pens and talked Edwin into forking out company money for some cute ones just for her. "We'll get Cherish these boring white ones with the black caps."

"You are so mean to her." Edwin laughed as he watched her put the pens in the orange buggy.

"I've lived with her. Enough said."

"Yet, she's the one who talked me into hiring you."

Faith leaned on the end of the cart, her black sweater falling open allowing Edwin to see all he wanted of her round globes. "Aren't you lucky she did?"

Edwin leaned forward and took a good look down her sweater. Glancing back at her unashamedly, he said, 'More than you know."

"Good."

They finished their shopping and loaded the supplies into the truck bed. When they got into their seats, Edwin flipped up the middle console and patted the empty spot beside him.

"Aren't you afraid someone might notice me that close to you?"

Edwin rapped his knuckles on his driver's window. "Tinted glass."

"Oh, yeah." Faith smiled as she eased over next to him. "Nice."

He started the truck and began the trip back. Once he pulled out into traffic, Edwin placed his hand on her thigh and squeezed. She glanced at him with a taunting arch of her eyebrows. Slowly, he ran his hand up and down her thigh, lightly caressing. Faith could feel her breathing get heavier as she placed her hands by her ass, bracing herself and giving him more freedom. He took it.

Sliding his hand up to her crotch, he began to massage her sex through her jeans. Faith moaned as she opened her legs wider. He slid his fingers up to her jean's button and slid it back through the hole. Then he slid her zipper down, opening her jeans. Slipping his hand inside her pants, he found her sensitive folds. "Nice and wet."

"Always lately," she said as she slid her ass to the edge of the seat, giving him easier access.

He inserted a finger into her wet slit and began to work it in and out. Faith moaned louder as she closed her eyes in pleasure. She put her hand under his and began rubbing her swollen clit. It was a tight fit with his hand in her pants but the pressure forced his hand tighter against her mound as his finger worked in and out. He added another and she felt her passion swallow it eagerly. With two fingers pressed against her swollen nub she rubbed harder, making small circular motions.

Edwin turned left off Wickham onto Eau Gallie Boulevard. "Almost home. You can make yourself come before we get there. Show me."

Faith nodded, her hips pumping against his hand. Her whole body tensed at the sensation of all the fingers playing with her. She pressed down harder on her clit as she felt the truck come to a stop at a red light. She reached a hand out and gripped his forearms as she felt her orgasm wash through her. She opened her eyes as her jaw fell. Grunting, she felt her body push upward, trembling, until her climax was over.

Breathing heavy, she sat back down while Edwin slid his soaked fingers from her slick channel. He wiped them on the seat as Faith slid back up, zipping and buttoning her pants as she did. She glanced over at her boss as she scooted back to the passenger side of the truck. He was smiling as he glanced over at her.

"Thank you," she whispered, her heavy breathing taking her voice.

"Oh, it's my pleasure." He grinned. "I'm having fun helping you enjoy life."

"So am I. Wow, so am I."

He pulled into the office parking lot and drove around to his spot between the two wings of the building. "Do I get to help some more?"

"All you want." She opened her door and walked to the back of the truck.

"What about Selby?" He met her at the back of the truck and opened the cab flap.

"He knows all about it. It's our game, remember?"

Edwin nodded. "I think I'm going to enjoy this game."

"Isn't that the point?" She grinned at him as he opened the back door.

Twelve

Faith lounged back in her deck chair, bare feet propped on the middle railing as she watched the seagulls glide in the air just skimming the waves. She held a mug of orange spice tea in one hand while the other rested on the arm of the chair, her thoughts lost on her trysts with Edwin over the past two days. As she sat staring at the cresting waves, she realized she wanted more. The playfulness with Edwin was just that, playful. While it was hot, it wasn't really intense. Paul had been intense. Edwin had given her choices. Paul had taken her, used her, and tossed her back to Selby. It was that part that turned her on the most.

She shook her head. How twisted was she? Yet, she still wanted more. She wondered if Edwin could take her like that. He was nervous, she knew. They both risked their jobs if they were discovered and who knew what the ramifications would be in her family. Yet, Faith wanted him, wanted him to use her harder.

Still, what if he did? How far was she willing to allow him to go? It was all equally scary and exciting.

She had called Selby at lunch and told him of her supply run. She could tell he was getting stiff by how his voice got deeper, and it was obvious that as she gave him every detail he was jacking off. That made her even hornier as she sat in the car and she started fingering

122

her clitoris again. That was even more daring as her windows weren't tinted.

He then told her of Tracey's visit to the bookstore that afternoon and Faith had her second orgasm of the day.

She heard the sliding door open, bringing her out of her reverie. She turned to watch Selby walking through it with take-out Chinese in hand. "They forgot my hot sauce again," he said as he set the bags on the table. "Why do we keep going back to them? They screw up every order."

Faith turned and helped him open the containers. "Because the food's good and they're cheap."

Selby sighed. "True."

Both fixed a plate and returned to the chairs looking out at the beach. "So, what have you been thinking about out here by your lonesome?"

Faith took a bite of her crab rangoon, crumbs falling onto her shirt. She slipped into shorts and a T-shirt as soon as she walked in the door after work. "Just the excitement of the past few days. I wonder how far it'll go."

"How far do you want it to go?"

"I really don't know. It would be interesting to see how far I can take it, the sexual aspects of it. The thought of just being used and taken just makes me drip with excitement. Weird?"

"No more so than me getting off on letting you be used and getting the leftovers; sexually, that is. As long as your heart stays mine, you can loan your body out all you want." He grinned at her, his face alight with playfulness.

"And what of Tracey?" Faith glanced over at him, her green eyes playful.

Selby laughed, shaking his head. He finished chewing his bourbon chicken before answering. "She's daring, I'll say that much. We almost got busted by two old ladies. She seems to think everything is 'interesting' so far."

Faith scooped some fried rice into her mouth as she thought of the whole situation. So many different scenarios went through her head. "Would you want to watch Edwin fuck me?"

"Would be fun. Do you think he's up for it?"

"I have no idea. I'm surprised he's gone this far. Although, he has asked me to stay late tomorrow to return the favor."

"You going to?"

"Oh yeah, even though I'm nervous as hell."

"You'll be the best head he's ever had."

"And I'm not for you?"

Selby rolled his eyes. "I should have known better than to try to be sweet."

"I love you. I'm just teasing, dear."

As Faith finished her orange chicken she wondered if Edwin had passions such as hers. She smiled at herself as she remembered his tongue gliding over her body, his hands strumming her like a fine instrument. He had wanted more of her, but how much more?

Her cell phone went off. She flipped it open and saw she had a text message from Edwin. *Looking forward to our meeting tomorrow.*

Faith glanced over at Selby who was sipping his Corona. He was watching her face and so she showed him the text. "I bet he is," Selby chuckled.

"What should I say back to him?"

"It's your game. Tell him whatever you want. Tell him you're looking forward to it as well."

Faith looked down at her phone, a school girl grin on her face, *So am I.*

She folded the phone and sipped her tea. This was different than her other experiences. When Selby and she took a trip to find play partners that was it. They met, they fucked, and then they said goodbye. This was a chase, a chase she was having fun being caught up in.

Within a few seconds her phone went off again.

I'm walking the dog, thinking of your naked body.

That's sweet of you, but I'm sure there are better looking girls for you to picture.

I liked what I saw yesterday. Can't wait to see more.

Oh, really?

Really.

Faith stared at her phone a moment, a wicked idea brewing in her head. Finally, she texted back, *How safe is your phone?*

Very safe. Why?

Hold on. Faith stood up, setting her phone on the railing. She unbuttoned her shorts and slipped them off along with her thong.

"What are you doing?" Selby asked as she sat back down.

She smiled at him as she draped her legs over the arms of the chair causing her slit to open slightly. She then pulled her T-shirt off, exposing her perky tits. "Playing the game. Get my phone and take my picture."

Selby shook his head as he reached for her phone. "You are brazen, Mrs. Greer." He snapped a picture of Faith, naked and inviting, with the camera on her phone. "I get a copy as well, you hussy."

"But of course, dear heart." Faith slipped her shirt back on since it was still daylight enough to see their deck from the sand. She sent Edwin the picture with the note, *Something to anticipate.*

A minute passed. Then two. Faith grew nervous wondering if she had gone too far. After four minutes her phone went off again.

Sweet. Now I have something to jerk off to.

Anytime I can help.

You will tomorrow. See you then.

Bye.

She set her phone back down as she thought of what she had just done. Suddenly, she grew scared. What if someone opened his phone and saw that picture? What would they think of her?

"Exactly what you want them to think," Selby told her once she had voiced her thoughts.

"Thinking is one thing. Knowing it and having proof is another." Faith set her tea down. It had already grown cold and she was no longer in the mood for it anyway. Her stomach was in knots over her rash behavior. "I'll get his phone tomorrow and make him delete it."

Selby shrugged. His corona swung back and forth, held by two fingers and thumb, his elbow on the arm of his chair. "Up to you."

"You don't care that another man has a naked photo of your wife?"

"That man's had my wife naked on his desk. Tomorrow he's going to fuck my wife's mouth. At this point, a picture is harmless, don't you think?"

Faith turned her gaze back to the ocean. Two teenage boys with surfboards under their arms walked down the beach. She took a deep breath. Selby was right. She was past the point of worrying about a picture.

"And besides, as long as you and I are okay with whatever's going on, what do we care what other people think? You wanted him to have the picture. You wanted to tease him and I knew you were sending it. Hell, I took it *knowing* you were sending it to him. I thought that's what you wanted."

Faith sighed. "I do. That doesn't mean it doesn't scare me sometimes."

Selby scooted out of his chair, dropping to his knees on the wood planks of the deck flooring. Evening had grown to the grayness of dusk and their deck was draped with heavy shadows. He knee-walked over to where she sat and ducked under her leg, dropping to all fours. He kissed under her knee as he passed, his tongue licking her flesh, cooled by the March evening air. He kissed her inner thigh, making a trail toward her exposed slit. He stayed on all fours.

"Admit it. You wanted him to have that picture of you." He licked around her labia, his tongue gliding up the outer edge of one side and back down the other.

Faith took a deep breath as the pleasure of his warm tongue against her chilled flesh sent shivers of pleasure through her body. She placed her right hand on his blond hair as she slid her left hand behind her head. "Yes," she whispered. "Yes, I did."

He pulled his mouth away from her moistened folds. She could feel the heat of his breath as he spoke. "Tell me why." His tongue started at the entrance to her honey and glided upward between her nether lips, reaching the sensitive bead of her clit.

She moaned. Ripples of pleasure washed through her. "I wanted him to see me." Her voice was low, raspy with the lust that was building within her. "I wanted him to remember what he had had and fantasize about having more."

"What else do you want, Faith?" His tongue flicked her swelling clit, sending tremors through her.

"To be used. I want Edwin to use me." Her hips pressed into his face. She knew it was Selby pleasuring her, but her mind was on

Edwin, on his mouth and fingers, on his cock that she wanted to feel again, wanted to feel in her pussy and not just her fingers.

"Keep going. I want to hear it all." Selby bit at her cunt lips, licking the piece of flesh in his mouth. She felt his finger slide across her ass and slip into her heat. Her hips bucked at the intrusion.

"Your wife wants to be Edwin's slut, Selby." She held his head in place as he licked her closer to the edge of ecstasy. "I'll do whatever he asks me to. I want him to take me." She cried out as Selby sucked her swollen clit into his mouth. He added two more fingers into her pussy and pumped them with a fierceness that had her whimpering. "I want him to use me and send me home to you fucked and filled with his cum." Another finger stretched her open. She placed her other hand on his head and ground her snatch against his face as he knelt between her legs.

The power of their positions filled her and she gave herself to her fantasies. Her hips forced her pussy harder against Selby's face. "I want him to use me at work. I want his cock, his mouth. I want him to fuck my mouth and use my pussy."

Faster, she felt the fingers pumping in and out of her wetness and was surprised at the ferociousness Selby was going at her. "I want you to know your wife is another man's toy." He sucked her swollen pearl, licking the sensitive nub as he did. She could feel her orgasm breaking like the waves in front of them, crashing through her and onto Selby's face. She cried out as it hit, not caring if people heard her whimpers of pleasure as they echoed off the ocean surface.

Her inner walls pressed against his fingers as her body tensed. Her legs stiffened as her body shuddered with ecstasy. Her whole body trembled, rocking the chair she was in. Her breathing slowed as the waves subsided and she was able to relax. She felt Selby's lips leave her and his fingers slip from her passage. She glanced down at him as he sat back on his heels and could see the bulge making a tent in his jeans from his excitement.

"Pull out your cock." She stayed spread before him, the glistening of her wetness running down her ass cheeks. She knew what she craved, to be with Edwin in a way that was the complete opposite of what she had with Selby. This was her game now, and she wanted it played by her rules.

Selby stayed sitting as he was as he unbuttoned his pants and pulled his manhood out with his balls. It was harder than Faith had seen it and she was amazed at how turned on he was by everything she had said.

"Jerk off. Now." Her voice was stern as she watched him, knowing that he wanted to sink his hardness into her.

He gripped his cock with his right hand and began stroking it up and down. She could see her honey still on his fingers. "You liked all of that, didn't you? You liked hearing how I was going to give myself to Edwin."

Selby stared at her, his lust strong in his eyes. "Yes." His voice was hoarse from pent-up passion.

"I'm going to let him fuck me. He's going to use my mouth tomorrow at the office and I want to make him give me his cum."

Selby pumped his cock harder with her words. She found herself getting even hotter as she watched him, taunting her husband as he sat there, down on his knees. He nodded as he masturbated in front of her.

"When I come home tomorrow my mouth will be warm from him using it. I'm going to kiss you with that used mouth."

"Yes." His body was tight. His cock throbbed.

"Just as Paul gave you his leftovers, I'm going to give you Edwin's."

Selby grunted and she watched as the white liquid erupted from Selby's cock splashing her legs and the wooden deck. His breathing was heavy as he slumped in on himself, emptied, but not spent. "I know," he whispered.

They both knew.

They tried to carry on a different conversation, but there was too much sexual tension for either of them to concentrate. Instead, they grabbed the bottle of wine and retired to the bedroom where they finished stripping each other before climbing into bed and making love for the rest of the evening.

Around midnight, they had worn themselves to a frazzle and Faith drifted into a peaceful slumber. Selby had too much going on in his head to sleep. He slipped from the bed, still naked, and went to the kitchen for water. His mind replayed the events of the past four days and his stomach knotted at the same time his cock twitched.

It was college all over again.

Selby left the kitchen, passing through the dining room and entering his office, second door on the left. Sitting behind his desk, he spun in his chair to the shelf and cabinet behind him on the back wall. Reaching into the bottom cabinet, he pulled out a photo album. He had attended college in Georgia on a full scholarship for literary arts. In August of '88, he moved out of his parents' home and into the dorms of Georgia University.

He laid the photo album on his desk and flipped through the first three pages, looking but not seeing the snapshots that documented his college years. On the fourth flip of the cardboard stock, a loose picture slid out of the album and into his lap. He picked up the photo as he settled back into his chair, his back sensitive to the cold leather. The photo had captured a young Selby Greer in the beginning of his junior year at Georgia. With him was a fair-complexioned, autumn haired lady, smiles plastered over their faces as their heads leaned into each other. They sat under a massive maple with the multicolored leaves of fall.

Chelsea Lanford.

She was a senior to his junior and surrounded herself with powerful players, or at least those destined to become the runners of major corporations. She had bought breast implants her first year in college thanks to a very generous and appreciative professor, if rumor held true, and she owned no outfit that didn't flaunt her blackmail price. She worked out two hours every morning so that she could play hard every evening.

"Men wield their pricks as swords to feel powerful," she had said once. "I use my body to control their swords."

Selby was far from a virgin when he entered college, but being with Chelsea had made him feel like one. She took him into a world that had almost cost him his soul, in a dramatic play of words.

He placed the photo back into the album and the album back on the shelf. He lifted himself out of the chair and made his way back to his bedroom, back to Faith. Chelsea had grown to crave the power she took from men, even from Selby. He had to admit that he had craved what she did to him, as well. Craved it a little too much in the end.

He slid into bed next to Faith, propping himself up with one elbow as he watched the rise and fall of her chest with her breathing. Her mouth was parted just a bit as one arm, crooked at the elbow, outlined her face and the other rested across her stomach. He smiled as she made little snoring noises in her sleep, noises she swore on her mother's Bible she never made.

Selby knew why he was uneasy. Faith was traveling the same road with Edwin, at least in her mind, which he had journeyed with Chelsea. He brushed a strand of her hair from her forehead. Furthermore, she wasn't alone. She was taking him with her. He realized it when he dropped to all fours in front of her and pleasured her; realized it when she made him do the same to himself. Memories twenty years buried had been resurrected from their cold tomb with fresh heat.

She wanted this journey. He had to have faith that she was ready for it. He needed to have faith in himself to keep them from losing themselves.

He knew he had Faith, but did he have faith?

Thirteen

Selby parked in front of his bookstore and locked up his car. His mind was still foggy with images of his past that had kept him tossing throughout the night. He was eager for a cup of coffee and a smile from a certain fiery redhead. However, as he turned to make his way across the street, he stopped dead, his heart a cold weight in his chest.

Against the beige concrete wall outside of Joe's Bakery stood Tracey deep in conversation with a man Selby had never seen before. He was tall, probably over six feet, with short black hair and an oblong face. He was clean-shaven and wore circular glasses. He wasn't muscular, but he wasn't scrawny, either. Fit is what went through Selby's mind.

And he was more than a friend.

The man had his hands on Tracey's upper arms as he spoke. He wasn't arguing, but he was passionate about whatever they were discussing. Tracey stood with her arms crossed over her chest, her face turned away from the man. Everything about her posture told Selby she was trying hard not to cry. Or run.

At first, Selby wanted to go over and make sure she was all right. He took a step toward her, but then the man pulled her into a tight embrace. She pulled her arms out from between them and wrapped them around him, her head on his chest, eyes closed. Just before Selby turned to go inside, feeling like a peeping tom, she opened her eyes and saw him standing across the street. They both stared at each other for an eternal second before Selby tucked his head and turned back to the store. He had intruded on her enough as it was.

Once inside he flipped on the lights before heading to the back to brew his own coffee. If she had been seeing someone why hadn't she told him about it? Why keep it a secret? And what about her visit to the store yesterday? He dumped yesterday's grinds into the trash and grabbed a new filter. He set about the mechanical task of fixing coffee while his mind jumped from one possibility to another.

"Oh my god, you're being dramatic," he said as he hit the brew button. "Maybe it's just a good friend having a bad morning. Maybe it's her brother come back to make amends. Maybe you need to stop talking to yourself and get to work."

~ ~ ~ ~ ~

The morning at Rutherford Construction was chaotic at best. Five men were late to jobs and two had simply walked off. Edwin called Nessa in to help man the phones and both, Grady and Jed, took to the field to fill empty spots until replacements could be hired. Terrence Ballard was in a snit as several workers had taken supplies without his knowledge, and Deon was hung over from a friend's bachelor party. It was not a happy hump day.

Cherish was on the phone all morning calling men in for interviews or trying to find subcontractors to finish jobs. Faith was calling clients, promising that things were under control and the jobs would finish on schedule. Ashlynn painted her nails.

Faith left her desk to give Edwin a quick update. She entered the hall, turning right and saw Edwin by the white board that hung on the wall outside of his office, his arms crossed, a scowl covering his face.

"Hey, everyone's confident we'll get things done except Mr. Polawski of the office buildings on Babcock and Laurie Street. Of course, nothing makes him happy." She stopped a foot away from Edwin as he pulled his eyes from the board.

Edwin, however, must not have been satisfied with the distance as he reached a hand out and pulled her closer. He returned his eyes to the white board as he slid an arm around her waist. "Mr. Polawski needs to get laid and perhaps he wouldn't be so cranky."

Faith laughed.

Edwin turned and glanced at her, one eyebrow arched. "You liked that, huh?"

"Selby said the same about Cherish just a couple of days ago."

Edwin just nodded as he turned his attention back to the board, his arm slipping from her waist. His face took on another expression she couldn't quite make out. "The Hartford Building is a week ahead of schedule. Pull the drywall crew off there for now and send them to the Polawski Development. Tell them it's just temporary until Cherish puts another crew together. And..."

"I know. Get the trucks ready." Faith cut him off, batting her eyelashes.

He nodded, a smile creasing his face. "Such a good girl."

"I can be." She wiggled her eyebrows.

"Oh, I remember." He grinned as he turned back to her. "And thank you for my surprise last night. It made sleeping, um, difficult."

"Maybe I can relieve some of that tension later."

"I can hardly wait."

"I'm excited, as well. Nervous, too."

He reached out and squeezed her to him one more time with ardent desire before allowing her to return to her work. She forced herself not to skip as she traversed the hall, still feeling the pressure of his arm around her. She loved the tingling it gave her, as well as the naughtiness of being held by him right there in the hall.

By the time the clock struck lunch, the day had settled in and jobs were getting accomplished. Faith locked her desk and escaped to the break room for some food and quiet. When she walked in, Jed, who had just arrived back at the office, was sitting in one of the black plastic chairs telling Terrence of some doctor drama he watched the night before.

"Hey gorgeous, come here." Jed reached out for Faith and, as soon as she was within arm's length, pulled her into his lap. "Miss me today?"

Faith could feel his cock under her ass as he pulled her down hard on top of him. "I always miss you when you're not here."

"Oh, yeah? Prove it. Wiggle for me."

Faith glanced over her shoulder at him, giving him her most seductive smile. She held herself up by the arms of the chair and glided her ass slowly back and forth over his crotch. "Doesn't feel like you missed me, though."

"Keep that up, babe, and I'll not be leaving this chair anytime soon."

"Might be fun to watch you walk down the halls," Faith giggled as she stood back to her feet.

"Thanks, thanks a lot." Jed laughed.

"Hey, what about me?" Terrence set up straight in his chair, arms out, waiting.

"What about you?" Everyone looked up as Cherish barged through the door, lunch box in hand, scowl set firmly in place.

"Rough day?" Jed asked as he crossed his legs trying to hide the erection Faith had just rubbed to life.

Cherish plopped down in a chair dropping her lunch on the hard table. "This day sucks. I hate when people don't just do what they're supposed to. Why can't people just show up and do their job?"

Faith winked at Terrence and mouthed the words "next time" while her back was to her sister. When she turned around, she said, "True. It's always harder on the people who do show up for their jobs when others blow theirs off."

Jed arched an eyebrow at Faith and then glanced to Cherish, waiting to see if she would take the barb.

"I know, right?" Cherish shook her head as she twisted the cap off her Mountain Dew. "Pisses me off."

Faith clasped her hands behind her back and rocked back and forth on her feet. She grinned like the proverbial cat, but didn't antagonize further. She already knew Cherish never saw her own failings, just those of other people. Jed just glanced at Faith, shaking his head.

Edwin walked through the door, hand raking through his dark hair. Everyone turned as he came in. Faith just stared at the strength in his arms that seemed to ripple with every move. "Morgan's visiting this afternoon. Apparently, someone called Neal about our chaos this morning."

"Mr. Polawski more than likely," Faith offered.

"Would be my guess, as well. Let's make sure everything's ship-shape when he arrives, however. I hate it when bosses visit." He turned and left the break room as abruptly as he entered.

Faith watched him leave, paying close attention to the firm curve of his ass as he walked. She hoped Morgan's visit wasn't going to screw up her afternoon dalliance.

~ ~ ~ ~ ~

The cowbell sounded as the front door to Selby's Downtown Books opened letting in the chill March breeze. Selby didn't have to look up to know who had entered. It was lunchtime. It could only be one person.

"I hope BLTs are okay. Do you have drinks in that broken down fridge of yours in the back?"

"Diet?" He started for the back, leaving the stack of books he was putting away on the floor.

"Do you have any grape left? I feel like being different."

"Coming right up. Never could understand how you could drink that diet shit anyway." Of course, his thoughts went a different direction. Was that what he was to her? Something different?

He grabbed two grape sodas from the fridge and when he returned to the front, Tracey had taken his chair and left him the stool. He paused at first, confused at the change in seating arrangements, but said nothing. She sat folded in on herself. Whatever had happened that morning was still affecting her. It seemed they both had things on their minds.

Selby reached over and opened her can of grape soda. "You doing okay?" He slipped the cold can into her hand as she offered him a weak smile.She took a long sip and he watched her throat bob with the action, the same throat that had swallowed his cum in that seat yesterday. She drank what she wanted and handed him back the can. Without thinking he took it and placed it back on the counter.

"Yeah, I'm fine. Just some unfinished business that needs tidying up. It's where I was last week when I canceled our lunch. I had some legal matters to straighten out." Her gaze rested on the can on the counter, but Selby doubted she saw it. "Some things just take longer to finish than others."

"Who was the guy?" Selby opened his container, trying to act casual about everything. She probably didn't need twenty questions at the moment. As he stared at the sandwich, he realized that he wasn't really hungry. Still, he forced himself to pick up the sandwich and take a bite anyway. The bacon was crisp, just the way he liked it. Tracey always made the best sandwiches.

She shrugged. He didn't think she was going to answer and was about to change the subject when she sat up in her chair, taking a deep breath. "He was part of my past and I need to stop allowing my past to fuck with my future. Today was the last day I'll ever see him and that's for the best."

Selby swallowed the bite he had taken. "You want to talk about it?"

"No. Not now." She grabbed her sandwich and held it in her lap. "Maybe later." She smiled up at him. She seemed a bit more relaxed. "But, thank you. I appreciate the offer."

He returned her smile. "Seems we both had our pasts pop up. Last night, some old memories came back that I had thought were long buried. They hit me as Faith told me about her road trip yesterday and what she wanted out of her relationship with Edwin."

"Bad memories will do that to you. What were they about?"

"It was about a relationship I had in college," he said around a mouthful of food.

"I didn't know you went to college."

Selby nodded. "Georgia University. I dropped out halfway through my junior year."

"Because of this bad memory?"

He took another bite of his sandwich, using his chewing to delay answering. How did he describe his time with Chelsea Lanford without seeming weak or weird? He sipped his soda before speaking.

"Shortly after my junior year started, I met a senior named Chelsea Lanford. She was a power all her own." He let his hands fall to his lap, sandwich still between his fingers as he stared at the counter without seeing it. "At first, I was intrigued by her and then I was in love with her. She owned a flat and had me move in with her after a month of dating and I waited on her hand and foot. It was like she owned me. I had rules. She had none. She would humiliate me and my cock would explode. Our last month together, I wasn't allowed to fuck her. She would make me masturbate while she told me of some man or woman she had just slept with. Weird thing is, I craved it all the more every time she did it to me."

Tracey nodded. "So, she dominated you and you got off on it. What's wrong with that?"

"Sex became my life. I lost myself and grew scared of never finding myself again." He shook his head. "I don't know. It was more intense than I was ready for, so I ran. I dropped out of college and eventually wound up in Florida where I took odd jobs here and there to feed myself. For two years I just wandered, never staying in one place for very long. My mom calls them my missing years. I was homeless and just dropped out of sight.

"Eventually, I wound up back home and started rebuilding my life. I bought this bookstore with some backing from my parents and set down roots. A few years later I met Faith and my life took on a brighter glimmer." He looked down at his sandwich for a moment having forgotten that he even had it. Lifting it to his mouth he took a bite, chewing without tasting.

Tracey was quiet. She chewed the last portion of her sandwich and licked crumbs from her fingers. She reached for her grape soda and drank it down, settling back in the chair. Her silence was driving him crazy. He should never have said anything. He was positive she now thought him totally deranged, some kind of emasculated sissy. That had been his opinion of himself back then.

Finally, she put the can in the trash beside her and sat back in the chair, looking at him with that soft smile decorating her lips. "Are you afraid for you or Faith?"

"Both."

"And that's why you'll be fine." She shrugged her shoulders. "You know what to watch for and you *are* watching." She kicked her white tennis shoe off her right foot and placed her toes on the stool between Selby's legs, stroking his cock through his pants. "She's having fun and so are you. Admit it?"

"I never said I wasn't, but I've been down this road. It's easy to lose yourself in it, especially if the other person is in it for themselves and could care less what happens to you."

She pressed harder with her toes. "Or find yourself."

He gave her a puzzled look. Thinking back on his experience with Chelsea he had to admit that until the end of the relationship, he was very content. Furthermore, he was satisfied. Had he found himself? He had admonished Faith to open her horizons and find what made her happy. There was no denying that she was having the time of her life with this adventure.

He felt Tracey's toes slide down to his jewels and press on them. Pain shot into him at the surprise of the pressure. "You want Edwin to use Faith and you get off on the thought of her bringing her cum-filled cunt home to you."

Selby looked at her. He could only nod.

Tracey pressed harder. "My dear Selby, I think that girlfriend of yours showed you who you are and that's what really scared you."

Was that really it? He's the one who talked Faith into taking this journey. Could he have done it for his own selfish desires more so than hers? Faith's journey was his as well and both of them had intense feelings about it. He had to admit that even though he had buried the memories, he had not buried the underlying desires. It was what made him excited and Tracey had made him face it.

She was still watching him, her foot pressing into his balls. "I love watching the light bulb go off in people's minds." She smiled. "Now, tell me some more about Chelsea Lanford. She seems like someone I might like."

Of that, Selby had no doubt.

~ ~ ~ ~ ~

The day slowed down to a newborn's crawl and Edwin sent Nessa home for the remainder of it. Faith took it upon herself to make sure Morgan's office was dusted and cleaned, ready for his arrival. Both, he and Neal Rutherford, had offices at each branch of Rutherford Construction for their own personal use when in that town. Mostly, they were kept locked and empty so Faith went in to air it out and open the drapes for light. Nessa kept the plants watered usually but was not very good at cleaning.

Edwin gave Grady more jobs in the field to keep him away from the office. Faith only chuckled and shook her head. She would never understand why he kept a man no one really liked. However, Edwin was smart enough to keep Grady away when the big bosses were in town.

"If I had known you'd be the one taking care of my office, I would have visited sooner." Turning, Faith saw the six-foot Morgan Brewer standing in the doorway to his office, water bottle in one hand, briefcase in the other. His short-cropped hair reminded her of mourning doves with eyes the color of fresh cut grass. He was a fit, trim man, but not buff like a muscle magazine.

"Well then, you should have come sooner." Faith finished wiping down one of the bookshelves before considering herself done. "I see you have water. Would you care for anything else?"

"I would at that." Morgan raked her curvaceous body with his eyes. "But I need to see Edwin first."

Faith nodded. "I'll tell him you're here."

As they passed through the room, Morgan caught her arm and stopped her. "Just so you know, I hear great things about the way you're keeping the office in shape. You're doing an awesome job. Even Neal has been saying great things about you. He's very impressed."

Faith felt herself blush as she said a soft "Thank you" before going to find Edwin. She could feel the satisfaction and pride busting from her face as she walked the halls to find her boss. Perhaps it was time to ask for that raise.

Edwin was in his office, sitting on the edge of his desk reading a file. Faith walked in catching his eye and went straight to where he was perched. She gave him a wicked grin as she slid her hand up from the base of his crotch and back down again. "Morgan's in his office."

He took a deep breath at her touch. "And you just thought giving me a hard-on before going to his office was a good idea?"

"You don't want me to touch you?" She pursed her lips into a pout as she stroked his cock through his pants.

He shook his head. "That's not what I said. Remind me to spank you later."

"Oooo, now that sounds like fun." She turned, leaving him with an obvious bulge in his pants and wiggled her fingers in goodbye. "I'll be at my desk if you wish to punish me, sir."

Back in her office, Faith busied herself with contracts and truck inspections. Cherish was playing some computer game, not seeming to care that Edwin's boss was in the building. Everything else stayed fairly quiet and time passed. Close to quitting time, Edwin entered the girls' office followed by Morgan.

"Cherish, I need you to look up everything on a carpenter we let go about a month ago. Richard Sykes."

"Okay, easy enough. What's up?"

Morgan sat in the chair at Nessa's desk, legs crossed, hands folded behind his head. "He seems to think we failed to pay him properly." Morgan then turned to Faith. "Faith, what would that husband of yours think of you going to the West Coast with me for about a week?"

"You taking me to Hollywood? I'm game whether he says yes or not."

Morgan laughed as he shook his head. "Not that West Coast, I'm afraid, but I'll keep that in mind. I meant the Tampa office."

"Why would she be doing that?" Cherish tried to appear nonchalant, but it was obvious she was bristled.

"That office just went through some major personnel shifts and most of them still don't know their heads from their asses. Faith's got this place running smooth as clockwork and I want her to teach them how to do it."

"I'll talk to Selby and see what he says. Do you know when?"

Morgan shook his head. "Not yet, but find out if you're allowed first. We'll go from there. I'll be around for the next week."

Faith glanced at Edwin, but she couldn't read his face. What would this do to their game?

Edwin and Morgan left the small room and Cherish immediately pounced. "I'm the HR person. Why does Morgan want you to go to Tampa instead of me?"

Faith shrugged her shoulders. "I don't know. You heard what I heard, so you know what I know."

Cherish just narrowed her eyes, but Faith only smiled back.

Finally, the day dragged to a halt and Cherish left without so much as a goodbye or kiss my ass, the silent treatment her normal weapon when she was miffed. Faith was done for the day as well, but didn't want to miss her promised dalliance with Edwin. The game was just getting started and already it was having delays. She was at a loss as to whether she should wait or leave with Morgan there.

Locking her desk, she decided to risk a look around before giving up on returning Edwin's surprise. Upon entering the hallway, she heard voices off to the left toward the conference room, and decided to investigate. The break room was empty as was the conference room. She turned the corner to the hall that lead to Neal and Morgan's offices and saw Edwin and Morgan in the hall chatting. Morgan once again held his briefcase, which showed he was leaving, and Faith couldn't stop the nervous jitters in her stomach.

"Faith, what's up?" Edwin turned as he noticed her.

She shook her head. "I was just getting ready to leave for the day and was saying goodbye."

"Don't leave yet. I need to go over something with you," Edwin said. "I'll be in my office in a moment."

"Goodbye, Faith, and don't forget to talk to your husband."

Faith said she wouldn't and then said goodbye. It was all she could do to refrain from skipping as she went back to Edwin's office and waited, the knot still in her stomach. Edwin hadn't forgotten after all. Entering his office, she sat on the edge of his desk, her feet swinging slightly as she waited. It wasn't long.

He walked in, that cocky grin on his face that warmed her passion. "Good girl for waiting."

Faith smiled back, her heart pounding in her chest, her ears. Her blood was pumping at what she hoped was going to happen. "I told you I could be." Her voice almost cracked as she spoke. *Get a grip, Faith.* She took a deep breath, hoping to steady herself.

He walked over to her, reaching a hand out to brush the hair from her shoulder. "Like earlier when you were stroking me to an erection before I had to see Morgan?"

She looked up into his eyes, the deep green mesmerizing. "Just being playful."

He eased his hand into her hair, taking a handful and pulling her head back exposing her throat to his mouth. He bent down and kissed her neck. "And what is this I hear about you rubbing your ass all over

Jed's cock in the break room today?" He bit her neck, and his teeth felt delicious on her skin.

Her desire came out in her voice, husky and low. "Again, sir, I was just being playful. He pulled me into his lap." She wanted him to keep biting her, to keep his hand in her hair.

He suckled kisses up her neck until his mouth was at her ear. "You were going to leave a moment ago?" His voice was a deep whisper.

"I...I wasn't sure what to do with Morgan here." She closed her eyes, his hot breath in her ear sending heat to moisten the triangle between her legs. "Trust me, I didn't want to leave."

"Why? Tell me why you wanted to stay?" He sucked her earlobe into his mouth, his tongue gliding across the edge of her ear.

"To be with you again." Her words were mere groans as she pressed her head against his mouth. His grip tightened on her hair holding her firm.

"You were here for a purpose, weren't you?"

Faith felt his hand slide up her thigh toward the dampness hidden behind her jeans. She parted her legs, not realizing that she had until she felt the pressure of his hand against her sensitive womanhood. She pushed her passion onto his hand. "Yes."

"Tell me Faith. What are you here for?" He began to kiss down her neck again, sucking harder. Tendrils of excitement shot through her. His hand making her pussy ache for him.

"Your cock. I'm here to suck your cock. Please, I want to taste you." She couldn't believe she was saying it out loud. Yet, she knew he wanted to hear it.

"You're a little high up for that, aren't you?" His teeth sunk into her throat and she would be surprised if he wasn't leaving marks on her.

Faith, with reluctance at pulling away from his mouth, slid off the desk and dropped to her knees in front of him. She slid her hands up the front of his legs, over the bulge of his pants until she reached the button. With her eyes glued to his crotch, she opened his pants, reaching in and pulling his cock out. His hard column of flesh throbbed warmly in her hand as the black curls poked from the base of his shaft. Faith leaned in and nuzzled her nose into his balls, breathing him in as her hand slowly slid up and down his hardness. With a deep breath, she took her tongue and rolled one of his balls into her mouth, sucking on it gently.

His moans filled her ears as she felt him shift so that he was leaning against the desk. She then slid her tongue up his cock from base to hood, twirling her tongue around the tip of his manhood, enjoying the salty taste of him as her tongue licked away the pre-cum that waited for her.

She took him fully into her mouth then until the head of his cock hit the back of her throat. There was still room for her hand to wrap around the base of his shaft. She began to work his hardness with both her mouth and hand, the latter following the former as she sucked. She ran her tongue around him as she pumped him with her hand, her mouth suckling on him, urging his seed to fill her mouth.

He grunted and whispered sex noises to her as his hips pushed his cock in and out of her mouth. "Good girl. That's a good girl." She bobbed her mouth back and forth on him as she jacked him off. She wanted it, wanted his cum.

She felt his hand grip her head as his cock twitched in her hand. He grunted loudly as he said her name. Then the hot liquid hit the back of her throat and she swallowed it, relishing every hot drop. She kept sucking on his cock until his trembling subsided. She then pulled away, licking the remaining drops from the tip of his cock before pulling her lips away. She ran her tongue over her lips, lost in the salty taste of him in her mouth.

His hand slid off the top of her head down to her cheek where he tucked her hair behind her ear. She glanced up into his satisfied smile feeling proud of herself. He helped her back to her feet and kissed her softly on the lips. Her breath left her as the warmth of his mouth pressed against hers, brushing her fire into greater flames.

"So," he said as he broke the kiss, "about this being playful."

She smiled at him. "Yes?"

"Pull down your pants."

Faith unbuttoned her jeans and then lowered her zipper. Without hesitating, she slid her pants and thong down her legs until they bunched around her ankles. She straightened back up, staring at

Edwin whose eyes were soaking her in. She followed the tilt of his head until his eyes met hers again.

"Turn and put your hands on the desk."

She grew a little nervous thinking that he was going to take her now just as she was without even looking her in the face. She felt sad and turned on at the same time. Still, she did as she was told.

His hand caressed her naked ass and she could feel each callus on his palm as it glided along her curved flesh. She felt the goosebumbs covering her body from the softness of his touch.

"You were a naughty girl today in your playfulness, weren't you, Faith?"

She bit her bottom lip feeling the warmth grow between her legs. She could feel the moisture from her passion drip. "I didn't mean to be." She glanced over her shoulder, pursing her cherry lips into a pout.

"Still, I believe ten good swats should be in order on that cute little ass. What do you think?"

She took a deep breath realizing that he was serious. She nodded, giving him the permission he sought.

She felt his hand caress her derriere and then it was gone. Faster than she could blink, her ass stung from the hand print that she knew was left on it. She braced herself as she felt her body lunge forward from the impact. Again, his hand left her ass and then she felt the sting of it on her other cheek. A small yelp escaped her pressed lips, but that was all. She waited for the next blow to leave its mark.

His hand slid from her ass to her slick channel and he slipped a finger into the dripping honey. She moaned as she pushed back against his probing.

She heard the pleased grin in his voice. "Seems someone is enjoying this."

She wiggled against his finger, fucking herself with it in answer. Faith could feel the heat drip from between her legs, covering his finger as desire coursed through every nerve. She needed him.

He withdrew his finger and, before her body could scream at the void left behind, two more smacks, hard, fell upon her soft flesh. She cried out this time, the surprise of the blows taking her.

"Maybe I should punish you like this when you mess up from now on. What do you think, love?" Two more blows and she felt the heat on her ass where his hands marked her.

"Yes! Please."

"Please what Faith?"

"Punish me. Spank me. Use me."

Two more swats rained down on her ass and she realized her body was pushing itself back to meet his blows.

"Should I do it right here at work? Bring you in like they did in school, only I'll make you strip for it."

She moaned at the image. She could picture Edwin calling her into his office telling her she had done something wrong. He would tell her to strip right there and make her bend over his desk where he would spank her, calling her a bad girl.

Two more smacks with his hand, the hardest ones yet, made ten. "I asked you a question."

Her ass was burning, making her wetness lava that oozed from her deep cavern

"Yes! Oh god, yes, Edwin. Do whatever you wish to me."

He caressed her ass. "Whatever I want, huh?"

She glanced back over her shoulder. "What would you want, Edwin?"

Then his eyes took on an evil glint and Faith felt more than nervousness as she stood there half-naked. At the same time she ached to know his heart.

He glanced at his watch, and then looked at her with a smile. "I wish we had time to explore that question. I have to meet Morgan or I'd give you something for this." He slid his finger into her sex, stirring the fire within her.

Faith groaned and tried to fuck his finger. She needed it, craved it. She wished he had the time, as well.

Fourteen

Selby glanced at the clock on the wall behind his counter. Closing time. By now the offices of Rutherford Construction were being locked down and Faith was about to give Edwin the experience of her mouth. He could picture it in his mind and felt the mixture of excitement and jealousy knot in his stomach at the same time his cock twitched in his pants.

He snatched up his briefcase and locked the store. Pausing at the door to his Accord, he glanced at Joe's Bakery. Another girl was behind the counter by now as Tracey always went home around three, which made sense since she was usually there at five doing the morning baking and prep. A sigh lifted and lowered his chest. He wasn't sure just how he felt about Tracey, yet.

That wasn't true. He knew how he felt, but he was worried that Faith was feeling the same toward Edwin.

He opened the car door, sliding behind the wheel as he plopped his briefcase onto the passenger seat. Soon he was backed out and heading east on New Haven towards the Melbourne Causeway and home. An empty home more than likely awaited him. He found himself wondering what tales Faith would come home with this time.

As he crested the bridge, his conversation with Tracey replayed itself in his mind. Was she right about his true reason for leaving Chelsea? College was all about finding yourself. Everyone experimented and explored with anything and everything, from drinking to drugs to sex. Most girls tried girl-on-girl sex during their college years. It was the place to lose your inhibitions and let loose before life came in and kicked your ass.

He had with Chelsea and she stripped him of all shame. Before Tracey, he had told no one, not even Faith, his experience with Chelsea. His parents thought he had burned himself out and couldn't take it anymore. The two years that he wandered homeless he had left notes on postcards that he would mail as if on some soul searching quest. Yet, if Tracey was right, he had found what was in his soul and it scared him.

Yet, it wasn't the same with Faith. Chelsea took over his life. Faith was allowing someone else to have his way with her and then coming back and telling him about it. It was sex, not life. At least, not yet.

He pulled into his drive, pushing the garage door opener as he did. The garage was empty. It was going to be an interesting night.

~ ~ ~ ~ ~

When Faith arrived she found Selby in the fireplace room with a mug of Earl Grey and a Terry Brooks' novel. He was stretched out lengthwise, feet aimed at the cold hearth, ankles crisscrossed. He closed the book, using his index finger as a bookmark and smiled up at her as she entered the room.

She flipped her eyebrows at him as she walked over to him, turned her ass to him and yanked down her jeans. Bending over she practically stuck her slightly bruised ass into his face.

He let out a soft whistle and she felt his soft hand caress her exposed backside. She immediately felt the difference between Edwin's hands and those of her husband's. Both were strong with long thick fingers. However, where Selby's were soft and those of a bookstore owner, Edwin's were rough and callused. They belonged to someone who had worked for years with his hands.

"Someone was a bad girl, it seems."

She turned back around, sliding her pants into place as she did. "Apparently Mr. Coldwell doesn't appreciate being given a hard-on before going to see his boss." She shrugged, but could feel the grin that wouldn't leave her face. She leaned down and kissed his forehead. "I need to fix dinner." She stood, pulling him after her. "Come sit with me so I can tell you all about my day."

Selby laughed as he rose from the couch and followed her into the kitchen.

Faith let loose of his hand as they passed through the doorway, Selby taking a seat on a barstool and Faith going to the fridge. "It was an interesting day. I had my little adventure and was able to piss Cherish off."

"How were you able to do that, although I'm not surprised you did?"

"Morgan came into town today with a proposition for me."

"You're going to fuck your boss's boss?"

Laying some chicken on the cutting board, she looked at Selby and almost rolled her eyes. However, with a tilt of her head she thought of Morgan and his cocky swagger and changed her mind. "It might be fun. But, no, it wasn't that type of proposition." She went back to preparing dinner. "At least, not this time. No. They're having problems with the staff at their Tampa office and he wants to pay me extra to go and spend a few days there and train their people."

"Really? And not Cherish?"

She shook her head and then flipped her hair back over her shoulder. "Nope. And that's what pissed her off. He said he knows I'm the one that does most of the office work and that even Neal Rutherford has noticed how smooth our office runs. They want me. He asked me today to talk to you about it before he puts it in motion."

"A few days? When? Will Edwin let you go?"

Dinner went into the oven and Faith pulled a bottle of water out of the fridge, twisting the top as she turned back around. "If Morgan tells him to let me go he won't have much choice. Besides, it might be fun."

"Should I even ask what you mean by fun?"

She gave him a smile before taking a long swig of her water. As she screwed the top back on she just said, "Any fun is good fun, right?"

He just laughed at her. "I guess so. Won't Edwin be jealous, though?"

Faith set her water bottle on the table before walking around the counter and wrapping her arms around Selby's neck. "If he is, then he is putting more into this than he should. This is just fun. I'm your girl and no one else has any claim on me." She stared into his eyes, making sure he understood what she was saying. Her heart was his, as was her life. It really was none of Edwin's business who else she slept with.

She felt Selby wrap his arms around her and squeeze her to him, his head on her shoulder. "Good to know."

~ ~ ~ ~ ~

After dinner, Selby helped Faith do the dishes, grabbed a bottle of wine, two goblets, and headed for the fireplace room. He was ready for a quiet night in front of the fire with a good book. When their little adventures had remained out of town, it allowed the weekdays to be subdued, holding a semblance of normalcy. Now, with the game players in their everyday lives, all hints of routine had been shoved out the door. Tonight, he wanted to regain some of that quietness again.

Faith grabbed one of her smut books as he called them and sat with her back on the opposite sofa arm and her feet in his lap. She held her book with one hand and her Pinot Noir with the other. Selby stared at her for a moment, enjoying how lost she was in what she was reading. His wine sat on the glass table beside him, his book in one hand. With the other, he reached down and massaged her feet as he returned his attention to the novel he was reading. Faith moaned with the first squeeze of his fingers and he just smiled. This was a normal night. This was what he would have to make sure they kept experiencing in order to keep from losing who they were as a couple.

As Selby flipped the page, Faith's phone chirped. He ignored it. She didn't. As she snatched it from the table where she had left it, her face broke into a schoolgirl grin. She ignored her book and typed out a quick message. When she was done, instead of sitting the phone back on the table, she plopped it in her lap and went back to her reading, the smile still on her face.

Selby decided to ignore it. He had no doubt by her smile who had sent the text, but he wasn't going to allow their night to turn into another conversation centered on sex. While it was a big part of who they were, it was not the only part. It wasn't even the biggest. He took a deep breath and continued reading.

Faith's phone went off again.

She was quicker snatching it up this time, not even bookmarking her place in the novel she was reading. Her smile was even bigger and she actually giggled.

He took a deeper breath and reached for his wine. A short conversation was not usurping an entire evening. He could be patient.

Out of the corner of his eye he watched Faith drop her phone again and then fumble through her book trying to find her place. She had just found it and probably only had time to read three words before her phone chirped again. She began to drop her book this time, when he reached over and slid his fingers between the open pages. "Do you want a bookmark?"

She smiled at him, oblivious of his frustration. "No, I have one. I must have dropped it."

He nodded without saying anything as she sent off another text before taking her book back from him. "Thank you, sweetie." She squeezed his hands as she blew him a kiss.

Again, Selby refused to say anything. He took another sip of his wine and turned his attention back to the marauding elves in his novel. So far, his night had been anything but quiet, and normal was well out the window.

He had just lost himself in the story line once again when her phone chirped. This time he just sighed. A loud dramatic sigh.

"Oh, babe, I'm sorry. You're trying to read."

"It is a bit distracting," he said, glad she had finally caught on. Perhaps now they could enjoy being just the two of them.

"Edwin's just teasing me about this afternoon and what else he'd like to do to me," Faith explained. "I'll move to the bedroom so we don't ruin your quiet night." She scooped up her wine goblet and book, kissed Selby on the forehead and left the room before he had a chance to say anything.

He watched as she left, her step a bounce that had no clue that it had just used his heart as a springboard. He jerked his wine glass up, the amber liquid sloshing over the rim and sprinkling his shirt. He didn't care. He gulped the warm liquid, using the chugging to absorb his frustration. He wanted to charge after her and blast away, but how could he? He had been the one to give her the thumbs up to her new exploration. He had always been proud of not being the jealous sort. Yet, he was jealous. Extremely. He couldn't be the one to call it quits, even though, right then, he very much wanted to put an end to it all. One night was all he had wanted and that had been yanked from him and Faith didn't even realize what she had just done. She was lost in the thrill of a new chase and Selby felt as if he was being left behind.

He tried to continue reading, but all he could do was stare into the flickering flames as they licked around the burning wood, turning everything it touched to ash. His temper burned just like the logs, smoldering as he sat and glared.

From the bedroom, he heard his wife giggle. He closed his eyes and forbade the tears to fall.

~ ~ ~ ~ ~

Faith finished washing her face, drying her hands on the towel that hung by the sink when she was done. She hadn't read much of her book, but she hadn't needed the sex in the book to moisten her panties that night. Edwin's texts had done that plenty. She was glad she had left the fireplace room for the bedroom. They had texted for well over an hour and she knew that would have ruined Selby's peaceful night of reading. She knew how much he enjoyed those nights with a book and a glass of wine. She had not wanted to be the cause of him not having his evening. She glanced at his prone form on the bed through the mirror, a smile on her face. He deserved those nights and more for everything he did for her.

She had to keep herself from giggling as she thought about how much Edwin shared what he wanted to give to her as well as how explicit he had been. She had encouraged him in all of it. This side of giving control was still very fresh to her and she wanted the abandon. She craved to be used and she had told him so.

"You wanted to know what I wanted to experience. That's it," she had texted. "I want to know what it feels like to be a toy. Whatever you want, I want to do. I don't want to be given a choice. I have that now. I want to experience something different."

"Whatever I want?"

"Yes. No strings. No emotions. Just use me. However you want. Whenever you want." She had felt her pussy drip at the exchange. Every time her phone chirped, her pussy burned even hotter.

It was still dripping.

She hung the towel back up and slid her naked body next to Selby. He rolled over onto his side, but she wasn't allowing that to deter her. He had never been able to refuse her when she wanted his cock. And she wanted it.

Pressing up against his bare back, Faith snaked her arm around his waist. She slipped her fingers into his waistband and her hand down to his limp prick. She was ready for both Selby and his cock to stir to life and come awake.

He stirred, but didn't roll over.

Wrapping her fingers around his member, she began trying to gain his attention. She knew he couldn't have fallen asleep that fast. Could he? She kissed his shoulder, the warmth of his skin feeling good against her lips. She ran her tongue over the flesh of his shoulder as she massaged his shaft to life.

Selby rolled over, pulling her hand away. "It's time for some sleep." He never even opened his eyes.

Faith stared at him. *He's turning down sex?* "I just thought you'd want to hear about my afternoon." She attempted to slide her hand back to his cock. "You always enjoy the details."

"Not tonight. I'm tired."

She couldn't believe it. How on earth could he be tired if all he did was read a stupid book all night? He never turned down a chance at sex, especially if it meant hearing how slutty his wife had been. "What's wrong?"

"Nothing's wrong. I'm just tired."

She watched as he settled himself back into his pillow, his eyes still closed. Not sure what to make of his reaction, she rolled over and settled in for a night of restless sleep.

Fifteen

"I'll just have water with lemon," Faith told the waitress. She slid her napkin over her lap as Tracey mimicked her order.

"I'll be right back while you take a peek at today's specials." The waitress bounced away as Daisy's Café began to fill with the lunch crowd.

"You know your husband is going to pout because I left him to eat by himself, right?" Tracey had dropped off a bagel club sandwich to Selby as she told him she was having lunch with Faith. He wasn't thrilled about it, but at least he wouldn't starve. The two of them had been having lunch together almost since Tracey bought Joe's Bakery & Café.

"How did he seem to you this morning?" Selby had been as quiet that morning to Faith as he had been when they had climbed into bed. There had been no playfulness, no smiles, no "How about a quickie before work." Something was obviously on his mind, but Faith had no idea what it was.

The waitress bounded back with their waters, taking their orders while Tracey took a sip of her drink before answering. "Subdued, as if he hadn't slept well. You two have an all-nighter between the sheets?" After setting her glass on an open napkin, she began to wrap the paper around it to soak up the condensation.

Faith let out a sigh as she said, "I wish." She then filled the fiery redhead in on her night and her failed attempts at getting a goodnight romp. "He's never turned down sex before. He could be on his death bed and still want a piece of ass. It was weird."

"Let me get this straight. He created a quiet environment for just the two of you at home and you left him alone so you could sext with your new boyfriend and you're surprised Selby didn't want to play Hide the Sausage before going to sleep. Is that right?"

Faith had started to sip her water, but stopped as she just stared at her friend. She had summed up their entire evening in one blunt sentence and Faith hadn't been able to see it even though she had lived it. How could she have been so stupid? She set the glass back on the table as she stared at the lemon floating in the glass. To add to her sin, she had just assured Selby that she would keep her focus on him before abandoning him for a cell phone conversation. No wonder he had been hurt. How was she ever going to believe her if she didn't back up her words with actions? It didn't matter that Selby had started them down their current path. The new door was one she had opened and she needed to be sensitive to her husband's feelings. She had failed to do that last night, caught up in the giddiness of the chase. *How could I have been such a bitch?*

"I wouldn't sweat it," Tracey said as the waitress brought their food, the smell of crispy bacon overpowering the table. "He'll get over it as long as you make time for him. It's a balancing act you've never had to do before. You'll get used to it."

Faith pulled a stray piece of lettuce from her sandwich and slipped it into her mouth. "But is it worth it?" She asked as she chomped down.

"I think so, but then again, I don't believe one person can be everything to another. I have always believed we are too complicated to have all of our needs met by any one person. Besides, I crave adventures." She waggled her eyebrows at Faith.

Faith laughed at her friend as they both picked up their sandwiches and took a bite. Tracey had given her quite a bit to think about and she was determined to take it to heart. She had just begun to explore with Edwin and had no doubt that it was going to be an interesting journey. She didn't want to give it up just yet. It wasn't that she had feelings for her boss. No, there was only room in her heart for Selby. However, her body had plenty of room and she was going to allow this new game to play itself out all the way. She would be more careful as to how she balanced her home life and her exploits with Edwin. Of course, the fact that Selby had grown jealous at all gave her heart a fluttering boost. She had never seen him react that way. His cock had always been the hardest right after she had been with another man. He had always been eager, never jealous. Of course, this was entirely different. He wasn't with her when she was with Edwin and only received the leftovers. She understood now how it could have an unsettling effect. Being alone could spark emotions. Add to that fact that she already had a working relationship with Edwin and Selby feeling threatened was even more understandable. He had always been the one to make her feel secure. She now needed to do that for him.

Tracey quizzed Faith on her after-work meeting with Edwin, asking for all of the delicious details. Not just how it was, but his size and did he make noises. She asked things Faith hadn't really paid attention to and she found herself laughing at each question that came out of her friend's thin lips.

"Okay, so since I've answered all of your questions, I have one for you," Faith said as the barrage of inquisitiveness began to subside.

"Shoot." Tracey picked up a stray piece of bacon and began to toss it into her mouth.

"When are you going to fuck my husband?"

Tracey choked, causing a coughing fit to rattle her insides. Faith silently applauded her timing as she just smiled at her friend, pulling herself together. After all of Tracey's nosy questions, Faith felt it only fair.

Eyes watering and hand over her mouth, Tracey finally managed to pull herself together. "That was mean," she said, her voice more of a wheeze.

"I know." Faith grinned as she popped a fry into her mouth. "Fun, too."

Tracey took a long drink of water. As she set it down, she shook her head. "For you maybe."

"Well? What about my answer? It's obvious you and Selby are attracted to each other and I've already given the green light, so what's going on?" It had dawned on her that part of Selby's problem could very well be that he was being left out of the fun. She didn't think that Tracey had turned him down, but she wasn't sure why they were waiting. They could have had time while she was with Edwin, but instead Selby had gone home and moped.

Tracey shrugged. "Timing, I guess. I really think Selby prefers you there when he explores. We've known each other a while, so maybe he's having problems crossing that line."

"He also prefers the woman to make the first move. If you want it, you may have to just take it."

"Perhaps. We both know I'm not the shy one." Tracey laughed a little, but it was an uneasy mirth.

Faith laughed with her friend, but she wasn't sure she believed her. Oh, it was probably true if Tracey was out in a bar looking for a one night stand. However, she knew crossing that boundary with Selby was probably different. They were either afraid of ruining a friendship or that it wouldn't just be sex. Faith wondered if she was the one who should be worried.

~ ~ ~ ~ ~

Faith decided not to wait until she returned home to make things right with Selby. As she slipped past Ashlynn and into the halls of Rutherford Construction, she passed the Girls' Den and headed for Edwin's office. She wasn't even going to talk to Cherish about taking the rest of the day off, because Faith already knew what her sister would say.

"And leave me here alone? It's too late to call Nessa in to help and Ashlynn is useless for anything except blowing bubbles—or the men. No way! Get back to your desk." Of course, it didn't matter that Cherish left her alone every time she could without a care as to what it did to Faith's day. But then, Faith didn't mind working and actually preferred it when her sister wasn't there. However, Faith wasn't giving her the chance to put the nix on her plans, so she bypassed her sister and went straight to her boss.

Or at least she thought she had. As she neared Edwin's office she heard Cherish arguing with him about something Faith couldn't quite make out. She wasn't sure what they were talking about, but Cherish seemed quite adamant about something, her voice a strained whisper. Faith peered around the corner before knocking on Edwin's door and saw him sitting on the corner of his desk, arms draped over his lap as he gave Cherish a disarming smile.

"You have a wild imagination," he said to Cherish as he reached up and touched her upper arm. "No one is replacing you. Morgan knows how valuable you are to this office and doesn't want to take you away from it. Faith is great at what she does, as well, and would be better at training those in the Tampa office, that's all." He squeezed her arm and then dropped his hand back into his lap.

By the look on Cherish's face, she wasn't buying what he was selling. Faith didn't know why her sister was so upset about not being asked to go to the West Coast. It was more of a hindrance to daily life than an honor.

"But what about…" Cherish began, but Faith wasn't allowing her to finish her question. She needed to get home to Selby.

"Excuse me," Faith said as she knocked on the door. "I need to take the rest of the day off. Something has come up."

"And leave me to do it all myself? No way!"

Edwin ignored Cherish. "Everything okay?"

Faith nodded slightly. "Yeah, I just have to take care of something important."

"No problem. We're kind of slow today anyway. Go ahead." His smile brightened as he spoke to her. "If you need anything just let me know."

Whenever he smiled, Faith found herself smiling with him. "It'll be fine. I just need to correct a screw up. Thanks."

Cherish's face was a storm ready to explode, but Faith didn't care. Selby came first, even before the job, even before the game she was playing with Edwin, even before her sister. Faith turned and left as Edwin told her to "Take care." Cherish, of course, said nothing.

Why her sister was being such a bitch, Faith had no idea. She would get out of whatever extra work she had to do anyway, so why Faith leaving early mattered to her made no sense. It didn't matter to Faith, however. She was doing what she had to do, not just to keep the game going, but to make sure she kept her husband happy. Tracey had been right. Faith had totally screwed up last night and hadn't even known she was doing anything wrong. She was so caught up in her texting fun with Edwin that she had been clueless as to what she was doing to Selby. She would make sure he knew how she felt today.

A grin pushed her cheeks upward as she decided what she was going to do. It was time to give Selby a little adventure of his own.

~ ~ ~ ~ ~

The lunch crowd was trickling out of Downtown Melbourne when Faith pulled up in front of Selby's store. The day was bright with a slight chill rustling the trees that lined the sidewalk. Faith found herself giggling as she locked her car and stepped up on the walkway to Selby's Downtown Books. This was even more fun than her games with Edwin.

The bell over the door called out her entrance as she passed through the doorway. Selby stood close to the counter, shuffling through a stack of paperbacks. He turned at the sound of the door and she loved the look of confusion on his face when he saw her. It was obvious he wasn't sure how to react and that he was expecting someone else, like a customer.

"Is everything okay?" He set the books on the counter and turned toward her, taking a step as he did in her direction. "What's wrong?"

She smiled at him. "Everything is fine. How is business today?"

"It's a mad rush of customers as you can tell." He gestured at the empty bookstore aisles as he laughed.

She smiled and gave him a wink as she turned and locked the front door, turning the OPEN sign to CLOSED as she did. "Just the way I wanted it." She turned back around and started to slowly unbutton her blouse.

Selby's eyebrows went up and his eyes wide as he watched her saunter over to him, her shirt opening more with each step. Once she pushed the final button through its tiny slot, she slowly eased the fabric off her shoulders and allowed it to fall to the floor. By then she had reached her husband, and with one hand she caressed his cheek while with the other she reached behind her and unclasped her bra. It fell to the floor, her breasts exposed as she lowered herself to her knees, her eyes never leaving his.

Selby just watched as she knelt in front of him. As she unbuttoned his pants, she ran her tongue seductively over her lips. With gentle motions, she moved the pants down his legs, pulling his boxers with them. His cock was already perking to life and she could see his chest rise with a deep breath. She gave another grin as she leaned forward, her tongue gliding over the bulbous head as her hand stroked his hardening shaft. A groan escaped his lips as she swallowed his cock into her mouth, sucking on it as she pulled her head back up, running her tongue around the swelling member.

Just then someone tried to open the door to the bookstore, scaring Selby and sending him into a short panic. Faith didn't move. She continued to devour her husband's cock as she knelt on the gritty floor of his store. She ignored the stiffening of his body as nervousness took him. Instead, she ran her hand up his leg and cupped his balls in her hand, massaging them as her head bobbed up and down on his hardness. She grew hungrier for him by the moment.

Releasing his cock, Faith grabbed at his pants and pulled them the rest of the way to his ankles. She popped to a standing position and released her own pants, sliding them down her thin legs as soon as they were loose. She turned and gripped the glass counter as she glanced over her shoulder at him, her most wicked grin decorating her lips. "Take me. Right here. Right now."

"Yes, Ma'am," Selby said as he slid in behind her, his hands on her hips, thumbs pressing her fleshy cheeks. She could feel the head of his cock at her entrance and knew as he squeezed her hips that he was ready to shove his stiff cock all the way, hard and fast. And she moaned, the sound echoing in the cramped bookstore as she felt him plunge deep into her cunt, spreading her open less than ten feet from the front door. His fingers pressed into her flesh as he continued to pump, his balls slapping her clit as she opened herself to him.

One hand left her hip and she felt it glide up the middle of her back, pressing her down further on the counter. She could feel the cold glass against her swollen nipples, the shiver causing her to yelp as she cried out. He kept pounding into her. She had never felt him so hard before. She cried out to him, begging him to fuck her. "I need it, Selby. I want it. It's yours. Take it." His hand squeezed tighter, pressed harder. His breathing echoed in her ears and she could feel her pussy sucking at his shaft, swallowing every inch of him. She started pushing back, driving him deeper into her channel. His hand snaked up her back and into her hair, wrapping it around his fingers and pulling her head back. She grunted. He groaned.

She felt the tremors begin to rattle her insides, her body tensing as electric shocks seemed to course through her. His cock twitched as he plummeted into her. She screamed for it not caring if those outside could hear her. Her orgasm crashed down on her as his explosion filled her insides. Her knees gave out and his hands were all that kept her from hitting the ground as her body shook and trembled. Her screams filled the place as his groans mixed in sexual harmony. She could feel his rhythm slow as their juices streamed down her bare legs. She laid her head on the counter as her breathing eased in heavy gasps.

She expected him to pull out of her and step away, but instead he laid his head on her back as he stood there. With a raspy voice, he said, "I love you."

Faith stood, forcing him to rise with her. She turned to face him and even though the sex they had was some of the hottest she had had to date, she felt tears welling up in her eyes. She wrapped her arms around his neck and laid her head on his chest. "I love you, too. Very much."

She felt him squeeze her, her nipples tingling against the fabric of his shirt. They stood that way for a few minutes, pants around their ankles, sex dripping from their bodies, lost in the emotion of being in sync and together.

Sixteen

"And did you get to talk to your husband last night about taking a trip with me?" Morgan Brewer came in first thing that morning and propped himself on the corner of Faith's desk. She tried hard not to stare at the outline of his cock in his khaki pants, but it was proving difficult.

She nodded, forcing herself to look into his eyes. "I did and he said it was all right with him. We're just curious about the specifics. You know, room, food, my job here."

After Selby had taken her bent over his counter, they both decided it was best to just close up shop and spend the rest of the day home in bed. They turned their phones off and left their clothes piled on the floor. When they weren't having sex, they were talking about everything going on in their lives and Morgan's request for her company on his trip west was one of them.

Morgan shrugged. "Edwin will deal with it while you're gone, although you'll probably have a mess to clean up when you get back. Expenses will be paid and I'll add some hours in for bonus time. As far as rooms go, I suppose I could give you your own if I can't swing getting you into mine."

Faith laughed. "Enticing. Of course, I''m not sure the company would appreciate it."

"But I sure would." He grinned at her as he squeezed her shoulder. "I'm going to shoot for two weeks then, if that's all right?" She nodded. "Good. I'll give you the details as I get them all figured out." He pushed himself off the desk and left as Cherish entered the office. They each said "Good morning" as they passed and Cherish dropped her purse onto her desk.

"What did he want?"

Faith filled her sister in on the brief conversation with Morgan as she flipped on her computer and prepared for the day. Morgan wanted them to leave in two weeks. She wasn't sure how long they'd be gone as she forgot to ask, but even one night away from Selby would be the first since they were married. Faith glanced at the open door to the Girls' Den, picturing the departing boss as she did. Morgan had always flirted with her, making it quite obvious that he would fuck her in a heartbeat. She wondered if he would make an attempt while they were in Tampa. She smiled to herself. It should be an interesting trip.

"I still don't get it. Why you?" Cherish opened and shut her desk drawers with frustration, pretending, it seemed to Faith, to be looking for something but never pulling anything out. "I'm the H.R. person. I've worked here longer. It should be me going west."

"Then go." Faith said as she faced her sister. "Makes no difference to me." And, in truth, it didn't. She had only agreed because she thought it would be fun. Sure, it was a huge feather in her hat to be asked and it gave her a sense of pride, as well. However, she knew there wasn't much room for advancement for her within Rutherford Construction. It was, after all, a man's world. So, while it was a pat on the back to be asked, it wouldn't ruin her if she didn't go. Besides, she had plenty right here to keep her occupied.

"They didn't ask me. They asked you." Cherish didn't look at her.

Faith turned back to her desk and started typing up job lists. Her sister had always been handed everything. Yet, she was still the bitterest person Faith knew. Well, except for her mother, of course. She dreaded to see what Cherish would be like in twenty years.

"I can't believe Selby is letting you go off with another man and spend the night."

You don't know my husband. She didn't say that, however. "I'm not spending the night with Morgan and you know it. I'll have my own room and it's just work."

"I know nothing of you lately." Faith turned to see her sister staring at her with a disgusted look on her face. "You've been walking around this place, teasing the men and making brazen overtures. You're not the same Faith you've always been."

"That's good to know." Faith shrugged. "I didn't like the stuffed shirt that I was back then. I'm enjoying life and having harmless fun. That doesn't mean I'd run off and sleep with Morgan. Just what is it about me having fun that bothers you?"

"It's disgusting to watch!" Cherish snatched her purse and practically leaped out of the chair. "I'm going to the bathroom."

Faith just watched her pound out of the office. She sat there staring at the door, not sure what to think. How had anything she had ever done angered her sister so much? Was Faith not allowed to have fun and enjoy life? Was she not allowed to be happy? Where had all of that hostility come from? None of it made sense.

Edwin walked in as Faith was still staring at the door. Her confusion must have shown on her face because he stopped two steps in. "What?"

Faith looked up at him and shook her head. "I just don't understand how people can get so pissed off because someone else is happy."

He glanced at Cherish's empty desk and seemed to know who Faith was talking about. He continued into the room. "I wouldn't let it bother you or change you, especially the change in you." When he reached her he leaned closer and whispered. "I'm having fun with you enjoying life."

She glanced up into his eyes and smiled. "So am I."

"Did you get everything taken care of yesterday? I never heard back from you."

"Sorry. We turned off our phones and spent the remainder of the day alone."

"Everything all right?"

She nodded. "I screwed up the night before and just needed to make things right. It's all good now."

163

"And our adventure?"

Faith leaned back in her desk chair and smiled up at him. "Is completely in your hands. I meant what I said to you and Selby is still fine with everything. We just needed to reconnect a bit."

"Good, because I would hate to see my fantasies dashed to pieces just as we're beginning to have some fun."

"I'm looking forward to it, as well."

Edwin glanced at the door and then turned back to Faith with a devilish grin. "As a matter of fact, I'd like to enjoy some of that fantasy right now."

Faith felt herself blush. "I would too. Too bad we're at work, though."

Edwin shrugged. "I'"m going to the warehouse while Terry goes for some materials. If you need or want anything..." He tapped the front of his pants. "I'll be out there. Alone."

"Where'd Morgan go?" She couldn't believe what he was suggesting. Did he really expect her to meet him in the warehouse for a quickie while everyone was there? Was that how he intended to put his cock inside of her for the first time?

"He went to soothe Mr. Polawski. He'll be back this afternoon."

Cherish walked in and went straight to her desk. "Not interrupting, am I?"

Edwin laughed. "Not at all. Just had to give Faith some information."

"Is that what they call it now?" Cherish rolled her eyes as she opened the web browser on her desktop.

Faith and Edwin glanced at each other and Faith looked at him as if to say, "See what I mean?" Edwin just shook his head and made a quick exit.

Faith turned back to her computer and brought up the daily job roster. She went through random personnel trying to figure out where everyone was. Grady was supposed to be touring jobs in Micco to the south. Morgan was with Mr. Polawski and Dion was doing punch-out at the Hartford Foundation. Jed had Thursdays off since he worked Saturdays and Nessa didn't come in until three. Ashlynn was stuck at the reception desk. That only left Cherish who was playing FreeCell on her computer.

Faith stopped herself, realizing what she was doing. She took a deep breath. It was scary even for Edwin to have suggested it. It was too risky. The warehouse was always open and anyone could pop in for anything. Men stopped by to say hello to Terry all the time. No, it was definitely too risky. What if they got caught? They'd be fired for sure. Cherish would know that it had all been true. It wasn't worth it.

But she couldn't stop thinking about it. Nor could she deny the wetness that grew between her legs, the warmth that was building to distraction. Isn't this what she had told him she wanted? To be his whenever or wherever he wanted. The only rule was that it wasn't to interfere with Selby's time. And Edwin wanted her, right there, right then. Surely he knew the risks and would account for their protection. He'd be just as worried about getting caught as she was. He had more to lose.

Wouldn't he?

It was a bluff. Surely, it had to be a bluff. Yet, he hadn't been bluffing so far. Perhaps it was just a test to see if she meant what she said.

She couldn't think. She glanced at her watch. Nine. Everyone would have already been there for whatever they needed and left.

No. She shook her head. She couldn't allow those thoughts. It was way too risky. Work. That was it. Focus on work.

She printed out the job list, picked it up off the printer and headed for the door. "I'll be back." She tried to slow her pace, walk normally. She couldn't believe she was doing this. She must look like a silly school girl to Edwin by now, chasing after his attentions.

Her breathing was a heavy mess as she turned in the hall heading for the back door. She knew how silly she would look if Edwin had only been teasing. Still, she had made the rules. She couldn't go back on what she had said the very first time he made a demand of her. Of course, it wasn't a demand, but more like a suggestion. She suddenly felt foolish but she couldn't stop. Her sex was a molten mess as she thought about what Edwin could possibly do to her in the warehouse.

The March air was still a little chilly as she crossed the grounds to the warehouse. It was quiet. No other trucks were around. Maybe he was truly alone. She hoped so. She hoped not. She didn't know what she hoped, to be honest. This was a mistake. She needed to go back to her desk.

She entered the first open bay door, stopping just inside. She listened for a sign as to where Edwin would be. The warehouse was a huge building with an office and three huge bay doors for the trucks to back in. Behind the office were two bathrooms—men's and women's. On the other side of the bathrooms was an open space where Terry kept spools of rope and wire. It was back there that she heard noises.

Following the noises, she found Edwin rearranging some of the round wooden spools. "Terry's not going to be very happy with you doing that."

Edwin turned and smiled at her. "He'll get over it." He walked over to where she stood and took her hand, pulling her the rest of the way behind the wall. He pressed her to him, his hands holding her waist firm. She could feel his growing excitement.

She felt his hand slide up her back and into her hair. She had to force herself to breathe as the sudden sensations sent tendrils of electricity through her body. She could feel the honey dripping from her tender slit, felt the ache between her legs that yearned to be filled.

He wrapped her hair around his hands and pulled her mouth to him, pressing his lips hard against hers. The air rushed from her as the heat of his passion overtook her. His other hand pressed her to him as he parted her lips with his tongue and teased hers to join the lusty dance. A groan escaped her as she surrendered to the kiss. Her knees grew weak and she knew the only thing holding her up was his hand on one side of her and his body on the other.

She couldn't believe she was doing what she was doing. Someone could come in at any moment. She should stop...

His hand slid from her back to her jeans button and before she could finish her thought, he had her pants open. She felt his strong fingers slide into her pants and between her lips, dipping into her wetness. She gasped, pulling from his mouth as he roughly began to fuck her with his fingers. She knew her eyes were wide with the shock of the sudden intrusion.

"Is this what you came out here for?" He was smiling, his eyes sparkling with mischief.

She couldn't answer. She felt his fingers clawing inside of her, her wetness dripping over his hand.

He let go of her hair and pulled his fingers from her pussy. She felt his hands grip her waistband as he yanked her pants down around her ankles. The cool air assaulted the warmth of her flesh as she stood half-naked before her boss. "Isn't this why you came out here, Faith." He returned his fingers to her pink slit, teasing her sensitive pearl. He leaned down to her neck, nibbling softly at her throat. "Answer me." His voice was a low growl.

"Y…Yes." It was true. She closed her eyes, but popped them open as she felt his hand grip her arm and spin her around. The spools were in front of her and he pushed her over them so that her ass was aimed upward, her slick channel beckoning.

"Tell me, Faith. What did you come out here for?" She heard his pants being unzipped and knew he was going to take her. She felt his hand smack her bare ass and she yelped slightly. "Tell me, Faith."

"Your cock! I came out here for your cock."

And then she had it. His hands gripped her hips as he plunged his thickness deep inside of her. "You came to be fucked, didn't you?" He thrust in and out of her, pounding her pussy with a fierceness that sent shudders through her.

"Yes. Oh god, yes. Please." She pushed back at him, fucking him as he fucked her. She knew where she was and that thought drove her crazy as he took her like a simple slut. She moaned, her body begging for release. Harder, she met his cock, felt his balls slapping her as his hips slammed into her ass.

It wasn't long before the tendrils of her orgasm shook her and she felt the tensing squeeze of her body. She straightened her arms as she pushed her body back into him. She needed to feel all of his cock buried in her. His cock twitched inside of her as her inner walls sucked at his hardness. With a jerk, she felt the hot liquid erupt inside of her, coating her warm cavern with his passion. He held her to him until he had emptied himself into her.

Her breathing came in quick pants as the wave slowly ebbed from her. Edwin slid his cock from her and she heard him zip up his pants as he left her bent over. "Is that what you wanted?"

Faith took a deep breath. She felt their wetness sliding down her leg and suddenly felt dirty. She pushed herself into a standing position and reached down for her pants. Her heart was racing as she zipped and buttoned her jeans and straightened her shirt. Once she was all put together, she looked into his dark green eyes. "Yes. Yes, that is exactly what I wanted."

With hands on his hips, he stared at her. A slow grin crept across his face. He nodded. "I can play this game. Can you?"

She stared at him. Faith knew without a doubt what he was asking. He had heard her and was going to give her what she wanted. He wanted to make sure she was ready.

Was she? Suddenly, the idea of giving herself to his desires at his whims and times scared her. Yet, at the same time, she was turned on more than she had ever been.

She took a deep breath. "Let's find out."

He smiled, his eyes twinkling. "Good girl. Let the game begin."

~ ~ ~ ~ ~

Selby reached into his briefcase and pulled out the picture of Chelsea that he had retrieved from his office that morning. He wasn't sure why he had gone and pulled the picture from the album. He just felt compelled. It was probably due to everything that had been going on with Faith.

As he glanced down at the picture in his hand, he remembered with vivid clarity what had overtaken him eighteen years ago. Tracey had said that he hadn't lost himself, but rather had found who he was inside. He had struggled ever since with whether she had been right or not. As he thought back to his college years, specifically his time with Chelsea, he knew that the sex had been extreme and addicting, even the humiliating aspects of it. Yet, it had been during those brief months that he had had the most intense orgasms.

With a sigh, he slipped the picture back into his briefcase. He picked up his Grumpy mug and sipped the lukewarm coffee. Work was the last place he wanted to be. The mood he was in required the sandy beach and a cold beer. Sooner or later, he knew he needed to discuss his inner turmoil with Faith. She didn't know about Chelsea or the real reason he dropped out of college. Whenever she asked about his missing years, he had merely shrugged and said it was a soul-searching period.

"And did you ever find your soul?" She had teased.

"Not for another few years when I found you." He had pulled her to him and kissed her.

And it had not been romantic syrup. He had found himself when he had found Faith. Twelve years had passed since he had left his ambitions behind at Georgia University. He had taken nothing with him. He simply walked out of Chelsea's flat and onto the streets.

Two years had passed before he showed up on his parents' doorstep, hair matted, body filthy and a stomach growling from days without eating. Selby glanced out the window as he recalled his mom's tears at both his appearance and his return, and his father's shake of the head.

Tracey left Joe's Bakery, crossing the street with their lunch. Selby glanced at his watch. 12:05. He smiled at how predictably patterned she was. He kept watching as she crossed New Haven, the sway of her hips, the smile that always decorated her face and the way the sun glistened from her hair giving it more of a coppery look.

Where she would factor into his life or even if she would, he didn't know. But it was going to be fun making the journey.

Selby stood and opened the wood framed glass door, allowing Tracey to slip in. He could smell the bacon hiding within the Styrofoam container and knew that he had a BLT on a croissant waiting for him. He loved her sandwiches. Since she had taken over the tiny bakery, business had doubled if not tripled. Joe never had a lunch menu. Tracey saw the opportunity and capitalized on it. When it came to business, she was an innovative thinker.

"So, tell me the latest Greer happenings." Tracey perched on the stool. She propped her feet on the bar between the legs since her feet just dangled otherwise.

Selby sat in his chair and opened the lid of his lunch. As he opened the chips and dumped them in the empty lid, he began to recite the adventures of his day. Faith had told him about her lunch conversation with Tracey and he knew it was because the small redhead had probably told his wife she had screwed up. Their conversation had led to the rest of Selby's day and some exciting conversations with Faith about the direction they were going. Together, they had come to a better understanding of their adventures and he felt more secure. He was still a little nervous, but not as he had been two nights ago.

Tracey wiped some mayonnaise from the corner of her mouth. "Good. I'm glad she heard what I was saying and chose to fix it." She smiled at him. "Now, perhaps we can explore our own little private game without you worrying over dear little Faith. Unless, you changed your mind, of course."

He felt his stomach begin to churn with nerves. "No, I haven't changed my mind. I suppose I've just been waiting to see where things go."

Tracey tucked her red hair behind an ear as she began to clean up her lunch mess. "Well, they're not going to go anywhere unless you decide they are. When you figure it out, let me know." She snatched the grape soda that Selby had had waiting for her from the counter. "Thanks for the drink." She was just about to leave, but before she rounded the counter, she stopped and glanced back at him, her features softer than they were a moment ago. She set her can of soda on the counter and stepped toe-to-toe with him. He glanced into her eyes, waiting for whatever smart ass comment she was about to make. But none came. Instead, she reached an arm up, wrapping a hand around the back of his neck, her face a mask of seriousness. "I know you're worried about our girl and I understand if you need to move slowly. I'm willing to wait. I've *been* waiting, so a little longer is no big deal. Just know that I'm here when you're ready." She pulled his head down until she could press her lips to his and then she kissed him, her lips warm and soft against his. He wrapped his arms around her, pressing her to him as he surrendered to the moment. His tongue parted their lips, searching for hers and together their tongues danced the dance they wanted their bodies to be dancing.

He couldn't believe it was happening and he sure as hell didn't want it to stop. He had been waiting just as long.

Seventeen

Faith locked up her desk and shut down her computer. The day was done and she was ready for her deck and a glass of wine. Cherish had been in another of her mad-at-the-world phases and refused to talk to Faith even if Faith spoke first. When the ice queen finally went home a few moments ago, it was as if a shroud had lifted and life could begin again.

Locking her office door, Faith went past Edwin's office, which was already locked and dark. She stopped in front of the door, knowing that a smile pushed upward on her cheeks. He hadn't even said goodbye for the day. She shook her head, shocked that it mattered.

"It's just a game," she whispered to herself as she turned and made her way to the back door. One more weekday before the weekend and Faith wasn't sure if she was excited or depressed. While a weekend was a much needed break from her work and her sister, it was also two agonizing days away from Edwin's hands. She didn't know what he had planned next, but she was dying to find out.

As she unlocked her small truck and slid behind the steering wheel, she found herself more worried about being away from Edwin than excited about being with Selby. She sat behind the gray rubber steering wheel and stared at the dash. And what about her trip with Morgan? Selby would be there when she got back. Would Edwin? He had already had his fun with her. What if her absence cooled the embers of his passion for her? What if he realized how wrong it was and stopped? Faith let go of the wheel realizing she was rubbing her skin red.

She didn't want to come back to business as usual. She was enjoying the game too much.

Her phone went off. It was a text from Edwin. *Meet me behind the old Riverside Motel.*

She stared at it for a moment, her heart pounding at what she was reading. He didn't ask. He ordered. What would she tell Selby? She dropped the phone in her lap and started the car.

The Riverside Motel was a closed down two-story motel, vacant for the past three years. It sat on the east side of Highway One along the Indian River. No one went there. Faith pulled in and saw Edwin's truck facing the river. She parked beside him, got out of her truck and into his, her chest a cage of fluttering butterflies. He was leaning against the driver's door, his cock already a bulge in his pants aimed at her. That cocky grin that warmed between her thighs just stared at her.

"You know why you're here?" His voice made it more statement than question.

She ran her tongue over the desert of her lips. She nodded, not trusting her voice.

"Then do it." He settled back against the door, one arm draped across the headrest of his seat, the other along the dash

Faith took a deep breath as her hands went for the button on his pants. She had to will her fingers to stop shaking as she pulled his hardening shaft from his pants. She leaned down into his lap, nestling into the dark curls at the base of his manhood. Faith could smell herself on him from where he had taken her in the warehouse. She breathed both of them in as she stroked his cock with her hand. She kissed his testicles, the taste salty in her mouth and she could feel the tightening of his hips under her.

She pushed from her mind their location; that they were in a truck. Pushed from her imagination what it would look like if someone were to happen upon them. She sucked on his jewels, running her tongue along the roughness of his sac. His moans seemed loud in the cab of the truck and she felt the wetness drip from her.

As her hand slid up his shaft, she followed it with her tongue until she reached the dome. He spoke to her but her lust pounded in her ears, drowning him out. She ran her tongue over the small slit that leaked and tasted the beginnings of his release. She felt the rising of his hips and gave in, swallowing him whole until his head hit the back of her throat and he grunted.

Faith sucked on him, her head bobbing up and down in his lap like a whore he picked up on the side of the road. Her hand twisted around his cock as she stroked it in rhythm with her mouth, her tongue licking around him, tasting him as she felt the throbbing of his cock and the pulling up of his balls. She relished the feel of him on her lips. Faster she worked, knowing what the jerk of his cock felt like as he emptied himself into her mouth. With every burst of hot liquid he fed her, she hungrily swallowed, loving the warmth in her throat and the taste of his passion on her tongue.

As he relaxed back into the seat, she licked the moist head of his cock before pulling up from his lap. She gazed at him as she slid her tongue over her lips. Out of the corner of her eye, Faith could see the river and the sluttiness of their location. A thrill went through her at her daring.

He smiled at her as he tucked his manhood back into his pants. "Thank you."

Faith ducked her head slightly as she said a demure, "My pleasure."

He reached a hand out to her and stroked her cheek. "You're doing pretty well, coming as you're told."

She grinned at him as she pushed her cheek into the palm of his hand. "Is that a play on words?"

He tapped her nose with his thumb, a chuckle coming from him. "Nice. Now, get home to your husband before we get in trouble for stealing his time. Any chance I could have time with you outside of work? It would be nice to move a little slower for once."

She placed her hand on his. "I'll see what I can do. I'm sure he'd love some time with Tracey."

"Tracey?"

"His adventure. I'll see what I can do." She tilted her head and kissed his thumb.

"Good girl."

Faith felt herself blush at the praise and was surprised at how much it meant to her. She squeezed the hand she was holding. "I'll see you tomorrow."

"Wear a dress; no panties."

Her face flushed hotter. "Yes, sir."

He smiled at her as she slid from his truck, and then he drove off, leaving her alone behind an abandoned motel with the taste of him on her lips. Her heart did a drum line in her chest as the entire situation cascaded over her and a grin decorated her face. And then she giggled. And giggled. Then she busted out in triumphant laughter. She had dared to do something she would have fainted from a few short months ago.

Still laughing, she slid back into her small truck and headed home. She contemplated what she was going to tell Selby about being late. He'd be turned on that she did it, but also upset at the dangerous location. The adrenaline of what had only been a fifteen minute adventure was still streaming through her when she pulled into her garage.

The front of the house was quiet when she dropped her purse and keys on the bench by the front door. Selby's briefcase was already there. Passing into the kitchen, she heard music playing from the back deck. She could smell hot food—lasagna?—but the kitchen was cool. Faith passed through the Florida room to the sliding doors leading to the back. The Righteous Brothers were singing Unchained Melody from the deck speakers. Two candles flickered on the small table as Selby was finishing opening the Olive Garden take-out containers.

Hearing the door slide open, Selby turned to gaze at her. She stood staring at the romantic setup. He followed her gaze to the table and then glanced back at her, his smile, the smile that had melted her heart ten years ago, softened his face and, as always, weakened her knees.

Faith gestured to the table. "What brought this on?"

Selby left the table, reaching for her hand. As he pulled her to him, he was already swaying slowly as "the lonely rivers flowed to the sea" crooned in the background. "What can I say?" He leaned in and planted soft kisses on her neck and the goose bumps returned for another reason. "I've hungered for your touch."

She felt his hands slide around her waist as he pulled her to him, their bodies rocking back and forth. Faith laid her head on his chest, thoughts of Edwin gone. "I like that."

Selby kissed the top of her head. After a couple of more turns, he escorted her to the table and held her chair out for her. She watched as he poured them both a glass of Rosa and then took his seat. As he reached for her plate, the Righteous Brothers faded into Elvis. He filled her plate and then his. She sat, watching the pampering. She was smiling as he took his wine glass in hand and gestured for her to do the same.

"To a nice, quiet evening."

"Amen." She sipped as he did and her heart felt as if it grew in her chest.

They ate their meal as the sky faded from blue to gray and by the time night had swallowed the sun and the stars twinkled into existence, the wine had soothed over-excited muscles. Selby took her hand and pulled her to the deck steps, grabbing a blanket off one of the lounge chairs as he went. The ocean breeze teased at her hair and filled her breath with a tangy taste. Halfway down, she felt him pull her down to sit beside him as he wrapped the blanket tight around them. He slid his arm around her waist and pulled her tight against him. With a contented sigh, she rested her head against his chest.

The entire evening had been small talk, each sharing their day without revealing the adventures at work. Faith wanted to tell him about the warehouse and behind the motel, but not now. Wanted to talk to him about Edwin's request for time outside of work, but not tonight. Tonight was theirs and only theirs. She held tight to her knight and refused to allow anything to break in to their bubble.

"Do you remember that Emily Dickinson poem you quoted me that first night at the beach?" She nestled her head into him, wanting to be closer.

"Wild nights - Wild Nights!
Were I with thee
Wild Nights should be

our luxury!
Futile - the Winds –
To a Heart in part –
Done with the Compass –
Rowing in Eden –
Ah, the Sea!
Might I but moor - Tonight –
in Thee!"

Faith could feel herself smiling. As he spoke each word, she could feel the memory of the coolness of the hood of the car and his hands rubbing up and down her thighs. It took her back to a simple time. Not better, just simpler.

"I love you," she whispered.

She felt his arm tighten around her. "I love you, too."

They stared at the foamy waves that battered the shore as they cuddled in silence. Couples occasionally walked the shoreline, hand-in-hand, their whispers carried up to them, secrets that they thought kept safe by their soft voices. Yet, the ocean pushed the voices with the crashing waves to be carried to the dunes by the ocean wind. The beach was for the dreamers and lovers. Everyone came there, businessmen on vacation, families with their screaming kids digging holes and building lopsided castles. Yet, only the dreamers could feel the soul of the beach. Only lovers could put the ocean's arms around them like a deep, thick blanket to warm them even in the chill air. It was they who spoke to the sea and to whom the sea spoke.

Faith loved the beach. It was for her that Selby bought the house with the Atlantic for a backyard. "It'll give you someone to talk to when I'm not here," he had told her. And she had spoken to the ocean every day. The back deck was her favorite place in the house.

Selby shifted slightly beside her, pulling her closer as he laid his head on hers. Suddenly, she was regretting her decision to go west with Morgan in two weeks. She had never been away from Selby, except for a couple of overnight women's retreats at the church her mom guilted her into attending. Yet, this was for a week, in a cold, strange bed alone. She shuddered at the future loneliness.

"You okay?" Selby squeezed her.

"Just thinking of my trip and already missing you." She rubbed her head against his chest wanting to be inside of him.

He nodded without lifting his head. "I'm not thinking about it."

~ ~ ~ ~ ~

He straightened a little and kissed the top of her head. Placing his index finger under her chin, Selby lifted her face and gazed into her eyes. "You'll be great." Softly, he tasted her lips, eyes closed, his breathing heavy. He felt her hand slide up his arm to squeeze his bicep as she tenderly returned his kiss.

Selby turned her slightly, his arms wrapping around her. She continued the circle until she was kneeling on the step below him. Their lips never parted. He slid his tongue between her hungry lips, tasting her passion, her heart. He glided his hands up and down her back, pressing, massaging. He could feel her hands on his thighs, rubbing with the desire that burned between them. With a hunger, he sucked her bottom lip into his mouth.

As her lip slid from his mouth, he could feel her kiss down his chin and throat as her hands pressed down his abdomen to his waistband, fumbling with the buttons. He leaned back against the wooden steps, giving her more room. She took it and soon her hand was stroking his cock. He closed his eyes at the pleasure, then opened them, suddenly quite aware of where they were. The day turned to grayish night, but still they were visible. Selby took the blanket from their backs and wrapped it around their fronts, or rather Faith's back as she was now kneeling in front of him.

Her teeth nibbled around his throat as she worked his hardness, her hand pumping with slow delight. A groan slid from his lips as he felt his sac being fondled gently. He gripped the step behind him trying to remember to watch for beach wanderers.

Faith leaned back on her knees and her eyes sparkled with mischief as she smiled at him. She stood, slowly unbuttoning her jeans as she did. Her eyes never left his as she slid out of her pants, leaving them over the railing. She whipped the blanket back around her as she sank into his lap. She slid her feet and legs through the opening between steps and with a hand wrapped around the base of his cock, guided him into her wet slit.

The slow sensation of her warmth opening before him made his body tense with pleasure. He felt her arms slip around his neck as she pressed her lips hard against his, her tongue sliding into his mouth and gliding across his teeth, teasing. She was using her calves against the wood to push herself up and down onto his hard shaft, riding him in slow, steady movements. He could only sit and stare at her as he remained pinned in place.

She broke the kiss, her head tilting back, eyes closed. Selby slid his hands to her waist and held on as she pumped up and down. The tight muscles of her secret cavern sucked on his manhood, begging for the nectar he kept in his stem. Her moans were soft to his ears as she pushed herself up, and then dropped down on him, over and over, again and again.

"My clit, Selby, touch my clit." Her arm swung freely behind her as her hips rose and fell.

He slid a hand between them and pressed her sensitive pearl, rubbing it back and forth.

"Harder."

He pushed inward, making small circles. He felt her body tighten in moments as her arms squeezed his neck. Her mouth opened but no sound issued forth as a tidal wave orgasm crashed over her. His cock twitched and hot fluid erupted inside of her, his ass tensed as he felt his orgasm tighten his balls. Together, they rode their passion to shore on the crest of ecstasy.

Faith's body relaxed as she settled on his lap, his shrinking member still nestled inside of her pink slit. She lowered her head to his shoulder and whispered, "I love you," as she exhaled deeply.

Selby wrapped the blanket around her and held her tightly. "I love you, too."

Eighteen

"A dress? On Friday?" Selby finished running the towel through his hair as he gawked at his wife as she put on the finishing touches of a tan business dress. "I thought Fridays were all about being casual and comfy. What gives?"

Faith weaved the belt through the loops as she checked herself out in the mirror. Not bad if she did say so herself. "I was told to wear a dress today, so a dress it is."

"Told, huh? Edwin is getting into his role, I see." Selby walked over to her with a smirk on his face. The towel dangled in one hand as he lifted the hem of her dress with the other and exposed her bare pussy. His smile widened. "The only reason to ask a lady to wear a dress. Easy access." He let the hem fall back into place as he tossed the towel onto the bathroom counter. "Are we planning some work day frolic?"

Faith brushed the dress back into place, smoothing it out where Selby had lifted it. "To be honest, I don't know what he has planned. That's the point of the game, to allow him to call all the shots and for me to just do whatever he says."

"With the stories you've shared so far it sounds like he enjoys taking chances. Hopefully, he is conscious of where you both are and doesn't risk your jobs because you both were horny."

Faith ran a brush through her hair one more time. "I doubt he would risk his lucrative position over a quickie. I trust him or I wouldn't be doing it. I have more than a job to lose. My sister works there. It could cause some horrendous family drama if she were to find out and take it back to Mommy Dearest."

She set the brush down on the counter and turned to Selby. "However, Edwin did have one request. He wanted to know what the chances were of getting together outside of work. It would limit the risk and offer a little more chance to explore. It would also give you time to see Tracey." Her stomach was a jumble of knots and she wasn't sure why she was so nervous, but it seemed worse asking for a night alone with Edwin than it did to just fuck him. This was almost like a date. "What do you think?" She found herself fumbling with her hands, twirling her fingers.

He seemed to think for a moment, but then nodded his head. "It might be the only way Tracey and I get a shot at being together. I don't see why we can't try it and see how it goes. Make it at the same time so that neither of us is here at home alone wondering what the other is doing."

"I hadn't thought about that. I'm sure it would drive me crazy. I'm not sure how you've done it so far."

His eyes twinkled as he said, "I read a lot."

She laughed with him. "Thank you."

Selby had slipped on his boxers and jeans and picked up a shirt from the foot of the bed. With the shirt dangling in his hands, he walked over to where she stood and wrapped an arm around her waist, spinning her so she faced him, pressing her to him tight. He raked her with his eyes, the smile still plastered across his lips. "I love you," he said. He leaned forward and sucked her bottom lip into his, before devouring her in a deep kiss.

Faith wrapped her arms around his chest, one hand slipping into the wetness of his hair as she returned his morning passion. She could feel the hardness of his chest against the swelling of her nipples as their embrace brushed the fabric across her sensitive flesh. As they pulled apart, she whispered back, "I love you, too."

As she left him to finish getting ready for his day, which happened to always be a casual dress day, she wondered what Edwin did have in mind for her to make her dress the way she had been told. Everyone at work would be surprised that she had chosen an outfit that wasn't jean material and wasn't painted onto her ass. That was all right. It paid to keep people on their toes once in a while and surprise them. Driving into work, she thought once more about how Edwin had taken her in the warehouse and used her, how he had made her ask for it, telling him that she wanted it. It had been exactly what she had wanted him to do. No boundaries. No rules. His to command. She wondered if she had surprised him by not only showing up in the warehouse, but following through with everything he had asked of her. She had definitely surprised herself.

The offices of Rutherford were quiet when she finally arrived. Glancing at her watch, she realized that she was early, way early. No wonder Selby had still been dripping wet when she left the house. She was surprised he hadn't said anything. She shook her head. *I am a silly school girl.*

Terrence was just opening the warehouse as a few other early birds were showing up for supplies. As Faith walked the small concrete steps to the main doors, Jed was just unlocking them. He opened them as he saw her approaching through the glass door, his face revealing how happy he was that it was Friday. "You are eager to get this day over, aren't you? You do know that just because you get here early, doesn't mean you get to go home early." His voice held a soft chuckle.

Faith slumped her shoulders in mock despair. "But that's not fair."

"Welcome to Rutherford Construction," he said with a slight laugh. "Why are you here so early, anyway?"

Faith stepped through the door and together they walked toward the den of offices. "To be honest, I didn't realize that it was this early until I pulled up and saw the empty parking lot. I must have woken earlier than I thought. It's probably going to make the day seem twice as long now."

"Well, nothing like getting a jump on the day. I dropped some files on your desk for a couple of new proposals. Edwin will be in a little later. He is having breakfast with Morgan before the big boss heads back to wherever big bosses come from. And it's your lucky day, Grady called out sick."

"There is a silver lining to this day."

At the door to the Girls' Den, Faith slipped in and Jed kept going. At the doorway, Faith paused and glanced at Edwin's dark office. *What* does *he have planned for today?*

~ ~ ~ ~ ~

Selby locked his car and slipped the keys into his front pocket. It was time for a steak bagel from Joe's. Faith had left so early and in such a hurry this morning that breakfast seemed a moot point. As he turned and started across the street, he caught a glimpse of Tracey coming out the side door that led to the kitchen, her arms across her chest. Her face seemed to be twisted in rage and Selby wondered what Joe had said to her to get her so irritated that early in the morning.

However, as Selby continued walking toward her, the man he had seen her with the other day followed her out of the bakery, his arms gesturing wildly at whatever he was trying to articulate. From the looks of Tracey, she wasn't buying any of it. Selby was about to turn and skip his breakfast, when he saw the tall man grab her and spin her around. It was obvious that he was yelling at her.

Selby sped up his pace. He had left her alone the other day, but not today, not with the man's behavior. "Tracey, you okay?"

As soon as the other man had heard his voice, he released his grip on the small redhead and took a step back. "We're fine," the man said. He was a few inches taller than Selby, with short dark hair and a slight mustache. He was thin and pale as if he worked indoors and never ventured out. What stuck out to Selby the most, however, was the wedding ring on his finger.

Selby ignored him and stepped closer to Tracey. "I wasn't asking you."

Tracey, her dusting of freckles now moist with tears he hadn't noticed, smiled up at him as she reached out and touched his arm with her hand. "I'm fine. Ryan was just leaving. For good." She turned and faced Ryan with that last phrase. "Goodbye, Ryan. And good luck." She stood there with her arms crossed waiting for the other man to leave.

Ryan stared for a moment, but then nodded his head. "Goodbye, Tracey," he said before turning and walking away.

Selby watched as he left. He wanted to wrap an arm around Tracey, but wasn't sure if he should or not. "Are you really okay?"

Ryan turned the corner and was out of sight before she answered. "Yes. Sometimes the past is stubborn."

Selby glanced at her as he slid his hands in his pockets just to put them somewhere. "Ryan is your past? Tracey, he has a wedding ring."

She turned on him, her face an angry twist. "So do you, Selby Greer. Do not be naïve nor hypocritical. And before you do something stupid and ask, yes, his wife knows. It was a complicated relationship that needed to end, so I ended it. Ryan just had a hard time accepting it and has been trying to force me into returning to something that I knew was going to cause people pain. I can't do it. I won't do it."

"He seems to be the one hurting pretty bad."

"Well, I wasn't in the relationship for him." She took a deep breath and before he could ask her what she meant, she turned back to the bakery. "Come on in and I'll hook you up with some breakfast for being my knight and coming to my rescue."

She walked away and he dutifully followed, his eyes trying to see through her back and into her heart, to see what she had meant and what she was really feeling. If she wasn't in a relationship with Ryan for Ryan, then who was she in the relationship for?

Joe's Bakery was buzzing with activity when they walked back in and Joanie was glad to have the help again as the line had backed up to the entrance. "Your girl's falling behind," Joe called out as Tracey entered the front of the bakery.

"What? You forget how to work the counter, old man? With as much free coffee as I serve you, you could have pitched in a bit." Tracey ignored the customers that were waiting, put a steak bagel together for Selby and thanked him again. "I'll come by at lunch."

"Good, because I want to talk to you about something."

She arched an eyebrow at him with a questioning look. He just winked at her. "Trust me."

"Please, I've heard that line too many times in my life."

He reached out and touched her hand briefly. "Not from me."

Their eyes locked and he tried to put as much meaning as he could into that gaze. "Go," she finally said. "I've got people to help."

He just smiled as he left. He wasn't sure why he had said it, but he meant it. He was going to prove to her that he wasn't Ryan. He wasn't naïve. He knew that if she would sleep with him, then she probably would have with others who had caught her attention. Selby knew he wasn't anything special for someone to change their moral code for. What he was asking of her, he was sure others had, but he was going to be different. He would show her.

But first he had to get her alone where they could talk.

~ ~ ~ ~ ~

Faith had managed to accomplish quite a bit before Cherish graced them with her crabby presence. She barely spoke to anyone once she arrived and slammed her purse onto her desk, not even offering an explanation as to why she was late. She merely grumbled that she was going to have a cigarette. Faith just shook her head. Arrive an hour late and then take a cigarette break. Cherish really was a prima donna.

It was after lunch before Edwin arrived at the office. He didn't offer an explanation as to where he had been, either. But then again, he didn't need to. He was the boss. Faith did notice, however, that his mood seemed to match Cherish's and decided perhaps it was best to steer clear of both for a while.

However, she wasn't afforded that luxury.

"Faith, may I see you in my office, please." Edwin stood in the doorway as he spoke, but didn't hang around to see if she was busy or available or even if she heard him. He just turned and walked away.

Cherish's face seemed to shrivel into a grimace even more as she made a point to avoid glancing at her sister or the doorway.

Faith gave a mental shrug and then followed Edwin's path. With Cherish, you never knew what had her panties in a wad and usually you didn't want to know anyway. Edwin was another matter, however. Faith wanted to know what had soured his usual chipper mood and, if there was a way to alleviate it, she was eager to do so.

He was already sitting in his chair when she passed through his office door. She didn't stop or wait or even think for that matter. She walked around the desk and stood behind him, her hands on his shoulders, massaging the tightness in his muscles. "Someone did not have a good morning."

He let out a deep sigh as he allowed her to work his shoulder muscles, enjoying the attention. "No, someone didn't." He was quiet a moment and then she heard a deep moan escape his lips. "You really have some talented hands, you know that?"

"So, I've been told."

"Did you do as I instructed?"

She assumed he was referring to his no panties order. "Yes, sir."

He reached around and took her hand in his and pulled her until she was standing in front of him, the desk slightly blocking anyone's view if they were to pass by. He gazed up into her eyes and she felt herself moisten at the glance. He continued to hold her hand as he glided his other up her thigh and under her dress. She felt her body stiffen and she had to force herself not to jerk her gaze to the door to see if anyone was watching. He just smiled as if he knew exactly what was going through her mind. Knowing Edwin, she assumed he did.

His hand continued until his fingers grazed the satin lips of her pussy lips, the wetness covering his fingers. His smile grew bigger as he slid two fingers into her, slowly pushing them until his bottom knuckle hit her flesh. She bit her bottom lip to keep from crying out, her breath caught in her chest.

"Good girl," he said as he pumped his fingers slowly, in and out, twirling them inside of her.

She felt her body tense even more, the passion stirring within her as she fought to remain standing. She held herself up with her free hand, bracing her knees, which wanted to buckle and drop her to the floor. "Thank you." It was a breathy whisper, but it was all she could get out.

"And did you ask about time outside of work?" He continued to finger fuck her as he spoke. He didn't even glance at the door to see if anyone was watching. His attention was solely on her and it sent shivers through her that tingled at every nerve ending.

"Yes, sir. Selby said it was fine."

"Good. Then tomorrow night, I want you. You pick the time. But I want you."

"Yes, sir. I'll text you after I talk to him and we pick a time."

He shoved his fingers in harder a couple more times before he yanked them from her wetness. He kept his eyes on her as he wiped her juices from his fingers onto her legs. "Good girl. My day has gotten better already. You may go back to work."

She took a deep breath to steady her knees. "Thank you." She smiled like a silly school girl with a crush, which is exactly how she felt.

As she turned to leave she was relieved that the doorway was empty, but who knew if anyone had passed by and saw them. Did she really care at this point? She took a couple of slow steps to allow the nervousness to leave her legs before she walked out of his office, hopefully with a normal gait, and back to the Girls' Den. Cherish was still there, pounding away at her keyboard. Nessa was ruffling through some old files as she listened to her iPod. Normal. At least, this part of the office was predictable.

Faith didn't say anything. As she slid into her seat, she could still feel the wetness where his fingers had been and even the moisture from her cunt dripping onto her legs. She wouldn't have been surprised if a steady stream had been running down her legs to be seen at the bottom of her dress. He had toyed with her right there in his office. Her eyes flew wide as she remembered that she hadn't even shut the door. A panic settled in as she realized anyone walking by could have heard them even if they hadn't seen them.

She closed her eyes and took a deep breath. The whole thing had been crazy. Risky. Exciting. And now he was going to have her all to himself tomorrow night. She couldn't help but wonder what he had planned for her and she felt her fire get even wetter. Time was going to drag. She knew it.

Nineteen

Faith sat in her truck for a moment as she stared at Edwin's front door. He had a western-style home with a circular drive that curved in front, leading in and out of his street. He lived out in the middle of nowhere, isolated from neighbors, and rarely did people drive by his home. He said he liked it that way. He could walk nude down to get his paper and no one would even know. Shrubs outlined the house and a giant oak brought shade to the front yard, making it inviting on a Saturday afternoon instead of suffocating. Her stomach was in knots and she thought she was going to throw up. Not the impression she wanted to give on their first outing alone.

Selby and she had agreed that Saturday afternoon would work best for the first date with their new playmates. It allowed them the evening to reconnect and didn't stick them with rising early in the morning. Their weekend was still basically their own. Both Tracey and Edwin had agreed and then the rule was made that it had to be somewhere other than the Greer home; at least for the first time out. Faith wasn't sure she wanted Selby to have sex in her home without her just yet.

She took a deep breath and opened the door to her truck. She was here to be fucked. Plain and simple. They were alone, no chance of being caught. This wasn't a romantic date nor was it about work. It was all about sex. Somehow that made her even more nervous. There was no prelude. No real foreplay of cat and mouse. She had already been caught and now Edwin was claiming his prize.

As her foot touched the first of the three steps leading up to his front porch, the door opened and there stood Edwin. He wore only jeans, his chest bare and his muscles toned. Even his bare feet seemed to hold a strength in them that made her pussy drip with just a glance. He *was* strength. It radiated from him in ways that made people follow him without question. His smile caught her breath and she stopped walking for a moment as her nerves tightened her stomach.

"Did you change your mind?"

She forced her nervousness into a smile. "No. It just caught me off guard when you opened the door, that's all."

He nodded, a smile bringing a mischievous twinkle to his eyes. "Would you like to come in and play?"

"That *is* why I am here, right?" She found herself swaying back and forth and forced herself to stop as she grinned up at him. "You wanted me on a weekend. I am here as you asked."

His smile widened as he crossed his arms and leaned back on the door frame. "If you wish to come in, you must strip and leave your clothes in the truck."

Faith's eyes went wide and she felt her jaw drop. "Right here? In the middle of the day? But what if people drive by?"

He just shrugged his shoulders. "It's your call."

She stared at him for a minute. Was he serious? He looked very serious. Was it another test? She took a deep breath. If it was, she was going to pass it. "Yes, sir."

Faith walked back to her truck, opened the driver's door, but didn't hide behind it. She kicked her sandals off and tossed them onto the seat. She slid her blouse over her head, her eyes never leaving his and then tossed it in after her sandals. Reaching behind her, she unclasped her bra and pulled it from her shoulders, leaving her breasts bare to the cool March breeze. She could feel her nipples shrivel immediately. She then unbuttoned her pants and slid them down her tan legs, leaving her wearing nothing except her lacy thong. She smiled at him as she turned her back to him, slipped her thumbs into the waistband and then made a slow show of sliding the thong down her tanned legs, pushing her ass out as far as she could. She turned her head as she stood, continuing to smile at him and then she tossed the panties into the truck and shut the door. With her hands clasped behind her back and her legs spread slightly, she waited. "May I come in now, sir?"

He raked her with his eyes, his grin crooked, cocky. He nodded. "You may." He then turned and went inside, not waiting to see if she followed. He knew she would. It was his confidence that made her drip as she did, made her want to follow him, please him. She climbed the three steps to his front porch, walked inside and shut the door on the outside world.

The air inside his home was cool, bringing her nipples quickly to attention and sending goosebumps up her arms. He led her without a word through the front room to a sitting room in the back of the house. She was surprised at how well-decorated his home was for a single man. It didn't look like a bachelor pad, but resembled a family home. She wondered if it had been left over from his ex-wife.

When they reached the sitting room with its two recliners, loveseat and a circular coffee table covered in car magazines, Edwin finally ceased his walking and turned to face her. Again, he swallowed her nude form with his eyes, a smile of admiration breaking his face. She stood with her hands clasped in front of her, hiding her womanhood, elbows in front of her nipples as best as she could. She felt bashful all of a sudden and had no idea why. It was probably due to the fact that she was completely nude while he was still mostly dressed. It made her feel vulnerable, a feeling he probably wanted her to have at the moment. Power. Strength. It cloaked Edwin like a mantle he was born to wear and made Faith drip with nervous anticipation.

"I don't remember you being so shy before," he said, his eyes twinkling to match his smile.

She dropped her arms to her sides and stood naked before him. "Sorry. Nervous."

An eyebrow perked up over his right eye. "More so than in my office or in the warehouse where people could have walked in on us?"

She nodded. "I knew that place and, although it sounds weird, felt secure. I am not sure of my surroundings here, so it is throwing me off a bit. There is nothing stopping us from doing anything we want, no risks, so no safety measures, if that makes sense."

He cocked his head to the side. "And do you need safety measures?"

She took a deep breath. "No. I am here because I want this. And I trust you."

He nodded as he crossed the room to where she stood. He reached out to her, his warm hand cupping her pale cheek, cradling it. She leaned into his touch, pulling the strength from it that was offered. She closed her eyes, relishing the gentleness as she took a deep breath. Her nervousness seemed to fade with his touch.

She felt his hand slide behind her neck and, as she opened her eyes to gaze at him, she felt him pull her toward him, his lips searching out hers. They were soft, warm, as they meshed against hers, softly at first and then with a tender hunger that pressed harder as his mouth opened and his tongue parted her lips. She wrapped her arms around his waist as she surrendered to him, pressing her lips to his as she felt the passion fill her most sensitive of parts.

As well as her heart. She felt the sudden growing feeling in her chest as if something had suddenly filled her. Her breath caught and she almost pulled away from his kiss. Yet, at the same time, she didn't want it to end.

She tried to think if they had kissed before and couldn't remember a time. This was her first from him and she was naked, alone in his house, and open for whatever he wanted. And she hoped she knew what he wanted, because she craved it.

His hands slid down her back, his fingers scratching trails along her flesh until he cupped her ass and squeezed her to him even tighter. She felt the growth in his jeans, the hardening of his cock against her, and her pussy dripped with a hunger that she needed to feed. She slid one of her hands down the back of his pants and cupped his ass as well. She could feel the tiny curls of hair and relished the firm flesh that filled her hands. God, how she wanted him right then to take her, bend her over a chair, and just pound into her.

She opened her eyes and he was staring at her, his eyes searching hers as if they were windows to what was inside of her. She knew that she could get lost in those eyes. He smiled back down at her. "I have waited quite a while to be alone with you like this," he said, his voice a bare whisper.

She felt her face flush as she smiled back up at him. "And why is that?"

"Because, you are one of the most enticing women I have ever met."

"So why did you wait so long to take me?"

He smiled as he shrugged. "How was I to know you were serious with all that seductive teasing and taunting?"

"Well, now you know."

"Now I know." He leaned down and swallowed her breath in another kiss, his lips meshing into hers as he held her to him with a grip that didn't seem to want to let go. She hoped he never would.

The kiss was finally broken and both took a deep breath. She watched as he stepped back, his hand sliding into hers. He didn't say a word. He just smiled as he led her out of the sitting room and down the hall to his bedroom. The furniture was all maple, the bed a king with thick comforters and wide pillows. A door led off to the south, probably a bathroom, Faith figured.

Edwin guided her to the bed and turned her so that she was facing him. Slowly he pushed her back until she was sitting on the soft, beige comforter and then continued to push her backward until she was lying down. She laid there, her legs dangling over the side of the bed. He knelt between her legs and she could feel his breath on her flesh as he leaned down, his mouth inches from her legs. He opened her up before him, his eyes watching her as he did, that mischievous smile plastered on his face. He bent forward, kissing her on the inside of her thigh, his lips warm, his tongue wet. She felt her chest rise with the breath she took at his touch, her pussy becoming even more wet, if that was even possible. The fluttering of her stomach moved up to her throat as she moaned. He continued to kiss upward until his mouth was almost touching her sweet mound. He blew his hot breath on her wetness and then dropped back down to the other leg, repeating the trail of kisses. However, this time when he reached her pussy lips, he didn't stop. She felt his tongue glide between her folds, spreading them before him until he could taste her sweet pearl.

She wanted to wrap her legs around him, hold him in place, but his arms kept her spread open before him. Her back arched as his lips surrounded her clit, sucking it into his mouth. She felt one of his hands slide up her leg and then his fingers were shoving inside of her. She gasped, her groan loud in her ears. She pushed her hips down, wanting to cram his finger into her. She needed it. Craved it. She put a hand on his head; fingers intertwined in his short hair, and held his face to her sex as she ground it on his face.

He held her stomach down with his free hand, so she couldn't move her hips. She couldn't guide him, press against him. She could only lay there and allow him to have his way with her. His tongue swirled around his finger—fingers, he had added another—two more maybe? She gasped as she felt herself being stretched.

He began to move his hand faster, finger fucking her the way she wanted him to fuck her with his cock. She desperately wanted to move her hips, but his hand held her firm. She could feel his tongue gliding around her slick lips, tasting her. Her moans echoed off the walls, the ceiling, and she was grateful that for once she could cry out without worry.

He nibbled her inner thigh and she was sure he had left teeth marks. At first, she worried about what Selby would say when he saw them, but then she didn't care and surrendered herself to the sensations Edwin was giving her body. She gripped his head with her hands, trying to move his mouth where she wanted it, but he refused to obey. This was his game, his rules.

She felt his fingers slip from between her lips, his breath pull away from her. Opening her eyes, she watched as he stood, his fingers going for the button on his pants. She leaned up on her elbows as she soaked in the image of him sliding his jeans down his powerful legs before stepping out of them. His cock was at full attention, pointing at her like a daring finger—a very thick, long daring finger.

Faith slid from the bed, dropping to her knees as she glanced up at him. Gliding her hands up his legs, she leaned forward and buried her face in the dark curls that surrounded his manhood, breathing in the musty smell of his sex. She felt the weight of his hand on her head as he guided her mouth to his cock and she didn't resist. She was his to use as he wished. She licked the shaft as she cupped his testicles with her hand. A drop of pre-cum bubbled at the tip and she licked it away, her first taste of him that day. His fingers tightened. Her mouth opened. Before she could brace herself, he shoved his cock into her mouth and began to face fuck her. The hand on his balls, went to his ass, gripping it for balance, while her other hand went to the base of his hardness so she could control how deep he went inside of her. Then, she began to suck him off, her head bobbing back and forth, swallowing as much of him as she could. The muscles in his ass tightened under her hand as she relished every slide of her mouth. She could feel the pulsing within her.

He only left her on her knees for a couple of moments, moments that passed way too quickly for her. He lifted her and slid her back toward the bed as he followed her. She lay sprawled out, running her hands over his body. She couldn't get enough of the touch of him. He climbed on top of her, his eyes never leaving hers, his mouth partly open in a smile that stirred her insides. He kneed her legs apart as he slid between them, his weight bearing down on her. "I have had you playfully, taken you, toyed with you. Now today, I make love to you." She watched as he brought his mouth down to her neck, his lips warm, his tongue gliding across her flesh.

And then she felt his hardness spear into her, shoved deep inside of her. She screamed at the suddenness, her hands digging into his back. Then his arms wrapped around her, under her arms and over her shoulders as he continued to pound her. She cried out with each thrust as her hips moved to meet his, their bodies slamming into each other in cadence to what was pumping through them, the passion that inflamed them. She wrapped her legs around his, holding him to her, trying desperately to drive him deeper. She kissed his neck as he suckled hers, his small chest hairs rubbing her sensitive nipples.

Faster, she could feel him drive into her, his groans matching her whimpers. Deep inside she felt her passion begin to climb, her body shudder as it tensed. Her back arched and she dug her nails into him as her orgasm crashed upon her in a violent tremor. Her screams ricocheted.

As did his name.

He continued his thrusts, his hips slapping hers. She took a deep breath in-between her moans and could feel another wave of climax about to crash down upon her. Her body tensed, her mouth opened, but this time no sound came out. She felt his cock twitch inside of her as his body stiffened. He grunted. She groaned. Their bodies shook. She thought for sure he was going to rip her shoulders apart with his hands as he tightened every muscle and filled her with his passion. She felt the warmth explode inside of her to mix with her own honey and then her body eased in to shallow breaths, a loosening of muscles, an easing of tension.

She opened her eyes and Edwin stared down at her, his eyes sparkling. Before she could say anything, his mouth covered hers and his tongue danced with hers. The pressure of his lips meshed into hers drove her into more of a heated state. She wanted more. She needed more.

He glanced down at her as he pulled his lips from hers, his body sliding off her to lay cuddled along her side, an arm draped over her stomach. His mischievous grin was back in place. "Not bad for round one."

She grinned back at him as her hand slid between his legs to stroke his soaked cock. "I'm already ready for round two."

He placed his hand on the back of her head and pushed her face down to his cock. "Good," she heard him say just as she ran her tongue along his semi-erect shaft. She could see their sex coating his manhood, taste herself, but as she swallowed his hardness, she didn't care. She wanted him again, whatever it took.

Twenty

Selby stared at the front of her apartment. It was a quaint complex with a rustic feel to it. The buildings were a light brown and the trim a rough chocolate. Giant oaks and pines grew throughout the complex, shading the parking spaces as well as the two-story buildings. Luckily for him, Tracey's was on the bottom floor.

He twisted his hands around the steering wheel, his body one giant nervous knot. He wondered if Faith was having the same feelings at Edwin's. He hoped so, although he doubted it. She had been too hyped up when she left. He was more nervous, which tainted the excitement. He wanted to be with Tracey, but he had always pictured them with Faith and not alone. Teasing at the bookstore was one thing. Meeting at her apartment was quite another.

Stop acting like a teenager, you idiot. With a deep breath, he opened the car door and slid out into the cool March air. The breeze tugged at his short hair, making it an even messier nest than usual. He slid his keys into his pocket as he strolled up the small walkway, shoving his hands into his pockets as well.

When Tracey opened the door after his faint knock, she wore a short sundress and a cocky smile. "I've watched you sitting out there. I thought you were going to chicken out. You could hurt a girl's esteem, you know."

He smiled as he ducked his head in a sheepish apology. "Sorry. I just don't want to disappoint you."

She grabbed his hand, his wrist really since his hand was stuffed back into his pocket, and dragged him inside. "Oh, you won't."

Tracey's apartment was bigger than the outside would allow you to believe. To Selby's right was a small kitchen with dark stained cabinets and a beige counter serving as a wall between the kitchen and the living room. She had decorated it in chocolate leather with oak end tables and a matching entertainment center. A picture of a swan gliding across a calm lake decorated one wall while gold metal butterflies flitted along another. Both were beautiful animals, but neither began life that way. Selby wondered if that was symbolic in some way to how Tracey felt about her life.

A small bookshelf set against the south wall, the top of which was covered with snapshots in dollar store frames. One was Tracey dressed in her floral blouse and beige shorts wearing her apron pointing to the sign, Joe's Bakery. *Probably opening day.* There was another of an elderly couple, obviously Tracey's parents unless she had a sister twenty years older than her. Right beside it was another picture of Tracey and what appeared to be an older brother and sister. All three wore white, long sleeve shirts and jeans as they walked barefoot on the beach. *That would be a fun shot with Faith.* As he looked closer, he recognized Ryan from outside the bakery.

Selby glanced back at Tracey who was still standing by the door. She had noticed him looking at the picture, her face a mask of apprehension. The last time they had talked about Ryan, she had almost bit his head off. He glanced back at the picture, this time paying attention to the woman in the photo. Tracey had said that she hadn't been in the relationship for Ryan, so that must have meant she had been in it for the wife. She was a tall blonde, athletic build with a playful face. If her smile in the picture was any hint at her personality, he could see Tracey getting along with her quite well. He stepped away from the pictures and glanced around at the rest of the apartment.

"I like it. The place suits you quite well," he said. He pulled his hands out of his pocket, noticing that he had stuffed them back inside, a nervous habit Faith had pointed out to him on numerous occasions.

Tracey just stared at him. "You might as well ask."

He nodded. "Will you please tell me about Ryan and I'm assuming his wife?"

She walked over to where Selby stood and picked up the picture. She stared at it although he didn't think the picture was what she was really seeing. "I met Chelsea Criswall while I was out dancing one night. She was having a girls' night out and I kind of crashed the party and attached myself to her. I was younger, of course, and still in my rebellious stage. I wanted to try everything my parents said I should stay far away from. It turned out that Chelsea was one of those things." She placed the picture back on the top of the shelf and grabbed Selby's hand and led him to the couch. "We hit it off and decided to keep hanging out with each other. She was married to Ryan and I found myself over at their house quite often. The three of us seemed to always be together. I fell in love with Chelsea and then Ryan. Chelsea said she loved me, but I think I was really a phase she was going through. Ryan, however, did fall in love with me.

"After a few months of what I guess you would call dating, Chelsea moved me in with them and declared us a relationship. We slept in the same bed, shared the bills, shared the household chores, everything a normal married couple would do, except there were three of us."

They sat on the couch, Tracey never letting go of his hand. Their clasped hands were her focal point during the story. "My parents found out about the relationship and, when I didn't obey and leave Ryan and Chelsea, quickly wanted nothing to do with me. Only Michael, my older brother, still talks to me.

"We were together, the three of us, for almost four years. Then Chelsea wanted to move away and decided she didn't want me to go with them. Ryan fought for me, but I refused to go where I was no longer wanted." Tracey shrugged her shoulders. "I wasn't going to force people to want to be with me. I haven't done it with friends and I refuse to do it with lovers. So I left.

"Ryan has been trying to convince me to go with them. He swears he can get Chelsea to change her mind and has even threatened to leave her for me. I don't want anyone to leave their wife for me. I told him it was over and what you saw today was a last ditch effort on his part as we signed some legal papers to finalize our divorce, so to speak. I'm sorry I took it out on you. That wasn't fair."

Selby watched her for a moment, her gaze still focused on their hands. He reached out and lifted her chin so that she was looking at him. "You don't have to apologize for anything. I should have been more sensitive. I tend to open my mouth before I know why and issue dramatically romantic statements. It's one of my faults."

She did smile then as she squeezed his hand tighter. "I tend to like your faults."

Without realizing he was even doing it, Selby leaned forward and kissed her, his lips gentle on hers, warm, sensitive. He slid his hand around her neck and held her as their kiss continued. He felt her hand drop to his thigh, relaxed as she fell into his kiss. He breathed her in and relished the fragrance, a jasmine with peach overtones. He would never forget it and knew from that day on he would always associate that scent with her.

He pulled away and gazed into her eyes. She had confided in him, which meant she trusted him. He would be deserving of that trust. He leaned in and kissed her again, harder, their lips meshed together as their tongues danced. She pulled him down on top of her, his body blanketing hers, his hands on each side of her face as they continued to kiss. He felt her arms wrap around his back, sliding under his shirt. Her nails dug into his skin, pressing him to her.

His cock grew to life between them.

Tracey pushed him off to the side and onto the floor, following as he rolled over. She straddled his chest as they continued kissing, their lips seemingly locked. She placed her hands on his chest, her fingers around each side of his button-down shirt, and pushed herself to a sitting position. She grinned down at him, her eyes sparkling with mischief, then she ripped his shirt open, the buttons flying everywhere. She laughed and he just took a deep breath.

He watched as she lowered her auburn-haired head. It was like a waterfall of phoenix colors as she bent over and started kissing his chest. He felt her tongue glide around his left nipple, swirling it into her mouth as she kissed and sucked. Selby gripped her hips with his hands, not knowing where else to put them. She moved to his other nipple, kissing, her tongue gliding and flicking across the swollen nub, and then he felt her hand slide between them to begin working his pants button. She slid her body downward as she unzipped him, her hand darting into his pants and under the waistband of his boxers until she had his shaft firmly in her hand. He felt her body continue to glide down his legs as she kissed her way down to her hand and what awaited her within its grip.

Selby propped himself up on his elbows and lifted his head to watch her. He could feel the tightness in his chest as his body tensed at her movements. Her mouth was but a breath away from the tip of his cock when she stopped and looked up. Gliding her tongue across her lips, she kept her gaze upon him as she lowered her head and licked the tip of his cock, taking his droplets of cum into her mouth.

He moaned as he took a deep breath. She grinned again and then lowered her eyes and her mouth onto his manhood, swallowing him inside of her as far as she could take him. Her hand twisted around his shaft as her head bobbed up and down, sucking him, devouring him. His back arched at the sensation and his moans grew louder. Her hair was like a fiery waterfall engulfing him as her face vanished beneath it to swallow his cock.

Selby groaned when she pulled her lips from his shaft and sat up, her face a radiant mask of lust. She crossed her arms in front of her and grabbed the waist of her dress, pulling it over her head and tossing it to the side. He just stared, memorizing every curve of her body, nude before him for the first time.

He smiled as he slid his hands up her sides to toy with her nipples. She pushed them out to him, offering herself, her body, for his pleasure. He took it.

With one hand he rolled her over to her side while at the same time kicking his pants the rest of the way off. He slid out of his shirt and tossed it after her dress, and then, he dropped, a hand on each side of her bracing him up as he stared, grinning, into her eyes. "I have longed for this moment."

She reached up with a hand and caressed his cheek. "So have I." She slid her hand behind his neck and pulled him to her, her mouth searching out his as their bodies pressed together, the heat of their passion a fire that was not going to go out. Her lips found his ear and nibbled slightly. When she pulled away, he heard her whisper, "Selby, take me. Please. Take me."

And with a sudden thrust into her most sensitive of parts, he did.

~ ~ ~ ~ ~

Selby leaned back against the kitchen counter and watched as Tracey reached up on her tiptoes for a mug to pour him some coffee. She had put his button-less shirt on after they had spent an hour on the floor in one position or another and now the bottom cup of her ass cheeks poked out from under his shirt. He couldn't stop himself from smiling as he stared, remembering how her flesh had felt in his hands and against his body. "You know you owe me a shirt."

"A shirt? What shirt?" She turned and gave him a confused smile. "This is my shirt now."

He laughed, his chuckle bouncing off the cabinets. "You want me to leave here half dressed? What will your neighbors think?"

"I don't care what they think." Her eyes twinkled as she said it and he knew she meant it. He doubted she ever cared what anyone thought. *You cannot live your life by other people's perceptions of what is right or wrong.*

She poured the coffee into two mugs, the steam rising between her breasts, which kept peeking out from within his shirt. She handed him the mug and he set it on the counter behind him, taking hers, as well, and placing it beside his. He pulled her to him, wrapping his arms around her waist as he leaned down and kissed her, her lips flush from their lovemaking. He felt her hands slide up his back to his shoulders and hold on. He loved the taste of her.

When he pulled away, he could feel himself smiling like a school boy who had just had sex for the first time. "This was a great idea."

"I know. I thought of it, remember?"

He paused a moment, his head cocked, as he tried to think. "You did, you little vixen." Her eyes gleamed as she tried to give him an innocent look, but failed. "You brought up the idea of Faith and I having solo adventures at that Italian restaurant. Was this what you had in mind?"

"Who? Me? Whatever do you mean, Selby Greer? What are you accusing me of?"

He pulled her to him and kissed her again, this time with more passion. "Of being adorable," he whispered as he pulled away.

They picked their mugs back up and she led him back to the couch. Their knees were touching as they sat facing each other; she grazed his arm with her fingers. He smiled at her as they made themselves comfortable and it surprised him that he *was* actually comfortable. He wasn't worried about Faith or in a rush to get out of there. He was relaxed, enjoying the moment, wanting it to last. And that part, he had to admit, scared him just a bit. This was supposed to be sex. Only sex. He stared into her eyes; her lips were curved up into a soft smile, her face a gentle glow.

It was quite a bit more than sex.

"May I ask a question?" He fidgeted a bit, pretending to reach for his coffee.

"Of course."

"You weren't in the relationship for Ryan, but for Chelsea. If your preference is for women…"

"Why am I here with you?"

Selby nodded.

She was quiet a moment, thinking. She sipped her coffee and then took a deep breath. "To be honest, I'd love to be here with both Faith and you, but I don't think Faith sees me that way." She shrugged. "So I at least get half of you." She took another sip of her coffee. "Half is better than none."

He leaned over and kissed her. "I'm glad you settled for me."

Tracey bit his lip as she called him a brat through her clenched teeth. He took her cup from her hands and set it back onto the table. He then brushed her hair out of her eyes before leaning down and kissing her again. This time, however, he didn't stop there. He continued pushing her back down as he kissed his way down her neck, her chest, until he found her swollen nipples. He sucked one into his mouth as he squeezed her to him. He was definitely glad she had gone for half.

Twenty-One

The one thing Faith truly loved about Florida is that even at its coldest, it wasn't ever really cold. Oh, it had its below freezing moments, but they came and went with the breeze, never lasting long. That Sunday afternoon was no different as she walked hand-in-hand with Selby along the sands of the Atlantic shore. The wind blew in over the white crested waves, pulling at her light jacket and her quickly tangling hair. The music of the persistent waves drummed its cadence just a few feet away from the path they made in the sand. It was peaceful, just the way she preferred her Sundays.

Selby and she had both arrived back home before dinner the previous night and he had treated her to a meal out. Back home, with glasses of wine and a fire flickering in the fireplace, she had told him about her time with Edwin. It had been intense. He had ordered her around and even taken her out into his backyard and fucked her in the grass. There was no privacy fence. He seemed to enjoy the daring aspects of their play. They had showered together and then he sent her back to her truck just as naked as he had made her enter his home. He sent her a text that morning saying that he was staring at the piece of ground where he had taken her and couldn't wait until he saw her again on Monday.

Selby had been open about his time with Tracey, but close-lipped about what they had talked about. All he would say was that she had shared some of her past with him and that she had wished Faith had joined them. Faith laughed as she said, "Maybe another time," with a look that really said, "No way in hell."

She made love to Selby in front of the fire and then the two of them made it to their bed and drifted off to sleep. They had slept in and had breakfast on the deck while deciding against planning out their day, choosing instead to just go with whatever popped into their head. So far, nothing had popped into their head besides a walk on the beach, and Faith was fine with that.

"Isn't that your father?" Selby pointed at a set of rickety stairs that led to one of the small access ways to the beach. Arni Driscoll sat there, the wind pulling at his hair as he stared out at the water, a cigarette dangling from his fingers as his arms rested on his knees. A notepad dangled from the hand that wasn't holding the cigarette, a typical accessory for Faith's father. "I never pictured him as a beach-goer."

Faith changed course as they walked, making her way to her father. "He's not."

As they drew closer, Arni turned and got a glimpse of them. He smiled, his cheeks pushing upward brightening his eyes, as he waved at them.

"Dad, you okay? Where's Mom?"

"Oh, she's at that church. I decided to let her do it on her own this morning and came over here for a smoke." He gestured to the waves breaking on the shore. "I can see why you two like it. Very peaceful out here in the morning."

"You should have stopped by the house," Selby said. "I could have offered you coffee to go with the morning."

"Yeah, why didn't you stop by?"

Arni waved their statements off. "I didn't want to disturb your morning. Besides, sometimes, it's nice to be alone when it's quiet."

"I bet Mom wasn't too happy that you skipped church. How did you swing that?"

He flashed a devilish smile at them. "I waited until she was out of the car and then told her I wasn't going. She stood there fuming a moment, but you know your mother, didn't want to make a scene where people could see. And then I drove off."

Faith rolled her eyes. "A scene that makes her look bad, you mean. She doesn't care what she does to make others look bad."

Arni reached out and squeezed Faith's hand. "She doesn't mean to. Your mother just has her ways about her."

Faith chose not to say anything more about the issue. Her mother's ways were quite often mean and selfish, but for some reason, Arni loved her and always stood by her, even when he was avoiding her. "And what is on your agenda today besides ducking church?"

He shrugged. "Not much. Probably take your mom out to lunch and then just piddle around the house. How about you two?"

Selby moved so that he could lean against the railing as another couple started descending the steps. "A whole lot of laziness."

Arni smiled before taking another drag from his cigarette. "Now, you see," he said as he blew the smoke out in a small stream, "that's the kind of life to be living. At your own pace, doing what you enjoy doing." He squeezed Faith's hand again. "I'm proud of you for doing what you want to do, sweetie. Don't allow anyone, not even your mother, cause you to not follow your own path. You only get one shot at this life. Live it your way."

Faith blushed at the compliment. She had never heard her father sound so sentimental before. "Thank you. I don't think Selby would allow me to live any other way."

"Good for him." Arni took another hit off his cigarette and then tossed it in the sand dune as he blew out the smoke. "Now, I better go pick up your mother. You know how she hates standing around. Any other day, she'd be yakking everyone's ear off, making me wait around, but since I left her, she'll be waiting at the curb as soon as the final amen is said." He stood and leaned down and gave Faith a hug, squeezing her tight. "I love you," he whispered. He then shook Selby's hand as he wished him a lazy day and then turned and headed back up the steps.

Faith watched him go. He put up with quite a bit from his family, Cherish's wild side, Dennis' snobbery, her mother's cantankerous ways, and even her own distance at times. Yet, no matter what, Arni Driscoll stood by his family. She never wanted to disappoint him or give him a reason to shake his head at her. That had always been the hardest part of being disciplined by him as she grew up. It wasn't the spankings or the groundings; it was that tone that told you he was disappointed in you and that hurt more than anything else.

The breeze picked up and Faith felt a shiver go down her spine. Selby grabbed her arm and led her away from the staircase, back the way they had come. "Come on, I'll make you some hot cocoa."

She leaned into him as they walked, her head on his shoulder, her hands wrapped around his arm. Her father had been right. Living your life your way was truly the only way to live it. She was lucky in the fact that she not only could, but that she was married to a man who made sure she did. She squeezed his arm as they walked. "I love you."

He kissed the side of her head. "I love you too, princess."

~ ~ ~ ~ ~

Edwin texted Faith several times throughout the day. Selby hadn't asked and Faith didn't offer. He could have asked, he knew, but for whatever reason, he just didn't feel like hearing about it. Faith's reaction was probably the reason. Whenever a text came in, she giggled. Giggled! It was beyond annoying. It was as if Edwin's text made her entire day.

Tracey sent him a couple of texts, but had told him that she wouldn't intrude on Faith's time with him. If he wanted to talk to her, he was free to text or call her. She would answer; she just would not initiate. Edwin needed that restraint.

Selby sat on the back deck, a Terry Brooks novel resting on his lap and a mug of coffee in front of him. He tried to read inside, but Faith's phone was distracting him again. She had agreed to keep their time, their time. Edwin had supposedly agreed as well, but it seems the newness of their little adventure was too much for either one of them to keep their word. He had found Faith making excuses to go into another room for whatever reason she could come up with just so she could check her phone without being caught. Selby finally told her to just talk to Edwin, grabbed his book, and escaped to his sanctuary on the deck.

He reached down and pulled his cell phone from his pocket, tempted to text Tracey since Faith was otherwise occupied, but decided not to do it. He wasn't going to get annoyed at Faith's behavior and then copy it out of revenge. Tracey deserved better.

He did, however, flip it open and browse through the pictures. Before he left her apartment the other day, he took a picture of her curled up on the couch with nothing on but a thin throw blanket. You couldn't see any vital body parts, but the image of her bare shoulder peeking out of the blanket, her red hair cascading down her back, was extremely sexy. She could come across harsh at times, but when she did show her soft side, it took his breath away. He smiled down at the picture, wondering if she giggled when he texted her. He somehow doubted it. Tracey Williams was not the giggling sort, not by a long shot.

Selby closed his phone and slipped it back into his pocket. He picked up his book and held it in his hands, but didn't open it. Instead, he stared at the sea grape that blew along his deck railing, his mind somewhere other than that back deck.

The sliding glass door opened and Faith stepped through the doorway. "You about ready for dinner?"

He turned and smiled as he noticed her cell phone was no longer in her hand. "The fun over for a while?"

She walked over and knelt down between his legs. "For the night." She leaned forward and kissed his hand. "I'm all yours for the rest of the evening."

He could feel his smile grow. "That makes me happy."

She pulled on his arm and he allowed himself to be dragged out of the chair. "Come on. Let's go inside and I'll fix you something to eat." She cocked her head over her shoulder, a devilish gleam in her eye. "Any idea what you'd like to eat?"

He reached out and tugged her hair. He had plenty of ideas.

~ ~ ~ ~ ~

She had watched him brooding through the sliding glass doors. It was then that she put her cell phone away and told Edwin that she would be his tomorrow. Tonight, she had to make sure Selby did not fall back into his mood from Thursday. It was up to her to make sure the game did not interfere with her home life.

Still, it was hard. She could still feel Edwin's hands on her body, his breath against her flesh, his commands in her ears. Yesterday had hooked her to the game. She wanted more. Wanted Edwin. He had made her scream with ecstasy. She wanted to scream some more.

But not tonight. Well, not from Edwin anyway. Selby could make her scream pretty well, too. And she was ready for it. Hungry for it, actually.

She was trapped between both of them. Edwin had shown her a soft side that she wasn't expecting. He had been tender. Loving. She hadn't wanted or expected loving from him, just sex. She relished every soft stroke, however.

Yet, she had to admit, she was confused by it. He knew what she wanted. To be taken. Used. Forced. Not to be made love to. No, she had Selby for that. Selby was for love while Edwin was for fucking, pure and simple.

It wasn't simple anymore.

It wasn't pure fucking, either.

Edwin had reached out with a soft hand and touched her in places she didn't expect him to touch. She found herself wanting more of it. For him to take her deeper into his bed as well as into his heart. Could she have both worlds with him and, if she did, what would she do with it? And where would that leave Selby? Selby was her life, her world, while Edwin seemed like another world entirely. She never knew the strength he had shown her during sex. Selby was playful, fun. Edwin was forceful, demanding. She needed both, wanted both, but now had to figure out how to make it all work without destroying either one.

Together, Faith and Selby fixed a steak and potatoes dinner, and opened a bottle of merlot. Music filtered through the house as they teased each other, their fingers brushing against each other with light touches and gentle caresses. She watched as Selby smiled at her, his eyes sparkling, and yet, she couldn't get Edwin out of her vision. She forced a smile upon her face and kissed Selby's cheek as he made some crack about her cooking. It was going to be a long night.

Twenty-Two

The next couple of days were quiet at Rutherford Construction. Yet, Edwin had still been able to sneak a feel and grope in here and there. Tuesday morning he ordered Faith to start arriving early to work so he could take her in his office. She jumped every time he snapped his fingers and, every time he did, her cunt became a molten mess. She was not permitted to wear underwear to work anymore, either, and was required to always be in a dress, no more slacks. Edwin wanted complete access to her sensitive parts even if he never had the chance to use them. Of course, he was always good at generating those quick opportunities.

Cherish was a grumpy pain in the ass for the first half of the week. Faith didn't ask or care, but assumed it had to do with her being asked to go on the business trip to Tampa instead of her sister. Every time Edwin would walk into the Girls' Den, Cherish would find an excuse to leave. It was the same with the break room. She did whatever she could to stay out of Edwin's way and Faith thought it was a drastic response for what was really Morgan's fault. Edwin already told Faith that he didn't want her to leave. He would have much preferred Cherish to go, but it had not been his decision. Morgan wanted Faith and Edwin couldn't fault him for that. Faith had done a remarkable job putting their office in order and Cherish had only slacked off more and more with each new week. Furthermore, most of the crew hated to go to Cherish for anything. She had become bitter and angry at life and took it out on everyone who came across her path. If she was going to be miserable, she was going to take as many with her as she could.

On the opposite end of the spectrum, Faith was a bubbly mass of giddiness and that drew people to her. She was not uptight and enjoyed every moment of every day. Of course, to be honest, she was just excited about each new day and the adventures it brought. It was the game she was playing that made her wear a constant smile.

And that game was getting more and more exciting. Perhaps Selby had been right a few days ago when he said that Cherish needed to get laid. It had definitely done wonders for Faith.

Edwin walked into the Girls' Den carrying a stack of manila folders. "Faith, I need you to go through these and make sure we're up to date on all of the registrations and licenses. Also, you'll need to give Nessa a crash course on what needs to be done while you're on the West Coast. She'll be working all day Friday with you. Will that be enough time?" As soon as he walked into the room, Cherish stood without a word and walked out. She didn't even glance in his direction. To his credit, Edwin didn't pay her any attention, ignoring her childish behavior.

Faith, however, was never one to pass up a chance to criticize her sister. "How long are you going to put up with that?"

At first, Edwin gave her a confused look, and then glanced at the door Cherish had just passed through. He shrugged his shoulders. "She'll get past it. There isn't much I can do about it."

"You can tell her to stop acting like a bitch. You are the boss, you know. That alone should make her treat you with greater respect."

He laid the folders on Faith's desk. "How do you know I don't deserve her cold shoulder?" He gave her a smile as he slid his hands into his pockets. "She'll come around. As long as she keeps doing her job, she can act anyway she wants. It's part of her charm." He laughed, but Faith could tell it wasn't genuine.

She just tapped the stack of folders. "I'll take care of it."

Edwin nodded and said thanks before turning and walking back out of the room. Faith watched him walk away, wondering why he would put up with behavior he didn't have to, especially from

Cherish. He usually nipped stuff like that right off. Of course, he also put up with Grady who was a total waste of a paycheck. She smiled as she shook her head, reaching for the top folder. She would just have to chalk it up to one of the many mysteries of Edwin Coldwell.

"That pretty girl at the front desk said I'd find you back here. Where's your sister? She said she'd be back here, as well."

Faith looked up and saw her father walking through the doorway toward her. "Dad!" Faith bounced out of her chair and met him halfway across the floor. She wrapped her arms around him, giving him a tight hug. "What brings you here? Cherish just stepped out. I'm sure she'll be back soon."

He glanced behind him as if the mention of her name would bring Cherish through the door. He turned back around and smiled at Faith. "I took the day off and thought I'd pull one of your mother's tricks and treat you two to lunch."

A laugh escaped Faith's lips before she could stop it. "Sorry. Mom has never taken me to lunch. She just takes Cherish."

"Ah. Sorry. She said differently."

Faith shrugged. "No worries. Mom is Mom. I'd love to join you for lunch."

"Lunch?" Cherish stood in the doorway staring at father and daughter.

Arni turned and walked over to his youngest daughter and gave her hug. "Yes, lunch. That meal that you eat in the middle of the day. I wanted to take the two of you to lunch. We can go to that café just up the road. Can you both get away at the same time? I mean, you have to eat, right?"

Before Cherish could refuse, Faith said, "I'm sure we could. It's not often we get treated to a meal. I'll have Ashlynn hold our calls and let Edwin know we're stepping out."

Cherish shot a dirty look at her, but kept her mouth shut.

"Great," Arni said, and he actually meant it. Faith didn't know if her father knew about the animosity his daughters had for each other or his wife's role in bringing it about, but she didn't care. Any chance to sit with her dad was to be grabbed, even if it meant eating with the enemy.

Faith stepped out and popped her head into Edwin's office. "Cherish and I are going to lunch with my dad. Is that okay?"

He smiled. "Of course. Just work on those folders when you get back. Enjoy your lunch."

"It's with Daddy. I'll enjoy it."

She hurried back into the Girls' Den before Cherish could ruin the afternoon. To her surprise, she stood there with her purse over her shoulder, waiting.

"We're all set," Faith said.

Arni rubbed his hands together. "Great, because I'm famished." He held his arms out for his daughters. "Shall we?"

Faith slipped her arm through his. Cherish grudgingly followed suit. "Lead on," Faith said.

~ ~ ~ ~ ~

Selby forced himself to pull away from Tracey, breaking the kiss that he could have sworn lasted the entire lunch break. He took a deep breath as he did. When he opened his eyes, Tracey was staring up into them, a smile on her face, her hands still pressed against his chest. "Shall we eat now?" She said.

"Sure. Hop up on the counter and spread your legs." Selby wiggled his eyebrows at her. He was teasing, but he half hoped she would do it. He had started closing for lunch as of Monday, so the two of them could enjoy their brief lunch period in private, just in case they decided not to eat the food that was brought and enjoy some other treat instead. So far it had mostly been heavy petting and some major kissing. It was enough to hold him over until their weekend date.

Tracey walked around the counter and began to set up their midday meal. Selby found himself watching her, a smile plastered on his face as if he were a schoolboy. In the beginning he had shared his afternoons with Faith, but he found himself sharing less and less with each day. It wasn't that he was trying to hide anything, more that he just felt protective of his time. Besides, Faith seemed lost in her game with Edwin and didn't really want to hear anything of what was happening with Selby. She was getting addicted to the risk factor of having a lover at work and how her behavior raised eyebrows. Sometimes, Selby felt he had created a monster in his wife.

Tracey glanced up, probably about to announce that lunch was served, and saw him staring at her. Her face flushed slightly as she smiled back at him. "What?"

"Nothing. Just thinking how I love our afternoons."

She nodded, the smile still decorating her face. "So do I. Now, eat."

He picked up his pastrami on rye. "Has Ryan stopped his attempts at stealing you away?"

She shrugged as she slid up onto the stool. "He texted me last night saying I will always be his. He's a persistent twit."

"He left town though, right?"

"He was supposed to, but with Ryan, who knows." She bit into her sandwich, pushing a stray piece of pastrami into her mouth. "How's our girl doing on her adventures?"

Selby noticed the quick subject change. He wanted to push it, but didn't want to upset Tracey more than the topic of Ryan usually did. "She is like an addict with a new fix. They text all night and I think she is even sending him pictures I don't know about. She's changed her style of dress for him and I don't think she even opens her panty drawer anymore."

Tracey's eyebrows went up in surprise. "Seems Mr. Edwin has taken quite a bit of control."

Selby finished swallowing the bite in his mouth, which suddenly felt very dry, before answering. "It's what she wanted." He gave a halfhearted shrug.

"Are you okay with that?"

He stared at his sandwich a moment. Finally he said, "I opened the door. I can't back out now."

"She's your wife. You can back out whenever you want."

She was right, Selby knew. However, it wasn't that easy. At least, it didn't feel that easy to him. Faith was excited and giddy and if he was honest with himself, their sex had been better than ever, even when they had first stepped out into the lifestyle. He didn't want that to change. Yet, he did fear the path she was walking. He had been lost in that fantasy before and it had almost ruined him. He was single at the time, so the only one hurt would have been him. However, would

Faith realize what her fantasies might cost their marriage if she became too immersed in it? Would she be able to back out in time?

Tracey ate her sandwich as she watched him fight his demons. He glanced up and then reached out and squeezed her bare knee. "I'm glad you're here."

"Why?"

"What?" The question confused him. He assumed she would know why he was glad.

"Why are you glad I'm here? Am I just a distraction while your wife bends over for another man? What purpose am I serving?"

He stared at her. "What purpose? You're not serving a *purpose*. You're here because we both want you here and I'm glad you want to be here with me. You're not just a distraction." He took a deep breath. "To be completely honest, I wish Faith were here with us, but I am glad that at least I can be with you. This isn't casual to me. I didn't think it was for you, either, but perhaps I was wrong."

Tracey left her chair and he watched as she took the two steps to reach him where he sat. She slid her arms around his neck and nuzzled into him. "It's not just a casual diversion for me, either. I just wanted to make sure we were on the same page, that's all." He felt her lips, soft and warm, on his neck. "And to be honest, I want Faith here, as well."

Selby slid his fingers into her hair and pulled her back so he could look into her eyes. He knew that he loved the fiery redhead on his lap and it scared him. He pulled her to him and kissed her deeply, his breath lost as well as his heart.

~ ~ ~ ~ ~

Arni Driscoll sat on one side of the table while Cherish was directly across from Faith. Cherish had been quiet as they sat in their father's small Ford pickup, Faith in the middle seat. If he noticed the tension, their father didn't acknowledge it. He was chatty, making jokes about the weather and other drivers, asking questions about work and their private lives. Faith tried to stay as vocal as he was, but Cherish barely grunted. Faith didn't doubt that Cherish loved their father, but she had always been their mother's girl. Mainly because their mother allowed her to get away with murder and spoiled her into being the brat she had become. That kind of behavior demanded a certain loyalty.

"How's Glen doing these days?" Arni asked as he lifted his water glass. They had already placed their orders and were nibbling on a basket of bread while they waited.

"He's doing well. Work is slow, but it's allowed him more time to do some projects around the house." Glen worked for Melbourne Decks and Piers installing wood decking and boat piers for those who could afford them. Lately, not many people could. Faith wondered if perhaps that had something to do with Cherish's bitter mood. Then again, she didn't really care. Cherish was Cherish.

Faith's phone went off and she glanced down. A text from Edwin read, "I wish you were eating me right now." She felt her pussy grow wet at the thought and hoped her face didn't show her blush of excitement.

"I'm sure things will pick up soon," Arni said. He glanced at Faith looking at her phone, and then turned back to Cherish. "Summer is almost here and people will be getting their play areas in order. He's had these slumps before, right?"

"He has. They just have never seemed so severe."

"Well, if you two need anything just let me know, you hear?"

She smiled as she said, "Thank you."

"And how about Selby? How is the book store doing?"

Faith's phone went off again, vibrating on the table. A quick glance revealed another text from Edwin. Faith fought the urge to read it. "Business is doing pretty good. He's thinking of adding a magazine rack like the bigger brick and mortar stores as well as newspapers. He thinks he can pick up some more downtown business that way." Her phone vibrated again.

"Do you need to get that?" Arni asked.

Cherish glanced at her with an eyebrow cocked as if she dared Faith to say yes. "No, it's just work. I'm at lunch. It can wait."

"Good. I don't get your attention very often anymore. This is a nice treat."

Faith glanced at her dad. "Is everything okay? Not that I don't love the treat to lunch, but usually you're at work. Is school closed today?"

He shook his head. "I just needed a day off. Middle school kids can be....loud," he said with a slight chuckle.

Faith wasn't buying it. Her father loved teaching and rarely ever took a day off. She stared at him as if sheer willpower was going to make him reveal his true motives. The waitress arrived with their burgers and set them in front of them, double checked their drinks and then left them alone. "Dad?" Faith stressed the word as if demanding to know what he was hiding.

Her phone vibrated again.

"If you need to check that go ahead," Arni smiled. "Work is work, after all."

"For some of us," Cherish mumbled.

Faith glared at her sister. Still staring at Cherish as if daring her to say something else, she spoke to her father. "Dad, why aren't you at school?"

"I quit."

Both women stared at him with jaws dropped. There was no prelude to his announcement. I quit. That was it. But her father loved teaching.

"You quit? Why?" Cherish demanded to know. "What are you going to do now? What does Mom think about this?"

Faith held her comments and questions, wanting to hear the rest of what he had to say first.

"Well, I'm going to write that book I keep talking about. I've always dreamed of doing it and now I'm going to go for it. I've got some money put away to hold me over for a while along with some investments to lean on. I've made enough excuses. Live life on your terms, isn't that what you and Sclby believe, Faith? Well, that's what I'm going to do. I'm tired of working for someone else and I can teach through my writing. So, that is the plan."

"What the hell did you do?" Cherish turned to Faith and glared.

"I didn't do anything! Why the hell do you think I did something?"

"No one did anything." Arni held his hands up as if calling for a ceasefire. "I decided this on my own. Life is short and you only get one chance to get it right. This is my dream. I've waited long enough.

Your sister has the right idea. Live life to the fullest. Cherish, don't you have something you dream about doing?"

"Yeah, I dream of taking care of my family."

"Well, I did that. All of my children are grown and can take care of themselves, so now it's my turn to do what I want."

"What about Mom? She's your family. How are you going to take care of her if you aren't working?"

"I will be working, just not for the school system. And your mother will have everything she has always had, don't you worry about that. I was hoping you would be happy for me and encourage me on."

Faith reached across the table and squeezed her father's hand. "I am proud of you, Dad. It takes a lot of guts to do what you're doing and I know you didn't just do it on a whim. I'm excited for you and I'm sure Cherish is, as well." Faith glanced across at the table at her sister, her look a challenge to deny her father his dream.

Cherish was quiet a moment, her face a stern expression of anger. Finally she surrendered. "Whatever makes you happy. I wish you the best of luck with it." She lifted her hamburger and bit into it.

Faith squeezed her father's hand again as she wondered how on earth she could be the sister of such a class A bitch.

Twenty-Three

Their father dropped them back off in front of Rutherford Construction and Faith and Cherish stood side-by-side as they watched him drive away. Faith waved and smiled, her mood lightened with the visit.

It didn't last long, however. With Cherish around, it never did.

"What the hell did you do?" Cherish whipped around with a look as if she wanted to punch Faith and just keep swinging.

"Do? I had lunch with my father. What are you talking about?" Faith shook her head as she turned to walk back inside. She was not going to have a shouting match with her sister at work.

Of course, Cherish didn't care where they were. "You let him think it's all right for him to just up and quit his job. He's in his fifties for crying out loud! Do you know how hard it's going to be for him to find another job?"

"He doesn't want another job, Cherish. He wants something different. He has a dream and he's chasing it. I'm not going to be the one to tell him not to go for it. He needs support, not condemnation."

"He needs a paying job!" She ran to get in front of Faith and blocked her from going up the steps to the offices. "What about Mom? How is he going to take care of her?"

Faith took a deep breath. "That's between them, don't you think?"

Cherish slammed her fists onto her hips. "You and all of this damn follow your dream shit is going to ruin the lives of others. Maybe you don't care about what it does to you and Selby, but others are getting caught up in your nonsense and it's destroying the great things in their lives. Keep your dreaming to your own bed and leave everyone else out of it."

"Excuse me? I'm not making anyone do anything and I sure as hell didn't tell Dad to quit his job. He's done that on his own. And you know what? I'm glad he did. Life is too short not to do what makes you happy." She pushed past her sister and stormed up the steps, jerking the front door open when she reached it and marching inside. If it hadn't been one of those doors on a slow return glide, she would have slammed it. How dare Cherish blame her for her father's actions. He was a grown man capable of doing whatever he wanted. He didn't need them babysitting him and dictating his life. There were enough people in his life now doing that to him. He had always wanted to write a book and she was glad he was actually going to make it work. She knew absolutely nothing about the publishing business, but she did know her father. He would not risk their security no matter what. Cherish needed to trust him. Faith always had. After all, it had been Arni Driscoll who made her realize that her life was hers to live and no one else's.

"Good lunch?" Ashlynn asked as Faith passed through the reception area.

"Perfect."

Faith jerked the door leading to the warrens of Rutherford Construction open and barreled into the hall. *And who else does she think I've swayed into doing something reckless? What else is she blaming me for?* It had been obvious that Cherish was upset about more than just their father quitting his job, but she hadn't elaborated. Who else, heaven forbid, was following their heart's desire?

Edwin stood outside of his office. At her thundering steps, he turned, eyebrows raised. She didn't stop to even say a hello. She stormed into the Girls' Den and threw herself into her chair, punching the power up button on her computer. Leave it to Cherish to ruin a perfectly good lunch.

Less than a minute later, she felt Cherish enter the room. It was as if a wall of ice blew in through the doorway. Not a word was spoken and Faith refused to turn her eyes from her computer. She could hear her sister bumbling around her desk, trying her best to draw Faith's attention. She wasn't going to have it. Not this time. Faith was tired of fighting with her family and being blamed for everything when really none of it was her fault. They could all stay stuck in their boring, routine lives for all she cared. Her life was hers and she was fed up explaining it to them. Work was work and that was all Cherish was going to get out of her from then on. She didn't need them. She had Edw...Selby...and that was all she needed. She would show them. She would show them all.

~ ~ ~ ~ ~

The bell over the door jingled and Selby called out, "Welcome to Downtown Books," as he sat on a step and loaded up a shelf of paperback fantasy novels.

"What? No special treatment for your father-in-law?"

"Arni?" Selby stood, leaving the books on the floor beside his stool. "What brings you by?" He asked as he passed down one of the aisles.

"I've come to impugn on my son-in-law's business." Arni leaned on the front counter, his thin arms folded in front of him. "I was hoping to steal some books from you on writing if you have any."

"On writing? Like how to write a book type stuff?" Selby cocked his head, thinking over his inventory as he made his way to where his father-in-law stood.

"Exactly like those types of books. I'm going to write a book. I've written a few articles for history magazines, but I know a novel is a horse of a different color. I figured I'd try here before heading to the old brick and mortar stores and see if I can save some money. Have to watch the pennies for a while."

Selby gave Arni a puzzled look. "Something happen at work?"

"I quit."

Selby just stared at him. "You quit?" He asked in disbelief.

Arni nodded. "Yup. I quit. I decided to follow my dream and try and make it as a writer. I'm going to do more with magazines, but I really want to write that novel I've always dreamed about."

Selby pressed his lips together and nodded his head, impressed that his father-in-law was making such a bold move. "A pretty gutsy move. I'm all for people chasing their dreams. What does Valerie think of your plans?"

The older man chuckled as he shook his head. "She thinks I'm a crazy old goat who is going to land us in the poor house, but she'll deal with it. She always does."

Selby merely nodded, not sure what to say and even less sure that he believed Arni. Valerie was a stubborn person who was used to having money and her way. It was unlikely she had taken his announcement with a smile and pat on the back. Crazy old goat was probably the nicest thing she had called him.

"I know, I know. She doesn't give you the impression that she can be supportive sometimes, but she has always backed me whenever I wanted to do something. She helped me get through college so I could become a teacher. She'll help me make a go of this."

Selby smiled. "I'm sure she will. I'm excited for you. Really. Anytime anyone goes after their dreams, it's a scary thing, but an exciting thing as well. I was nervous as hell when I opened this bookstore."

"Well, listening to Faith lately and how bubbly she is I'm impressed with how she has grabbed life by the horns and ridden it her way. It's time I began to do the same thing."

Selby laughed as he gestured Arni toward the back of the store. "The books you want are probably this way. Help yourself to whatever you want." It was a good thing her father didn't know what horn she was grabbing and riding that had put that bounce in her step.

~ ~ ~ ~ ~

Faith stared at the truck, glancing at tires and bumpers without really seeing anything. She needed a break from her sister. The tension since lunch had been thicker than London fog and she had had all of it she could tolerate. Selby was going to be massaging her neck that night for sure.

"Another fun day for the Driscoll sisters?"

Faith turned at the sound of Edwin's voice to see him walking toward her from the main building. She took a deep breath as she turned back to the truck. "Apparently I am now responsible for what my father does with his life." She stared at the clipboard in her hands wondering what she had inspected last. Her irritation was distracting her from her work and that was causing her to be even more distracted.

Edwin walked up behind her and started massaging her shoulders, his strong fingers squeezing and rubbing her muscles. Faith closed her eyes and lowered her head, relishing the feel of his touch on her body even if she was wearing clothes. "So, I take it lunch did not go well," he said.

Faith gave him a brief rundown of lunch with her father and sister and how Cherish had blown up at her on their return to work. "I just couldn't be in there anymore. She drives me crazy with her judgmental mindset. No one has ever told her she couldn't do something, but heaven forbid if someone were to choose to do something precious Cherish didn't approve of. She just hates for people to be happy."

Edwin didn't say anything as he continued to rub her shoulders. His silence bothered Faith. "What are you thinking?"

He squeezed her shoulders tighter. "I'm wondering if perhaps you're not too hard on your sister."

Faith spun as she pulled away from him, her face a mask of disbelief. "Too hard on her? Are you kidding me? You weren't there when she blamed me for our father quitting his job as if it were my fault he decided to chase his dream. You haven't been there when she has spit her venom-laced barbs into my back. Too hard? Since when are you on her side?"

"I didn't say I was on anyone's side," he said as he slipped his hands back into his pockets. "I'm just saying maybe she's going through something you don't know about and lashing out at you is just her way of getting some of her anger out. Maybe she can't go after the real problem."

"And I'm the stand in? No thank you. She can take it out on someone else. I have enough family drama in my life without being her punching bag." She gripped her clipboard tighter in her hand and walked off toward the warehouse. She wanted to get away from her sister and now she wanted to get away from Edwin. That was a switch from how she felt as of late.

She marched into the warehouse and as soon as she was out of sight came to an abrupt halt and took a deep breath trying to calm her agitation. It didn't last. A firm hand gripped her arm and spun her around. She gasped as she stared into Edwin's eyes. "What the hell was that about?"

She stared into his green narrowed eyes as they penetrated into her. Words left her as his angry gaze bored into her nerves, her anger.

"I wasn't defending Cherish. You forget, I know her too. I know what a snarky little snit she can be and how vindictive she is. However, I see her from a view that you don't because you're her sister. And I am telling you there are things she is going through that you aren't privy to and you need to just cut her some slack."

"What is she going through? Why does that give her the right to blame me and chew my ass out for something that isn't my fault?"

Edwin released her arm as he took a deep breath to calm his own nerves. Faith reached up to where his hand had been, the ache of his grip still throbbing, and rubbed her muscles. His face softened as he spoke. "It doesn't give her the right. No one has the right to use someone else as their punching bag. However, try being the bigger person and give her the benefit of the doubt."

Faith narrowed her eyes at him as she crossed her arms. "What is she going through, Edwin?"

"It's not my place to say and I'd appreciate it if you didn't say anything to her about it." He looked almost frightened of Cherish finding out that he had spoken to Faith. She had never seen him like that. Whatever her sister was going through, it must have been pretty big for him to be worried and defending her.

"Edwin, is something wrong with my sister? Is she sick or something?" She wasn't sure what else it could be that Cherish wouldn't have announced to the world. Then again, Cherish would have shouted that she was dying even if all she had was a cold just for the attention. "Is Jordie okay?"

"Oh yes, yes, it's nothing like that. As far as I know everyone is healthy and doing well."

"Then what the hell could it be?"

"I'm sorry, Faith, but I can't say. I just know she is hurting right now."

Faith wanted to growl, but knew it wouldn't make a difference. When Edwin made his mind up about something it stayed that way. "Fine." She turned away from him and walked further into the warehouse. "Where is Terry?"

Edwin crossed his arms and watched her. "What does it matter? You didn't come in here to see Terry. You came in here to get away from me."

She turned and glanced at him, wishing he was wrong so she could prove it to him, but he wasn't wrong. It annoyed her that he knew what she had been about when she stormed away from him. She continued to search for Terry as if Edwin had been wrong.

"He's not here. I gave him the rest of the day off to do something with his son at school."

Shit. She heard his boots on the concrete floor as he moved closer to her. He gripped her shoulders and turned her around to face him. A smirk creased his face. It was that smirk that constantly made her panties soaked without even a sexual word being spoken. He pulled her closer to him and kissed her, his lips soft, his whiskers coarse against her skin. He split her lips with his tongue and tasted her. Her moans filled her ears, echoing in the cold warehouse, as he pressed her body to his and raped her mouth with his tongue.

When he finally broke the kiss and pulled away from her, she quickly scanned the area for anyone who might have seen them. He chuckled at her slightly. "Worried? I thought you were mine to do with as I please, anywhere I please."

She had to swallow the nervousness that had crept up into her mouth. "I...I am."

His smirk widened. "Good. Remember that." He kissed her forehead and then turned and left.

She watched him leave, his back straight, shoulders firm, his ass....his ass capturing her attention. He drove her crazy with how he could swoop in and take her like that. And it was only a kiss!

Yet, it was more than his kiss. It was that presence; that power that radiated from him, that had drawn her to him and made her melt when he demanded something from her. And she knew she would give it no matter what it was. He owned her and she relished the ownership.

Twenty-Four

Faith held up a turquoise blouse, inspecting the ruffles down the front. "I just don't see why I am supposed to be nice to her when she never is to me," she said to Tracey, who was inspecting her own blouse from the clearance rack. "I mean if something is going on that makes her a bitch, she should see a therapist."

"And Edwin didn't give you a clue as to what it was?" Tracey had met her at the mall to help her pick out a new outfit for her trip next week. Selby was at home waiting for the call to start the grill and open the wine.

"No. All he said was that it wasn't his place to tell me something Cherish didn't want me to know. He just stood there with a guilty look on his face. Then he kissed me."

Tracey glanced up at her, a confused look on her face. "He kissed you? Just like that?"

Faith nodded as she slipped the blouse back on the rack. "He said it was to remind me of our agreement."

Tracey stood there, the blouse in her hand now simply dangling from her fingers. "I take it he doesn't care about being caught at work or the position that would put you both in."

Faith took another blouse, this one a dark burgundy with gold fringe around the collar. "It doesn't seem to. Or rather according to him, he had it all under control. Still, I have to admit, the excitement of where we were stopped my ranting and took my breath away. That's the part of being with Edwin I like the most, the risk factor."

Tracey laughed and shook her head. "You're crazy, you know?"

Faith laughed. "This coming from the woman who made my husband come in his bookstore with the door unlocked, adding the risk of anyone coming in possible. I think risk is what we both enjoy." Faith nodded at the shirt she had chosen. "Let's try some of these on, shall we?"

Tracey followed her into the dressing room, both showing their selections to the attendant on duty. They took stalls next to each other and continued talking as if in the same room and not stripping down.

"And how is Selby handling your half of the arrangement?" Tracey asked through the thin wall separating them.

"As long as I dote on him once in a while he seems okay with the way things are going. Why? Has he said something to you?"

"Not really. He wishes we were all together, but he hasn't complained about anything."

Faith laughed. "I bet he does."

A knock came on Faith's dressing room door. "Open up. I want to see what this one looks like on you."

Faith stared at the door a moment before shrugging and slipping the latch up. Tracey walked in, not caring that the other woman was half dressed with a shirt in her hand. "Nice bra. I love that shade of blue. Here, try this on. I think it would go better with your eyes." Tracey took the shirt that had been in Faith's fingers away from her and handed her a turquoise blouse with butterflies up one side. Faith paused a moment, but it was obvious that Tracey wasn't leaving the small room. With a sigh, she slipped the shirt over her head.

Once she had it smoothed out, Tracey reached out and adjusted the way the material hung on Faith's breasts, not caring that she seemed to be manhandling the other woman. Satisfied, she stepped back and nodded. "I thought so. It looks better on you than on me. You should keep it."

Faith laughed as she shook her head. "Yes, Ma'am."

"Here. Try it on with these pants you picked out." Tracey stood holding a pair of beige slacks in her hands, waiting on Faith to strip out of her jeans.

Faith stared at her. "Um, are you going to step out?"

"Why? You think I'm going to see something I haven't seen before?"

"No, but I'm not used to getting dressed in front of people."

"You and your sister never tried on each other's clothes?"

"I've told you about my sister, right?"

Tracey nodded. "Right. Well, get used to it. Now, out of those jeans."

Faith couldn't help but laugh as she unbuttoned her pants and slid them down her hips.

Tracey whistled and Faith felt herself blush. "Matching thong. Nicely planned. You meeting Edwin later or does Selby like the pretty stuff on you?"

"Selby prefers me naked," Faith laughed. "Edwin prefers me to dress this way."

Tracey leaned back against the dressing room wall as Faith slid the slacks up her long legs. "Doesn't it get hard to keep up with both of them like that? I mean, two men, each wanting something different?

"Not really. Selby never asks for anything, so it hasn't been a conflict. He seems to like the small changes."

Tracey nodded. "It would drive me crazy if I were a guy."

"Well, what do you think?" Faith held her hands out to her side as if putting herself on display. "Why would it matter if you were a guy?"

"I like it. See, another new outfit." Tracey slipped the other blouse back on a hangar. "And most guys don't like to compete for their woman's attention and seem to prefer their own way in a relationship. Most don't share things like that well."

Faith slid the pants back down her legs. "Well, so far, Selby doesn't seem to care. At least, he hasn't said anything to me about it if he does. What has he said to you?"

"Only what I shared with you, that he wishes we were all together. He hasn't complained." Tracey snatched up the scattered clothing. "I'll meet you out there."

Faith watched as Tracey left the small dressing room. The usually fiery redhead didn't seem perturbed, but something in the way she had just suddenly left gave Faith an odd feeling. It was abrupt. Faith could understand Tracey wanting to defend and even protect Selby, but what exactly did she think she was protecting him from? Swinging had been his idea. He had agreed on the separate play time adventures. Surely, he wasn't second guessing his choices and whining to Tracey about it and not her.

Faith continued to stare at the door. *Or was he?*

~ ~ ~ ~ ~

Selby stood by the grill, the aroma of the ribeyes mixing with the salt spray from the Atlantic. Over the sounds of Foreigner singing Jukebox Hero, he heard the girls coming through the Florida Room and onto the deck. They were laughing, so he assumed the shopping trip had cost him plenty of money.

Faith crossed the deck toward him and leaned in and kissed him as she asked how the steaks were coming along. Tracey followed her and to his surprise, when Faith moved, she stepped in and kissed him as well. "Miss us?"

He stared, silenced by confusion for a moment. After a quick second, he said, "Always. And the steaks are almost ready. Why don't you ladies fix yourselves some drinks and I'll set everything else up."

"Sounds like a plan to me," Faith said as she turned back toward the house.

"How about you? Need another of whatever you're drinking?" Tracey stood with her hands in her jean pockets as she smiled at him, all innocence and sweetness.

"Sure. I'll take another glass of the merlot that's on the counter." He handed her his glass as he gave her a puzzled look, which she ignored.

Tracey had never kissed him in front of Faith before, so it caught him by surprise that she had done it just as naturally as his wife had. Even more so that Faith hadn't blinked an eye. Of course, things between them had recently changed in a drastic way, but did that mean it should be out in the open? Were there rules about what could be done in front of Faith and what couldn't?

He found himself smiling. He had to admit that he liked the new way of doing things if this was how it was going to be. Not that it wasn't going to take some getting used to. Before, when Faith and he had met other couples, they knew it was sex and they fucked their partners and everyone said goodnight. This was different. With Tracey it seemed more intimate, almost like he was cheating in some way.

He shrugged. He wasn't going to complain.

With the steaks steaming on the platter, he turned the grill off and began to set up the table. The girls passed back through the sliding glass doors with the rest of the meal and fresh drinks. The music had switched to Jimmy Buffet as everyone made themselves comfy around the table. The girls told him all about their shopping trip and promised a modeling show after dinner.

And they did. Selby stretched out on the bed, feet crossed and hands clasped in his lap as one by one the girls stripped and showed off their new purchases. It didn't seem to bother either one that they were both getting naked in front of him and twirling around. Both seemed to need his approval on what they had bought and he was more than happy to give it with the show he was getting. He continued to sip his merlot and smile.

Once the show was done, they slipped back into what they had been wearing, made some popcorn and snuggled on the couch, each girl taking a side, and they watched *While You Were Sleeping*. At times, Selby had his arms around both of the ladies, and their heads were on his chest. When he noticed it, he suddenly grew self-conscious and shifted, making everyone move.

It was definitely going to take some getting used to, if they kept this up.

Once the movie was over and the credits rolling across the flat screen, everyone stretched, restoring blood flow to muscles that hadn't moved in an hour. "As much as I hate to say it, I have to get going. Four comes early."

"Four?" Faith asked. "You get up at four in the morning?"

"I have to be at work by five to make sure those early risers have their breakfast of sweets and coffee. Someone, not mentioning any names, but his initials are Selby Greer, would pout if everything wasn't fresh and hot when he came in."

Selby laughed as he stood. "What can I say? I hate cold coffee and sweets."

Faith gave Tracey a tight hug. "Well, be safe going home. I'm glad you came over tonight. Shopping was fun."

"Girl time is always fun."

"I always enjoy being with the girls," Selby said as he wiggled his eyebrows at them.

Faith patted his stomach as she shook her head. "Be a nice guy and walk your girlfriend out. I'll meet you in the bedroom."

He watched as his wife turned and walked out of the television room and into their bedroom, leaving him alone with their friend, or rather his girlfriend as Faith had just called her. He turned back to Tracey, an eyebrow raised in baffled surprise. "I guess I'm walking you out."

"Nice," she said as she smiled up at him before turning to the door. "I can get used to this."

He stared at her back as she walked away. *Me too.*

At the car, Selby took her keys from her and unlocked the door. He opened it as he handed her back the keys. "Your chariot is ready, my lady."

"Yes, I could definitely get used to this." She glanced back at the house. "What do you think has brought this change upon our dear Faith?"

He took a quick glance at the house as if he could see Faith inside. "I don't know but I am not going to argue with it." He turned back to Tracey. "I'm enjoying it way too much." He reached out and touched her cheek with his palm.

She placed her hand over his and pressed it tighter to her face. "Me too."

He pulled her closer to him and pressed his warm lips to hers. Her small body fell into his as he felt her arm wrap around his waist and hold him tight. When they broke away she was gazing up into his eyes, a bashful smile creasing her eyes. "I'll see you tomorrow morning."

"With my hot coffee."

They both chuckled as she slid into the car. He watched as she drove away, not returning to the warmth of the house until her brake lights were out of sight.

~ ~ ~ ~ ~

As he entered the bedroom, Faith was already dressed for bed and snuggled under the quilt reading a Lisa Jackson novel. "I thought for sure you would be longer saying good night." She closed the book and watched as he strolled across the carpet pulling his shirt over his head.

"What? You thought we would have had a quickie in the driveway? The neighbors would have loved that."

"I'm glad I didn't peek through the window and watched. I would have been disappointed."

Selby shook his head as he slid his pants off and tossed them toward the closet. He found himself smiling at the image of Faith watching in the window as he took Tracey right there against her car. "That is a pretty hot vision. Maybe next time we'll have to give it a shot."

"Don't make promises you won't keep. You'll get me all hot and bothered just to be dropped into frustration. You might come in and find me taking care of business on my own."

Naked, Selby slid under the covers and snuggled up to Faith. "Now there's motivation not to do it. What would I come in and catch you doing?"

Faith closed her eyes. "One hand would be massaging my tits, pulling on my nipples, twisting them." She slid her left hand onto her breast, and began carrying out her words. "My other hand would be between my legs, fingers pressing onto my clit making small circular motions." She moved her right hand between her legs and began to masturbate her swollen pearl. She moaned softly as she felt Selby nuzzle close to her ear, his warm breath on her neck. "Every few minutes I would dip my fingers into my wetness, finger fucking myself as I pinched my nipples. I would be picturing you bending Tracey over the car, taking her from behind. Your cock would be pounding her, your hands on her hips as your cock speared into her tight little cunt." Her fingers returned to her clit and she rubbed it back and forth with quick, jerky motions.

Selby ran his tongue over her ear. "And you would be getting hotter and hotter as I took her right there in our driveway?"

"Yes." Her hips moved upward to meet her fingers. She rubbed harder, faster, her breathing coming in short gasps. "Oh god, yes. It would be hot."

Selby kissed his way down her neck. "Would you be playing with yourself while you watched?"

"Yes!" Her voice rose higher as she pinched her nipple harder. Her hips bucked against her fingers as she rubbed harder. She could feel it building inside of her, saw the images in her mind, felt Selby's warm lips against her flesh. "Ohh, ohh…Selby..oh, godddd…unnnggghhhh…" Her moan filled the room, her hips raised off the sheets as her orgasm ripped through her tense body, shaking her, her head rolling back and forth as she groaned.

She opened her eyes at the peak and saw Selby watching her, a grin splitting his face, his eyebrows raised. She took a deep breath as she collapsed back on the bed. "Oh god, that was good." Her chest rose and lowered with her heavy breathing as she opened and closed her eyes a few times as her climax subsided. Selby merely leaned on an elbow and watched her.

"It looked good," he said with a slight chuckle in his voice. "I can imagine me fucking Tracey and then turning toward the house and seeing you standing in the window with your hand between your legs getting yourself off as you watched. Definitely a hot scene for sure."

She reached over and wrapped the hand that had not been between her legs around his neck and pulled him to her. Their lips met and she kissed him with a satisfied hunger. "Something to look forward to."

He smiled at her as he watched her lay back on her pillow, her eyes half closed as sleep was beginning to take her. The scene still played in her head as she drifted off.

Twenty-Five

Edwin ran his hand over Faith's bare ass as she stood by his desk, her hands on his shoulders as he sat staring up into her eyes. "Did you have a good evening?" She had started coming in early to work at his request, so that they would have a few minutes alone before the chaos began. The first morning he had bent her over his desk and fucked her, her dress hiked up around her waist, both of them fully dressed. It was quick and hard and had left her pussy sore for half the day. The next day he made her get on her knees beside his desk and give him a blow job, not allowing her to drink anything that morning in order to taste him for a couple of hours. This morning he was merely groping her as he talked to her, a hand on her ass and a finger fucking her pussy.

Between her moans and gasps, she told him of her night and how she had masturbated before going to bed. She told him about her fantasy of watching Selby fuck Tracey on the hood of her car.

"That would be fun to watch, you playing with yourself."

She smiled at him, her eyes half closed. "Anytime you want to see it just say the word."

"Oh, I will." He slid another finger into her, pumping them in and out as his thumb rubbed her clit. "Today, however, I just want to tease." He seemed to know when she was right on the edge of her orgasm and slipped his fingers out of her heated channel. He wiped them on her thighs as he smiled at her sudden frustration. "Tomorrow you will train Nessa on your responsibilities so she can take your place while you're gone."

She smiled down at him. "Do you want her here in the morning just like this? I'm sure I could train her to handle your teasing as well."

He laughed as he pulled her dress back into place. "No, I still have you for a few days. I'm sure I'll be fine. Just teach her your paperwork."

"You're the boss."

"Don't forget it," he said with a grin.

She touched his cheek as she gazed into his dark eyes. How could she ever forget it? He had brought out the risk-taker in her and she would not give up his hands on her reins. He knew just how to take her and make her melt. She loved the strength in his every movement. Leaning down, she kissed him roughly as if wanting to show how much he ignited her flames. As she pulled away, she gazed into his eyes again. "Never."

Outside of her quick trysts with Edwin, Faith enjoyed the quietness of the Girls' Den in the morning. Cherish was not there to get under her skin so fast and she was able to accomplish quite a bit more without the distractions of the workers coming in and out. Of course, the quiet never lasted because Cherish did eventually come into the office, bitter attitude and all.

"This is the third morning in a row you have come in early. You trying for a raise or something?"

Faith didn't turn to look at her sister. "Nope, just getting a head start on things and enjoying the quietness."

"And what's with the dresses all of a sudden? This is a construction company, not a bank."

Faith continued to click away at the keyboard. "Nothing wrong with dressing up and looking professional. Makes me feel good. You should try it."

"What's wrong with the way I dress?"

Faith took a deep breath, stopped what she was doing and turned to face her sister. "Nothing is wrong with the way you dress, just like there is nothing wrong with the way I dress. If you don't like the comments, then you should stop making them yourself. Now, I have work to do." She spun back around and resumed keying in her numbers.

Cherish remained silent, but Faith could hear her slamming around her desk taking out her frustration on the furniture. One of these days she would break something important. *If I'm lucky it will be her fingers.*

"Mom came over last night," Cherish said after a few silent moments.

"That's nice."

"She's not happy about Dad's new venture. She thinks he's being reckless."

"I'm sure she does. Dad knows what he is doing and deserves to give his dream a shot."

"Even at the risk of their security, the chance of going broke?"

Faith dipped her head back and stared at the ceiling. Why did God make idiots? She turned around and faced Cherish. "Every dream has its risks. I know our father. I'm sure he has weighed them and taken as many precautions as he could before quitting his job and chasing his. I trust him. Mom should and so should you. Regardless of whether you do or not, it's his life to do as he pleases. You and Mom have the same problem. You both want to control the lives of other people and make them do what you want them to do regardless of what makes them happy. For once, let Dad be happy." She stared at her sister, watching as the blood boiled inside of her and filled her face with anger, her eyes narrowing to pissed off slits.

"I'm not trying to control anyone's life, especially not yours. You can run yours into the ground for all I care. If Selby can handle you being the company whore than by all means have at it." She turned back to her desk and jerked a drawer open searching for anything that would take her attention off Faith.

"Company whore? You are such a....never mind. You aren't worth the effort." Faith turned back to her desk and stared at the screen. She knew she shouldn't allow Cherish to get under her skin, but it seemed to be her sister's super power. Faith was not the company whore. She was Edwin's whore. A smile creased her face as she thought back to his fingers in her pussy that morning. Yes, definitely his whore.

~ ~ ~ ~ ~

"Something wrong with our girl?" Tracey asked as she opened their lunch containers and Selby set his phone on the counter.

"Nothing more than usual. Apparently, she got into it with her sister. It's another one of those I'm-only-going-to-talk-to-her-when-I-have-to days. It happens at least twice a week."

"I never hear you two talk much about her brother. Do they ever talk?"

Selby popped open the cans of grape soda before taking his Styrofoam container and his seat. "He's deep into his church activities, so we don't see him much. He's all right as far as people go. Sticks mostly to himself and out of the family drama."

"Smart man."

"It would be me if Faith didn't work with Cherish. As it is, I'm neck deep in the family drama." He bit into his sandwich and talked around the food in his mouth. "Sometimes, I think her family is bat shit crazy. They are mostly egos and self-righteous bullshit. All except Arni, that is. He's the only one with any sense in his head. Poor man."

"What do you think they would think of how you two are living your life?"

"It would be worse than it is now, I'm sure. They may even stop talking to us all together." He widened his eyes and stared at Tracey. "You may have something there."

She shook her head. "Family is important. Trust the girl whose family disowned her."

"But it didn't stop you from making your own choices."

Tracey stared down at her sandwich and Selby could see the pain in her eyes. "No. No, it didn't. In the end you have to be true to yourself and your heart, regardless of what anyone else thinks of your choices." She glanced back at him. "We can't help who we fall in love with. It just happens to us."

He nodded. "True. Faith's mother wished Faith had never fallen in love with me."

"Can I ask you something? Are you afraid Faith will fall in love with Edwin?"

Selby didn't answer right away, which scared him. Yet, he didn't want to just spout off with a denial without really thinking it through.

The truth was he didn't really know. Sometimes people confused sex with love or that rush of excitement of something new as love. Then they would get a few weeks into it and realize they were just horny. "I'm not afraid that she will fall in love. I'm afraid that she will get lost in the excitement of her adventure and forget what's really important."

Tracey cocked her head to the side as she looked at him, the sadness having left her eyes. "And what's important to you?"

Selby smiled. "Family. And Edwin is not family."

"What about me?"

"You've been family for quite some time now."

Her smile made his heart jump. It wasn't just a sappy saying and it had nothing to do with the fact that he was having sex with her now. It was the truth. Even Faith would agree. Tracey had been hanging out with them for quite a while and had become a natural part of them. Edwin was work and a diversion. Not family.

Tracey blushed when he said it and looked away, suddenly interested on what was on her sandwich. He wondered how she felt about things, about him, about them since they had finally been together. He must not have disappointed her because she kept coming back.

She glanced back up at him, her smile a gentle softness. "I like that, being part of your family."

~ ~ ~ ~ ~

Faith stared at her plate, tenderloin over noodles, and wondered why she had even ordered it. She was not in the least bit hungry. Ever since her verbal bout with Cherish, she had not been able to shake the funk she allowed herself to slip into. Or rather that Cherish had shoved onto her. She tried her best to be civil to her sister, but she was damned if she was going to allow her family to continue to place her on the executioner's block. How they lived their lives was up to them and how she lived hers was up to her.

Well, her and Selby.

He tried his best to get her out of her sour mood, such as taking her out to eat. Even Edwin had attempted to swing her back into a cheerful demeanor as well, but both had failed. She was just too tired of being blamed for the decisions of others. It seemed to be the theme of her life of late.

"Would you folks like another drink?" The waitress stood, smiling, beside their table.

Selby didn't ask if Faith wanted one. He just ordered another round to go with the meal that had just arrived.

"Well, look who's out for an evening on the town."

As Faith glanced up, she saw her father standing there beaming as if his whole night had just been made. Beside him, purse over her crossed arms, stood Valerie Driscoll, a permanent snarl on her face.

"Care if we join you? I know you already have your food, but I feel like it's been forever since we've seen you two."

"You had lunch with her yesterday," Valerie reminded him.

Arni glanced over at his wife, an indulgent smile ignoring her correction. "I meant together. I haven't seen them together." He turned back to Selby and Faith. "May we?" He gestured to the empty seats at their table.

Faith wanted her dad to join them, but could do without Valerie gracing them with her presence. Still, you can't have one without the other usually, so Faith said yes as she motioned for them to take the empty chairs. Selby appeared as if he was trapped and wanted to run.

"So, what brings you two beachside?" Faith asked.

"We can't eat on this side of the bridge?" Valerie said as she draped her napkin over her lap.

"You can…"

"Eat wherever you like," Selby cut Faith off, probably expecting her to snap at her mother like she had her sister at work. "If you would have told us you were coming out we would have waited for you. It's always a treat to go out with you two."

Arni shot him a look that told Faith he knew Selby was lying, but trying to be nice. Her father gave a soft chuckle as he waved to the waitress. "Thanks, Selby. This, however, was a last minute idea. Valerie had liver planned and I just wasn't in the mood. Besides, a small writers' group meets over here and I was thinking of sitting in and seeing what it was all about."

Valerie rolled her eyes. Faith was about to make a biting remark, but Selby placed his hand on her arm and gave a slight squeeze. When

Faith turned to glare at him, he just smiled, brought her hand up to his lips and gave it a soft kiss. "That sounds like a great idea," he said as he turned his attention back to Arni. "Have you decided what you're going to write about, yet?"

Arni's face lit up, excited to be asked about his dream. "I want to write a Civil War story about two brothers fighting on opposite sides of the war and the girl they both fall in love with. I want it to take place in Mississippi and I plan on visiting there for some research as well as vacation time."

Selby nodded. "Sounds like a pretty good basis for a story. Have you written anything so far?"

The two men talked back and forth about Arni's book, Selby asking a question and Arni then going on for lengthy periods about what he foresaw in his story. Faith and her mother just sat and stared at their glasses. Her parents ordered their food and the waitress did her best to put a rush on it. Still Selby and Faith were finished with their meals by the time the other food arrived. Faith was ready to leave, but to her surprise as well as annoyance, Selby ordered another round of drinks and continued talking to her father. Both women glared at him.

Faith should have known, however. Selby could talk books for hours and her father always loved talking about a project of his when he was in the beginning phase. They could be there all night.

"Well, I'm excited for you, Arni," Selby said. "Not many people have the courage to follow their dreams. It's great to see you going after it."

Valerie made a grunt as she cut through some of her sirloin. "He could have written his book while teaching."

Arni took a deep breath. "I told you. I couldn't focus properly. Besides the after school activities, there are papers to grade and reports to read. Then you are always dragging us to those church functions you're so fond of. There just wasn't enough time in a day to get any real words in. This is my shot and I'm taking it."

Valerie spun around and glared at him. "I drag you to church? You don't want to be there? Well, don't make me force you to do anything, especially take care of your family. You can write your way into perdition for all I care. It's your life as you keep saying."

"It is his life," Faith snapped. "He has taken care of his family all of his life and done a damn good job of it. He deserves to take this chance."

"Another dreamer," Valerie said as she rolled her eyes.

"What's wrong with having dreams and going after them?"

"Nothing as long as your family doesn't suffer while you fritter your life away."

"Who is suffering by him taking this time to make it as a writer? His kids are grown and have families of their own. And Dad has always taken care of you, so I highly doubt you would ever suffer."

Arni reached across the table and tapped Faith's hand. "It's okay, honey. You don't need to defend me. Your mother will get used to it once she sees it will work out."

Faith turned to him. "Then I would love for you to convince your other daughter of that as well, because she is blaming me for you quitting your job."

"Blaming you? Whatever for?"

Selby sipped his drink and glanced at his watch. "Time to go, I think."

"Because she thinks that me living my life the way I want has forced you to quit your job and follow your dream."

"Well, it hasn't forced me to do anything, but it has given me the courage to take the chance. Life is too short, as you say, to not live life the way you want and do what makes you happy. I've seen how happy you two are and decided it was time to do the same. I see it more as you inspiring me than anything else."

Faith blushed and Valerie rolled her eyes. Selby called for the check and Arni changed the topic. "I hear you're going away for a week due to work. Is this a promotion or are you thinking of moving?"

Faith laughed, slightly. "Neither. Morgan wants my help getting an office back on track. They've had some personnel changes and things have become disorganized. He's impressed with the way I do things at Rutherford and has asked for my help in showing the new employees how to do things."

"Isn't that really Cherish's job?" Valerie asked, an eyebrow raised.

"It's not Cherish who has Rutherford running so smoothly," Selby interjected. "Faith has organized things at her office. Cherish likes to call out sick."

"She can't help that," Valerie said. "Jordie gets sick easily."

"Well, then it's a good thing she wasn't asked to go away for a week, huh?" Selby sipped the remainder of his drink as he signed the credit slip the waitress had left beside him. He stood and reached a hand out to Arni. "Thank you for joining us. I wish you the best with your writing. I really am excited about what you're doing."

Faith walked around and hugged her father goodbye and kissed his cheek. "So am I. I love you. Sorry for anything I said that may have upset you."

"Not at all, sweetie. Thanks for allowing us to join you. And trust me, it will be all right."

Valerie Driscoll remained seated and kept eating.

Twenty-Six

"You ready for your big weekend?" Edwin stood behind his desk buttoning his pants back into place. Faith still knelt on the floor by his chair, the office lights low.

"Yes and no. I'm excited for the opportunity, but nervous about being away. I'm also afraid of the mess I will find when I return."

"You don't think Nessa can handle it?"

"I'm afraid Cherish will drive her away." Faith was still angry about her sister's accusations and about her run in with her mother at dinner. She was tired of being the brunt of their unhappiness. Cherish would sabotage Nessa just so she could say that Faith hadn't trained her properly before leaving. She wanted Faith to fail and didn't care if it ruined another in the process.

"It'll be fine. All Nessa has to do is keep up with everything. There aren't any new jobs, so she won't have to worry about getting crews set up with stuff and even if there was, Terry can handle it."

Faith placed her hand on the desk and lifted herself to her feet, a look on her face that said she didn't believe Edwin's version of how things would go. "How about you? You going to miss our morning sessions?"

He walked over to her and placed his hand on her cheek as he gazed into her eyes, his filled with a longing she had not seen before. "More than you know. It's going to seem like an eternity."

Faith stepped into his arms as she slid hers around his waist, laying her head on his chest. "It is. I'm going to hate it. I just got used to this. I don't want you to forget me while I'm gone." She glanced up into his eyes, her face a serious mask. "And Nessa is only to take my place at my desk, not under yours."

Edwin laughed, his head tilting back as if he were laughing at the ceiling. "Promise. No hanky panky with Nessa."

"Or anyone else."

Edwin gazed down into her eyes, a soft smile on his lips. "Or anyone else."

She sighed as she laid her head back onto his chest. "I better go get set up for my training session."

She felt his lips on the top of her head. "Yeah, I guess you better. I'll check in on you."

She squeezed him tight. "I count on it for my sanity around here."

Nessa arrived as the doors opened, excited to learn something new and to do more than just answer the phones. Faith took her through the short steps of contracts and filing, what to do if a truck needed to be issued, and how to handle the job assignments in the computer. Regardless of Edwin's assurance to her that there would be no new jobs while she was gone and that Nessa would merely be handling normal paperwork, Murphy's Law dictated something unplanned was bound to happen.

"Could you teach a little quieter," Cherish snapped. She arrived thirty minutes late without as much as an "I'm sorry" or even a "Good morning." For the most part, she kept to herself, which was just fine with Faith.

Faith patted Nessa's hand as she ignored her sister. "Every once in a while, throw the lion a bone. She gets cranky if not fed properly."

Faith ignored the daggers she knew were being aimed at her back. Nessa's eyebrows rose with surprise, but she said nothing. With that mindset, Faith figured Nessa would survive the week filling in for her. Of course, Faith wasn't at all sure what she was going to be doing in Tampa with Morgan, but the trip was set and ready to go. A note had been waiting on her desk when she arrived that morning, telling her to be at the office by seven Monday morning and to pack for a week. There was a chance they might not stay the whole week, but it was better to be safe than sorry. The entire trip would be on the company checkbook—meals, room, transportation. Of course, Morgan was driving so no issue with transportation. Plus, she was going to be getting paid extra for making the trip. It would be like a working vacation.

"Are you excited?" Nessa asked.

Faith nodded. "Nervous. I've never been away from Selby that long. It's going to be strange."

"Is he jealous? Morgan's not a bad looking man." Nessa gave her a playful, mischievous look.

Faith laughed. "It's a business trip. Get your mind out of the gutter. Besides, Selby doesn't get jealous."

Nessa shrugged her soft shoulders, a knowing smile on her lips. "The gutter's more fun."

"How did you get Selby to allow you to go anyway?" Cherish cut in.

Faith glanced at her sister from over her shoulder. "I asked him. Are you saying Glen wouldn't trust you on a business trip?"

"I'm saying I'm surprised Selby trusts you. He must not be aware of your current behavior."

Faith spun around to face her sister, arms across her chest. "And just what is my current behavior?"

"I'm going to go get some water." Nessa stood and left the sisters to duke it out.

"You know what your behavior is like, you little slut. We've already had this conversation. You've been throwing yourself at anything with a penis. And what's with the sudden early mornings? Are you trying to fuck your way to the top? You think you're the only skirt Edwin chased around the office? You're not. He's a walking hard-on poking his way around for his next notch."

Faith glared at her. "So, have you been one of those notches and you're talking from experience or has he turned your advances down? Is that it? You're jealous that people pay me attention and you get ignored? Perhaps you should try loosening up a bit and having some fun. No wonder Glen looks so sad. He's married to a nun." Faith propelled herself out of her chair and flew from the room. It was probably better than flying into the rage she could feel boiling up inside of her.

Cherish was so judgmental about everyone except herself. She couldn't just be happy that Faith was happy. Oh, no. Cherish had to destroy it; call it ugly. Faith wasn't going to allow her to tarnish what was truly none of her business. She was having fun, and she was going to continue to have fun. Screw what Cherish thought.

"I take it that didn't go well." Nessa stood just inside the break room door, leaning back against the wall, sipping a bottle of water.

Faith shook her head. "Not hardly. She can be so damned condescending. It pisses me off."

Nessa turned and walked back into the break room. "C'mere and sit down."

Faith looked at her, confusion covering her face. "What?"

Nessa tucked some of her dark tresses behind her ears and gestured to one of the hard plastic chairs. "Here. Sit."

Faith finished entering the room, nervousness filling her. Nessa spoke to her as Edwin did when he wanted her to do something. It had instantly put her stomach in knots and made the nectar drip from her sweet lips.

Still, Faith obeyed, crossing the break room threshold and taking the seat in front of the honey-skinned woman, each step placed hesitatingly in front of the other. She wasn't sure what had started the butterflies in her stomach, but she knew her lace thong was already drenched.

Nessa set the bottled water on the table before putting both hands on Faith's shoulders and began to massage. "Oh, wow. Your sister has you all in knots. Why do you let her bother you so?" Nessa's fingers were small but there was strength in them. She squeezed and twisted Faith's shoulder and neck muscles with determination, grinding the tension from Faith's body.

Why *did* she allow Cherish to rile her up so much? It was a good question. She should be used to Cherish's tactics by now. Faith almost shrugged, but Nessa's hands kept her still. "I just hate judgmental people. Cherish is so much like my mother in that area that I can't stand it."

Faith closed her eyes and could feel Nessa's breasts rubbing across her back as the younger woman worked her magic. Nessa's breathing was in Faith's ears, steady and strong, in rhythm with the massage. Faith took a deep breath trying to shake the lustful thoughts in her mind, but it was impossible. She kept her legs closed, pressed together, hands prayer-like in her lap. Her body was still a fire from that morning's activities with Edwin with no release for her. Nessa may not have been purposefully trying to ignite Faith's inner flames, but it was working nevertheless.

"Yeah, I hate those types as well. People need to be free to live their life as they choose as long as they're not hurting anyone. Everyone has a right to enjoy their life. I'm lucky that my family respects how I choose to live my life. They may not approve, but they love me and don't condemn my choices."

"Choices? You seem pretty normal to me. What wouldn't your parents approve of?"

"They're parents. It's their job to hate our choices, especially if we're enjoying our life in a way that doesn't exactly match up with their views."

Nessa's fingers slid further down Faith's chest and Faith felt her breasts being pulled upward. Her nipples tightened at the sensation, becoming sensitive pearls against the fabric of her bra. Her breathing grew huskier, lusty.

"And...Um...I am enjoying my life," Faith mumbled, her head lolling forward. "What's wrong with having fun?"

"Nothing. Trust me, I like having fun."

Faith, lost in the pleasure of the massage, could only moan. "So do I." As Nessa worked her muscles, all Faith could think about was Tracey. At first, it caught her off guard that it wasn't Edwin in her thoughts, but then she thought it was because Tracey had become more aggressive in her thoughts and actions. The fiery redhead had taken charge while they were shopping and didn't seem at all hesitant about making Faith strip in front of her. While Edwin was the one Faith was exploring with, it was different with Tracey. The smaller woman was more like...family?

Faith popped her eyes open at the thought. *No. She's a friend. She's Selby's play partner. We're close, yes, but...*

245

Nessa squeezed tighter on Faith's shoulders jerking her thoughts back to the massage and who was actually giving it. "You're really good at this."

Nessa squeezed harder as she leaned close to Faith's ear and whispered, "You'd be surprised what my fingers are good at."

Faith heard herself moan at the thought of what those fingers could be massaging.

Faith focused on the Formica table in front of her. She could feel the naughty thoughts making her smile. "Perhaps one day I'll find out." Nessa may have thought Faith was referring to her, but it was Tracey consuming Faith's mind at the moment.

~ ~ ~ ~ ~

Tracey closed her Styrofoam container, lunch over for the day. "We should go dancing tonight. The clubs down here hop pretty well on the weekends. Might be fun before our girl leaves for a week." She dumped the trash into the waste basket behind the counter. "Unless, of course, you were planning to keep her all to yourself all weekend."

Selby watched as she tidied up from their afternoon meal. "No way. If I can have my two favorite ladies with me, I'll take it every time."

Tracey pushed up on her tiptoes and kissed his nose. "Good answer."

"I've been practicing." He smiled at her. "It's true. I stand in front of the mirror wondering what you might say and then rehearse my answers so I look sharp."

"I'm sure that's what you practice in front of the mirror." She leaned against him, her breasts firm against his chest, and gave him a slow, soft kiss. Her eyes were still closed when she pulled away, savoring the moment. When she opened them, his eyes were smiling at her. "I'll meet you at the Upper Floor around nine." She patted his thighs as she pushed away from him.

"We'll be there." He squeezed her hands tight before allowing her to walk away. As she closed the door, he couldn't help but think how wonderful his life was going at the moment. He never imagined having anyone else in his life besides Faith. Not only was he allowed to be with Tracey, but his wife had even suggested it. *Eat your hearts out, men.*

He walked to the door and stepped outside to the sidewalk. The March breeze blew, rustling the fallen leaves and keeping the day cool even though the sun beat down. With a quick nod, a decision was made.

Reaching back inside, he hung a sign on the bookstore door. "Closed due to illness." It wasn't really a lie. He *was* sick of working. He locked the door and started walking. It was a beautiful Friday and he didn't want to waste it by sitting in his musty bookstore. That was, after all, why he had gone into business for himself, to be able to enjoy moments such as this.

The March breeze was brisk, low seventies with no humidity. In Florida, you enjoyed those days to the fullest, because all too soon the temps hit the high nineties.

He crossed New Haven, walked down Glover to Melbourne Avenue and turned east toward the marina just past the railroad tracks that crossed Turkey Creek. Manatee Park sat along the waterline and bench-sitters could watch the round, gray sea cows floating around. It was popular with children and lovers. Selby liked it for the peaceful romance of the place. Something about being near the water calmed a person's spirit. He needed to come here more often.

Mullets broke the creek's surface every once in a while enjoying the sun for a brief second before falling back into the murky water. A bum slept on a white concrete bench under a massive oak and a couple strolled hand-in-hand along the wood deck path. Boats, the size of small houses, rocked slightly in the water where they were moored until whoever owned them needed to show them off again.

Selby watched the couple, their arms gliding back and forth, fingers interlaced, as they whispered the things lovers whispered to each other when alone. Their bodies pressed into each other, as if not able to get close enough.

Suddenly, Selby missed Faith. Next week would be long. Too long.

He pushed his hands into his jeans pockets and walked on, letting the future loneliness fall from his mind. It was just too gorgeous of a day for depressing thoughts.

~ ~ ~ ~ ~

Cherish had been stubbornly quiet the rest of the day for which Faith was grateful. It had enabled her to focus on Nessa's training until the younger woman was seeing dancing numbers in her vision. Finally, it was time to go home.

Edwin poked his head into the Girls' Den as Faith slung her purse over her shoulder. He glanced around the office. "Nessa gone?"

"As fast as she could." Faith laughed as she walked toward the door. Cherish punched away at her keys, ignoring both of them.

"How'd she do?" Faith gave him a rundown of the day and of Nessa's progress. Cherish pretended not to listen, but it was obvious she hung on every word, because her typing slowed a bit.

Edwin nodded, obviously satisfied at all he heard. "You ready for your night of dancing?"

"You keep pretty good tabs on your employees," Cherish said, her focus still on the monitor.

Faith knew it irked her sister that Edwin had known her plans and she didn't. "I am at that," Faith said as she crossed the room. At the door she patted Edwin's cheek. "Try not to miss me too much." She smiled as she slipped through the doorway.

"I'll walk you out," he offered as he turned to follow her out.

"An escort. Nice." Faith crooked her finger and motioned him to follow her.

The office was pretty deserted. Ashlynn had already left, Deon was on a job, and Grady had never shown up. Jed was in the back poring over blueprints and Terry was locking down the warehouse. As soon as they were out of earshot of any stragglers, Edwin said, "I have a meeting tomorrow with Mr. Polawski." Faith thought he was about to cancel their Saturday date, which would suck since it was only their second and would be her last before her trip. Instead, however, he asked to see her on Sunday.

"Going to miss my services while I'm gone, are you?" She smiled as she unlocked her truck.

"Yes, as a matter of fact. But, I'm going to miss you more than your talents."

She smiled as she turned to face him. "Good."

To be honest with herself, she knew she was going to miss Edwin's attention as well. She had grown to look forward to their bantering every day and their short but satisfying rendezvous.

"When?"

"I'll be here till 5:30."

"At the office?" Didn't they play enough at work?

"Grady's covering for me on Saturday, so I'm covering his Sunday. It's quiet. If anyone works it's in the morning. Will that be all right?"

She smiled up at him. "Yes, sir. You're the boss." She realized that she hadn't thought about clearing it with Selby first. She was going to do it. She had to. It was her last chance to be with Edwin before the trip. Selby would just have to understand.

"Good girl." He held her door open as she slid in, giving her a wink before walking away.

Her stomach was a gymnast competition as she thought about Edwin and wondered what he had in mind for Sunday. She fantasized about it all the way home, putting Cherish, her mother, and their bitchiness out of her mind. It would be something for her to remember while she was gone.

And she would need it.

Selby's car was already there when she pulled into the garage and Faith felt envious that he had started his weekend early. Still, that was her carefree husband, always at the whim of the weather. It was worse in the fall when leaves were falling and the air cooling. Then his mind was always drifting off with the breeze and she never knew where he would land. Of course, it was one of the things that had endeared him to her heart. Selby was never a nine to five type of guy, at least not for very long. It was probably due to the two years he wandered the mountainsides and Florida highways. He loved roaming and exploring. He had settled down for her and she couldn't begrudge his day trips

Faith passed through their front door at five thirty-five and Selby was already dressed in slacks and a long-sleeve lavender shirt, sipping hot tea. "There's my girl."

She slid up beside him, purse dangling from one hand as she wrapped the other around his neck. Their lips pressed in a tender lock of longing. She tousled his hair with her fingers as they pulled away. "I missed you, too, lover."

He patted her ass with that rogue grin plastered on his face. "I took the liberty of laying out your attire for the evening," he said. "I was thinking of dinner at that new sushi place before tripping the night fantastic."

"Dinner *and* dancing? I'm such a lucky girl."

Selby chuckled as he pushed her to the bedroom. "Yes, you are. Now, go get ready."

Twenty-Seven

Dinner was a succulent array of oysters, crab cakes, and salmon washed down with a crisp Chardonnay. Faith found herself giggling more and more as they talked across the table. Selby had reached across and caressed the back of her hand as she rested it on the hunter green table cloth. She couldn't take her eyes off him; his whole face seemed alight.

He had dressed her in three-inch heels, black, which matched her knee-length skirt. Her blouse was a silky lime, which he had her keep unbuttoned enough to allow her cleavage to turn several heads. She found herself blushing quite a bit, but had to admit, she loved the attention. He also laid out her black lace bra, but no panties. She loved the twists of her husband's mind.

"You are beautiful."

She felt the blush heat her cheeks. "You are blind." She felt beautiful, though. There, with him, dressed as she was. She felt sexy. Alive. She had never felt that way before.

He grinned at her. "That means I get to read you like Braille and run my fingers all over you."

"Now, that sounds promising."

After dinner, Selby drove them over the bridge to the Downtown night life. Old fashioned lamp posts lit that section of New Haven as streams of people flowed along the sidewalks and even into the street.

It was one giant party with pit-stops for alcohol and dancing. The Upper Floor was a two-story pub with the band blaring from the top floor and an outside deck that filled up quickly. It was popular with the upper-twenties crowd with their jeans and untucked shirts and short skirts and cleavage down to the navel. Sexuality oozed from every pore of every patron. Everyone in the place was beautiful, even the ones who weren't very pretty. Couples snuggled in the corner, groups of friends huddled over a two foot by two foot table, and men as well as ladies prowled for that night's hook-up.

Faith had never been to a dance club before meeting Selby. Her mother thought them cesspools of sexual deviance and so Faith had dutifully avoided them to keep her mother appeased. Of course, that never stopped Cherish from enjoying the smoke-filled dens of iniquity. She would go out two or three times a week, staying out until dawn and only then slinking back into her room, still intoxicated and smelling like yesterday's ashtray. Their mother never quizzed her or scolded her. Cherish got away with everything. She still did.

But not Faith. The one time Faith had even tried to taste a glass of wine with dinner, her mother had gone off on her as if she had put Christ on the Cross herself. Faith never asked again. Of course, that didn't stop her father from taking her to the garage and allowing her to have her first taste of everything. Wine. Beer. Bourbon. Coconut rum. Faith's father had a locked tool cabinet that didn't have any tools in it. He kept his secret fun stuff tucked safely away, out of reach of the long arm of Valerie Driscoll. He followed his wife to church and supported Dennis' ministry ambitions, but thought too much religion shrunk your smile as well as your heart.

Faith always wondered how her father stayed married to her mother for forty-four years. He'd always shrug and say, "I like her meat loaf." Truth was he thought everyone was quirky and you just took people as they were. Her mom wasn't always so bitter and Faith could remember some hilarious moments. Just none recently.

"Malibu and cranberry?" Selby asked as they found a table in the corner and he helped her slide in.

"Please." She smiled and knew his next comment.

"Predictable."

"I'll be more adventurous later," she said.

"Now *that* sounds promising." He wiggled his eyebrows as he disappeared into the mayhem for their drinks.

Selby had been the one to take Faith to her first club. He had noticed her swaying beside the car to a Brittany Spears song and asked her if she liked to dance.

"Southern Baptists don't dance," she told him.

He just laughed. "Everyone dances, little lady. Some just never do it outside their homes. I promise you, the preacher who told you not to dance will grab his wife around the waist and grind against her in the kitchen while she's trying not to burn the potatoes."

Faith laughed at the image because the preacher at the time was a short, balding man in his late sixties while his wife was a plump, blue-haired lady. Not the grinding couple.

Selby took her that very weekend to a restaurant on the beach that turned night club after nine and helped her ease out onto the dance floor. The crowd was a mixture of gray-hairs all the way to barely drinking age, but everyone was dancing away as the live band rocked through the music that spanned four decades. She had loved the place and the freedom. No one knew her there and she was able for the first time to cut loose and have fun. She danced to almost every song. Selby had bought her drinks while he sipped on water, so she felt safe.

Faith glanced across the dance floor as Selby weaved his way among Upper Floor's patrons, drink in each hand. She always felt safe with Selby—then and now. He was always her safety net for when she wanted to try some new stunt. She smiled as he slid up beside her, comforted in the knowledge of their love and strength.

Selby slid the drinks in front of her as he scooted into the booth. "And what's brought a smile to your face?" He leaned in and nuzzled his nose against her neck before kissing her ear.

She squirmed a little, feeling the electricity shouting from her neck to the pinkness between her legs. "Just thinking of how much I love you."

"And here I thought you were having dirty thoughts."

"With you, always." She giggled as she felt his hand caress her thigh, fingers just lightly brushing her skin. She sucked in a breath at his touch and braced for more of his pleasure.

He teased her flesh only slightly more as he sucked her ear lobe. When he pulled away, he wore that Cheshire Cat grin that screamed mischief. "You, Mister, are bad," she said.

His grin grew until it crinkled his eyes. "I know." He sipped his Maker's Mark and then said. "Let's dance."

Lady Gaga gyrated from the house speakers as the people on the dance floor twisted and gyrated against whoever was next to them. It was a free flowing groove with people just lost in the music. Faith draped her arms around Selby's neck as his went to her hips, crotches sliding up and down, simulating what they both wanted to be doing instead of dancing. Soon Enrique took over for Gaga, but Faith never let go. She loved the tightness of his muscles when he danced and couldn't deny how sexy it made her feel.

After a couple more dances, Faith was ready for another drink and Selby needed to hit the head. "You get them, gorgeous. Tab's open. I'll be back in a couple of shakes."

"Gross." Faith kissed him, while she laughed at his attempt at humor. "Now, go."

Selby squeezed her hand and then began the winding path to the men's room. She watched him leave, her eyes enjoying the tightness of his ass until he disappeared through a bright orange door. Once he had vanished from sight, Faith weaved her way to the bar where a young man dressed in black pants and black dress shirt waited to take her order. As soon as she placed it, he turned to his bottles and Faith leaned on the bar, fingers intertwined, waiting.

"Having fun?"

The feminine voice startled her out of her private reverie and she turned to see Tracey perched on a bar stool beside her, smiling and toying with a strand of red hair. Faith felt her cheeks flush as she thought of her fantasy from earlier while Nessa had been massaging her shoulders. The auburn-haired woman wore a simple blue dress, low-cut and at mid-thigh. Faith glanced at the tan flesh of her exposed breasts and felt the heat rush out of her even more. She quickly glanced away, hoping Tracey hadn't noticed.

She heard the other woman slide closer, felt the warm touch of Tracey's hand on her thigh, grazing upward. Faith tried not to move, but her legs seemed to part of their own. The redhead's fingers were cool and a little damp from where she had been holding her own drink a moment before. She raised her eyebrows at Faith who had forgotten she had been asked a question.

"Y-yes. Yes, actually I am." She tried to control her voice, but was having problems as Tracey's hand inched upward.

"I saw you dancing with Selby earlier," Tracey went on as if her fingers weren't inches from Faith's sweet passage. "You two looked great together out there."

Faith glanced around, praying it wasn't obvious what was happening. The place was dark and everyone else was lost in their own pursuits. Turning her head back to the mirror behind the bar, Faith leaned in closer, trying to hide herself. The bartender returned with her drinks and she gave him Selby's name for the tab. As the man thanked her, she felt Tracey's fingers brush against her bare pussy. She gasped at the touch and even though she knew she should have pulled away, she felt her body push against the fingers lightly caressing her.

"Thank you," she said, but she wasn't sure if it was for the compliment or the fingers.

Tracey continued to talk, asking questions of Faith's night, how she enjoyed dancing. The conversation was normal if anyone happened to be close enough to hear. Except, they would have noticed Faith had a hard time answering. Tracey's fingers pressed against the standing woman's sensitive pearl, pressing on it as she twirled in small circles. Faith could feel the moisture building, the orgasm cresting as a wave on the ocean. She struggled to hide what was going on. She opened her eyes and stared into the mirror.

And saw Selby staring at her with a confused look on his face.

~ ~ ~ ~ ~

Selby washed his hands, tossing the Eco-friendly towel into the over-flowing trash bin as he pushed his way back out to the crowded bar. The place seemed to have doubled in occupancy since he had entered the restroom. Most of the tables were full with people lining the walls and crowding around the dance floor. First, he glanced at their table, assuming Faith had beaten him back, but it was empty. Glancing at the bar, he finally found her. He could see in the mirror behind the bar that she had their drinks, but she wasn't moving. It was then that he spotted Tracey perched on a barstool beside his wife. A smile pushed his cheeks up seeing the two of them together. He was glad Tracey had showed up since dancing was her idea.

He started to make his way to the girls and then stopped. Faith's eyes were closed and her facial expression was...different. He tried to get a better look at what was going on, but the crowded dance floor was between them and people gyrated across his line of sight. Faith opened her eyes and they saw each other.

He grinned. Selby knew that expression.

~ ~ ~ ~ ~

Tracey could see Selby watching them through the crowd thanks to the mirror behind the bar. "Keep watching your husband, Faith," Tracey whispered. "It was nice of you to leave the panties at home."

"It was Selby's idea." She almost panted the words.

"Remind me to thank him."

Faith started to groan and then bit her lower lip against it. She stared into Selby's eyes, focusing on him as Tracey strummed her slit. Faith felt the other woman's fingers slip inside her slick channel as a thumb replaced the fingers on her swollen clit and gasped before she could stop it. She wasn't sure what had brought out this aggressive side of Tracey or if Selby had set it up, but she would have to thank him, as well.

"You're such a good girl," the other woman whispered. "And also a very naughty girl. Is this what you meant by taking risks? Think of it, Faith. A crowded bar, your husband watching, and I'm about to make you come. And Edwin's not here. You want to come, don't you? Right here? Right now?"

Faith kept her eyes locked onto Selby's as she nodded. "Oh god, yes."

"Right here at the bar?" Tracey's fingers worked faster, curled inside just enough to reach that sweet spot.

"Please."

"Such a naughty girl, aren't you?"

"Yes! Yes, I am. Please."

Faith felt her knees weaken and held herself tighter to the bar. The bartender came over noticing that the two of them were still there. "Anything else I can get you ladies?"

"No!" Faith almost screamed. "No, thank you."

She felt the thumb dig into her clit and the wave crashed upon the shore of ecstasy. Her mouth opened in a silent "Oh" as her release sent tendrils of pleasure through her.

The bartender walked away, a confused smile on his face.

As Tracey's fingers slid from her sex, Faith groaned with sensitive want. She felt the other woman wipe her fingers on the black skirt before bringing them up and grabbing her sweaty glass. With a smile, Tracey caught Faith's eyes in the mirror. "Shall we join Selby now? Before his drink totally waters down."

"I'll buy him another."

Twenty-Eight

The midmorning sun beat down upon Faith as they lay in lounge chairs along the sandy Atlantic shore. She wore sunglasses over closed eyes and tried not to move. She had downed half a bottle of aspirin and an equal amount of coffee. It had been way too long of a night. Tracey joined them for the rest of the evening, dancing and drinking. Faith wasn't sure when they had arrived back home. Or how.

She heard Selby turn the page of whatever thick volume he was reading and she winced at even that slight noise.

"It's not fair," she said.

"What's that?" His voice was distant and she knew he hadn't even taken his eyes off the page. She'd smack the book out of his hand if she could move.

"Why aren't you in as much pain as I am?"

Now she heard him close the book. "Let's see, three shots of tequila, five of your Malibu and cranberries, and two Alabama Slammers. I do believe your pain is self-inflicted, my love."

"So? You drank as much as I did."

At that he chuckled and the urge to smack him increased. "Hardly. I only did one shot and after my second drink, I switched to water."

"Only you and I kept drinking," Tracey said as she walked in front of them.

Faith tensed, her eyes opening wide. Tracey had spent the night? Where did she sleep? She hadn't seen the other woman when she woke up that morning.

"Here," Tracey said, "I brought everyone a bacon and egg sandwich. I hope you don't mind. I raided your kitchen."

Her voice was way too chipper after a night like they had. Faith lifted her sunglasses and stared at the redhead. She had raided more than the kitchen. She was wearing one of Faith's two pieces, one of the skimpier ones.

"I never turn down food no matter where it comes from," Selby said as he reached for a sandwich.

Faith took the offered food with a whispered, "Thanks." Confusion mixed with residual intoxication in her mind.

"You two were pretty hilarious, matching each other drink for drink. I almost didn't make it to the car with both of you."

"Were we that bad?" Tracey asked around a mouthful of egg muffin.

"Oh, I'm sure everyone loved the show you two put on on the dance floor. I'm surprised we didn't get tossed out for indecent exposure."

Faith looked at Selby with a shocked look. "What did we do?"

Selby grinned at her. "Well, the way you two were grinding against each other, they knew you weren't wearing undies."

Closing her eyes, Faith allowed her head to fall back on the lounge chair, embarrassment reddening her face. She would never drink again. Hell, she'd never leave the house again.

It didn't help that Tracey was only giggling. "Did she really scream out, 'Make way for my lesbian lover'?"

Selby started laughing harder. "She did, clearing a path on the dance floor to the exact middle. Then, when I finally got her to the car, she had to pee, so she lifted her skirt and went right there in the parking lot."

Faith covered her face with her hands, the heat of the sun no match for the heat of the embarrassment on her face. "And you didn't stop me?" How could she have allowed herself to get so out of control?

"And let you pee in my car?"

Tracey must think her a fool, but all the other woman did was laugh.

She felt Tracey's lips on her fingers, which were covering her face. "It's okay, sweetie. We all get that way once in a while."

"I want to die." What she really wanted was to kill Selby, but not in front of a witness. It was one thing to behave the way she did when Selby and she were in another city surrounded by strangers. Or, in a private spot with Edwin, but in a bar where people who knew her could see her? How could Selby allow her to get that far out of control?

"It's fun to cut loose. No harm; no foul," Tracey said as she sat on the sand in front of the couple.

Faith dropped her hands to her sides and stared at the redhead smiling up at her. "Did we ..?"

Tracey and Selby both chuckled, but it was Tracey who answered. "Did we have hot, amazing sex? No, sweetheart. We didn't. I wouldn't let you take advantage of me." She grinned around her bottle of water.

"I tried....to...you know?" She felt her face going even redder.

"Oh. Yeah," Selby said through a mouthful of his sandwich, pushing some egg back into his mouth with his finger. "In the bar, the car, the driveway, and the house. You even said you had been thinking about her all day."

Faith focused on her food. No more drinking for her. She finished her sandwich and then laid her head back and allowed the sun to punish her. She couldn't deny that she was having fun. And she had been thinking about the smaller woman. So, why the embarrassment afterward? Tracey talked as if it were all a natural occurrence in life. Perhaps for the redhead it was. For Faith, it was still all very new. She had never thought of having sex with a woman before. It went against everything that had been ingrained into her. So had fucking someone other than your husband for that matter, but she wasn't having any problem with that.

She glanced over at the two beside her and suddenly, she was regretting agreeing to go to Tampa. The adventure was here, right in front of her. And it was just kicking into high gear. What would happen in a week's time? Would momentum wane? And then she wondered why Morgan asked her instead of Cherish. True, Faith was the one busting her ass the whole time while Cherish took numerous smoke breaks, but her sister had the position and the seniority. Faith was just a grunt. Was it possible Morgan wanted to promote her? Rutherford was putting together a traveling team to open new offices and expand. Perhaps this was his way of seeing if Faith could handle it.

She turned and saw Selby stretched out on his lounge chair, his nose buried in Emma by Jane Austin. He was one of the few people she knew who could get absorbed in any genre. Books were like music to him. He liked them all. The question was did she want to be away from him for week long periods of time? What if it was longer?

Faith glanced at Tracey and found herself blushing. This woman had inserted herself deeper into their lives, and not just Selby's life, but both of them. She made Faith do things she had always been repulsed by before and Faith wasn't sure what to do with it. There was that voice telling her it was wrong. Yet, she couldn't deny the flutter of her heart and the warmth that heated her sweet passage. She found her eyes drawn to the fall of auburn locks as they hung free as Tracey tilted her head back to catch the sun with her face. The taut skin of her graceful neck led to her tender globes encased in a flimsy white bikini top that Faith had forgotten she owned. Selby must have loaned it to her. The material was thin and Faith could see Tracey's nipples pushing against the fabric, straining for freedom. Her stomach was flat and firm and while her body had small dustings of freckles, they enhanced her beauty instead of detracting from it. Her legs were not long, but they were dancer legs, strong and beautiful. Her arms were slender and fingers small, but they carried a strength that Faith had felt between her legs. She felt her face blush at the memory of the two of them at the bar. She made herself look away from the woman stretched out before her and gazed at the ocean.

A sand crab skittered sideways along the grayish sand avoiding the foamy pounding of a wave redecorating the shore. The soft roar of the ocean drifted over them. Faith stared at the choppy sea. How could she be thinking of Tracey the way she was? And what of Selby? Or Edwin? Where did Edwin even fit into all of this? He was fun, no doubt, and the game that they had started was a thrilling rush that

Faith was enjoying too much to abandon. She had no idea where it would go or how far, but she didn't want to lose it. To be honest, she needed it and she had no idea why. She knew she couldn't have gone through with it if her marriage wasn't secure. Selby and she had never been stronger. Her adventures with Edwin actually excited him as much as they did her.

She took a deep breath. What Bizzaro world had she stepped into?

~ ~ ~ ~ ~

"I think I overdid it," Faith said as they passed through the sliding door to the Florida room. Her skin was the color of the inside of her favorite steak. She felt microwaved and she was sure her flesh had shrunk on her body. How long had they been out there?

"You are kinda reddish," Tracey said, her face puckered in empathy at what Faith must be feeling.

Selby merely chuckled and shook his head.

"I know, I know." Faith dropped her towel on a wicker chair as she passed through to their bedroom.

Tracey glanced back and forth between the two. "What am I missing?"

Passing through the inside slider and into the bedroom, Faith reached behind her and pulled her bathing suit top loose. "He has no sympathy for Floridians who get sunburned. We should know better."

"Bully." Tracey swatted Selby as she took Faith by the arm and led her to the king-size bed. "Here, dear, lay down. We need to get some aloe on those burns." Tracey pushed Selby toward the bedroom door. "You can get us some water with lemon slices."

Selby grinned, giving the fiery redhead a mock salute before leaving the two girls alone.

Faith allowed herself to be eased onto their chocolate comforter. She wasn't sure how to refuse Tracey, even if she had wanted to. That was also her confusion. She didn't know if she wanted to refuse the other woman anything.

Tracey's fingers grazed her sensitive flesh as Faith's bikini top was pulled off her scorched flesh. She winced, both from the sting as well as the sudden exposure.

"Oh, baby. Ouch." Tracey tsked, looking at the lobster color that encircled the death white flesh that had been hiding under the bathing suit. "You really did a number. Now, we've got to get the rest of you tanned." She caressed the pale flesh with her fingers as she pushed Faith backward, making her lie down. With tender fingers, Tracey gently pulled the bottoms down Faith's scorched legs and off her body. She tossed them toward the closet door without thought.

Faith tried to cover her intimate parts only to have Tracey smack her hands away. "I've fingered this body, silly girl. Besides, we have the same parts. Now, roll over."

With embarrassed reluctance, Faith rolled onto her stomach, the backs of her hands overlapping as a make shift pillow for her right cheek. She closed her eyes wanting to hide her nakedness. Why was she giving into this woman? She gasped as the cold of the aloe gel bit her heated skin and was inwardly glad that she was sun burnt to keep Tracey from feeling how her body was reacting. Of course, if her fingers came near Faith's pussy, she'd know for sure.

With slow but strong circles, Tracey worked the healing gel into Faith's reddened skin, massaging as she went. Faith quickly forgot her unease about being naked, lost in the working of Tracey's hands. A moan squeezed past her lips as she heard Selby come back into the room, glasses clinking with floating ice.

"Now, this is a sight I can get used to," he said as he set the water glasses on the oak nightstand.

"Spoken like a man," Tracey said.

Faith felt the depression of the bed on her left side and then Selby had one of her feet in his hands massaging with his thumbs. She laid there, a gelatinous mass under the two sets of hands that worked her body over. More lotion was applied and rubbed in as Tracey massaged down her back and over her rounded ass-cheeks, putting lotion even on skin that didn't need it. She moved to Faith's thighs before the prone woman could get nervous about the other's hands. Selby set one foot down and picked up the other, his hand kneading at her muscles.

When Tracey finished with the front of Faith's thighs she swatted Faith's ass and told her to flip over. Faith hesitated. Her exposed ass was one thing, but to open her most intimate parts for casual observation? It didn't help that she was the only one naked.

Tracey swatted her ass again. "Over."

Faith felt Selby pulling her foot around, twisting her to the left so that she would flip to her back. She took a deep breath and followed his lead. She avoided eye contact with either of them as she shifted to her back, choosing to focus on the dark ceiling fan above her.

"So shy," Tracey said softly in a tsk-tsk voice.

The cold of the aloe fell above Faith's breasts and her body tensed as Tracey's hands started massaging the gel into her reddened skin.

"Relax."

It was easily said, but not so easily obeyed. Faith felt the tiny hands massaging her pale globes, the soft fingers flicking over her nipples as they hardened under the touch. Did she moan? Oh god, she hoped not. How embarrassing to be getting aroused at the woman's touch.

Tracey slid her hands from Faith's breasts to stomach, rubbing the lotion in with slow, steady circles. Faith tensed as she felt Tracey's fingers getting closer and closer to her...

And then Tracey was massaging Faith's thighs, squeezing, caressing. Faith let-out a slow breath, relaxed that the other woman had not...

But then she felt Tracey's fingers slowly inching higher, closer to the wetness that Faith knew was glistening from her soft mound. She felt her body tense again as her legs slid apart allowing Tracey access to work—or play.

Faith opened her eyes and glanced down at Selby who was on the edge of the bed watching, his face wearing a soft smile. Tracey was sitting at Faith's knees, her hands massaging the inner thighs. Faith glanced at her, the auburn haired woman smiling down at her, her face a light dusting of freckles that the sun had brought out. Their eyes met and stayed locked for a moment.

Then Tracey lowered her mouth to Faith's slick channel and blew softly on the tiny pearl, her hair cascading in a canopy around her, hiding her face. Faith felt her body arch, her hips rising to meet the other woman's lips. Her body wanted the forbidden kiss, craved it no matter how her mind fought against it.

With one hand holding Faith's thigh and another on her hip, Tracey brushed her lips against the soft folds of Faith's labia. Shots of passion went through Faith, her body tensing and a moan escaping her lips. She felt the warmth of Tracey's tongue slip between her pussy lips, licking its way up to the sensitive bud at the top of Faith''s sex. Fingers gripping the quilt, Faith found herself pushing upwards to gain more of Tracey's touch. Her breath panted as her body tensed. Tracey kissed her clitoris before sucking it into her mouth, flicking it with her tongue.

Faith moaned louder, spreading her legs, giving Tracey full access to her warm channel. She felt the other woman slip between her legs and continue to love on her honey.

The bed moved beside Faith and she glanced over to see Selby kneeling beside her, his pride aching for attention. When he had stripped, she didn't know. With a hunger she took him into her mouth, her tongue swirling around the rim of his bulbous head. She slid a hand under him, cupping his hairy balls, massaging them. His hand fell to her head as she bobbed back and forth on his hardness.

She moaned as Tracey slid two fingers into her, pumping as her tongue lapped at the swollen pearl. Faith's body shuddered and rocked as it cried out for release.

Selby slipped from Faith's lips and slid off the bed. Faith watched with glazed eyes as he ran a hand down Tracey's back, fingernails grazing the woman's flesh. When he reached the skimpy bottoms of her bathing suit, he slid them off, leaning down and kissing the softness of her ass. With the bathing suit bottoms tossed to the floor, he eased two fingers into the tight red curls between her legs. Faith saw the passion in his eyes, the grin on his face. He was watching her as he toyed with Tracey's wetness.

Faith smiled back and nodded.

Selby continued to watch Faith as he knelt behind Tracey, his hands on her hips. With a steady push he speared the pink slit with his hard cock and slowly rocked back and forth. Tracey moaned into Faith's pussy and pressed harder as she licked with faster relish. Faith moaned and it was all she needed to let herself go. She gripped the comforter, pulling it to her as her body arched. Her cries of pleasure, passion, filled the room, mixed with Tracey's whimper as Selby rammed into her.

As Faith's body started to relax, Tracey laid her head on her thigh as Selby took her. Faith watched the pleasure on both their faces, felt Tracey's hands gripping her hips, saw the woman's body tense and knew the climax that ripped through both of them. It was as if she felt both of their orgasms in her body as the bed rippled under her.

Selby slowed the pumping of his hips as their bodies relaxed. He slid from behind Tracey and laid beside Faith, kissing her softly as his fingers pulled at strands of her hair. Tracey crawled up to Faith's other side and Faith pulled her toward her, brushing her lips against the other's. She felt Tracey's arm slide over her belly and squeeze. Everyone was still breathing heavy as Selby draped a leg over Faith's thighs.

She didn't know what to think. Cocooned between semi-naked bodies, she decided not to think and instead closed her eyes and slept.

~ ~ ~ ~ ~

Selby felt sleep pull at his eyelids as he laid there, his fingers entangled in Faith's hair. His leg lay draped across Faith's and he could feel the warmth of Tracey's thigh with his knee as well as her hand as it rested between Faith and himself. Both ladies were already sound asleep, exhausted from the previous night, the warm sun, and their recent escapade atop the sheets. He was ready for a nap, as well.

Yet, his mind wouldn't shut down enough. He stared over Faith to Tracey and wondered where she fit into the whole scheme of things. She was no longer the friend who ran the bakery. He felt drawn to her in ways he had never felt since Faith walked into his life. As he told her the other day at lunch, she was family.

He smiled at the way her eyes never completely closed when she slept; her lips slightly parted, as well. He could smell the aroma of their passion mixed with the aloe and he couldn't help but be content.

He picked up a strand of Faith's hair between his fingers and pulled it gently into the air, smiling as each strand slipped free and fell back to the bed. She was the woman who had saved him, really. She taught him to open up and trust again, to love. She had his heart. So why was he feeling this tug toward Tracey?

By the time sleep had captured him, he still had not found an answer to where Tracey fit in the scheme of things. She was no longer the friend who ran the bakery. He felt drawn to her in ways he had never felt since Faith walked into his life. As he told her the other day at lunch, she was family.

He smiled at the way her eyes never completely closed when she slept; her lips slightly parted, as well. He could smell the aroma of their passion mixed with the aloe and he couldn't help but be content.

He picked up a strand of Faith's hair between his fingers and pulled it gently into the air, smiling as each strand slipped free and fell back to the bed. She was the woman who had saved him, really. She taught him to open up and trust again, to love. She had his heart. So why was he feeling this tug toward Tracey?

By the time sleep had captured him, he still had not found an answer.

Twenty-Nine

"Have you thought about what you're going to wear on your trip?" Tracey sat cross-legged on the bed as Faith folded a basket of towels. They had taken almost a two-hour nap and when they awoke, Selby decided the night called for Ribeyes and Merlot, so he headed to the market.

Faith decided she needed to do some laundry before the trip and Tracey wasn't leaving until she had her steak. So, Faith loaned the other woman some gym shorts and an old Green Lantern T-shirt, much to Selby's dismay who was hoping the girls would stay naked for the remainder of the day. He was even willing to grill the perfect steak for them in return. They, of course, laughed as they shook their heads, but promised perhaps after they tasted the steaks they might accommodate the pouting man.

Faith had laughed at the time, but later was shocked at her quick agreement to the promise. All of their sexual exploits, not that there had been many, had either been with single men or couples, never just a woman. Selby had always wanted to make sure Faith had someone to focus on. She had never been confident as to how she would feel with just two women and him since she wasn't into women. Yet, even though she still wasn't interested in having sex with another woman, with Tracey it just seemed...different. She wasn't sure how to explain it to herself nevertheless anyone else.

"I'm not sure I like this two-on-one," Selby said as he scooped the keys to the Accord off the counter.

"I'll remind you of that," Tracey said with a grin.

With an over-dramatic sigh, he said something about never winning and left.

Tracey volunteered to do the dishes while Faith sorted the laundry, a task that seemed so mundane after their morning. Eventually, however, the two women wound up back in the bedroom.

Faith shook her head. "Not really, other than my Mario Brothers pajamas."

Tracey raised her eyebrows. "You're kidding, right? That's not sexy at all."

Faith laughed as she put a navy blue towel on top of a growing stack. "I'm not going for sexy. I'm going for work."

"So? Who says you can't have both? The two of you have opened up your sex lives to others. Is this a no-play week?" Tracey pulled a red towel from the basket, shaking it out before folding it. "A solid week surrounded by construction workers and a free room? Sounds like party central to me. And don't tell me you don't mix work with pleasure. I know better, remember? Or would your *boss* get upset?"

Faith walked over to the closet and slid the pocket door open. How would Edwin feel about her fucking someone else? Since she had started her game with Edwin, she hadn't even thought about playing with anyone else. He had consumed her attention and time. They had also never talked about it, so she wasn't really sure how he would feel about her with a man outside of Selby and him. For that matter, how would she feel? The game she was playing with Edwin was one thing. To go to Tampa with Morgan for business with some fringe benefits was something else entirely. Morgan was a cocky bastard who had ruined three marriages because of his habits. Faith thought it too much to get involved in. Of course, as Tracey pointed out, there were other possibilities.

"I do need to dress to impress, however. Right?" She shot a grin over her shoulder at the redhead on the bed.

Tracey returned the grin as she pushed herself off the bed and practically hopped to where Faith stood. "Now, *that's* my girl."

"Funny, I thought she was *my* girl." Selby stood in the door frame, one arm stretched across, leaning on the wood.

Tracey shrugged and then patted Faith's ass. "Not today."

Faith smiled with a tilt of her head. "Sorry, love. Looks like I've been stolen." Both ladies dove back into the closet, clothes on the brain.

~ ~ ~ ~ ~

Selby watched as they disappeared into the walk-in closet, both giggling about whatever women giggle about as they plot and plan in closets. He had never seen Faith have so much fun, not with another woman anyway. Faith didn't mix with other females well. She preferred simple things, non-frilly things. She was a tom boy at heart while most of the women she grew up with preferred prissy things and mindless chatter. Or, they were the abrasive, feminist type who hated men and saw them merely as sperm donors and if they could get the sperm without touching the cock they would. Faith had always gotten along with men better. In high school her best friends had always been boys. Not much had changed in almost fifteen years.

Selby pushed himself off the door frame and left the women to the dress up. He decided then would be a good time to get lost in a book. It was obvious the women were bonding. He just wasn't sure where that bond was leading. They were both loners for the most part and, outside of family, Tracey was the first to enter their home. Selby and Faith thrived on each other, reading, traveling, and the beach. Unless there was a required family gathering, they were quite comfortable with just the two of them, alone, exploring their minds and bodies. Both had been severely hurt by the outside world, by friends and lovers, even by family. Those few they had met on their weekend adventures were never contacted again. Faith had her coworkers, but up until Edwin, they had remained at work. Selby had had Tracey.

Now they both had her.

He stood in his library, staring at a book shelf, not really focusing on any one book. He turned his head in the direction of the master bedroom as if he could see through the walls to where the girls were pulling outfits off hangers. Tracey was bringing down both of their defenses and it scared him. Fulfilling fantasies and exploring their desires was one thing. This was more. He wasn't sure what it was, but it was definitely more than sex.

~ ~ ~ ~ ~

The day started to cool as the sky shifted to the gray of dusk, storm clouds in the west causing a cool breeze to blow in from the river. Selby stood at the grill thinking more of the two girls bantering in the kitchen over salad as they sipped a cheap Merlot. He flipped the steaks and then closed the lid. Cupping his own goblet, the stem dangling between his index and middle fingers, he crossed the deck to the railing over-looking the dunes. The ocean reflected the approaching night with a ripply streak of white where the rising moon grazed the Atlantic.

The sliding glass door opened and closed behind him and he heard the soft pad of bare feet on wood. He didn't turn. It could only be one of two people and he would welcome the company of either. A hand started at his waist and slid upward to his neck, a small hand.

Cocking his head to the left, he smiled as Tracey, her hand back at his waist, joined him at the rail. She held a full glass of wine in her other hand. "I was sent to check on the steaks as the rest of the meal is almost ready."

Selby reached a hand across her face and brushed a loose strand of hair from her eyes. "About five more minutes." He glanced back at her pale green eyes, searching her face, for what, he didn't know. "You doing all right?"

Tracey took his hand and squeezed. "Yes. I've had a great time with both of you. You finally had your fantasy of the three of us fulfilled, unless all of those teasing suggestions weren't really sincere." She smiled up at him, eyebrow raised.

"Oh no, it was definitely what I've wanted."

"How about you? You doing okay?"

He took a sip of his wine to delay his answer. The truth, however, was that he was doing great. Better than great, really. He licked the dry red from his lips as he nodded. "I am. Everything's seemed so, well, so easy, comfortable."

"You wanted it to be hard?" Her face held a wry grin.

He laughed. "Nice." Then, he shook his head. "I didn't want anything, really. Or rather, I never expected anything." He turned to her and ran a finger over her cheek. "But I'm glad I got it."

"So am I." They both stared at each other, their eyes speaking what their lips were not ready to say. "Now, I think your five minutes are up."

Selby downed his last swallow of wine before handing her the glass. "I'll get the meat, if you'll get the wine."

She took the glass in one hand and rubbed his cock through his pants with the other. "I've already had your meat, but I'll go ahead and get the wine." She squeezed his stiffening member once before turning and walking away. "Oh, and after dinner, I'm taking Faith to my place for a bit," she said over her shoulder. "The woman needs something sexy for her trip."

He watched her walk back into the house, her small rounded ass swaying slightly as she did. She probably knew he was watching. What man wouldn't be? Selby shook his head, a smile creasing his face, and went to check the steaks. Life was good.

~ ~ ~ ~ ~

The rain was like ice pelting them as Faith and Tracey ran from the small Toyota to the steps of Tracey's apartment. The overhang was just enough to keep the rain off Faith's head, but her backside was taking a shower, a very cold shower.

Once they were able to drip their way inside, the air conditioned air sent shivers through Faith's soaked body. She wanted to fling the water off her as she huddled within herself, arms wrapped around her, but she didn't want to drench Tracey's spotless apartment.

"I'll grab some towels," Tracey said as she darted through the apartment to a doorway on her left.

Faith continued to rub her arms as she stood trying not to drip on anything. As she stood on the tile foyer floor, she took in the apartment, surprised at how big the inside actually was. She smiled at the gold metal butterflies that Tracey had fluttering up one wall and loved the peacefulness of them. Everything seemed in its place and a perfect fit for where she had placed it.

The smaller woman walked back in and tossed Faith a thick towel. "Here, before you catch a cold and I have to listen to Selby whine. You should probably strip out of those clothes, as well. I can toss them in the dryer if you want or give you another pair of shorts to wear."

Faith laughed as she started to rub the towel against her hair. "You just want to see me naked again."

"Of course I do." Tracey grinned.

Faith had to laugh as she shook the water from her ears. "I love the way you have it. It all seems so...you." She slipped out of her shorts, but left her thong on. She then pulled her shirt over her head, leaving herself in the tan bra she was wearing. "Now for those extra clothes?"

Tracey grinned. "In time. First you have to try on the outfits to see what fits."

"I feel like I've been tricked," Faith said, still wearing a smile. Since she was dry, she made her way slowly around the apartment taking in all of the knickknacks and photographs that Tracey had scattered throughout. When she came to the one of Tracey with Ryan and Chelsea, she picked it up and took a closer look. "I didn't know you had a brother and sister."

Tracey glanced at the picture Faith was holding, her lips forming a weak smile. "I don't." She held her towel in one hand as she took the picture from Faith with the other. "This is actually a couple I lived with for about four years, Ryan and Chelsea Criswall. I'm surprised Selby hasn't told you about them."

Faith shrugged as she continued to look around the room. "Selby hasn't said much about what the two of you have discussed and shared. I know he didn't mention that you had had roommates before."

Tracey slung the towel she was holding over her shoulder as she placed the picture frame back where it was, a sad smile on her face as she gave the photo one last glance. "They weren't just roommates." She walked into the small kitchen and pulled two black mugs from the cabinet and filled each with water. Reaching into another cabinet above the breakfast counter, she pulled out two tea bags of orange spice, dropped one in each mug and put them both into the microwave. "The three of us formed a triad. We were a family, basically." The hum of the microwave counted down the two minutes she had punched into the timer.

Faith looked at her in confusion. "You used to be Mormon?"

Tracey snorted in a burst of laughter as she shook her head. "I am far from religious on any front. No, you're thinking of polygamy. We were a poly-fidelity triad. Most call it polygyny, but to me names are just names. It's the relationship that matters. We worked as a couple, except our couple had three people in it."

"Isn't that basically the same thing?" Faith stared at the small redhead wondering how she had managed to share a man completely with another woman. How would something like that even work?

Tracey shrugged. "To some it might be, but not to me. Polygamists seem to have some very bad connotations attached to it. Poly-fidelity to me is more about the emotions that go with the relationship, and not trying to appease some higher power." The microwave dinged and she pulled the mugs out, setting them quickly on the counter. "There's as many different types of polyamory, which poly-fidelity is a part of, as there are people in the actual relationships. Some, like the three of us, stay committed within the relationship while others may have a partner that doesn't really have anything to do with the rest of the family unit."

Faith wrapped the towel around her body, trying to stay warm as well as hide her partially nude body. She then turned her mug so the handle was on the left while she dunked the tea bag a few times, seeping it. "So like an open relationship?" Tracey put sugar, honey and Bailey's French Vanilla creamer on the counter along with two spoons. Faith used two dollops of honey and ignored the rest.

"Yes and no. An open relationship could include just as many things as a poly one does. Take you and Selby, for instance. You two fall into the swinger's category for right now and open relationships. You two are having fun sexually with others without the emotional attachments and responsibilities that come with a relationship. You fuck and move on, even though you're fucking Edwin repeatedly, it's still not a relationship in the sense of the word we are talking about. In a poly household, you'd be very much committed to the others with normal household and financial responsibilities."

Faith thought on that a moment as she blew on her tea to take a sip. She had never really cared for the term swingers as it made her think of massive orgies with hands and mouths everywhere all over everyone and anything attached to someone. Not something she pictured herself doing. Granted, Selby and she had had sexual encounters with others and technically that made them swingers. She just preferred to not use the term.

Edwin, however, was a different creature. So was Tracey for that matter. They both seemed more than fuck buddies. Selby and Tracey definitely had a relationship that went beyond sex as did Edwin and she. While they had just shared Tracey and both had a friendship with the woman, Edwin was all Faith's. She hadn't even shared everything that the two of them had done with Selby. Faith felt guilty about that as well, but how could she tell him now? Edwin had taken her deeper into his world than she thought possible, had made her do things she never thought she would even consider. And Selby was the ever faithful husband, waiting for her to come home to his arms and his bed, not even knowing how often his wife had been fucked anymore.

Faith held the mug in both hands as she brought it to her lips and took a tentative sip. "What happened that you three aren't together now?"

Tracey turned so that she could lean back on the counter, her cup warming her hands. She gave Faith the history of Ryan and Chelsea as she stared into her mug. Her voice was distant as if she was trying to separate herself from the story she was telling. It didn't take long and at the end, Faith could tell it was still a pretty raw subject for the usually chipper redhead.

"Tracey, I'm sorry." Faith was at a loss as to what to say. She wanted to just pull the other woman close to her and hold her, but wasn't sure if Tracey would welcome it. Instead, she just tried to change the subject. "I never knew there were so many lifestyles out there."

Tracey shifted where she stood as if shaking off the memories and Faith knew the sudden smile was forced. "Probably more than we know about or at least different versions of lifestyles." She shrugged. "I do what makes me happy and don't worry about labels. I follow my heart."

Faith sipped her tea as the last four words Tracey had spoken repeated themselves in her mind. *I follow my heart.* That's what she was trying to do, follow her heart. Yet, the heart could be a very fickle thing and Faith's lately had been a total roller coastal. Selby. Edwin. Now Tracey. There were so many directions she had allowed herself to be pulled in over the last month that her mind, body, and heart were all screaming different things.

What was her heart telling her? As she stared into her mug, she realized that, for the first time since she married Selby, she didn't know.

Thirty

Faith took a quick look around. The house was clean, her bags were packed and she had even prepared a couple of meals for Selby to zap in the microwave. Although knowing Tracey, he would be well fed while she was gone. *I wonder if she'll take the opportunity and spend the night.*

Satisfied that everything was done that needed doing, Faith felt grateful that the rest of her Sunday could be spent relaxing and enjoying time with her husband.

And her excursion with Edwin.

She was nervous about her afternoon rendezvous. They had had sex at Rutherford Construction before, but this was different. For one, it was Sunday. What if someone saw her truck and questioned why she was there? There was enough talk as it was about her and Edwin. They did not need to feed the gossip mill. Still, the excitement outweighed the trepidation. It meant something that he wanted to see her before her trip west and didn't just blow it off. She wanted to see him, as well.

Selby joined her in the fireplace room, handing her a soft cover Megan Hart book. "For those nights you need some stimulation."

"And what do I do after I'm stimulated?"

"Call me, of course. You did pack Fred, right?"

She smirked at the mention of the name they gave her cock-shaped vibrator as she glanced at him with lifted eyebrows. "How could I leave my favorite man behind?"

"Ouch. You know how to hurt a guy."

"Just keeping you humble."

The next couple of hours were spent down on the beach darkening their tans and enjoying the battering of the waves. She loved the soothing cadence of the ocean. With her eyes closed, Faith could allow the gentle pounding to lull her to sleep. It just about had when her phone dinged.

Opening her eyes, she looked for Selby, and then remembered he was up at the house making a pitcher of lemonade. She pulled her phone from under the towel and squinted at the screen through the sun's glare. Edwin.

In less than three hours you will be my plaything. I hope you're looking forward to it as much as I am. You are to shower with your husband's help. Pick out a sexy outfit. Have him help you. No panties, of course.

She read it again. And one more time. She truly couldn't believe her eyes. What's more, she couldn't deny that her body flushed with heat at the idea. She had had sex with Selby after Edwin, recounting all of the erotic details, but this would be completely different. Selby would be preparing her for another man. She could feel her honey flow between her legs.

She typed back simply, *Yes, sir.*

A couple of minutes later another text came through. *You are not to have sex before you see me.*

Yes, sir. She practically gulped as she sent the reply.

"Everything okay?"

Faith jumped at Selby's voice. "What? Oh, yeah, fine, everything's fine. Edwin was just making sure we were still on for today." Her breathing was heavy and she attempted to take a deep breath to calm herself.

Selby chuckled as he handed her a Rum Runner. "He must be an eager man," he said as he sat down beside her. "I can't say I blame him, though." He took a swallow of his drink and Faith stared at the way his throat rippled with the action. The ocean breeze tousled his golden hair and the straw-like curls that crept from the top of his board shorts beckoned at her with seductive tendrils. She was told she couldn't have sex with him and right then that's exactly what she wanted to do.

And Edwin wanted her to have Selby bathe her and get her dressed? It was going to be a painful three hours.

"Come on, let's hit the water." Selby grabbed her hand and refused to take no for an answer.

"Selby Greer, it's March! That water is freezing."

He never slowed. "You worried about shrinkage?"

The water was like ice, but Selby never slowed as he led her over the foamy waves into deeper water. "I'm worried about pneumonia..!" She screamed out as Selby just fell into a breaking wave taking her with him and she found herself sinking into the tumbling wave. Her hair!

Selby's hand slipped from hers with the violence of the wave and she felt herself tackled by the salty sea. She wasn't ready. Air whooshed from her lungs even as she tried to hold it in, save it against the undercurrent that tugged at her. She panicked and flailed her arms, reaching for the surface, reaching for Selby.

Her head broke the watery barrier only to be hammered back down again before being able to catch a breath. The water couldn't be that deep yet. They had only gone a few yards. She felt her foot hit the sandy bottom, sea shells pelting her ankle. She pushed upward and then a hand had her arm and she was being pulled. Selby held her tight, holding her as she coughed up the water she had swallowed. She wrapped her arms around his neck, fear sealing her to his body like a second skin.

"It's okay, babe. I got ya. Relax, I got ya." The words repeated over and over until she felt her body shaking only because of the cold water and not the fright that had ripped through her.

She coughed some more, the water at their waist now. Selby stood solid, his back to the waves creating a safe wall for her. "Don't ever let go again. I thought I was going to drown."

She felt him squeeze her tight. "Never, love. No matter what, I've always got you." With one hand he brushed her wet hair from her eyes and then very gently kissed her forehead. "Let's get you inside and warmed up, shall we?"

Faith only had the strength to nod as he helped her walk through the current that persistently tugged at her feet. It was too easy to drown in the ocean. A person could get trapped in a rip current and pulled out to deeper waters, too far out to swim back in. She clutched to Selby until the waves were mere licks at the bottom of her feet and even then she held on tight.

When they reached the blanket, Selby took a towel and wrapped it around her, rubbing her within it to chase away the chill. He held her close as he did and she could feel the strength in his arms, the safety.

"Come." He led her up the sandy dune to the stairs, allowing her to take her time. A good thing too as she was still shaky from the ordeal. Once inside, he left her at the bathroom counter as he drew her a nice hot bath. While the water ran, he stripped her of her suit and dried the icy sea water from where her body had been covered. "If you can make it into the tub, I'll get you some hot tea to warm the inside of you."

Faith smiled at him and only nodded. She watched as he left the master bedroom for the kitchen and then she eased her cold body into the steaming water. Her flesh tingled as heat hit cold flesh, but she relished the prickly sensation.

Soon, Selby was back with peppermint tea in a Tinkerbelle mug. She wrapped her hands around it as he knelt beside the tub, kissing the top of her head on his way down. Without a word he picked up her loofa, squeezed some of her vanilla bean soap on it, and washed the salty sea from her body. Laying her head against the tub's edge, she lingered in the sensations of the gentle caressing of her body. Her nipples tightened into hardened circles as the heat between her legs grew.

Selby took the tea from her hands and had her lean forward. With gentle massaging circles, he lathered her hair and washed the ocean from it. Completely relaxed, she could have fallen asleep with his hands on her scalp.

After he dried her off from the bath, Faith asked him to blow dry her hair and brush it out. He kissed her nose with an "Of course, my queen" and settled her in the chair at the bathroom vanity. Faith's valley grew wer at what she was doing, having him prepare her for another man. Did Selby know what was going on?

When her hair was dried, she asked him, "What do you think I should wear?"

His eyes swallowed her naked form. "That looks good to me."

She laughed, one hand on her hip. "Oh I'm sure I'll get down to this, but I can't start off this way. Dress me, sexy."

"Dress you?" She didn't think he'd go for it at first, but then he just shook his head. "Okay, let's see what Selby, the fashion designer hailed from around the world, can dream up." He waggled his eyebrows at her, his smile contagious. "It needs to be alluring, seductive, and easy to take off, eh." Selby took on a flamboyant air, waving his arms and flipping his wrists. He went to her bureau of drawers and opted for a dark lavender bra and thong set, leaving the thong in the drawer, with deep rich flowers strategically placed over the otherwise see-through fabric. He slid the straps over her shoulders and clasped it in place.

He took a step back and eyed the effect. "Now that's an amazing sight." He then stepped into her closet and came out with a violet sundress that stopped just above her knees. He held it open for her and slid it over her head and down her body, his hands gliding across her skin as he did.

She felt the tingle of her flesh at the grazing and her wetness increased. Edwin's words filled her head. *Do not have sex with your husband.* Oh, but she wanted to so bad. She closed her eyes and pictured her boss in his tight jeans, both hands on his hips. What would he do with her today?

Once the sundress was in place, Selby picked out a pair of off-white sandals and, kneeling in front of her, slid each one onto her feet. Her breath caught at the sight of him, practically bowing in front of her, serving her. It reminded her of the other night on the deck when he helped her take pictures for Edwin and then went down on her right there, kneeling between her open thighs. She wanted to rape him right there and dug her nails into her palms to fight the passion that inflamed her sweet channel. It was excruciating, the desire that was building within.

She watched as her husband stood, his eyes sparkling, and the swelling in his pants giving away his thoughts. "A radiant temptress if ever there was one."

She could feel her face blush. "Thank you." The words came out a husky whisper.

He leaned forward and gently kissed her lips, which were suddenly dry. "Enjoy your date, my queen."

~ ~ ~ ~ ~

Selby closed the book he was reading and sipped the Cabernet that warmed his glass. Dusk was claiming the night sky and it really was getting too dark to read outside without turning on the lamps. He glanced back to where the switch was and decided it was too much effort to move. Setting his book on the table beside him, he held his glass in both hands and stared out over the ocean. The breeze was light but still held a March chill to it along with the tang of the ocean.

Faith had been gone for an hour and a half and he really had no idea when she would be home. There were no time restraints on their weekend excursions so as not to rush the experience. The weekdays were for quickies. Weekends allowed for more freedom.

Selby thought of what the coming morning meant. A week. Faith would be gone an entire week and he was getting nervous about it now for the first time. He had wanted her to explore her fantasies, but he was afraid of how far those fantasies would take her away from him, and if he was honest with himself, he had to admit that he was afraid this trip would play into her exploration. They hadn't discussed whether she could have sex while she was gone. He wondered if perhaps they should.

"Anyone home?" A male voice called from the bottom of the stairs.

"Come on up!" Selby stared with confusion at the steps that led to the sandy shore below. No one used their beach access to get to their home. Usually it was the other way around, using their home to gain access to the beach. Selby watched as Faith's brother-in-law ascended the wooden steps.

"Glen?" Selby stood and shook the man's hand, more confused at who it was who had climbed his steps than the fact that someone actually had. "Never pictured you as a beach walker. Can I offer you a beer or something?"

"Faith here?" Glen asked as he looked around. When Selby said that she was out for a while Glen glanced at the near empty wine glass. "You got any bourbon?"

Selby nodded and led him into the house. The bar was situated in the Florida room so it would be close to the pool deck. Glen slid onto one of the wooden stools while Selby stepped behind the bar, slipping both glasses from the top shelf. He poured two fingers of Makers Mark into both glasses and handed one to Glen. Selby stayed behind the bar playing bartender and waited for Glen to talk. His eyes looked drained with dark semicircles underneath, his dark hair blown haphazard by the salty air. It was more than a tired look. He appeared beaten.

Glen took a swig of the bourbon, his lips taut against the smoky taste. He stared with tired eyes at the amber liquid without seeing it. His shoulders drooped as he slumped in the stool.

Selby sipped his bourbon and waited. It wasn't long.

"Something is eating at Cherish and I'm not sure how to handle it. She's going crazy, like she's obsessed with Faith and the sudden life that seems to have come out of her. She's cranky, snappy, and jealous as hell. I don't know what to do."

"What is she jealous of?"

"As crazy as it sounds—Edwin."

Edwin? Why on earth would Cherish be jealous of Edwin? Selby stared at his glass a minute trying to fit pieces together, but it could take several paths. *Either Cherish is jealous of the attention Faith's getting or...*

"Don't get me wrong. I love Faith and you. I love the way Faith has grabbed life and shed that timid church mouse side of her. But, since Faith's come into herself, Cherish has been on edge. I don't know what's gotten into her."

"Why do you think it's Edwin?"

Glen took another sip and a deep breath right after it. With a shrug he said, "That's all she talks about. Faith and Edwin."

Selby stared out the window, lost in thought. The two sisters had never really gotten along since Selby had known them. There were brief periods of civility, but it never lasted. Cherish was a spoiled brat and Faith a bullied pup, but they never really outright fought, not until recently, anyway. It was possible that Cherish felt threatened by Faith's new confidence. Hopefully, Edwin was smart enough not to risk their jobs with their game. Of course, lately it seemed like more than just a game.

"You know she actually accused Faith of sleeping with their boss for special favors? Now, I don't for one minute believe it, but that's how crazed Cherish has become."

Perhaps they weren't as careful as I'd hoped. "Glen, I can assure you Faith is not cheating on me." *Well, it's not a lie. I know she's fucking him.* "And Faith doesn't want Cherish's job. She's just having fun. I'm well aware of her antics at work, I assure you."

Glen leaned on the bar, drink forgotten. "How did you do it?"

Selby gave him a confused look. "How did I do what?"

"Get her to loosen up, have fun. You know, flirt and stuff." He took a sip of his bourbon. "Cherish is so rigid it keeps me flaccid."

Selby lost the battle with laughter. He couldn't help it. Glen's description just caught him way off guard to be able to stay serious. "I'm sorry. Really."

"Not as sorry as I am."

Selby never imagined having this type of conversation with his sister-in-law's husband and it really was TMI as the teenagers would say. Still, he could see Glen's frustration, but it was one thing to fantasize about a flirty wife and quite another to be able to handle the attention it brought about. Glen didn't seem the type to be able to cope with someone else touching Cherish. "Glen, we're a very different couple than the two of you. Are you sure you'd want men coming onto your wife all the time or her coming onto them? What if another man saw your wife naked? Or kissed her?"

Glen stared down into his glass and Selby could see the conflict in his face. Finally, the troubled man just shook his head. "I don't know. However, I do know I'd rather have the knowledge of her being attracted to someone else than her being a bitch to me for no reason."

If Cherish was panting after Edwin, Faith has stepped into a mess she knows nothing about. "Have you talked to Cherish about opening your marriage up?"

Glen glanced up at him, confusion and shock mingled on his face. "You and Faith have an open marriage?"

Selby shrugged. "Faith and I have fun within certain boundaries. No secrets. Maybe you should share your concern with Cherish."

The dark-haired man stared back at his glass, his fingers twirling it on the bar. The conversation in his head was very visible on his brow. It was true that many people couldn't handle seeing their partner with someone else. Yet, that's where trust came in and, as Selby always said, matters of the heart are not matters of the body. He glanced out the sliding doors at the darkening sky. *I hope Faith remembers to keep the two separate.*

Thirty-One

The ride to the office seemed to take forever with Sunday afternoon traffic being more congested than she could remember. Edwin said he'd be there until five thirty and it was only ten till five. Plenty of time to catch him. She had sent him a text telling him she was on her way if the plans hadn't changed. He had replied simply, *Come*. No playfulness. No flirtatious innuendo. Just *Come*.

Suddenly, Faith's excitement turned to a nervous anxiety. Had something gone wrong this weekend? What kind of mood was he in? He had given her instructions earlier and then just dropped out of sight. Was this all part of his stoic, stern demeanor as the one controlling her, his plaything?

She parked her Toyota around back next to Edwin's truck, took a deep breath, and opened her door.

The back door was unlocked, and, as soon as she opened it, she heard Edwin's voice calling her to stop. She released the door handle and turned to see him coming from the warehouse. He walked with determined strides, his back straight as the wind teased his eggshell shirt and raven hair. A smile parted his lips revealing the teeth she remembered on her neck. His jeans were tight and even limp she could see the outline of his cock in the material. Her breath caught. Her heart pounded.

"I'm glad you made it," Edwin said as he neared where she stood. "Your husband picked out a very pretty outfit."

Faith felt herself flush at the mention of her assignment. "Thank you."

"Did he go all the way with the outfit?"

"Yes, sir."

Edwin held out his hand. "Hand me the dress and let me see."

Her eyes widened. She could feel her heart pound even harder at his suggestion. "But, we're outside. Who all is here? What if someone sees us?"

He continued to hold out his hand. "Then they see you," he smirked. "Now, the dress."

She couldn't believe what he was asking her to do. Surely he wouldn't risk them getting caught. The sun beat down on her. They were hidden from the main road, but what if someone came back for whatever reason? She'd be standing there in just her bra in front of her boss. She could feel the lump in her throat as her hands went to the material at her waist and she pulled the dress over her head, handing it to Edwin once it was off. She stood, practically naked before him, the breeze kissing her skin. She wanted to cover herself, to hide, but instead she just stood there waiting.

He held her dress in his hand as if it were a rag as his eyes raped her. She felt his lust from where she stood and saw the tightening of his pants as his cock began to swell. She felt a flush of pride at being able to illicit such a response without even touching him. He tossed the dress on the hood of her truck. "Your bra." His hand was out again.

Faith didn't question the command this time. She just reached behind her and unhooked the clasps. No sense being modest or worrying about someone's sudden appearance at this point. Sliding the straps from her shoulders, she removed the bra and handed it to him. Edwin took it and grinned as he hung it on her truck's side mirror. He then gestured to the back door. "Now you may go inside. Remove your sandals once inside."

She left the cool March breeze against her skin for the cold, artificial air. Once on the beige industrial carpet she slipped her sandals off leaving them by the door. It seemed she'd be getting dressed again outside. At least, she hoped she would.

She waited just inside the door, her hands hanging at her sides. She never felt as vulnerable before as she stood in her work place in front of her boss totally naked. It wasn't the first time she had been naked while he toyed with her at work. She had stripped in his office and even been exposed in the warehouse. Yet, she had never walked the halls in only her birthday suit. She was as much frightened as she was turned on.

Edwin pointed her down the hall and with a deep breath, she turned and walked. *Why was he staying so quiet?* It was the silence that added to her nervousness. She could feel his eyes on her as she led the way down the hall, and it made her honey drip between her legs as she thought of his arousal at the sway of her naked hips.

She walked down the hall, pausing at the connecting corridor that led to the offices, but Edwin just motioned her straight. She continued on, but her stomach was spinning with new fear. He was taking her the back way to the main lobby. *Oh my god! What if someone's there? What if someone passes the big front windows?* She kept walking, but her legs were now shaky. The hall made a right turn and, way too soon, Faith was walking into the front lobby of Rutherford Construction, stark naked.

"Stop."

She obeyed, but her eyes swirled in every direction making sure they were alone. Then her eyes went to the tall window and she could see Eau Gallie Boulevard and knew that if someone looked in they would see her.

"Kneel facing the window."

No! Oh my god, someone will see me.

"At any time you fail to do as asked, whatever is asked, the game ends."

She looked at him with nervous eyes, silently pleading.

Edwin shrugged. "This is what you asked for. It's up to you to decide when it's too much."

He was right, of course. She had told him she wanted to be pushed, to see how far she would go. Edwin stood, hands on hips, waiting. She took a deep breath and then walked over to the window and knelt down facing out. *Please, let no one I know drive by.*

"Now turn your body to the side." She obeyed. "Good girl." Edwin walked in front of her, the bulge in his pants straining the fabric. "Do you want it?"

Faith nodded, her throat tight with her desire.

"No nodding. Do you want it?"

"Yes, sir. Please, may I have your cock?" She looked up into his eyes, begging for what she knew he wanted to give her, and for what she'd have to earn.

"Pull it out and use that talented mouth of yours."

"Yes, sir." She practically lunged for the button of his jeans, all at once forgetting the window in her desire to have him. Her honey flowed at the sound of his zipper, and her mouth, suddenly dry, ached to taste him. She slid his pants to his ankles, her lips pressing to his engorged sex even before they were completely down.

"No hands, just your mouth."

She left her hands pressing into her thighs as she buried her face in the dark curls of his balls. She breathed him in, loving the musky scent of him, and then she caressed him with her tongue. He placed his hand upon her head as she sucked one of his jewels into her mouth, sliding her tongue around and over the sac. His moans filled her ears, pushing her forward. Running her tongue up the underside of his thick shaft, she loved the feel of him on her nose and chin, every bump and ridge. As she reached the tip of his hardness, she took him as far into her mouth as she could, relishing the way he filled her. It was awkward, at first, without her hands guiding his cock, but she ravenously devoured it, her head plunging down on him, sucking him with a passion.

"That's my girl," his voice growled as he spoke. "Take your boss' cock all the way into that mouth. See yourself sucking me off right here in the lobby. You're naked, in front of this window, giving a blow job. You like being the little slut."

His words stirred her juices. Everything he said was true. She did love it. She would picture this scene now every time she came to work.

"Too bad we don't have cameras."

She moaned. Oh god, how bad would that have been? Proof that she was doing the boss. She grew wetter, hotter.

"Maybe I'll make a video of you one day."

She only moaned again as her head bobbed up and down on his hardness. She wanted to scream no and yes at the same time. She wanted him, his cock. Her passion was uncontrollable. She needed to be fucked! Right now. Right then.

She slid her mouth off his cock and begged, begged like the little slut she felt she was. "Please! Please, Edwin, please fuck me! I need you to fuck me." She dropped her mouth back onto his swollen member.

He gripped her head and pulled her from him. Without a word, he pulled her up by her hair and the pain made her scramble to her feet, the taste of him still on her swollen lips. He pushed her to the giant window facing the road. Her mind screamed. *Oh god, no! Not in front of the window.* But that's where he put her. She caught herself with her hands as she felt his hands on her hips, pulling her slightly back. As she felt his cock at her sweet passage she forgot the window and begged again. "Please!"

And he drove inside of her with one thrust. She couldn't believe how wet she was, how horny he made her. He gripped her ass with his strong fingers, digging them into her flesh, and pounded her with deep, violent thrusts. She could feel his testicles slapping her as his cock speared her. One hand left her ass and she felt it slide up her back and into her hair, gripping it and pulling her head back.

"Open your eyes."

She obeyed and could see the world driving by past her nude reflection. One group of air boaters slowed and stared, three men returning from a day on the lake. They cheered as Edwin took her right there for anyone to see. She no longer cared.

"They enjoy seeing my slut getting fucked, it seems," Edwin smirked. "I enjoy it as well."

His words, her reflection, the audience, it all pushed her over the precipice and she felt her body tense as her orgasm took over. She screamed, falling into the glass. The coldness pressed against her tits giving the men more of her nipples. She wanted them to see, wanted them to know what she was and what she was doing.

Edwin's cock twitched inside of her and she felt his climax fill her. His groan filled the lobby as she pushed back harder onto him, wanting every drop of his precious seed. He thrust twice more and then held her onto his cock, pinning her between him and the window.

Before she was ready, he pulled his hardness out of her and yanked her back around, pushing her to her knees. With a gentle tug, he pushed his cock back into her mouth saying only, "Clean." She sucked with the same passion, tasting herself on him as well as his own cum. With her tongue she wiped their sex from his manhood as their audience watched.

When she finally pulled away and looked up she saw his satisfied, proud smile. "Good girl."

"Thank you, sir." She felt the heat of her blush on her face as his words stirred within her.

"You may stand now, love." He held his hand out to help her to her feet. She took it, needing that extra leverage as her legs were weak and shaky. His smile never vanished. "Now I may survive the week."

She blushed even more. "I won't." And she truly wasn't sure she would. Edwin was a drug and she found herself very much addicted. She craved him like a junkie craved their next fix and a week apart seemed like she was being forced into rehab.

He grinned as he wrapped his arm around her waist and led her back down the hall. "Perhaps I'll have to find something to keep you busy on your trip. You are, after all, going with *my* boss. I could use you to earn me brownie points."

She wrapped her arms across her breasts, suddenly aware of being naked. "Um, like what?" She couldn't hide the nervousness in her voice. What was going through his mind?

He kissed the side of her head. "Who knows? Maybe I'll share your photo with him."

"Edwin..."

"Yes?"

She didn't say anything further. She wasn't ready for the game to end. Of course, she wasn't sure she was ready to have sex with anyone else and she was *quite* sure Morgan was willing to put a notch on his bed post with her name on it. Would Edwin really bring someone else into their game? She took a deep breath deciding to wait and see what he had in mind and then decide whether she would do it or not. Right now, she needed Edwin.

"Have you ever done this before? Controlled someone like this?"

Edwin entered his office and sat on the edge of his desk, leaving her to stand nude in front of him. "Not to this degree. I've had dalliances before, even affairs, but none like you or what you are wanting."

"What happened to those?"

He shrugged. "Most just ended. We either grew apart, found something else that interested us more, or just became bored with what was going on. I am a lot like you. I want the adventure, the excitement of new things and new experiences. You offered me that whereas my last encounter didn't"

"Encounter? You make it seem so cold."

"Trust me, it was. Oh, it didn't start out that way. They never do. However, it quickly became that way. I think she was actually looking for an escape from her marriage and was hoping I was going to be it. I hated to disappoint her, but I had made it perfectly clear from the beginning that I wasn't looking for a permanent thing. Relationships do not suit me over the long haul." He reached out to her and pulled her to him, her naked flesh shivering at the sudden brush of the fabric of his clothes, reminding her once again that she was naked and he was not. "That's what I am enjoying about this. You are quite content with Selby and I can just have fun pushing all of your buttons."

She grinned up at him. "And you do know how to push them well."

He kissed her nose. "Good." He placed his hand on the top of her head and then pushed her back down to her knees. "We're not finished here, by the way."

~ ~ ~ ~ ~

They had sex for another hour, Edwin bending her all over his office claiming he wanted visions to think of while she was gone. He didn't mentioned using her again to gain points with Morgan and she was afraid to bring it back up. It was his job, after all, to stretch her experiences.

She watched as he zipped up his pants and fastened his belt. "I guess I'm getting dressed outside."

"Only partially. I'm keeping the dress."

She stopped and looked at him. "What?"

He pushed her toward the door. "The dress is mine. I'm sending you home in just your bra. I could keep that too, if you like."

What will Selby think? She took a deep breath. It didn't matter. Edwin was in control. "No, sir. I would like to keep my bra, please."

His mischievous grin said more than words ever would and she felt the embers of her lust being fanned into flames. Luckily, the sun would have started to set by the time they were walking out. With any luck anyone who noticed her would only think she was in a bathing suit. *Now, Faith, just don't do anything to get pulled over.*

Thirty-Two

Faith glanced at the clock. Four. One more hour and then she would have two days finished of her little work adventure. It hadn't been bad, just comical. This office had been around as long as the Brevard branch and yet, it seemed so ass backward. Nothing was organized. Equipment was missing. People didn't even know how to fill out work orders. How it had survived, Faith had no clue, but she knew she was needed. Before she had left Friday, she emailed herself forms and copies of spreadsheets in order to print them out when she arrived. She was thankful she had planned ahead, because there was nothing there for her to even begin.

There was only one girl in the office, Patricia McClusky. She was a young girl, early twenties, with fiery hair and a dusting of freckles on her face and arms. Faith was pretty sure the freckles traveled the length of her. She was the same height as Faith and just a smidgen skinnier. She had a mouth on her worse than the men and, combined with her Irish temper, used it to control them. It was the administrative work Patricia couldn't get a handle on. When they arrived Monday morning, Morgan pointed Faith to a desk covered in folders and paper and said, "Fix this." Later that day, he introduced her to Patricia with almost the same words. "Fix her." Yet, Faith wasn't sure she could. She wasn't even sure why the redhead had a job. She had no office skills, she sucked at organization, and she was rude to the clients.

Office work was not her forte. The girl would have been better off out in the field rather than behind a desk, but Faith was determined to give it her best shot. Besides, she needed the distraction.

She had not heard from Edwin since he made her get into the truck naked Sunday and drive home. She thought for sure she would have heard from him last night since he knew she had a room to herself. Yet, he had neither called nor texted. Faith tried reaching out to him, but was answered only by silence. She was beginning to worry that she had made the wrong decision by accompanying Morgan.

She heard Morgan's booming laughter coming from the conference room and soon she saw him and Kent Dedmon coming down the hall. Kent was the manager at Rutherford's Tampa office and what he lacked in management skills, he more than made up for in appearance and personality. He wore round glasses that made her think of Radar in the old M.A.S.H. sitcom, and the cleft in his chin gave him a rugged look that was only increased by the size of his biceps and tall frame. His almond hair was parted on the right and just long enough to keep falling into his eyes as he talked. His smile immediately disarmed a person and made them feel totally at ease. That was also his problem. People took advantage of his easy disposition and because of it, his crew was walking all over him.

"Faith, it's time for an early dinner," Morgan said as he entered the main office area. "You about done here for today?"

She nodded. "I can be in five minutes. Just let me get Patricia started on how to do equipment inspections."

"Meet me outside when you're done." Morgan hit Kent on the back. "Where we eating tonight, Kent?"

Both men walked out the front door and Faith turned back to the girl beside her. It didn't take the five minutes Faith had asked for to get Patricia started on her next project and soon Faith was sliding into the passenger side of Morgan's truck. Dinner was at a country barbecue place and the drinks were on Morgan. Besides the two of them, Kent and two of his foremen joined them and the conversation went from work to relationships to sex as it usually did with men. Faith laughed and cracked jokes right along with them. She had learned a long time ago that construction was a man's world and she needed to toughen her sensitivities if she was going to survive.

And flirt. Flirting could get a girl far in a man's world as well as quite protected. By the time dessert was ordered, Faith had won Kent over completely to her side of any argument, including that he might need to replace Patricia.

Morgan sat close to her throughout the night and she felt his thigh press against hers several times. The first couple of times she thought it merely an accident due to proximity, but the third time it happened he had pressed it into her as he turned and smiled. There was no mistaking the meaning. Had Edwin told Morgan he could have his way with her just to earn himself some brownie points with his boss? He had mentioned it Sunday, but she assumed he had merely been joking. Hadn't he?

Yet, what if he told Morgan he could fuck her? Faith took a deep breath, conflicting emotions going through her. She couldn't deny the heat that was growing between her legs at the thought. The notion of being used in such a way, a barter for a better position, both excited and angered her. It wouldn't surprise her for Morgan to jump at the opportunity. He was a known womanizer, which accounted for his divorces as well as his current single status. Still, perhaps he was just testing the waters and Edwin hadn't said anything at all. Would he want her to sleep with Morgan? Would he even care if she did?

She took another deep breath and thought of Edwin again, and then she felt guilty that she thought of him before Selby. She casually adjusted herself in her seat allowing her to move slightly away from Morgan without being too obvious. She hadn't discussed boundaries with Selby before leaving, but he knew the game she was exploring with Edwin. Surely, this would fall into that category.

This was madness! In the past few months she had opened herself up to so much that she didn't know where the line was or even if there was one anymore.

"Faith? Faith. Earth to Faith Greer." Morgan was waving his hand back and forth in front of her face and only then did she realize that she had been staring at a plastic ketchup bottle, totally zoned out. "These guys have wives waiting for them, the poor bastards. Say bye-bye."

Quick hugs and handshakes were exchanged as Kent and his two foremen left. Morgan showed no signs of leaving and instead, ordered another round of drinks. "So, tell me where you went."

"What do you mean? I've been right here."

He laughed as he lifted his Jameson to his lips. "Your body was. The rest of you was elsewhere. So, what's on your mind?"

Faith stared at her drink. That was a dangerous question. She also wasn't sure how much to share with Morgan before crossing the wrong line and getting Edwin in trouble. Of course, that reasoning would be funny and extremely hypocritical of Morgan, considering the type of man he was and the attention he had been giving her thigh. Still, it was all a mess in her head. "Sorry. I didn't mean to be antisocial. I just have a lot going through my mind at present."

Morgan gave her a smart ass smile. "You mean my presence alone isn't enough of a distraction?" He took a sip of his drink, smiling around the rim. With a tilt of his head, he asked, "You and Selby doing okay? I've only met him a couple of times, but the two of you have always seemed pretty solid."

"We're great. It actually has nothing to do with Selby."

"Does this have to do with a certain boss back in Melbourne?"

Faith squirmed in her seat, but didn't say anything. There's no way Morgan could have seen them on any of their outings. If he knew, it was because Edwin had told him in some locker room type conversation.

Morgan took another sip of his drink and then just held the glass by two fingers in front of him. "Faith, I know about Edwin. He's had a thing for you for a long time. He's almost like a puppy dog with it, the way he follows you around panting. He talks about you constantly. Does Selby know about the two of you?"

She nodded, her gaze fixed on the drink between her hands, refusing to look at the man across from her. "We have an understanding between us. We're opening ourselves up to new experiences and adventures." She jerked her gaze back up to Morgan. "I would never cheat on my husband. He knows everything." *Well, almost everything.* Faith thought Edwin was more of a bulldog, but kept silent. "If Selby is up for you exploring your more adventurous side, what seems to be worrying you?"

She stared at her glass. "Getting lost. This is all new to me. I want the fun that comes with all of these experiences, but what if I get carried away and lose who I am? What then?"

Morgan shook his head. "You're stronger than that. Like I said, I've watched you and Selby together. You're a strong couple and I think that if he didn't believe it to be so he'd be keeping a closer eye on you. Life is about the experiences you enjoy and you only get one shot at it. As long as you're not hurting anyone, what does it matter what you do?"

"According to my mother it matters very much and my actions are going to cause me to burn in Hell."

Morgan just about choked on his drink. It took a couple of minutes for him to get his coughing fit under control. "You told your mother?"

Faith just laughed as the waitress brought them their check and Morgan's dessert in a to-go box. "Are you crazy? No, no one knows except Selby, Tracey, Edwin, and now you. I just happen to know what my mother would say and it wouldn't be good."

Morgan tossed a couple of twenties down on the table as he stood, scooping up his strawberry shortcake. "Who is Tracey?"

"A close friend. She owns the bakery across from Selby's bookstore." Faith slid out of the booth and followed Morgan out. "As I said, it's been life-changing these past few months."

Morgan only laughed as he held the door open for her. "You get more and more interesting."

"If you only knew," Faith said as she passed through the doorway.

~ ~ ~ ~ ~

When the doorbell sounded, Selby set the book he was reading on the coffee table and forced himself out of his recliner. His stomach growled as he stood and he realized that he hadn't eaten yet. "I should at least have a bowl of chips," he mumbled to himself as he walked to the door. He realized that he hadn't been eating as well as he should since Faith left Monday morning. The night before he had even skipped dinner and didn't realize it until he woke up still in his recliner at two in the morning, book in his lap. He had offered Tracey to keep him company, but she turned him down. "I don't want her to think I was jumping at the chance for her to leave so that I could play house with you." He wasn't exactly happy about it, but had agreed. What choice did he really have?

Three more days, Selby. Life will be back to normal in three days. As he opened the oak door, he wasn't sure he would last three more days.

Tracey stood there holding a bag that had steam rising from it. "My guess is you haven't eaten, yet," she said as she pushed her way into the house.

Selby just smiled and stared at her as she passed through to the kitchen. A spicy aroma led a scented trail behind her and his stomach growled again.

Closing the door, he followed the feisty redhead into the kitchen where she was already setting out the Thai food in its square aluminum containers. She reached into a cabinet and pulled out some plates without a word and started scooping out the food. Halfway through fixing one plate, she stopped and stared at him. "I bought dinner; the least you can do is pour me a glass of wine."

"Oh, yeah, sorry. I was just taken by surprise. I didn't expect to see you. I suppose waiting two days before visiting me looks good enough?" He walked around the counter and after retrieving a couple of wine glasses, poured each of them some Merlot.

"It's as long as I planned on waiting." When Tracey finished dishing out the food, she held both plates and looked questioningly at Selby. "Dining table or back deck?"

"What? Oh, eating, um, why not..."

"Forget it. Back deck. C'mon." She led the way, laughing as she spoke. "Since when did you become the indecisive sort?"

They passed though the Florida room and through the sliding doors to the back deck. Selby watched as her firm ass swayed back and forth. He remembered her naked form on his bed just a couple of days ago. His cock twitched inside his jeans. "I'm sorry. You kind of caught me off guard."

As she set the plates on the table, Tracey cocked her head and smiled up at him. "I prefer you off guard."

He smiled back as he handed her a wineglass. "I've noticed."

The night was overcast with a slight breeze coming off the Atlantic that made the evening cool and comfortable. The sound from the neighbor's television could barely be heard over the surf, the swords clanging as Johnny Depp and Orlando Bloom battled it out. Selby sipped his wine, thankful for the company.

"So, what made you decide to come over tonight?" He asked as he slid a forkful of pork into his mouth.

Tracey brushed her hair out of her eyes as she shrugged. "Most men do not do well on their own for too long. I figured by the second night without Faith, you'd be pathetic and, from the look of you, I was right."

"My savior," Selby placed his hands on his chest and bowed his head.

"What can I say, I'm a saint." Tracey sipped her wine and then asked, "How's our girl doing?"

Selby shrugged as he filled her in on what he knew of Faith's last couple of days. His wife sounded busy, which he knew she loved, but also sad. He had asked her about it, but she only said that she was tired. The Tampa office had been a bigger mess than she had thought. He was surprised that she had complained about it really, because Faith thrived in that area, bringing order out of chaos. She had done it at Rutherford Construction as well as the doctor's office where she had worked before that.

"Perhaps she's not getting the attention she craves," Tracey offered. Selby just gave her a puzzled look, so she went on. "She is the one at her office everyone fawns over and at night she has your attention. She's probably competing with another star female and it's not setting well with her."

Selby thought about it a moment. Part of what Tracey said seemed like it could be true. Faith had changed quite a bit since October and it could have been an overload for her to get taken away from her new comfort zone as well as the spotlight. However, he just couldn't shake the feeling that it wasn't him she missed.

"You can't think like that," Tracey said after he shared his thoughts. "She's having fun, the type of fun that you pushed her to explore. She'll lose her way here and there because it's part of the journey, but you have to believe that your marriage is strong enough to withstand the explorations."

Selby stared at the dark crimson of his wine. "What if it's not?"

Tracey settled back into her seat, her meal mostly gone. "Then you were doomed to lose her even before this path came along."

~ ~ ~ ~ ~

Morgan walked beside Faith down the hotel corridor. She had checked her phone three times between the restaurant and the hotel, but still no word from Edwin. Could she have been forgotten so soon?

"Stop worrying about your boy. Last time I talked to him, he was having an emergency at work as well as at home."

"At home? He lives alone."

Morgan just shrugged. His room was directly across from Faith's and as they neared it, he smiled at her and said, "I'll be over in a minute. I need to make a quick call."

Faith pulled her card key from her purse as she looked at him. "Okay," was all she said. She couldn't deny the heat between her legs at the thought of him in her room, but could she go through with it?

Not knowing how long Morgan was going to be or even what he really wanted, she decided to go ahead and slip into her night clothes and get ready for bed. After slipping into Selby's Mario pajama pants and an old Dr. Pepper T-shirt, she washed her face and then climbed into bed, flipping on the television as she did. Before settling back into the pillows she had stacked against the wall, she checked her phone one more time.

Nothing. No missed calls. No waiting texts. Not even a work-related email. She practically threw her cell phone back onto the nightstand. How could he have become so distracted? She fell back against her pillows staring at Hotches of Criminal Minds as she wondered what was going on back at the Brevard office.

A knock came at the door followed by "It's Morgan." Faith pulled herself from the bed, not really in the mood for company, and opened the door. She didn't wait for him to enter, but rather returned to the bed and sat back under the covers. She suddenly felt a little weird being in the room alone with Morgan and in her pajamas. It seemed—off.

He closed the door and, when he turned around, she saw the take-out dessert box in his hands. "We're eating dessert?"

He chuckled as he walked over to the bed. "You're not; I am."

As he stood there, she couldn't imagine ever seeing him look so powerful before. She felt a twinge of fear while at the same time a fire burned between her legs. Morgan reached for the blanket and, with a quick jerk, yanked if off her and onto the floor. He arched his eyebrows as he took in her pajama pants. "Mario, huh? Not exactly what I was hoping for."

Faith didn't move. She wasn't sure what to do or how to respond. "Sorry," she whispered. Edwin had given her to him, she had no doubt.

Morgan set the to-go container on the nightstand. He gripped her pajama waistband and yanked them off her just as he had the blanket.

She didn't move. She didn't cover herself. She just stared at the man beside her as he soaked in her naked pussy. "Edwin told me that you wanted this. He even told me you liked being controlled." Morgan glanced into her eyes as he slid his fingers up her leg to her inner thigh. "Was he right, or should I stop?"

Faith just sat there. Edwin had told Morgan to have his way with her. She should throw him out and call Edwin and tell him to fuck off. She should. She really should. But instead, she merely parted her legs, giving him access to her sensitive spots. She couldn't help herself. She wanted it, wanted whatever Morgan wanted to give her. Wanted it, because Edwin had set it up and she didn't want to fail.

Morgan smiled down at her, his eyes sparkling with mischief. "Edwin said you were a good girl."

Faith opened her legs wider as his hand neared her clit. As he slid his finger between her slick lips, she gasped as her hips rose to meet his hand. "I try."

Morgan pulled his hand away and reached for the Styrofoam container. "Now for dessert." His grin almost ate her up alone.

As he opened the lid, Faith saw the strawberry shortcake from earlier, the whipped cream filling the box surrounded by thick strawberries covered in syrup. With one hand Morgan lifted her leg as he sat on the bed, placing her leg across his, leaving her open to his fingers. He looked at her with a playful grin as he scooped his fingers into the fluffy cream. She followed his fingers as he painted her pussy with the whipped cream. She gasped, expecting it to be cold, but it had already warmed up to room temperature. She relaxed a little, but only a little, still not believing that she was allowing him to continue. Yet, this was her connection to Edwin, weird as it sounded.

Morgan looked into her eyes, his devilish grin toying with her as he picked up a strawberry and slid it between her lathered lips, spreading them as he rubbed the fruit up and down. Faith moaned as he pressed it against her labia, sliding it back down between her lips and then gently pushed it inside her cream covered opening.

Faith felt her hips moving as he pushed it halfway inside and left it. "Now, for dessert," he said, and his voice somehow sounded deeper, huskier.

Faith's mind screamed at her as she watched his head drop between her legs, his hands cupping her ass. She felt his tongue glide around her outer lips, lapping up the cream that covered her. She moved, her hips rising to meet his mouth. *Oh my god!* She couldn't believe what was happening, but she was lost to it. Morgan circled the strawberry with his tongue, pressing against her, pushing it in just a little more. She wanted it, wanted his mouth on her clit. She gripped the pillow under her with both hands and opened herself wider for his touch. *Oh, please, please...*

Morgan pulled the strawberry out of her pussy with his teeth, taking a bite of it before tossing it back into the box. He drove two fingers into her as his lips kissed her clit, his tongue flicking over it. Faith let out a loud whimper at the sudden intrusion, her head tilting back, mouth open. *Yes!*

Morgan sucked on her clit, nipping it with his teeth. She wanted him, wanted him to take her. She was just about to tell him to fuck her when her cell phone went off.

Selby's ring.

"Oh god, Morgan, I have to answer it. It's Selby." How was she going to hide her heavy breathing?

Morgan lifted his mouth from her almost clean mound. "So answer it." And he went back to licking her pussy.

Faith reached for the phone, unable to believe she was actually going to answer it while Morgan was between her legs. "Hey, Selby." *Oh god, he's going to know.*

~ ~ ~ ~ ~

"Are you okay? You sound out of breath." Selby stared out at the Atlantic as the moon cast its glow onto the breaking waves. Tracey had left with only a kiss on the cheek so that he could make his nightly call to Faith. He had wanted her to spend the night, but they agreed that since no discussion was made prior to the trip, they would wait until Faith returned. He wasn't happy about losing the opportunity, but he knew it was the right thing to do.

He heard Faith take a deep breath. "Sorry. I was trying to get a shoe that had been kicked under the bed. How's your night going?"

"Those shoes can be tricky. Everything else going okay?"

Faith gave him a rapid fire account of her day, rushing through every word and answering his questions in short...gasps?

"Are you sure you're all right?"

"I'm just bushed, Selby. It's been chaotic down here."

Selby nodded and then caught himself. "Okay. You should get some sleep then. I'll talk to you tomorrow. I love you."

"Goodnight, Selby. I love you, too."

He waited until the phone went dead before setting his cell phone down. He stared at it for a moment. That had to have been the strangest call he had ever had with his wife.

Thirty-Three

Selby stared at the clock on the wall. Five o'clock. Usually he'd already be flipping the OPEN sign to CLOSED and heading for his car. However, with Faith in Tampa his eagerness to go home was simply not there. The house was empty and he hated it. He hadn't slept well at all because of the abrupt ending to his phone call with Faith. It just seemed off to him and he wasn't sure what was going on. It wouldn't have surprised him if Edwin had made a special trip to visit her.

He sat back down in his swivel chair. *Might as well see if there's any nighttime business.* He opened up a Terry Goodkind paperback and tried to get lost with the Sword of Truth.

He couldn't focus on what he was reading, so he tossed the book on the counter and began rearranging his shelves and contemplating adding an online store for his books. He was running through his mental list of acquaintances for anyone who might know web design when the cowbell on his front door gonged. *Maybe I'll have a customer, after all.*

"Selby!" A voice boomed out as the door clanged shut.

As Selby weaved his way through the bookshelves to the front of the store, he saw Glen standing there holding a six pack of Shock Top. "I swung by your house, but obviously you weren't there. So, I thought I'd gamble that you'd be hiding here." He held a beer out for Selby.

Selby took it and the two men clinked bottles. "Cherish doing better with Faith out of the office?"

Glen shook his head as he leaned back on the counter. "Yes and no. She's busting her ass and working overtime, bitching that Faith isn't there to do anything. I don't know if she'll ever be happy."

Selby just laughed. "They all have too much of their mother in them." He took a long swig from his Belgian white.

"Bite your tongue. Why would you wish that on us?"

Selby shrugged. "Genetics. Arni's the only calm one." That itself was an understatement and Selby knew it. The entire time he had been married to Faith he had never seen Arni ruffled. The truth of the matter was that the Driscoll children all had their selfish sides and that was all Valerie because Arni would give you the shirt right off his back. Valerie and the kids were every-man-for-himself, even Faith.

Selby stared at his beer bottle. Could that be why she was going so deep into this game with Edwin? Was her selfish nature coming out to the forefront now?

"I asked Cherish if she was fucking Edwin."

Selby spit out some beer as he choked on what he was swallowing. His eyes watered as he tried to get his coughing fit under control. "You timed that," Selby's voice was strained.

Glen gave him a sheepish smile as he flipped through a children's book on the counter. "Sorry. I guess that was kind of random."

Selby took a deep breath as he said, "Don't worry about it. And?"

"She got pissed that I even asked." Glen looked so forlorn that Selby felt sorry for him. Glen looked up and his chocolate eyes were fighting back tears. "She's always laughed off comments like that before, but this time she actually got pissed."

Selby knew what his brother-in-law was thinking. Cherish's reaction made her look guilty. Could Edwin be screwing both sisters and if he was, did Faith know? No. He couldn't believe that his wife would go that route. She was too worried about her family finding out what she was doing. If Edwin was having sex with both, then Faith was clueless, but Cherish must have her suspicions. If it was just a fight between two women at work, that would be one thing, but this had the potential of involving the whole family. Selby drained his Shock Top and reached for another. It was time Faith's game at work ended.

~ ~ ~ ~ ~

Faith had risen out of bed that morning not knowing what to expect from Morgan. He had finished his dessert, so to speak, after Selby's call, but that was as far as it had gone. He had acted like it was no big deal and kissed her hand before returning to his own room, his own bed. However, the reaction she did receive was the last thing she expected—silence. Morgan had been on the phone talking work the entire way to the office and as soon as they arrived had driven off with Kent. Not a word had been spoken about the previous night and what had happened.

To make matters worse, there had still been no word from Edwin. Three days and not one "Hey, there. How's the trip?" How stupid could she have been? Out of sight, out of mind.

C'mon, Faith. It was a game. Why are you acting like a jilted lover? She stopped filling out the equipment release she was working on and just stared at the wall. Why was she behaving like a love sick puppy? Did she have feelings for Edwin after all? It was just sex, a game of the flesh for attention and excitement. Yet, if that were really the case, why was she so upset that he hadn't reached out to her?

Faith glanced over at her phone and realized that she hadn't heard from Selby in four hours and *that* wasn't bothering her. She leaned back in her chair. *I'm not missing Selby; I'm missing Edwin.* The realization made her sick to her stomach and she left her desk to go outside for air.

She held herself, her arms cradling her chest as her hands rubbed her arms. The temperature outside was nice, and yet, she found herself freezing. Edwin had told Morgan he could have her and even what she liked. She should have been pissed, but she was still panting for just one word from the man. Selby would lay down his life for her and she hadn't even thought about him the entire trip. What kind of a woman had she become? What kind of a wife?

"Everything okay?"

The voice startled her out of her morose train of thought and Faith looked up to see Morgan and Kent walking down the sidewalk. She took a deep breath and nodded. "Yea, just needed a break."

Morgan ran his hand through his almond hair and smiled at her. "Good, because we've still got a lot to do before we go home."

As the two men passed her, the word "home" echoed in her mind. She worried about what waited for her when she returned. She realized she had changed. Not Selby. Not Edwin. Her. She hadn't even been aware that it had happened until five minutes ago, and now she had to figure out what to do with those changes.

When she sat back at her desk, she picked up her phone and thought about texting Selby, but what would she say? She set the phone back down and shuffled the paperwork on her desk just for something to do. She had never felt so lost.

She leaned back in her chair with a heavy sigh. With so many emotions and thoughts going through her head, it was hard to concentrate. She sat there gazing around the room and she noticed Patricia doing the same thing, only the redhead's gaze was focused on one person, Kent Dedmon. Faith recognized that look, recognized it because she knew it had been on her face for a while now. Either there was an office romance already in bloom or Patricia wanted one. Now Faith wished she had kept her mouth shut at dinner when she told Kent that Patricia may need to be fired. How could she not have seen it before? What worried her more was that if she had that look on her face back home, then everyone knew about Edwin and her, including her sister.

Suddenly she felt sick to her stomach. No wonder Cherish had been acting the way she was; she knew her big sister was banging the boss. What on earth could she possibly think? Not that Cherish was such an innocent victim in their battles, but still, no one had ever seen Faith in anything but a good light. Now, she was the office slut. She closed her eyes as she squeezed the bridge of her nose. *Run, Patricia, run, and don't look back.*

Yet, really, she couldn't blame the girl for doing the same thing she was doing. That excitement that flutters up in her stomach, that rush of adrenaline that pumps through her every time she's about to be naughty, were addicting emotions. It was the same when she first met

Selby. The newness and giddiness of the relationship was the wave that she could ride unencumbered. Until it hit the shore of life, that is. Then work and bills and family left you standing on the soggy shore amidst the detritus of the wave that was being pulled back out.

Was that it? The game that Selby and she had begun had placed her back on top of that wave, only now it was with Edwin. There was no real responsibility there, just the excitement of exploration. She could let go of life and its monotonous cares and just ride the crest of the wave.

A hard knock woke her from her reverie as Morgan stood there, knuckles on her desk, staring at her. "Welcome back," he chuckled.

Faith took a deep breath as she rubbed the palms of her hands on her jeans. "Thanks. What's up?"

Morgan slid some of the desk clutter to one side and perched himself on the corner. "Something seems to have rattled you. Need to talk?"

Faith leaned forward on the desk staring at a spot in the wood, her hands folded in front of her. "To be honest, Morgan, I don't know what I need anymore." Faith took a deep breath as she looked up at the man, his eyes tender where they were usually wolfish. "I thought I did. I mean, everything was all fun and games until my mind caught up with me."

Morgan cocked his head and with narrow, questioning eyes asked her what she was afraid to ask herself. "Your mind or your heart?"

And there was the problem she had been avoiding. She didn't know. Edwin not contacting her all week was driving her crazy. Yet, her scarce communication with Selby hadn't bothered her at all. She had barely thought of her husband and that tore her stomach. *Oh god, Faith, what have you done?*

Morgan tapped the desk as he stood to his feet. "Let's call it a night, shall we? Your mind is definitely not on work."

She gave him an apologetic smile and nodded.

~ ~ ~ ~ ~

They ate dinner at the hotel restaurant. Morgan tried to keep the conversation going, but Faith's attention was inward, not outward. She wasn't sure when he stopped talking and began working via his phone again, but when their plates were cleared away, it surprised her. She didn't even remember eating.

Morgan paid for the meal as she gathered her stuff and the two walked to the elevators. She hugged herself as she rode the elevator up the four floors. She could feel Morgan watching her and felt guilty for her mood, but she couldn't help it. Too much was going through her mind and her heart. Morgan was probably disappointed, hoping for some more impromptu fun after the previous night, but Faith just couldn't bring herself to think about that at the moment. All she could think about was Edwin and Selby, and she wasn't even thinking of them in the right order.

"Look, if you need to talk, I'm right across the hall," Morgan said as they reached their rooms. "Of course, if you need anything else..." He wiggled his eyebrows. "I'm still across the hall. Don't hesitate to knock on my door for whichever you need." His playfulness turned sincere.

Faith nodded and tried to smile. She didn't think she pulled it off, however. "Thanks, but I think I just need some alone time."

Morgan slid his card key in the door and then opened it. "Well, the offer still stands." He smiled at her as he entered his room.

She stared at the closed door, wondering if it was somehow an omen. Her life had been just like this just a few months ago. She had stood in the corridor of her life, calm, predictable, and in front of her had been a door behind which resided fun, excitement, and adventure. Selby opened that door for her—for them, really—and yet, here she stood back in the corridor, worried that she had passed through the door too soon or if she should have passed through it at all.

With a sigh Faith went inside her room, tossing her purse on the floor as she entered. She wanted a hot shower, mindless television, and bed. Snatching up the remote, she flipped on the news channel. *That should be mindless enough.* Walking into the bathroom, she turned the water on and slowly began to strip her clothes off while the water heated up.

Faith stared at herself in the mirror. Her hair was a mess, probably had been for a while. She hadn't even cared to primp at all during the day. That wasn't like her; at least not the Faith of the past few months. Appearance had become so important to her, important because her appearance gained her the attention she craved that drove her attitude of wanton abandon. All of it, her low-cut blouses, her tight pants, her perfect hair, and make-up, gave her the confidence to flirt with the men at the office. She dressed in order to get their whistles and winks.

She turned sideways, taking in her profile, the curve of her ass, the roundness of her breasts with their perky—and now hardening—nipples. *And why shouldn't they whistle and wink at me? I've worked hard to make myself look damn good.* Faith caressed her ass with one hand, letting her fingernails scratch at her skin leaving white trails. She smiled at herself. *Yes, Faith, you have a fine ass.*

The bathroom was beginning to fill up with steam from the shower. Before she ran out of hot water, Faith stepped into the tub, pulling the shower curtain closed behind her. She allowed the hot water to beat her chest, turning her pale flesh first pink and then a bright red as the heat pounded her, water cascading down her tired body. The heat trickled over her tits, down the flat of her stomach, and waterfalled between her slightly spread legs. The warmth struck her clit in a constant wave and she stood there reveling in it. The beating water massaged her muscles, driving the stress of her thoughts from her mind. With eyes closed, she caressed her breasts, letting the water pool around her nipples in a pleasurable mass of heat. With her fingers, she pulled at the hardening nubs, stretching them slightly until she felt the tendrils of her pleasure-pain tingle through her. Tension left her as passion filled her.

Faith slid down to the base of the tub, positioning herself so that the pulse of the shower beat on her inflamed sex. The cold of the tub on her back only made the water feel hotter against her flesh. She glided her fingers down her body and stroked her swollen clit, rubbing it in small circles. *Oh god.* A moan escaped her lips as she pictured anyone—everyone—touching her body. She rolled her nipple and it was Edwin's fingers; her clit had Selby's mouth tonguing it; the water caressing her body belonged to the hands of Morgan. She arched her back, giving them access to all of her. She pushed the guilt aside and surrendered to the passion that she couldn't control. She wasn't losing herself; she was already lost.

She rubbed her clit harder, her body taut with need. She felt their mouths, their hands; felt their hot breath covering her. Her body shivered with her excitement, goosebumps covering her flesh. *Please, oh, please.* She felt her mouth open, wanting. The water hitting her in the face was the hot cum from the men who stood over her, covering her with their sperm. She looked down and saw Selby, his cock hard and thick, and as she pictured him driving it into her, it was all she needed to crest the wave of her orgasm. Her body tightened as she felt the ripples of pleasure take her beyond her fantasy and into bliss, real and pulsating. Her moans and whimpers echoed off the plastic walls and she was sure whoever was in the next room heard her. She didn't care.

How long she had been down there on the tub's bottom, she didn't know. Long enough for the hot water to run out and leave her soaked and chilled. Faith just wanted to lie there, but the icy water forced her up and out without showering. Once she had a towel wrapped around her, she leaned back against the wall, and it was then that the guilt returned. Her fantasy popped back into her mind and again she fretted. Had she lost herself? Was this who she was and what she truly wanted?

And what about Selby?

As she slumped against the wall, she heard her room phone shrilling. Faith pushed herself off the wall and went to answer it, wondering who would be calling her room instead of her cell phone. Sitting on the edge of her bed, she picked up the receiver. "Hello?"

"Hey. Where've you been? I've been calling your cell for twenty minutes." Selby's voice held an edge, part worry, part anger.

"I was in the shower," Faith snapped into the phone. "It was a long day and I wanted to wash it away."

"Well, I was worried. You could have sent a text saying you were in the shower."

"Do you want me to text you when I take a shit, as well?"

"Now you're being ridiculous."

"And you're acting like my mother." Faith had to stand. She would have paced except the cord wasn't long enough. "I'm a grown woman, Selby. I don't need to vouch for my every move."

She heard Selby take a deep breath and let it out slowly. *That's right, count to ten before you say something else totally asinine.* He should have counted longer. "Look, I'm sorry. I'm a little on edge. Glen just left and I think I know why Cherish has turned queen bitch."

"Something get stuck up her ass?"

"No, Edwin."

Faith had nothing to say. What in the world did Edwin have to do with her sister? "What are you talking about?"

"Glen thinks Cherish has been having an affair with Edwin," Selby said. "I think Edwin was sleeping with your sister and dumped her for you and Cherish knows it or he's juggling his hanky panky with both of you."

So Cherish was the girlfriend Edwin had broken up with after we started our game. It explained her sister's mood and why she suspected everything. Cherish had done it all with Edwin already. Then Faith thought back to what he said during their last time together. His girlfriend had been trying to escape her marriage. Yet, she had always believed Cherish and Glen were strong. Odd, perhaps, but still a strong marriage. Still, that was her business. "And what does this have to do with me? That's between Glen and Cherish."

She could hear Selby take another deep breath, preparing himself for a reaction. "I think you should stop screwing around with Edwin. It's hitting too close to home and I don't like how he put you in that position."

Every guilty feeling Faith had been feeling fled. "Wait. Cherish is a bitch because Edwin stopped his affair with her and you want me to just give her back her toys and walk away! Cherish has gotten her way her entire life. I'll be damned if I'm giving into her again."

"Faith, this isn't a doll you two are fighting over. If it comes all the way out that you've been fucking Edwin at the same time your sister was are you ready for the fallout?"

"Weren't you the one always telling me as long as we're happy who cares about others? What happened to that?"

"I still believe that, but Faith…this is involving family. This isn't about people accepting our choices. This could hurt others. Hell, it already has."

Faith found herself clenching and unclenching her hands into fists. Her body was tight, tense, and she really wanted to move around. She knew he was right. Her head knew, anyway. The rest of her was fed up with her sister. She also knew she should be angry at Edwin and she would be. Later. Right now, her rage focused on her hypocritical sister who called her a slut and a whore while Cherish had been playing private secretary to Edwin behind everyone's back. She was not going to give in to the little bitch no matter the consequences. "I don't care."

"You don't mean that."

"Oh, yes, I do. I am sick and tired of worrying about what others think. This is my life and I'll damn well do what I please."

"Even if I'm the one asking you not to? What about our agreement that either of us could call it quits if it became too much."

Anger is sometimes like a runaway train, barreling downhill. It keeps gaining speed until the only outcome is a collision of personalities. "You're the one that opened this door, Selby. You got us into this game. You're not going to stop it just because Cherish gets her panties in a wad."

"Is Edwin really worth all of this?"

"No. I am."

Thirty-Four

Faith slept like shit that night. Throughout the day her head pounded like it had a high school drum line following her around. She had a war going on inside of her and she was afraid of which side would win. If Selby hadn't called last night, Faith probably would have ended the game on her own, but hearing Cherish's name brought into it just sent her spiraling out of control.

The odd thing was that the battle within her was no longer about Selby and Edwin; it was about Edwin and Cherish. If he was sleeping with her sister, did it really matter? This was just a game about sex, not a relationship. Wasn't it? What difference did it make who else Edwin was doing the dirty deed with if it was just sex? After all, it's not as if she had an exclusive right to him. That wouldn't be at all fair considering she went home to Selby every night. There was no commitment, no future planned out. Edwin didn't check in with her. *That's obvious from how often he's called me since I left Brevard.* She didn't check in with him, either. Faith took a deep breath.

Yet, if all that was true, why had she kept checking her phone all week expecting to see some form of communication? She had never been jealous before, had never had these feelings. But she was jealous, she realized. She didn't want to share Edwin, especially with her sister.

Faith picked up her phone. *But is Edwin sleeping with Cherish?* The truth was, Glen suspected she was cheating on him. There was no real proof, however, even if all the signs pointed to it. She set the phone back down. This was not a conversation to be had over text.

"I've finished the equipment inspections and we found what was missing." Faith glanced up as Patricia McClusky handed her some chicken scratch on forms. "I'll say this, we're definitely organized now."

Well, at least I can do something right. "Now all you have to do is stay on top of it. Kent's going to hire a couple of more girls to help out in here, so you'll have your own office team."

Patricia shrugged. "I'll take the help, but I don't work too well with other girls."

Faith debated within about talking to the fiery redhead about her suspicions concerning the office affair, but really, it wasn't her business. She took a look around at the people who made up the small office. The truth was, her only concern was the business Morgan had recruited her for. This was work and she had crossed the line and mixed her personal life with her business world and that wasn't going too well. "Just keep it all business and you'll do great. Besides, you'll be the girl in charge, so that'll make it all the better."

"Thanks. I'll give these to Kent." The redhead smiled as she turned to leave.

Faith watched her walk away, her mind shifting back to her own office dynamics. Even if Cherish wasn't sleeping with Edwin, she was still the office manager and, in a way, Faith's boss. Yet, Faith had been acting as if she was her own boss, especially since starting her foray with Edwin. *No wonder Cherish is so pissed at me. I leaped right over her.* She knew she had to fix that when she returned home. She had allowed her selfishness to trump what was right. It might not calm things, but it would be a start. She had to regain some semblance of order out of this chaos even if she didn't necessarily agree with all of it.

The day passed and Faith lost herself in tidying up the loose ends of the tasks Morgan had given her. Kent's office and crew were now organized and running efficiently. With any luck he could keep it going this time. Patricia seemed determined to help him and do her fair share, which was probably due to her feelings toward Kent more than any ambition on her part. It would boil down to the fact that Kent just had to want to be the boss more than he wanted to be their friend. Edwin could teach him that balance.

Faith shut down her computer and reached for her phone, which she kept on top of the desk. She was about to check for messages, but stopped herself. *Why bother? He hadn't texted all week. Why would he start now?* She tossed the phone in her purse and pushed herself away from the desk.

"Ready to blow this Popsicle stand already?" Faith turned and saw Kent walking over to her.

She shrugged. "I've done all I can do. It's up to Patricia now to keep it flowing."

Kent nodded as he glanced over to where the redhead sat thumbing through applications. "Do you think she can?" His face held a soft hopefulness as he stared at Patricia.

"If she doesn't get too distracted, yes." He turned and glanced at her, a puzzled look on his face. She shrugged. "Office romances are never as secret as you think they are. Trust me on that."

Kent shifted where he stood, putting his hands in his pockets and then taking them out again. Finally he just stood there and nodded. "Thanks for all of your help this week."

"Faith, you ready?" Morgan called as he peeked his head in the door.

She waved at him as she slid her purse over her shoulder. Turning back to Kent she said, "No problem, that's why I was here. I'm only a phone call away if you need anything or have any questions." He said he would take her up on it if he needed help as he slipped back into his office. Faith said goodbye to Patricia leaving the girl her phone number and wishing her luck.

As she passed through the door without looking back, Morgan was waiting for her by his truck. "Ready for some food?"

~ ~ ~ ~ ~

Selby locked the door to the bookstore and made his way to his car. However, after stowing his briefcase in the passenger seat, he decided he wasn't ready to go home just yet. Three nights walking into an empty house had been bad enough. He wanted to postpone the fourth as long as he could. He glanced over at Joe's Bakery, but decided he really wasn't in the mood for company either. Scanning the downtown scene he decided clubs were out, as well.

Shoving the keys in his pocket, Selby crossed New Haven and decided to see where his feet would lead him. Maybe he just needed to walk.

The afternoon—early evening? He never knew which category five o'clock fell into—held a slight breeze that tugged at the small maples that lined the street. Selby walked with his hands in his pockets, watching the people as they browsed the antique shops and specialty stores. Couples walked hand in hand as they leisurely strolled the sidewalk. Some sat whispering at small tables outside the cafes that lined the street as the bar scene started to creep into its night life. He wanted some place quiet and not so crowded. As he passed the Gentleman's Cigar, he decided that was the place for his mood. A cigar, a scotch and his thoughts were the perfect combination for a brooding evening.

He picked out a Romeo and Juliet and allowed the girl behind the counter to cut and light it for him as he ordered a Glen Livet neat. He wished he had thought ahead and brought his book, but at least the place was quiet. Two men sat at the bar chatting up the female bartender while watching CNN. Other than that the place was empty, just what he needed.

He found a comfy chair, made himself cozy and took a long pull on his cigar. As he exhaled, he pictured all of the stress of the week leaving his body along with the smoke. It didn't work. How was he going to convince Faith to end her game with Edwin? It could only lead to a disaster. He never should have allowed her to play with anyone at work, especially with Cherish there. There was too much potential for something to go wrong and the situation with her family was tense enough as it was. Clubs and bars were one thing, but fucking someone at work was never a good idea.

He sipped his drink as he stared at the wall, the smoke from his cigar wafting upward in a thin stream. He was at a loss as to what was the right way to go about it. Getting Faith to loosen up and explore her fantasies was his idea, after all. Yet, he hadn't anticipated the depth that she would go in that exploration. She was having fun, that was a definite, but she seemed to also be getting too emotionally charged with it and he wasn't ready to share her heart, yet. But how could he get her to slow down without appearing to be the jealous husband that he constantly assured her he wasn't?

"I never pictured you as a cigar smoker."

Selby glanced to his left and watched as Edwin Coldwell walked around a sofa and joined him, his own cigar and drink in hand. It had been a while since Selby had seen his wife's boss and he had forgotten what a powerful build he had or how black his hair was, so much so that it almost shined. He could see why Faith was attracted to him. What woman wouldn't be? He was tall, dark, and handsome. Right now, it just made Selby sick.

He shrugged. "I haven't in a while, but felt like enjoying a peaceful night out."

"And I'm disturbing it." Edwin made to stand. "My apologies. I'll let you be."

As much as Selby wanted the man to walk away, he waved him back into his seat asking him to stay. "By peaceful I meant I wasn't in the mood for the club scene."

"Wouldn't your deck to the ocean be suitable for quietness?"

Selby took a swig of his scotch, delaying his answer. He really didn't want to tell this man how he was dreading going back to an empty house. "Sometimes a change of scenery is refreshing."

Edwin settled back sipping his own amber liquid as he nodded. "I will agree with you there. How's Faith doing in Tampa?"

Selby glanced at him a little confused. "Haven't you talked to her since she's been gone?"

"Actually, I haven't. I figured she'd be swamped with whatever Morgan had her lined up to do and, frankly, I've had my own crisis here. The place doesn't run as efficiently when she's gone. I'll be glad to have her back next week."

"Oh. I just assumed with as much time as you two were spending together you would have been talking to her." Selby wasn't sure he should have said anything. Had Faith told Edwin that Selby knew what was going on? It would be ballsy to have a drink with the man whose wife you were fucking behind his back, but weirder things have happened. Furthermore, if Edwin had been quiet with Faith the whole week that could very well explain some of her snappish mood. It was a total game with him while she had allowed her emotions to get involved.

Edwin crossed his legs, his ankle resting on his knee, his hand resting on his leg with the cigar perched between two fingers. "I've missed her, but I figured she was busy. So, how is she?"

Selby took a pull from his cigar and told Edwin what he knew of Faith's trip. She had said it was a disaster, but he knew his wife. Anything that wasn't done her way just wasn't being done properly. She seemed tired most nights and went to bed early, usually with the television blaring. He hadn't heard from her today, but he usually didn't until after dinner most nights. Selby was ready to have her back home, as well, but for different reasons; well, mostly different reasons. He hoped they would make tomorrow an early day.

"Well, from everything I've heard that office was one of Rutherford's worst. I'm sure Faith could straighten them out, though. I know I'll be glad to have her back in the office."

"Cherish not handling it?" Selby studied Edwin as the man talked. He was confident, well-groomed with slightly faded jeans and a long sleeve white shirt that made his skin seem that much darker. He probably did have every girl in the office swooning and tripping over themselves to gain his favor and attention. How far would Faith go with it, though?

Edwin stared at his glass as he shrugged. "Cherish has lost her drive and ambition. Work has become a bore to her, which she tries to avoid at all costs now. It wasn't as obvious while Faith was here because Faith picked up the slack and was eager to do it. She loves to work and throws herself into it."

Selby smiled. He could picture Faith working at a feverish pitch. "I've always thought that Faith found her identity in her work."

"I can see that," Edwin said as he nodded. "However, her sister doesn't, or at least, not anymore. Cherish used to be like Faith, but that ended several months ago. Cherish felt as if she were entitled and soon stopped caring as much about work. As Faith underwent her metamorphism and came out of her shell, Cherish grumbled and withdrew even more."

"Glen thinks she's jealous." Selby had been staring at the table in front of him when he said it and hadn't even realized that he said it out loud until it was too late to retract it.

"Glen? Cherish's husband? What would she be jealous of? It's not like Faith can take her job."

Selby shifted uncomfortably in his chair. He wasn't sure he wanted to dive into these waters, but couldn't back out once he had waded in. Family life was hitting business life and someone was going to drown. He needed to pull Faith out of the churning waters if he could, even if she came out thrashing and kicking. "He thinks she's jealous of you." He left it there waiting to see if Edwin would pick up his meaning.

Edwin stared at him a moment and then diverted his attention to the cigar in his fingers. He twirled it a bit, thinking, and then took a long pull, holding the smoke a brief moment before allowing it to slowly seep out between his lips. He was taking time to gather his thoughts before answering, but that already told Selby that his suspicions were probably correct. *Oh, Faith, what have you wandered into?*

Edwin seemed to study his cigar as he spoke. "I had a lady friend once that told me she had never found a friends-with-benefits guy. She said that every time she thought she had found a playmate they would fall in love with her and start demanding more of a relationship than merely a good time. It never ended well no matter how many of her male companions swore they were just there for the sex.

"It has been my experience that the same can be said about most women. Few can play the sexual game and then simply walk away. They soon mistake what they feel during their physical passion as true feelings of the heart." Edwin took a sip of his bourbon as he shrugged. "Hearts can often be a casualty when sex is involved."

Selby stared at him. "You had an affair with Cherish." Everything fell into place. Glen was right and Faith had wandered right into the middle of it.

"I did not have an affair with your sister-in-law. We fucked. There's a difference."

"And what the hell is the difference?" Selby shifted to straighten in his seat, his body tensing.

"Affairs are emotional and come with expectations. Fucking is just that, sex with no strings." He took a pull from his cigar, holding the smoke longer this time before exhaling. He uncrossed his legs as he leaned forward, placing his elbows on his knees, the hand with the cigar draping over his other hand. "Office romances happen all the time, but Cherish knew that I didn't want any emotional attachments. I had made it perfectly clear."

His eyes stayed focused on his hands. Yet, Selby knew Edwin wasn't seeing them, but was visiting a time when choices went wrong. When Edwin began to speak again, it was as if his voice came from wherever his gaze had centered. "The change started when we moved into the new buildings. She wanted to decorate my office and all the key rooms in the place. Conference room. Reception area. Cherish took to it like a wife redecorating her home. It reminded me too much of my ex-wife, as a matter of fact, and creeped me out.

"So I ended it. Not right away, but in a gradual pulling back. I was worried about fallout at work. I wasn't worried about being fired. Hell, Morgan's a bigger dog than I am. No, I was worried about Cherish's reaction and the scene she might cause. Eventually, I just stopped seeing her altogether."

"And then your attention went to Faith." It wasn't a question. For Cherish to be reacting the way she was, the time frame between dumping her and paying extra attention to Faith had to be the same. "Does Faith know you slept with her sister?"

Edwin just shook his head, his eyes still on the smoldering cigar.

Selby glared at him. "So you allowed my wife to walk into a family drama because you had an itch in your pants."

Edwin snapped his head up. "Hey now, Faith chased after me just as much as I chased her, and I was told you were okay with it."

"Faith didn't have all the facts though, did she? And I guarantee you that Glen wasn't okay with it." This was a mess. Selby wanted to tell the ass sitting across from him to stay the hell away from his wife, but Faith wouldn't understand that. No, Selby had to convince Faith that her game with Edwin was too much of a risk and that it needed to end. That wasn't going to be easy.

~ ~ ~ ~ ~

Her phone rang for the third time that night and, as she did the first two times, Faith allowed it to go to voice mail. She was not in the mood to deal with Selby right then. This was her last night away and she was going to enjoy it without worrying about anyone's consequences. Tonight was not about Selby or Edwin or Cherish or Rutherford Construction or her family. Tonight was about Faith. Fuck the rest of them; at least for tonight.

Morgan had taken her to a sports bar close to the hotel and she did not waste time ordering drinks. She had two Rum Runners before their meal arrived with no intention of slowing down. Televisions blared as well as music and Faith teased and joked with Kent and the two laborers that caught up with them. Patricia finally showed up, her eyes glued to Kent, and it was a proper send off. They were done with work and would be returning home in the morning. However, tonight Faith planned on having fun.

By the time dinner was finished, so was her third drink and Faith wanted to dance. Morgan just shook his head and laughed. "Well, let's go dance then."

Down the strip from the sports bar was a club with a live band and Faith led their merry band of revelers inside. She grabbed one of the laborers—Bob Harper, she thought his name was—by the hand and headed to the dance floor. As she walked, she glanced back at Morgan with a pout. "I'm thirsty."

He nodded and headed for the bar, a smile pushing his cheeks up.

The band on stage was halfway through the *Love Shack* when Faith managed to get Bob on the floor. She started wiggling her ass in front of him, batting her eyes, and suddenly she didn't care that she didn't dance. Music combined with alcohol transforms everyone into a dancer. Bob tried his best to sway and shuffle his feet, but his eyes remained fixed on Faith's ass as it seemed to grind closer and closer to his swelling crotch. She noticed the effect she was having on him and made sure to brush against him as often as possible. She had to admit he was worth brushing against. Construction had given him a taut, trim build, while being outdoors had added a bronze tone to his body. His hair was a dirty blond, cut short, and his eyes a deep blue. Faith smiled as she traced his broad chest with her fingers. Yes, Bob was definitely a nice piece of construction.

The band stopped playing and a DJ started a song. Bob smiled and gestured toward the others. Faith gave him a pouty look, but allowed herself to be escorted off the floor and to a booth where everyone was squeezed inside. She slid in across from Morgan who just gave a smirk as he slid another Rum Runner across the table at her.

"For little ol' me? How sweet." Faith blew him a kiss as she lifted the glass to her lips.

Kent was pressed against the wall on the side as Faith and Patricia were virtually mashed into him. From the reflection in the window Faith noticed that, while both of Kent's hands were accounted for, only one of the fiery redhead's were visible. They were doing their best to look at each other without anyone else knowing they were looking at each other. Faith, however, caught them several times in the reflection of the window beside them. If they were trying to hide their office romance, they were doing a lousy job of it. Of course, just like the office in Brevard, Rutherford Construction seemed to have a "don't ask, don't tell" policy.

Morgan sat across from Kent and next to him was Jeremy, one of Kent's foremen. Bob and his construction chest sat across from Faith. Two girls, four guys, Faith liked those odds.

She could feel Morgan's eyes on her and glanced over at him. She smiled as she set her glass down. "What?"

He shrugged, his smile more of a smirk. "Good to see you've come out of your funk. I should allow drinking at work."

"Wait. Drinking's not allowed?" Jeremy wore an exaggerated, shocked look. "No one check my cooler."

Faith just laughed. She then looked at Morgan and shrugged. "It is what it is. I don't see any sense in worrying about it now."

"Here. Here." Bob lifted his beer into the air. "Why worry when you can drink?"

"I'll drink to that," Jeremy said as he lifted his glass, as well.

Patricia lifted her glass and clinked the others. "I'll drink to anything."

Everyone else cheered and glasses were raised to clink beer bottles and everyone drank. The music blared as Usher serenaded them from the speakers and the girls dragged the guys back out onto the dance floor. They swayed, they swirled, and they stumbled, but to Faith it didn't matter as drinks kept coming and the pain was numbed. Faith rubbed up against Bob as she twirled her fingers through his hair. He lifted an eyebrow at her, but didn't move away. She was confusing him and she knew it. Hell, she was confusing herself. She was tired of feeling, though. Anger. Hurt. Frustration. Tonight was about not feeling anything, even though she knew she'd feel it in the morning in more ways than one.

For now, she twirled on the dance floor, arms stretched wide.

Thirty-Five

The morning came early. Faith hit the snooze button three times before she forced her eyes to creek open and tried to focus on the popcorn ceiling. Each time she had silenced the screeching wail, she negotiated with herself in order to remain in bed. She didn't need to wash her hair. She could wear her Polo pullover instead of her beige blouse, so she didn't need to iron anything. She would risk sandals and forget socks and shoes. Finally, there was nothing else to cross off her morning routine. She had to get up.

Her head throbbed as if one of those silly wind-up monkeys were clanging its cymbals behind her eyeballs. She slammed the alarm off as she squeezed the bridge of her nose between two fingers. Groaning, she pulled herself into a sitting position, the blankets bunched around her waist. *Oh god, what did I do to myself?*

Faith left the warmth of her bed and trudged her way to the bathroom, holding her head with her right hand. With her left hand, she turned on the shower, avoiding the mirror. She did not want to see what she looked like this morning.

They were done and heading home. Kent's office was running smoothly and, if Patricia did everything she had been shown, she could stay on top of it. Faith had done all she could. It was in their hands now.

The hot water scalded her body, but did little to wake up her mind. She should have known better than to get that drunk. Faith wasn't a heavy drinker and twice in one week now she had allowed herself to lose control. She placed her hands upon the plastic shower wall and hung her head into the pelting stream. Her hair draped around her head like a curtain. Last week, her drunken stupor was with Selby and Tracey, and Faith had just let go and enjoyed herself. Last night, she had been angry and hurt and simply wanted to stop feeling. Of course, this morning she was more than making up for it in the feeling department. Her head was pounding, her mouth felt drier than dirt, and her back ached from the stone slab the hotel called a mattress. It seemed as if her entire body felt something.

Once she was out of the shower and trying to dry her hair with a towel without throwing up, her cell trilled out its ring. She answered it just to shut it up. "Hello?"

"Whoa, you do not sound good at all." Tracey's voice on the other hand sounded way too chipper for seven in the morning. "You okay?"

Faith plopped on the edge of the bed, her naked body still damp. She held the towel across her as if Tracey could see through the phone. "Yeah. I just woke up with a headache."

"A headache or a hangover?" Faith could practically hear the evil smile.

"Yes."

Tracey started laughing and Faith had to hold the phone away from her ear until the other woman stopped. "Good for you. At least someone is having fun this week."

"I did last night, at least. Who isn't having fun?"

Tracey told Faith about Selby's moodiness and how he had been moping around all week without her. Faith felt both, happy and sad, hearing it. Happy that he was worried about her and missed her; sad that he hadn't enjoyed his week. She had no illusions that Selby would survive without her, but it helped knowing that he was miserable while doing it. Of course, she didn't know how much of his mood was because of the drama of Edwin, Cherish, and Glen or actually him missing her. She was sure the former had played a big part in it.

Faith then told the redhead about her conversations with Selby and Edwin's silence. "Hell, not only did Edwin not talk to me this week, the bastard told Morgan he could have sex with me!"

"Did you?"

"Did I what?"

"Have sex with him."

Faith felt her cheeks blush. "That's not the point."

"Ha! You did. Faith, you little slut, you."

"I did not!" Faith yelled into the phone. "Well," she said a little more meekly, "not exactly. He went down on me. That was it." By the end of the sentence, she was smiling.

"Does Selby know?"

"Not yet, but he called just as it was getting started."

"Okay, girl, tell me. I want it all."

"Oh god, it was good." Faith told Tracey everything from the dinner conversation all the way to Selby's call and her saying she was digging a shoe out from under the bed to cover up for her heavy breathing. Faith could hear the business of the bakery going on in the background and somehow the knowledge of Tracey's location started Faith's pussy dripping. Not only couldn't she believe she was telling the redhead about Wednesday night, but what's more she couldn't believe the other woman was at work, listening. It felt like sneaky phone sex and she couldn't resist slipping a finger between her legs to rub her swelling clit. Her breathing grew heavy and she tried to force it back to normal, but it wasn't going to happen.

How she could flip back and forth in her moods, Faith didn't know, but right now she just wanted to be touched. It didn't matter by who or how. She could feel the wetness between her pussy lips as she slipped two fingers into her channel and started massaging her clit again. She shared how Morgan had smothered her pussy with whipped cream and used the strawberry to fill her. She closed her eyes as she pictured his head buried between her thighs and remembered how his tongue felt on her as he lapped the silky cream from her body.

Tracey's breathing grew heavy in Faith's ear, a pant and moan. The noise in the background had disappeared, leaving the two of them alone with Morgan. Faith lay back on the bed, the towel falling to the floor. "He ate the strawberry out of my pussy." She rubbed her swollen nub in faster circles while Tracey's moans told her that the customers were being put on hold. Faith continued her story, feeling it all over again as her fingers caressed where his tongue had licked.

Faith heard the other woman moan and then catch a whimper before it became a scream. Faith's back arched as her own orgasm hit, her body shaking as her hips tried to fuck her finger. She no longer saw Morgan, but the redhead in her office chair, fingers mirroring Faith's. That was the image that caused her explosion. Tracey's was the name that she whispered into the phone. Her name was whispered back.

Both ladies were silent for a while except for the panting of their heavy breaths. Faith didn't know if that had been phone sex or mutual masturbation or both. She did know that she was still turned on and that the conversation had just made it worse.

"When will you be home?"

"Not soon enough."

~ ~ ~ ~ ~

Selby stared at the clock on the wall. Faith had been on the road for two hours with another hour to go. He had given up stocking shelves and just sat behind the counter staring at the rotating hands of the clock. They didn't move. Time wasn't just dragging; it had stopped altogether.

There had been no morning call, just a text saying she was leaving and she loved him. He wanted to keep texting her on her ride home, but didn't. She had ignored his calls last night and hadn't called that morning. She was making a statement, a loud one, and Selby had gotten the message. She needed some space and he was forcing himself to give it to her.

His fear, however, was what might happen on the other end of that space. Would Faith continue to see Edwin just for spite, even after Selby had asked her to stop? Then the next question was how much Selby would continue to allow. This went beyond their sexual exploration. Faith's relationship with Edwin had the potential to explode in her face and rain down into her family. If her mother was a bitch now, it would only escalate with the knowledge that Faith had fucked her boss. Life with Valerie Driscoll would become even more of a living hell.

The cowbell over his door clanged as Tracey entered the bookstore, two turkey on rye sandwiches in one hand and a couple of Cokes in the other. "Our girl make it in, yet?" The door slid shut behind her as she laid the food on his cluttered counter.

Selby shook his head. "Another hour, I'm guessing. I haven't heard from her since she left."

She just shrugged as she slid behind the counter and onto the black stool. "You'll get her all weekend. Well, not all weekend, because I plan on having some girl time, as well."

Selby glanced at the sandwich, but didn't reach for it. "At this point, Faith will probably want to see you more than me anyway." He caught himself glancing at the clock again, but stopped, closing his eyes instead. He forced a smile upon his face as he glanced up at Tracey. Reaching for the sandwich, he said, "So, how has your morning been?"

Tracey had been about to take a bite of her lunch, but stopped. "What was that all about?"

"What? I can't ask about your day?"

"Don't play stupid with me." She held her sandwich by her lap. "I've never known you to play the poor pitiful Selby act. Why now?"

Selby leaned back in his chair, shoulders slumped. "Because she's not talking to me." He went over their last conversation and how Faith had been ignoring his calls. His only communication had been the text that morning. He knew that Faith was upset, but he was confused as to exactly what it was that had her that way. Edwin? Cherish? Him? All three or a combination of the three? He didn't know and it was bothering him to no end.

"So she's mad; she'll get over it," Tracey said. "You're not giving our girl much credit here. She's being bombarded with a myriad of emotions and feelings, all very new and extremely raw. She has to sift through them and she will. She's just not going to do it as fast as you want."

Selby didn't say anything. He just stared at the sprouts poking out between the meat and bread. He could understand that Faith was going through a lot, but she had never shut him out before. They prided themselves on being able to discuss anything. They both said it was a major strength in their marriage. Selby didn't know how to handle the silence.

Tracey slid off the stool and walked around behind his chair. She slid her arms around his neck and her hands down his chest, holding him in place as she leaned in and kissed his ear. "She's not going anywhere, Selby. She loves you and the life she has," Tracey whispered as she squeezed him lightly. Any other time it would have been seductive, but right then it was simply comforting.

Selby lifted a hand to cover hers, giving it a gentle squeeze. "I hope you're right."

He felt the softness of her lips as she kissed his ear. "I'm always right." They gave each other another squeeze before letting go. Tracey waved at the lunch remains as she circled the counter. "Now, be a good boy and clean all of this up while I get back to work and give our girl a big, wet, sloppy kiss from me when you see her."

Selby watched as the small woman passed through the front door and stopped traffic as she crossed New Haven Avenue. She was always so positive, so upbeat. She didn't care if the glass was half empty or half full; she just drank it while it was there. He needed that in his life right now. He picked up the wax sandwich wrappers, then paused as he glanced back across the street. No, he needed Tracey in his life, not someone like her, not just her positive attitude. Her. He froze at the realization.

He closed his eyes and took a deep breath. It was an emotional time for him right now and he needed to make sure he didn't put feelings where none really existed. He loved Tracey in their life, but she was a friend. True, a friend with perks, but that was it. Faith was his wife and he loved her.

Selby opened his eyes and stared across the street at the entrance to Joe's Bakery. He could picture the petite auburn-haired girl tying her apron around her waist while flirting with the next customer. Only she could make pastries seductive. He found himself smiling. Was it possible to care about two people at the same time as Tracey had done with Ryan and Chelsea? Was this Faith's battle with Edwin?

He took the trash and dumped it in the garbage bin out back. He was eager for Faith to be back in his arms.

~ ~ ~ ~ ~

Faith was quiet for most of the trip, her thoughts sinking in the quicksand that had become her life. Morgan was stuck on his phone conducting business, making Neal money as he liked to say. Their conversation, when they did have it, was light, him telling her what a great job she had done and how he appreciated all of her hard work. He was heading back to Orlando when they returned and it'd be at least a month before he was in Brevard again.

"To be honest, Neal's thinking of taking me to Mississippi with him," Morgan said as they finally entered Brevard County. "Seems he's ready to branch out more and there's still quite a bit to rebuild after Katrina."

"Where in Mississippi?"

"Right around Biloxi. I was thinking you did such a great job this week, I'd take you with me to train a brand new office."

She couldn't help but smile at the thought and she hoped some of it was true. Of course, knowing Morgan as she did he was also probably hoping to finish their little tryst. She had to admit it would be fun to see what he was like in bed. However, traveling wasn't what she needed at the moment. "Thanks for the offer, but right now I need to focus on what I have at home."

Morgan nodded. "Have you figured any of that out, yet?"

Faith glanced out the window at the passing palm trees and oaks. Florida had such bizarre landscaping, like a hodge podge of plants and trees with no order or design. Her life had suddenly become a hodge podge, as well, and somehow she needed to sort it out and bring order to it. "Not really."

"Well, you're still on my dime, so take the rest of the day off with pay. Go see Selby, go to the beach, go home, whatever, but relax. You've earned it. Everything else will figure itself out. You're a strong woman, Faith, who enjoys her life. You'll know what to do when it's time."

She hoped he was right.

When they pulled into the parking lot at Rutherford Construction, Edwin and Cherish were standing by the back door having a cigarette. Things were back to normal, it seemed. Morgan parked beside her small Toyota and thanked her again for all of her hard work. Faith thanked him for the fun time in return and then both slid out of the truck.

Cherish was standing a few feet from Edwin, but as Faith came around Morgan's truck, she saw her sister slide closer to their boss. Faith took a deep breath. She was taking Morgan's advice and taking the rest of the day off. She was in no mood to put up with the jealousy nonsense.

"How did it go?" Edwin tossed his Salem into the distance as he left Cherish's side and approached Morgan and Faith. "Ready to return my girl to me?"

Cherish glanced at Faith. "Welcome back." She dropped her cigarette and went back inside, leaving the two men alone with Faith.

"Nope," Morgan said. "You get her back Monday morning. I gave her the rest of the day off." He turned to Faith and winked. Turning back around, he gave Edwin's arm a pat as he walked by. "I'll see you inside."

Edwin slipped his hands into his pockets. "So, how was it?"

Faith just glanced at him and then at the door Cherish had passed through. "Quiet," she said, her eyes returning to the tall man in front of her. "Very quiet."

Edwin nodded. "I figured you'd be busy, so I left you alone. Figured you'd reach out to me when you wanted."

"I did reach out to you, but gave up when you never responded. And you mean you thought I was busy with Morgan because you told him he could fuck me? And that's bullshit. An excuse for you to ignore me for a week." Anger coursed through her, ready to erupt and scald the man before her that a week ago she would have done anything for. "How long have you been fucking my sister?"

"Selby told you?"

"He told me Glen's suspicions and then everything fell into place. He shouldn't have had to tell me, though. The signs were all there. I should have seen it myself, but more importantly, you should have told me."

"That would have gone over like a fart in church. Do you want Cherish to know that we've been having sex?" He crisscrossed his arms over his chest and arched an eyebrow at her.

"Hell no! Are you crazy?"

"Well, I'm pretty sure Cherish doesn't want you to know, either. And really, Faith, it's not my place to tell you other people's secrets." He took a deep breath. "Look, I didn't plan any of this. I never dreamed you would actually follow through on any of it and when you did, I was too caught up in it to think about Cherish. You two are nothing alike." He glanced off into the woods in the back field. "I'm sorry. Maybe I should have told you. It was stupid."

"No, Edwin, it was selfish. Just like you ignoring me for the past week was selfish. And cruel." She shuffled into her purse and dug out her keys. Looking up at Edwin, she wanted to cry and scream and slap him, all at the same time. "I'm going home."

"But I want to see you."

"No, you want to fuck me. There's a difference. If you had really wanted to see me, you would have talked to me throughout the week. I don't need a welcome home booty call." She opened her truck door and threw her purse inside. Turning back around to face Edwin, she saw Cherish staring out the break room window. Her sister had been the wild one growing up. It shouldn't have surprised Faith that Cherish was sleeping with their boss. The fact that Faith had been screwing around probably shocked the hell out of Cherish, however. "I'll see you Monday morning." She slid behind the wheel and shut the door.

She caught Cherish's eye as she turned the key. If Glen knew that Cherish was having an affair, what did that mean for their marriage? Faith put the truck in reverse, not looking at Edwin, but with Cherish's face etched into her mind. She felt as if she betrayed Cherish, somehow, and the sad part was that the two sisters really didn't like each other that much. Still, she didn't wish her sister harm.

Faith slipped out onto Eau Gallie Boulevard and headed for the ocean. She dug her phone out of her purse and sent Selby a text. "Heading home. Please close the shop early." She plopped the phone in her lap as she pressed harder on the accelerator. She just wanted to be in her home in the arms of her husband.

Thirty-Six

Selby's arms wrapped around her like a familiar blanket, keeping her warm against the coldness of her thoughts. She had told him everything about her trip, including how Morgan had went down on her a couple of nights ago. He hadn't been mad that she had done it, only that she had waited to share it with him. "I'll ask for the kinky details later when we're naked in bed," he said while he smiled at her. He kissed her on the forehead and tightened his grip on her. She just dropped her head on his chest and breathed in the scent of him.

"Tracey says I'm not to hog you all weekend. She needs some Faith time, too."

Faith gave him a tiny smile. "Tomorrow. Tonight, I want it to be just us."

He kissed the top of her head. "I like that."

So did she. It seemed like forever since it was just the two of them. If someone wasn't visiting, then someone was texting. Faith knew that she had allowed her fascination with Edwin and the chase to consume her. Selby hadn't complained; at least, not until he discovered Cherish's affair with Edwin. At least, not to her. Still, Faith didn't want to lose who they were as a couple. She squeezed his arm as she buried deeper into him. She didn't want to lose any part of him.

She had beaten him home, but he wasn't far behind her. She had stripped and was just stepping into the shower when Selby called out her name, searching for her. As soon as he found her, he ran to her, taking her up in his arms and squeezing the breath out of her. He wasn't even going to allow her to shower in peace, saying that they had been apart too long and he wasn't going to be away from her for another second. As he spoke, he shed his own clothes, making a pile on the floor. Together, they entered the shower.

The scalding water had beat her pale skin a bright pink as he wrapped his arms around her, his lips on her neck, her shoulders. His hand caressed her flesh sending shivers through her even in the burning water. She just stood there, basking in his touch. She felt his fingers glide up her body, his hands cupping her breasts as he kissed her neck. As she leaned her head back against his chest, she reached behind her and pressed her hands against the outside of his thighs. She could feel the strength of his muscles as well as the intensity of how much he missed her with the hardening of his cock against her ass. She slid a hand around his stiff shaft stroking it slowly. She had missed him just as much.

His thumbs toyed with her already erect nipples sending bursts of heat between her legs. "I want you." Her voice was husky, filled with a need that kept growing. It was more than want. It was need.

He pushed her forward. Her hands left his thighs and pressed against the wet tile. The water beat the top of her head, pouring down and over her face. She pushed her ass back as she bent over, offering herself to him. She felt his hands slide from her tits, down her sides to her hips. He didn't wait. She was ready, eager. So was he. With a deep thrust, he was buried all the way inside of her, making her gasp. Water filled her mouth and she allowed it to fill her and flow back out as she pushed back, wanting Selby even deeper. He gripped her hips as he pounded into her, driving hard into her deep cavern as the water washed over her. She savored every thrust, her moans echoing off the tile walls. When her orgasm hit, she allowed it to wash over her as the water did. Her body shook; her inner walls sucking Selby's cock, milking it. She felt it twitch inside of her just before Selby's nectar mixed with hers. By the time his spent cock slipped from her pussy, the shower had begun to turn cold.

He washed her with loving hands afterward, and then dried her with the softest towel he could find. Now, they sat cuddled in a thick quilt in front of a small fire, sipping wine. She could still feel him inside of her and wanted to hold on to that feeling.

She felt Selby's lips press against the top of her head. "I missed you," he whispered. "I was afraid you were still angry with me."

She squeezed his arm again. "I missed you, too. Too much to stay angry with you."

"I'm glad for that." Selby put his chin on her shoulder. "Still, I've never known you to ignore me for so long. Ever, actually."

"I know. I'm sorry. Everything just turned into a cluster fuck. At least now I know part of the reason for Cherish's anger with me at work. What do you think Glen will do?"

She felt him shrug his shoulders. "I don't know. I don't think he does, either. You should have seen him, Faith. He looked so lost."

Faith liked Glen. He was a great father to Jordie and a hard worker. There was quite a bit of Arni to be found in her brother-in-law and she could see why Cherish had been attracted to him. What he saw in her sister, though, Faith would never comprehend. "I've tried to figure out when Cherish started sleeping with Edwin and I think it was when we moved into the new buildings. She spent quite a bit of time with him on interior design. She was even the one who decorated his office. Why had I never seen it?"

"You weren't looking. No offense, babe, but most of the time you have blinders on to everyone around you. If it doesn't affect you, you don't care about it."

"You make me sound like a cold, selfish bitch."

"No. It's just you. It's all of you, really. Your mom. Cherish. You. The Driscoll women have always been about themselves first."

"If I'm so self-absorbed, why do you stay with me?"

He kissed her ear. "Because I'm part of that self-absorbed focus. I love our private world, Faith, and I'm happy hiding here with you. Most of the time that is. However, that doesn't mean the people around you aren't living their own lives, as well, going through struggles and hurting. Sometimes, you have to force yourself to look up and around at others."

She kept quiet. There wasn't anything to say really. She knew who she was and she had tried hard to separate herself from the back-biting of her family. Of course, if she hadn't been so blind to what Cherish was doing, she would have known what a minefield she had been entering. As much as she wanted to blame Edwin, the truth was, it was just as much her fault as his. She had chosen to close her eyes to everything around her and live her life like a bull in a china shop.

"Look, I'm not going to tell you to stop seeing Edwin. I just want you to be careful."

She nodded slightly. At the moment that was the only answer she had, which she knew was no answer at all. She didn't have one, really. She had a notebook full of questions, but not one answer.

Well, that wasn't exactly true. She had Selby and he was the answer to her life. Now, she had to find the answers to everything else.

~ ~ ~ ~ ~

Selby groaned as someone persistently pushed the doorbell, sending its ding dong chime throughout the house. Through blurry eyes he tried to focus on the time. Eight twenty-seven. He dropped his head back on the warm pillow. He was going to kill someone.

He glanced over at his wife who was totally unaffected by the constant chime. They had talked way into the night and made love in front of the fire and once more when they finally slid under the covers. The future of their game had not been decided, but at least she wasn't still angry with him. And she was home. He brushed a stray strand of hair from her face as he smiled at the pillow marks on her cheek. He had needed her back home.

The doorbell screamed again. Selby slid from his side of the bed and grabbed his robe. As he covered his naked body, he stumbled to the front door, forcing himself awake and out of a murderous rage for the intrusion. As he peered through the peephole at the perky face on the other side, all he could think was that he should have known.

He opened the door with a sigh. "Tracey, it's too damn early for cheerfulness."

"And here I thought you were a morning person." She bounced into the house, a box of bagels in one hand and a drink carrier with three hot coffees, steam rising from the drink holes on the lids, in the other. "You're lucky I waited this long."

He didn't doubt the validity of her statement.

"Now, by your appearance, I'm assuming our girl is still in bed. You didn't wear her out did you?"

"I tried my best." He followed in her wake, wishing she would slow down long enough for him to snag one of the coffees. It wasn't going to happen.

He watched as her long red hair, which was pulled back into a ponytail, swished across her back in contrast to the sway of her ass. She wore a pair of faded blue jean shorts that barely covered the round cup of her ass and a brown spaghetti-strap blouse. She had kicked her sandals off as soon as she entered the house and pranced through as if she owned it. She didn't stop in the kitchen, but went straight through to the master bedroom and her sleeping target. He followed her, smiling and shaking his head.

"Rise and shine, sleeping beauty. I brought breakfast." She sat the box on Faith's nightstand. "Of sorts."

Faith rolled over, staring, but not seeing. "How late did I sleep?"

"Miss Williams, here, allowed you the privilege of sleeping in until eight thirty," Selby said as he took the drink carrier from the smaller woman's hands. "Gracious, isn't she?"

"I think I was." Tracey reached for the coffee carrier and pulled one of the cardboard cups from the container, handing it to Faith.

The prone woman stared at both of them as if they were crazy. Selby just shrugged as he smiled back at her. "Don't look at me. I've never been able to control her. She's like a playful stray that thinks it owns you and expects you to play with it."

Tracey reached for the sheet covering Faith's naked body and tried to peek under it. Faith kept it clamped tight to her body. The redhead winked. "We can play later." She kept the coffee held out for Faith until the other woman took it. "So, what are we doing today?"

"Not sleeping, obviously." Faith pushed herself up on the bed, keeping the sheet tucked around her. Once settled, she popped the lid off the cup of coffee and blew on the beige liquid inside. At least the coffee had been made the way she liked it. After taking a gentle sip, she said, "I have no plans except sleeping today. It was a long week."

"What? You can't sleep all day. You've been gone a whole week. We have to make up for lost time."

"And you thought a box of bagels at eight thirty in the blessed morning was the way to start?"

"And coffee. Don't forget I brought coffee." Tracey's eyes were mischievous as she practically bounced on the bed. "Now, let's get going. The day is wasting away."

Selby just laughed as he watched the two of them on the bed, one full of energy and the other still a morning zombie. It seemed natural, the three of them together. Faith seemed happier when the other woman was around. Even with all of Tracey's antics, there was a calmness when the three of them were together. He sat on the bed and sipped his coffee as the shorter of the two ladies pried his wife out of bed and into the shower. Of course, Faith stopped the redhead at the shower curtain and kept that part of her morning to herself. It was probably all she would be allowed.

Tracey sat back on the bed, legs folded and crossed in front of her. With a tilt of her head, she indicated the shower. "How's our girl doing?"

He stared at the closed door a moment. Finally, he gave a shake of his head. "I don't know. She was very clingy last night. Just wanted to be held and cuddled. She told me all about her week, but it wasn't with the same playful naughtiness she usually attaches to it." He glanced back at the redhead on the bed. "It's like she's made some decisions that sadden her. I'm not sure what's going on."

"Something happen we don't know about?"

He shrugged "Your guess is as good as mine."

"I guess we'll find out when she's ready to tell us," Tracey said. Selby just nodded.

They heard the shower shut off and changed the subject. "So, what are we going to get into today?" She asked with a glance at the bathroom door.

Selby smiled at her, causing her to blush when she turned back around and noticed. "I like this *we* by the way. Faith seems happier when you're around. Calmer, even."

"I enjoy being around. I'd rather be here with my two favorite people than home alone."

"Don't see me enough during the week?" His grin teased a smile out of her. The bathroom door opened and Faith walked out with one towel perched on her head holding her wet hair and another around her semi-dry body. Both turned and watched her as she walked out and joined Tracey on the bed.

The redhead leaned over and ran her finger down Faith's arm. "I don't think I could ever get enough of the two of you."

"Good, cause I like you here," Faith said as she took the other woman's hand in hers and squeezed.

Selby just watched the exchange, wondering what it was that was actually being said and feeling good about it, anyway. His wife had under gone some type of change within herself. That was obvious even though what that change was he couldn't even guess. He had noticed that there had been no mention of Edwin or her game with him since she returned. Even her stories about Morgan lacked her usual excitement in the telling. There was no rush to get back to the office of Rutherford Construction and the attention the men gave her there. For the first time since they had agreed to explore with others, Faith truly seemed happy to be at home.

He glanced at the redhead and somehow had a feeling that his home had gained a new member. As he watched the two ladies in front of him plan out their day, he realized he wasn't opposed to the idea of their family getting bigger. Although he wasn't sure what that meant, he knew he enjoyed watching the two in front of him getting along so well. They were happy and that brightened his world.

~ ~ ~ ~ ~

They spent the entire day dragging poor Selby in and out of every store that came into their minds. Faith could tell that, although he wasn't complaining, her poor husband was foot-sore and tired. Finally, the girls surrendered, picking up Chinese for dinner, and allowed him to take them home. He deserved a drink and his back deck. She had to admit, she was ready for another quiet evening with those closest to her heart, as well. However, when she saw her mother's Buick in the driveway, she knew quiet had just flown out the window.

"Were you expecting your mother?" Selby gave her a puzzled look as he pulled in behind Tracey's vehicle.

"I never expect my mother."

"I'm sure she just missed you and wanted to see how your trip went," the redhead said from the backseat.

Faith and Selby just turned and stared at her. "You don't know my mother."

"Oh," Tracey said. "Oops. This will be an experience then."

Selby popped his door open and the ladies followed suit. "Well, it *was* a nice day," he said as he stepped onto the driveway.

Valerie Driscoll stood on the front step, arms crossed over her chest as her handbag dangled from her right elbow. By her expression, it was a personal affront to her that they were not there waiting for her arrival. The fact that she hadn't called to even find out if they were home wouldn't matter to her. People were supposed to always be available when she wanted them, not living their own life. The stark woman just stared at them as they approached, her eyebrow arched as she took in Tracey.

"Mom, why didn't you tell us you were coming over?" Faith held the bag of Chinese in front of her as a shield. Her body had instantly gone tense.

"I wasn't aware I needed to call before visiting," Valerie said, her words an accusation.

"Only if you want to make sure we're actually here," Selby said as he climbed the steps. "We're about to have dinner. Would you care to join us?"

Tracey climbed the steps last, keeping a smile on her face as if nothing was going on underneath everyone's words. "Hi, I'm Tracey. We haven't met, yet."

Valerie's eyebrows arched as she took in the minuscule shorts of the smaller woman. "A little exposed, aren't we?"

"Mom!"

"Valerie, Tracey was invited. You weren't. You will be polite to our guest or leave."

Valerie physically bristled at the rebuke, but said nothing of it. "I need to discuss a family matter."

Faith knew Tracey was about to offer to disappear, but she cut her friend off before she could. "Tracey is family and we're about to eat.

So, either join us and say what you need to say or come back when you've called first."

Faith could feel Selby staring at her. She knew he was surprised, but she was fed up with cowering before her mother. Valerie Driscoll was no longer going to treat her like a doormat and wipe her shitty attitude off on her daughter. Faith was in charge of her own life and she was going to live it her way with whom she wanted. She turned and looked at an obviously impressed Selby. "Are we going to stand out here or go in and eat?"

Selby smiled as he pushed the door open. "By all means, my love. Your castle awaits."

Faith went inside, not bothering to see if her mother followed her or not. She didn't care one way or the other what the older woman did. As she entered the kitchen, Tracey and she set the bags on the counter as Selby pulled plates out of the cupboard. Four plates. Valerie stood just barely in the kitchen, her arms still folded together. Faith didn't say anything as she dished out the food. If her mom wanted to talk, she would. If not, she could leave.

Selby wasn't as patient, however. "If this is a family matter, where's Arni? Shouldn't he be with you?"

"My husband is at some writer's group living his dream while his family falls apart around him."

Selby nodded, already guessing as to what was coming, but asked anyway. "So, what's up with the family that brought you to our doorstep all cranky?" He pulled a Merlot from the wine rack and began to open it. He was going to need it. Tracey remained silent as she dished out the food.

"I would like to know what you did to cause Glen to leave his family."

Everyone stopped and just stared at Valerie. Faith and Selby glanced at each other, both, confused and ignorant, as to whatever was going on. Turning back to her mother, the accusation on the other woman's face apparent.

"What makes you think we did anything?" Faith said as she dumped lo mein on the plates. "I've been out of town for a week and haven't talked to either of them. I didn't even know they were having problems." Yet, Faith assumed that Glen had decided Cherish was lying about sleeping with Edwin.

"Yes, I heard. A business trip alone with your boss. Not a proper thing for a married woman to do."

"Mother, I don't care if you approve of what I do or not. It was business. I had my own room. However, even if I didn't, it's none of your damn business. You didn't approve when I was the perfect obedient daughter and I could care less what you think now." Faith stood, back straight as she faced her mother.

Valerie stared at her daughter. "What you do is your choice, but to accuse your sister of sleeping with her boss is ridiculous and vindictive."

"I never accused Cherish of anything and if she told you that, then your precious daughter is a liar."

"Not you. Him" Valerie pointed at Selby.

"Me?" Selby's eyebrows went up and Faith could tell he was equally confused. "I never told Glen that Cherish was sleeping with anyone. You have your facts wrong."

"Then where did Glen get the idea?" Valerie was like a dog with a bone when she had a notion in her head. There was no chance of her letting go.

"From Cherish," Selby answered. He poured three glasses of wine, grabbed one and downed half of it. He continued talking as he topped his glass off. "Glen came to me the other day and said Cherish had changed, become grumpier, if that's even possible. He told me that he thought she was sleeping with Edwin and her reaction confirmed it in his mind. I didn't offer an opinion one way or another, except to tell him to talk it out with her."

"And why didn't you just tell him that it was crazy? Cherish would never do that."

Selby took a deep breath. "I didn't tell him that because Cherish was cheating on him. Edwin told me so himself."

Valerie just stared at him. Faith could see the battle within her mother. The perfect daughter wasn't perfect anymore and Valerie Driscoll didn't know how to wrap her mind around it. "I don't believe it." She turned to Faith. "This is your doing."

Tracey, who had been standing quietly by the kitchen sink, laughed. "Faith forced her sister to fuck her boss."

"I don't care what you believe, Mother." Faith took a step toward Valerie. She had all she was going to take from her family. "I only care that you leave. Get out. Now."

Valerie opened her mouth to say something, but Faith took another step and cut her off. "No more. Just. Get. Out."

The older woman just stared a moment. Faith knew her mother had not expected such a reaction. It didn't matter what they said, however. Valerie could have walked in on Cherish being pounded by Edwin and still believe it was Faith's fault. Nothing was ever going to change in that area and Faith was tired of trying. She adored her father, but as far as she was concerned, the rest of her family could go to hell. Finally, Valerie just turned and left.

Faith watched her mother walk out the door. As it clicked shut, anger burst into sobs and she felt her chest constrict, making it hard to breathe. Four arms wrapped around her and she allowed herself to fall into them as she cried out her anguish.

Thirty-Seven

Sunday dawned with the temperature already pushing towards eighty. Winter in Florida was always short. Tracey had spent the night, nuzzled on Faith's right while Selby had draped her left. After Valerie Driscoll left, Faith had remained quiet in a numb aftershock. The others hadn't forced her to communicate and when she did speak it was to vent about her mother's audacity at blaming her for Cherish sleeping with Edwin. She never had to do anything for her mother to paint her out as the bad guy. What she had ever done to earn her mother's scorn, she could never fathom. And now....

Now, she didn't care. She was through being pushed around and made to feel inferior by her family. She didn't feel bad about standing up to her mother. However, she didn't feel good, either.

She felt lost. Separated. The gulf that had been there between her mother and her was now a chasm and she doubted it would ever be different. Cherish was the one who had screwed up her life, and yet, it was Faith who was bearing the blame. It would always be that way.

Once they roused themselves out of bed, Selby made breakfast while the two ladies decided what to do with their day. Faith didn't want to drive anywhere. A week away had made her just want to isolate herself from the world. However, the prospect of a leisurely walk on the beach was more than promising, so they each put on some shorts and tee-shirts, left their shoes on the deck, and hit the sand. The waves were choppy, two foot swells and the wind coming in off the Atlantic was cool enough to counter the late morning sun. They ventured out, more for enjoyment than exercise, stopping here and there to examine shells or some lone piece of driftwood.

Tracey spent half the time at Selby's side and half at Faith's, her normal bantering finally bringing Faith's smile back out. By the time they were heading back for a late lunch, Faith had forgotten all about her mom's visit and was laughing with the others. The day was bright and her spirits had finally decided to join it. That is, until they neared the weathered steps leading up to their back door.

There sat Cherish.

Faith stopped and just stared once she saw her sister. She could feel Selby glance at her, just waiting to see what she was going to do. Tracey stood with her hands on her hips and a confused look on her face. "I take it you two know the woman on the steps," the short redhead said.

"My sister." Faith took a deep breath and continued walking. "This should be interesting."

Selby just nodded. Tracey kept quiet, but moved to Faith's other side so that Selby and she flanked Faith. Her protectors. Hopefully, Cherish would see that Faith wasn't alone and rein in her normal attitude.

As she neared her sister, Faith could see her blood red eyes, swollen from crying more than likely. She had her arms wrapped around her chest, hugging herself as she bent over as if ready to puke at any moment. Her hair was more a mess than normal and Faith doubted it was from the wind. Cherish looked as if she hadn't slept since Faith had seen her on Friday. She couldn't really imagine what her sister was going through. A personal hell, more than likely, but Faith wasn't about to feel sorry for the woman. Not with the way Cherish had treated her.

Cherish watched as they approached and Faith stopped at the base of the stairs, arms crossed over her chest. Cherish was sitting far enough up that it made them eye-to-eye. She didn't say anything. She just waited.

Selby spoke instead. "Hey, Cherish. Your mom told us what was going on. I'm sorry to hear it's happening."

Cherish glanced at him and nodded. "Me too. Thanks."

Faith continued to stare. "Why are you here?"

Cherish looked out at the breaking waves, then down at the beach. It was obvious she was struggling to hold it together. Finally, she stared down at her hands. "I don't know what to do. I've lost Glen. You've got Edwin. I ..."

"I don't have Edwin." Faith's voice wasn't a shout, but it was cold and hard. "I have Selby."

Cherish snorted a short laugh. "You were fucking Edwin. I'm not stupid." She glanced at Selby. "He seduced your wife, too."

"No, he didn't," Selby said.

"Bullshit. Your wife isn't Miss Innocent. He got to her just as he got to me. She fucked him."

Faith started laughing. "You came out here to tell Selby I was fucking your boyfriend? Your marriage is screwed and you're way of fixing it is to try and ruin mine? You cheated on your husband, Cherish."

"So did you!" Cherish stood to her feet and Faith saw both Selby and Tracey take a step forward.

"No, I didn't," Faith said. "You are very much mistaken there."

"You fucked him!"

Selby placed his hand on Faith as he spoke. "Yes, she did, but she didn't cheat on me. As I said, Edwin didn't seduce Faith. She seduced him. She didn't cheat on me, because I knew it was going on."

"You knew? You *knew* she was screwing our boss and you were okay with it?" She jerked a finger at Tracey. "Are you two fucking her, as well?"

"Probably not now since you've shown up and ruined the mood," the redhead quipped. "Your family has lousy timing. First your mother, now you."

Faith reached over and gave Tracey's arm a gentle squeeze. When the redhead turned her focus to Faith, she just gave a soft shake of the head as if to say, "Not now."

"Cherish, you can't blame Faith for what you did," Selby said. "I'm sorry that your life is screwed up right now, but the way to fix your marriage isn't to come here trying to screw up ours. What we do is our business and I assure you, we both know what the other is doing."

"How can you be okay with it? It's wrong." Cherish stood with her arms across her chest.

"No. You fucking Edwin behind Glen's back was wrong. He didn't deserve it and he doesn't deserve you. He deserves better." Faith took two steps forward. "Now, get off my property." She walked past her sister.

She didn't look back.

~ ~ ~ ~ ~

Selby watched his wife climb the stairs, arms still folded across her chest. He motioned for Tracey to follow and keep an eye on her while he turned and faced his sister-in-law. She had been watching Faith's departure and was startled when she turned around and he was still standing there.

With a sheepish look, she ducked her head. When she spoke, her voice was a bare whisper against the ocean breeze. "I'm sorry. I'll get out of your hair."

"Not yet." He stepped in front of her, blocking her from walking way. His patience with the Driscoll family was at an end. "I have tried to keep my mouth shut, but you and your mother have pushed too far. I don't know where either of you get off blaming Faith for you cheating on Glen, but it's total bullshit."

"My mother blamed Faith? When?"

"Last night. She was here when we got home. Seems none of you know to call first." Selby stood with his hands on his hips. "Faith has never done a damn thing to you or your mother to deserve the abuse you both give her. I don't care what you two do, but you're not going to hurt my wife anymore. What we do with our life and in our marriage is our business and I don't care if you approve or not. I'm sorry that your marriage is on the rocks, but that's your fault. Not Faith's. Own it and leave her the hell out of it."

Cherish just stared at him. Her eyes were narrow slits and he could see the anger on her face. He knew she wanted to say something, but was smart enough to keep it to herself. Instead, she just turned and walked away.

He watched her for a moment and then climbed the stairs to check on Faith. The two of them had made a pact when they were first married that each would handle their own family. He stuck to that pact eight years too long. He wasn't going to do it a day longer.

As Selby entered the kitchen, both women were preparing lunch. Soft jazz played throughout the house and the smell of bacon along with sizzling beef wafted through the air. It was going to be a greasy lunch.

He opened the fridge and pulled out three beers. After popping the top off each bottle, he set one in front of each of the ladies. No one was speaking. Tracey glanced at him and just shrugged. He knew she was lost in what to do to help Faith. She had been thrust into a family drama that had been going on for years. He married into it, but Tracey had been plopped right into the mess. Selby knew what the Driscoll's were like before agreeing to marry Faith. Tracey had been clueless. She was definitely getting the full show now.

Faith was chopping onions and Selby could see her temper flaring, her chopping harsh and violent. At one point she slammed the blade on the counter as she glanced at him. "That little bitch thought she was going to ruin *my* marriage. She came all the way over here just to try and rat me out. The sneaky, conniving little bitch."

"I'd say she wasted a trip," Tracey said as she sipped her beer with one hand and flipped bacon with the other.

Selby reached into the fridge and began to pull out the rest of the fixings for their lunch. "She screwed up and needs someone to share her misery. It's how your family works."

Faith returned to slicing onions. Selby finished laying out the cheese and condiments and went to the pantry for the buns. He wasn't sure how he was going to salvage their day. Once Faith allowed herself to be inflamed, she usually stayed that way for days. He needed to talk to her about Edwin and her plans for their game, but now was definitely not the time. Knowing her, she would only continue the relationship to spite Cherish at this point. No, he needed his wife calm when they discussed Edwin.

They ate lunch on the deck, the afternoon sun a bright contradiction to the chill of the ocean breeze. Tracey tried to pull Faith out of her funk, but it wasn't working. His wife was determined to stew herself into a miserable evening. Finally, the redhead gave up and geared her conversation toward Selby. Faith remained quiet and stared at her food.

"I think after lunch I'll let you two have some space," Tracey said as she popped a stray piece of bacon into her mouth. "I need to get some laundry done if I'm going to have anything to wear to work next week."

"I don't know. I think a nude uniform might bring in more business."

"I'm sure it would bring in the voyeurs. However, I need paying customers." Tracey took a swallow of her beer. "What are you two going to do for the rest of the day besides pine away for my company?"

"Oh, that's all we'll be doing. Sitting here moping because you're not with us, thinking about how dismal our lives are without you around."

Tracey smiled as she nodded. "As it should be." Looking around at the empty plates, she scooped hers up. "C'mon, I'll help with clean up and then you can escort me to my car."

Clean up was quick and, true to her word, Tracey grabbed her stuff and headed for the door. Faith followed her as Selby stepped in front to open it. As the two women hugged, Faith whispered an apology. "This isn't how I wanted our day to go."

Tracey squeezed her tight. "I know you didn't, honey. It's not your fault. None of it is your fault. Don't allow your mother or sister to convince you any differently. Cherish made her bed and fucked around in it. That's on her. Don't let it cloud what you and Selby want for yourselves." Tracey leaned up on her toes and kissed Faith's cheek. "You're an awesome lady. Don't let them into your head."

Faith gave Tracey a kiss on the cheek and squeezed her arm. "I'll try."

Selby followed Tracey out to her car. Before she slipped behind the wheel, she turned and faced him. "You reassure that girl, Selby. She needs to know she's done nothing wrong. Her sister's a bitch and so is her mother."

Selby smiled at her as he leaned down and kissed her softly on the cheek. "Welcome to the party," he said as he stood back up. "I'll take care of her. This isn't the first time they've ganged up on her for no reason."

"Well, those party poopers don't need to be pooping on her party." She slid behind the wheel, her body still tight with the aggravation of what they were doing to Faith. "Call me if you two need anything."

Selby promised he would and then stood and watched the fiery redhead drive off. It made him proud that she had gotten so upset over how Faith was treated by her family. It was more intense than a mere friend's reaction.

But then Tracey was far more than a mere friend.

When he entered the house, he found Faith sitting in front of a cold fireplace, her arms wrapped around her knees holding them to her chest. He went up behind her, wrapping his legs and arms around her, and held her to his chest, his chin on her shoulder. He didn't say anything. He just held her and stared into the darkness of yesterday's ashes. He wasn't going to rush her, knowing she would speak when she was ready. While he was her shield from the brutality of a selfish world, he couldn't protect her from her own family.

~ ~ ~ ~ ~

She felt his legs press against her thighs as his arms wrapped around her chest, his breath warm and steady against her cheek. She fell back against him and willed some of his strength into the coldness of her heart.

Faith knew what her husband was thinking, that she had taken her family's words as proof that she had done something wrong. He had watched her practically grovel at her mother's feet all of these years for just an inkling of acceptance from the woman. She had tolerated her sister's harshness as a means of being close to her mother, afraid that angering Cherish would anger her mother and cause herself to be pushed away even further. She didn't doubt at all the course of his thoughts. The sad thing was that a few days ago he would have been absolutely right.

But not that night. Not then. Not ever again.

When her mother stood there the previous night accusing her for Cherish's indiscretion, a switch inside of Faith had been flipped. She wasn't worried about her mother accepting her any longer, because at that moment she realized that she hated Valerie Driscoll. She had cowered enough before the family matriarch. She would do so no longer. Her mother didn't deserve her love and had never earned her respect. She would receive neither, ever again.

And Cherish. Cherish had only earned her contempt and pity. Her sister was a spoiled brat used to getting her way. She was finally reaping what she had sown. Karma could be a bitch and Cherish had earned the Universe's scorn. Faith didn't take pleasure in what the other was going through, but she wouldn't pity her, either. She deserved every bit of it. Glen and Jordie, however, did not. It was selfish and mean.

Faith caressed Selby's arm. She had been just as selfish. He had warned her where her game with Edwin was leading and she had refused to listen. The truth was she hadn't wanted to listen. She was having fun and for once just wanted to abandon herself to the sensations that coursed through her. It was exciting to be so daring. She didn't want to give that up. She didn't want to sacrifice her desires for the greater good of her family again. She deserved to be selfish just this once. She had earned it by putting up with her mother all of her life, for being the good, obedient girl everyone expected.

She felt Selby nuzzle the side of her head, his lips pressing against her ear. She squeezed his arms as she tried to bury herself inside him. She had put herself ahead of him, something she had never done before, and it wasn't because of neglect or for her own protection. It was because of the thrill of being taken and used by another man. Usually it was men who thought with the head that dangled between their legs, but it had been her who had allowed her pussy lips to do the thinking for her.

"I'm sorry."

He squeezed her. "You don't owe anyone an apology, love. You haven't done anything wrong."

"Not to my family or Edwin, no," she said, still clutching his arms. "But to you. I ignored your warnings and forgot our rules for this adventure. When we started, we said that if either of us felt it needed to end, we would put a halt to it. You tried, but I ignored you. If I had listened to you, perhaps things wouldn't have become so heated."

He kissed her cheek. "We're good, babe. Always have been. It was a new adventure. There were bound to be some speed bumps along the way."

"I feel more like I crashed and burned."

Selby laughed and then spun her around so they faced each other. "You didn't have an accident, I promise. The whole idea was to have fun and try something new. Did you have fun?"

She couldn't deny that she had. Everything she experienced with Edwin had been a rush of sexual adrenaline. The risk of being caught as well as the chase had been most of the thrill, the two of them panting after each other, the whole cat and mouse game.

"So you're feeling guilty because Cherish wasn't the good girl and you're allowing that to cloud everything else," Selby said. "Don't allow her fuck-ups to determine your course in life. This is still just about you and me and whoever else we allow inside."

She smiled at him. "Like Tracey."

He nodded. "And Edwin if you still want him."

She stared into Selby's blue eyes, amazed at the softness. He was actually willing to allow her to keep her game with Edwin, even after all the chaos it had just caused. As always, he was putting her wants above everything else. Yet, did she still want Edwin? He had deceived her, in a way, concerning Cherish. However, she was sure her sister wanted more than Faith had ever intended. All she wanted was his cock. Was it still worth it, though?

She gazed up into Selby's eyes and suddenly knew what she wanted. Leaning forward, she pressed her lips to his and tasted his warmth. She continued to press, pushing him backwards until they were flat on the floor, her body covering his as she wrapped her arms around his head. Their kissing grew hungrier as she parted his lips with her tongue to taste him. She could feel his cock growing under her, pressing its need into her.

Pulling her lips away from his, she whispered, "I love you." He was about say it back, but her lips were already on his again.

Thirty-Eight

The offices of Rutherford Construction were quiet, almost in a funeral home sort of way. Even the ever perky Ashlynn seemed to sense the underlying mood and reined in her bubbliness. Faith waved at the buxom blonde as she passed her and received a limp wave back. Something must have happened before Faith had made it to work. She wasn't sure if it had to do with her or not. How far had Cherish taken her accusations?

As she stepped into the hall behind the front lobby, purse and lunch box dangling from her fingers, she noticed Morgan talking in hushed whispers with Jed Jorrell. She gave Morgan a curious glance when he looked her way, giving her a quick nod in greeting. He wasn't supposed to be there. Something was definitely off.

She said good morning to both and then passed by into the Girls' Den. Nessa was already there, but Cherish wasn't. Actually, as Faith took a closer look, nothing of her sister's was there. Her desk had been completely cleared off. That could explain why Morgan was there. *This is going to be a Monday to end all Mondays. Great.*

She glanced at Nessa who just shrugged. "It's been a tomb around here since I arrived. Edwin is MIA, as well, but his office isn't as empty as her desk."

Faith nodded. "Interesting." Had Glen killed Edwin? Had her mother?

Morgan popped his head through the doorway. "Faith, gotta minute?"

"Always." She tucked her purse into the bottom drawer of her desk as the boss of her boss vanished from sight. She glanced back at Nessa before leaving. "If I don't come back, it was nice working with you."

"Good luck," the smaller woman said with a slight laugh.

Morgan was waiting halfway down the hall toward his office. She started to speak when she reached him, but he held up his hand, holding off any comments. He then led her quietly to his office, remaining silent until they were tucked away. He sat on the edge of his desk and gestured for her to take a seat, but she declined with a shake of her head. She crossed her arms over her chest and waited.

He ignored the refusal. "Did you know your sister was going to quit?"

"No. I still haven't been told. I just noticed her desk. I also heard that Edwin hasn't shown up today."

Morgan nodded. He studied the carpet for a moment as if trying to decide what to say or perhaps how much to say. When he did look at her, his eyes were squinted as if examining her for a reaction. "I'll tell you how I would like this conversation to go, then you tell me if it can or not. It has to be your call. First, I would like to talk as friends, completely off the record. Afterward, we need a company conversation."

After a moment of silence, Faith realized he was waiting on her decision. She nodded, not sure to what she was really agreeing. "Friends, of course."

She could see a look of relief flow across his face as he visibly relaxed where he was sitting. "Good. It seems you and I came home to a hornets nest. I'd like to hear what you know, then I'll add my knowledge."

Faith nodded. "I assume this is about Cherish and Edwin?" When Morgan nodded, she continued. "Well, I haven't talked to Edwin since we saw him Friday and he tried to put the charm on. I told him he was an ass and went home. As far as Cherish is concerned, my mother showed up at my house blaming me for Cherish fucking Edwin and Glen leaving his wife. It was the first I had heard of it. Then Sunday,

Cherish showed up and tried to cause problems between Selby and me, but I've never lied to my husband, so he just laughed at her. That's it. I didn't know she was quitting until I got here."

Morgan took a deep breath. "Too bad it's too early for a drink. I could use one right now."

"So what's going on?"

"I received a call from Jed last night. Cherish asked him to let her into the office to get her stuff. She told him she was quitting and didn't want to face anyone this morning, especially, and I quote, 'that fucking egotistical jackass boss of mine.' Well, Jed had to call that jackass and both Edwin and Cherish arrived at the office at the same time. Jed was already here, even though Edwin had told him to stay home. Well, needless to say, Jed now knows about all of you screwing around. Apparently, Edwin and Cherish got into a huge shouting match, which ended with your sister drop kicking Edwin's balls into some unseen goal post. Cherish then retrieved her personal belongings and left and Edwin took off. I haven't heard from him and he isn't answering anyone's calls. I was actually kind of hoping you had heard from him."

Faith sat on the arm of one of his leather chairs as she took in all he had said. She could picture Cherish going off on Edwin, unleashing all of her anger, hurt, and frustration on the man's testicles. Yet, where would Edwin sulk away to? "He didn't talk to me the entire week we were gone, as you know, and I didn't give him a warm reception when we returned. I told him I knew about Cherish and he knew I was pretty pissed off. I doubt he'd run to one sister after the other just about took off his nuts."

Morgan laughed as he shuffled on the desk. "No. No, you're probably right." He shook his head. "I'll tell ya, it's a mess. I left a message that he needs to get in touch with me by the end of the day. If he does reach out to you, please tell him to call me."

Faith said she would. "So, what's the business part of this conversation? Am I fired?"

He gave her a puzzled look. "For what? Having consensual sex? I'd have to fire me, as well, and I like my job. No, I'm not letting anyone go unless Edwin refuses to call me. What I want to do is give you your sister's job."

She just stared at him. A promotion? She did not see that one coming.

"You're damn good at your job, Faith. Hell, you were better than Cherish, but I couldn't rock Edwin's boat. Truth is, that's why I took you with me and not her. I want someone with your work ethics in that head chair."

"Well, I don't know. I'd have to talk to Selby." She stood there stunned. "Pay raise, by chance?"

"Of course and a good one. More vacation time, as well. Talk to your husband and let me know as soon as you can. I don't want a hole left in that spot too long."

Faith said she would and then it was time to get back to work. When she entered the office, Nessa welcomed her back with a wink, but Faith could only smile at her, still confused by everything that transpired that morning. It was quite a bit to take in and she really wasn't sure which way she wanted to go. Of course, taking Cherish's job would piss her mother off and it wouldn't matter that her sister had quit without notice. She didn't care. At the moment, anything that angered her mother made Faith happy.

She was going to take the job.

~ ~ ~ ~ ~

Selby hung up the phone with a feeling of pride for his wife. She deserved the promotion. Faith had always been a hard worker, throwing herself into whatever was asked of her. He understood the conflict going on within her, however, an inner sense of betrayal to Cherish for stepping in where her sister had stepped out. Yet, she deserved the new position *and* the pay raise. She deserved the recognition.

The morning had been slow at the bookstore. Only one visitor had graced his door and they had only purchased a small paperback for fifty cents. He hoped his entire day wasn't going to follow the same track.

Soft jazz played in the background as Selby sat and stared at the picture of Faith in Key West that he kept at his crowded desk. He had given her permission to keep seeing Edwin if she wanted, but the truth was he wanted the relationship to end. It had already wreaked havoc within their family as well as Rutherford Construction. He wasn't sure where the damage would end or how Glen and Cherish would fare. Selby just wanted it over and life to move on. However, life didn't work that way.

Faith wasn't going to work that way, either.

Still, this had to be her choice. He wouldn't force it upon her because if he did she might resent him for it. He could only hope she would make the right decision.

He needed more coffee. Pushing himself out of his chair, Selby headed to the back of the store where his mini kitchen resided. As he finished refilling his #1 Husband mug, the bell over the door sounded. He suddenly regretted his earlier wish for more customers. He really would have preferred a nice, quiet day.

Taking a sip of his coffee, he almost choked on it when he saw Cherish standing there. He glanced at her, but said nothing as he walked back to his chair. Faith's sister fidgeted with her hands as she warred within herself about whatever had brought her to his store. Selby would have preferred customers to Faith's family.

He took another sip of his coffee and just waited.

Cherish took a deep breath that lifted her tired shoulders. "I'm sorry for yesterday. I was hurt and angry and took it out on Faith and you. I was wrong for doing that."

Selby stared at her for a moment and then nodded. "Faith's the one you should apologize to."

"I know. And I will." She stood still for a minute, obviously hoping he would say something more. He had nothing else to say to her. "Anyway," she went on after the silence dragged. "I just wanted to come by and apologize."

"Thank you."

She gave him a weak smile and then left. He watched as she slipped out the door, and as another hand grabbed it. Tracey walked in as his sister-in-law left, a shocked expression on the redhead's face. "What the hell was she doing here? Surely, not buying books."

Selby stared at the door. "I'm not even sure she reads." He took a sip of his coffee as he shook the feeling of pity for Cherish that was creeping over him. She didn't deserve it. "She came to apologize for yesterday. I think she expected me to blubber with gratefulness."

Tracey cocked an eyebrow at him. "I hope she was disappointed."

"She was." He gave Tracey a satisfied smile. "And what brings you out of your cave? It's not lunchtime, yet."

Her expression changed and for the first time since he had met the fiery woman, she seemed unsure of herself, almost afraid. She was always confident, upbeat. Now, standing there in front of him, she almost seemed like a frightened school girl.

"How did it go after I left last night?"

"Quiet. She was pretty edgy. We sat in front of the fire and talked most of the night."

"What is she going to do about Edwin?"

Selby shrugged. "I have no idea and I'm not sure she does, either. This whole thing is a fiasco. I'm not sure what direction we'll go, yet. Why?"

She went to run a hand through her hair, and then remembered it was pulled up in a ponytail and stopped. "I figured you two might be making some changes in your adventures. I guess I was just curious if we were still going to be friends and all. I have become quite attached to both of you and not really sure how I'd handle losing you both." Tears pooled at the bottom of her eyes and she wrapped her arms around herself trying to hold it all in.

Selby set his mug on the counter and walked around to where she stood, his heart aching at the pain in her eyes. Placing a hand on each of her arms, he gazed into her emerald eyes and smiled his most reassuring smile. "Sweetie, you're not an adventure; you're family. You're not going anywhere and neither are we." He leaned in and kissed her forehead. "You're a part of us," he said as he pulled her to him, hugging her tight.

He felt her arms wrap around him and squeezed as if she'd float away if she let go. She buried her face in his chest and he could feel the wetness of her tears soaking into his shirt. "Good. Because I don't want to go anywhere else."

He kissed the top of her head as he caressed her back. "You won't."

~ ~ ~ ~ ~

Selby called Faith during lunch and filled her in on all of his visitors. She was surprised that Cherish had shown up and even more shocked that she apologized to him. However, she knew it would be a cold day in Hell before her sister ever apologized to her. She didn't care. She didn't need it. She had made her decision about her family and nothing they could do would ever bother her again. She would stay in touch with her father, but the rest could go to Hell.

Her heart broke when he told her about Tracey, however. The fact that the other woman thought they could so easily dismiss her from their lives and turn their backs on her caused her to pause and consider how deep the three of them had grown together. Edwin had been a game, but Tracey had become intertwined in their daily lives. Faith immediately called the redhead and gave her the same assurances Selby had.

"Nothing going on has anything to do with you," Faith told her. "If anything, I am leaning on you just as much as I am Selby. I need you, Tracey. More than I thought."

"I need you, too. I just thought that with everything going on, you would want to return to just the two of you and a normal life."

"Normal would mean continuing to put up with my family. No, I don't want normal. I want extraordinary, and that means you have to stay put. We love you, midget, and you're stuck with us."

She could actually hear Tracey smiling and would have bet good money she was crying, as well. "I love you guys, too. I'm not going anywhere."

Faith hung up the phone knowing she had meant every word. She did love Tracey and she was tired of normal. She was tired of living her life to please everyone else. The people of Rutherford Construction. Her family. The only people she had to make happy were Selby and herself.

And Tracey.

Then it all clicked and Faith knew her future course of action. She called Selby and told him that she would be late coming home. There was something she needed to do. She told him to have Tracey join them for dinner and she would explain everything then.

She then made another call. "We need to talk."

Twenty minutes after she left work, Faith pulled up behind the abandoned hotel. The giant Tundra was parked with its tailgate facing the river. Edwin perched on the open gate, a cigarette dangling from his lips as he stared out at the churning river. He turned, facing her when he finally heard her wheels on the asphalt. He didn't stand or even move. He just watched her approach.

She parked her tiny truck beside his, facing the Indian River. With a deep breath, she shut off the engine as well as her feelings for the man waiting for her. He had caused enough damage with his secrets. Oh, the fault wasn't all his. She carried some of the blame, as well. She had been warned and had ignored the red flags that had been waving in her face for the thrill of the game. She could still surrender to it if she allowed herself. Yet, there was something better in store for her and it didn't include Edwin Coldwell.

Faith stood in front of him, arms across her chest. The wind tugged her hair, stray strands blowing across her face. She made no attempt to move them. His gaze had returned to the river, so she allowed hers to go there, as well. It would probably be better if she didn't look into his eyes for this conversation.

She knew what she needed to talk about, but didn't want to just blurt it out. "Did you ever call Morgan?"

"Yeah, I'm going to transfer to some offices in Georgia. They're going to promote Jed to my spot. I'm not sure who will take his place." He shrugged. "Not really my concern, I guess."

"When do you leave?"

"I start there Monday. Neal and I will be drumming up business, starting from scratch."

"Have you told Cherish?"

He gave a snort of laughter. "I doubt I'll ever talk to your sister again, not after she tried to drop kick my family jewels into a new dimension."

"You deserved it, you know. Don't get me wrong. Cherish slept with you, too. It's not your fault alone. Still, you played us against each other. Dumped her so you could get into my pants and didn't even give me fair warning that you had your own game underway. Now her marriage is over and my nephew has a broken home. You deserved what she did and a whole lot more." She stopped and took a deep breath as she felt her anger boiling over. "You're lucky that's all she did."

"I know." It came out as a sigh. "I screwed up. I hurt people I never meant to hurt. To be honest, if I had ever thought I had a chance to be with you, I never would have allowed anything to happen with Cherish." He turned and stared into her eyes. "Faith, I have always been attracted to you. We've been great together and you know it." He pushed himself off the tailgate and stood in front of her, his hand raising her chin, making her look into his eyes. "We still can be. Come with me to Georgia." Before she could even think, he leaned down and kissed her, his lips soft and warm, yet with urgency to them.

She wanted to melt into him, her body screaming for her to give in to his need. He had actually asked her to go with him, to runaway together. He would continue to take her the way he always had, possibly even giving her to others as he had done with Morgan. The thought made her pussy drip with hunger, ache to be taken right then and used on his tailgate.

Her heart, however, wasn't finished with the adventure that was waiting at home. Faith put her hand on his chest and pushed him away. Edwin had been fun. Selby was her life, though, and she could never leave his side. She pushed up on her tiptoes and kissed Edwin's cheek. "Good luck in Georgia." She patted his chest and turned back to her truck.

"Faith…"

She faced him as she opened the truck door. "Goodbye, Edwin." She slid into the driver's seat and drove away.

~ ~ ~ ~ ~

There were no regrets as she opened her front door. The decision had been the right one and she knew it the moment she stepped inside and the music of Rascal Flatt's filled her ears. This was home.

She weaved her way through the kitchen and the Florida room out onto the back porch. Selby was flipping steaks on the grill. Tracey was sitting at the table sipping a red wine. Both turned and smiled at her as she stepped through the open sliding glass door. She felt her heart beat just a little faster. This was her family.

And her adventure.

About the Author

Robbie Cox lives on the beach in sunny Florida where he spends his days playing taxi to the family while jotting down the many crazy thoughts inside his head. He enjoys a freelance career where he writes for several magazines, sharing some of his interesting viewpoints on life and the zaniness around him. He can usually be found on his back porch surrounded by family and close friends while he enjoys a cigar, a scotch, and the many characters that talk to him inside his head. He is also the author of *Reaping the Harvest*, the first book in the Warrior of the Way series, *A Confused Life: the Mess on Steroids, Losing Faith, Roll the Dice* and *Sibling Rivalry*.

Connect with Robbie online:

Website: www.robbiecox.net

Facebook: The Mess That Is Robbie Cox - https://www.facebook.com/themessthatisrobbiecox

Twitter: http://twitter.com/CoxRobbie

Pinterest: http://pinterest.com/themessthatisme

Goodreads ~ http://www.goodreads.com/RobbieCox

Instagram ~ http://instagram.com/robbiecox66/

Visit www.robbiecox.net to find out more about these great books by Robbie Cox!

Roll the Dice

Jacqui Karston has lost - her husband, her daughter, her mother. Now, she lives life with a purpose, playing it safe and leaving chance in the past. Her life is stable, predictable, that is until Rutherford Construction opens up an office in Biloxi.

Morgan Brewer, however, believes that unless you roll the dice, you'll never achieve that big payoff. He lives his life on the edge, making the most of every opportunity that comes his way, taking every gamble he can and wasting his winnings. That is until his roll of the dice brings him across Jacqui's path.

Can Morgan stop taking chances long enough to give Jacqui her chance? Does Jacqui even want a chance? Or does she just want to be left alone to grieve?

Sibling Rivalry

Will the rules be broken?

It had been a rule of the Harper twins since high school—no one gets to sleep with both sisters. However, Mitch Greenway doesn't like rules and is determined to break theirs. Yet, where does that leave Clint Asher? What starts out as a simple car repair can possibly tear the sisters apart. Sibling Rivalry pits the Harper Twins against each other as well as against the men they are chasing and who are chasing them in return. Set on Florida's Atlantic Coast, it's not just the weather that gets everyone all hot and bothered. With plenty of twists, sneaky moves, and under the covers fun, Sibling Rivalry will keep you turning the pages to see who wins in the end.

Reaping the Harvest

On his way home from a moving job, Rhychard Bartlett heard a scream and ran to help. That action changed his life forever and tossed him into a war between the Way and the Void. Given the Guardian Sword, assisted by an ellyll who only stands two feet tall, and bonded to a mind speaking coshey the size of a Newfoundland canine and a taste for pepperoni pizza, Rhychard must stop the demon Vargas from carrying out his plans. Once he finds out what they are, of course. In the meantime, he longs for the girlfriend who left him because he suddenly had too many secrets. Not only must he save the day, but he also must convince Renny Saunders he's not the cheating lover everyone thinks he is.